my hands
came away red

my hands came away red

LISA McKAY

MOODY PUBLISHERS
CHICAGO

Some Scripture quotations are taken from the *Holy Bible, New International Version*®. NIV®. Copyright © 1973, 1978, 1984 by International Bible Society. Used by permission of Zondervan. All rights reserved.

Some Scripture quotations are taken from the *Holy Bible, New Living Translation*, copyright © 1996, 2004. Used by permission of Tyndale House Publishers, Inc., Wheaton Illinois 60189, U.S.A. All rights reserved.

Some Scripture quotations are taken from the King James Version.

Editor: LB Norton
Interior Design: LeftCoast Design
Cover design by LeVan Fisher Design, www.levanfisherdesign
Cover photo by Susumu Yasui/Getty Images
Back cover photo by Martin Strmisla/licensed by Shutterstock/2007

ISBN: 0-8024-8982-6
ISBN-13: 978-0-8024-8982-1

Library of Congress Cataloging-in-Publication Data

McKay, Lisa.
    My hands came away red / Lisa McKay.
    p. cm.
    ISBN 978-0-8024-8982-1
    1. Teenagers—Fiction. 2. Missionaries—Indonesia—Fiction. 3. Missionaries—Crimes against—Fiction. 4. Americans—Indonesia—Fiction. 5. Suspense fiction. I. Title.

PS3613.C54517M9 2007
813'.6—dc22

                                                                          2007016719

We hope you enjoy this book from Moody Publishers. Our goal is to provide high-quality, thought-provoking books and products that connect truth to your real needs and challenges. For more information on other books and products written and produced from a biblical perspective, go to www.moodypublishers.com or write to:

Moody Publishers
820 N. LaSalle Boulevard
Chicago, IL 60610

3 5 7 9 10 8 6 4 2

Printed in the United States of America

To my parents, Lloyd and Merrilyn McKay
For not shielding me from the tough questions in life
For living your faith
And for never pretending to have all the answers

"The blood-dimmed tide is loosed, and everywhere
The ceremony of innocence is drowned."
—WB Yeats

prologue ~

It only takes a day and a half for the dreams to find me again.

I wake just before dawn sweating and shaking, the sheets all tangled around my legs. I can't get back to sleep. If I close my eyes, I can see the flames and hear the voices. I can't understand most of the words, but that doesn't matter. It's the anger that's important. Underneath the clamor I hear pleading. I see their blood. I taste my own. And the pre-dawn haze in the bedroom becomes the smoke.

I reach out for the lamp beside my bed and stare up into white space. Just because blood and smoke are not a reality for me tonight doesn't mean they're not for someone else. Mani and Tina are still out there, adrift in the sea of violence we left behind.

Stark against the blank terrain above I can see one thing clearly. My family nearby, my own safety, my bed and my pillow with their familiar scent of refuge and rest—none of that is enough to right things. My hope that it would be is just the latest casualty of a summer that started as a lark, and ended . . .

Well, hasn't ended yet, I guess.

I went to see another psychologist today.

It's been almost three weeks since I got home, and I'm still spending the early morning hours wandering softly around the house, tracing the scar on my left arm, thinking about the others, listening to the silence and the sound of my own breathing.

Mum and Dad are worried. It's in the quick glances when they think I won't notice, as if to reassure themselves that I'm still here. It's in the careful tone of voice, a blend of sympathy and patience I'd find annoying if I had any energy to spare.

It's not their fault. They're trying; they just can't know what it was like. They think that seeing a psychologist will help.

"It's nothing to be ashamed of, Cori," Mum told me this morning.

I'm not ashamed. I'm not anything, really. But I have my doubts about this whole psychologist thing. The counselor I saw last week didn't have much to say. She wanted to listen to me. I didn't want to talk. There was a lot of silence in the room. In the end she patted me on the arm and came out with the usual clichés. Stuff like "We know that God works all things for good for those who love Him." I refused to go back.

I can quote that verse from Romans too. But sometime during the last three months I've learned that there's a difference between being able to say the words and really believing them. What I want right now is to believe them the way I used to.

Before this summer those words were part of a whole set of trusty beliefs that defined my life. I knew they were true the same way I knew it really *was* good for me to eat my green vegetables. God is good, and everything works out for the best . . . and we all live happily ever after.

I was so naïve.

It's not that I don't want to trust those promises I've always believed in, but I just don't understand. I try to pray, but I run short on words, and God doesn't seem to be listening. The effort just makes me emptier.

I don't want to talk to anyone, not even Kyle.

Scott's tried to be there for me. The day I got home he turned up with a teddy bear and a hug. After weeks of imagining a reunion, all that went through my mind was how *clean* he looked. Even after three showers I still felt filthy. When he reached for me, I felt like crying for the first time since the soldiers casually turned their rifles aside and I thought it was over. But the tears wouldn't come. I still had the small, wounded bear I'd given Budi in my pocket, and Scott's present made me think of that little boy so far away.

Scott has changed. Before I left, talking about stuff like the meaning of life wasn't high on the list of things he liked to do. Now it's almost as if we've switched places. He doesn't have all the answers, but he is the one with the conviction and I . . . I don't really have doubts. It is more that I have nothing.

It was Amy, the psychologist I saw today, who suggested writing. I think she probably meant a poem or a letter, not an epic. But if I'm going to write, I need to write it all, because making sense of what happened and who I am now must be somewhere in the details.

If I knew where to start with those details, it might help. Eighteen years ago in Australia, when I was born? Two weeks after that, when my parents tell me they first took me to church? Nine years ago, when they packed up their three kids, we all moved to Kenya, and I fell in love with adventure? They must all play some sort of role.

Church probably came first—that's there as far back as I can remember. Whether we were in Australia or Kenya, Sunday morning found the five of us in church and afterwards in an ice cream shop. Given that African church services regularly go for more than two hours, Tanya, Luke, and I earned every bite.

Sweet bribery aside, God was a constant centering force in a kaleidoscope world of airports, cultures, and friends. I was baptized at our church in Nairobi when I was fourteen. In the middle of winter. In an unheated baptismal pool. Outdoors.

That's how important God was to me.

I guess I wasn't quite holy enough not to feel the cold that day. But I also felt something else—a deep surety, as warm as touch, that my life was an important piece in the huge cosmic puzzle. That God loved me. That I had purpose.

Even before this summer that was what I felt slipping away.

I was in the middle of my junior year at high school when Dad decided to take the position of principal economist at headquarters in Maryland. The new school was all shiny linoleum, cinder-block walls, and dirty snow, instead of flagstone corridors and hot sunshine. It was Spanish instead of Swahili. It was trying to make friends with people who watched MTV and thought Africa was a single country. Even as I went about the business of absorbing the hit songs, figuring out which clothes made me look the least odd, and learning that people who couldn't locate Kenya on a map probably still had other good qualities to recommend them, deep down I felt I would never be really happy again.

I spent hours every day wondering what my friends back home

were doing or thinking or laughing about at that moment. I even kept my watch on Kenyan time and learned to read it backwards. That way, with a glance, I could be transported out of my pre-lunch Spanish class and into the gathering dusk of an African evening. I'd stare out the classroom window, the skeletal branches of the oak tree tracing dark lines across the view, and see the flaming magenta of the bougainvillea in our garden and feel the warm tongue of our dog, Barnabas, swipe my ankle. There was no detail of the life we'd left behind that I could not wax nostalgic about. I even spent time missing our old school uniform —a horrible brown-and-cream creation with a green tie. In retrospect, it's not surprising that I failed Spanish that quarter.

It was Scott, more than anything else, who reeled me back into the land of here and now. I remember meeting him early on—with black hair, green eyes, and his ever-present leather bomber jacket, he was hard to miss. But he didn't become more than a face in the crowd for three months. Not until the day a pack of fifth graders cornered my eight-year-old brother, dumping the contents of his backpack on the hallway floor, knocking off his glasses, and taunting him with shouts of "monkey boy." It was Scott who stopped to help Luke gather up his papers, Scott who managed to find the words, whatever they were, that stemmed Luke's tears before I arrived on the scene. And, as Luke relayed the story, it was Scott who straightened up to smile down on me. Great smile. One perfect dimple. Even my sisterly fury didn't prevent me from smiling back, and it seemed that some silent bargain had been struck.

We had a good relationship. I mean, we hardly ever argued. The only serious conflict we ever had was about what I considered the really important stuff. I never grumbled when he wanted to put his private pilot's license to good use and take me flying. We had no issues deciding whether to go running or to the movies. Scott would just laugh when I grumbled that in Kenya *football* meant soccer, and patiently persevere in trying to teach me the rules. I usually didn't dispute his happy visions of us attending Georgetown together by reminding him that I didn't have a bottomless well of family wealth to draw upon, or that I still hadn't decided whether to attend university here or in Australia. Church, however, was a different matter entirely. I'd typically try and persuade Scott to come with me; he'd work just as hard to tempt me into playing hooky. He usually won.

As the months slipped past, the hollow yearning for everything that had been home in Kenya stopped being the first thing on my mind when I woke up. Scott was. And I think that's when Scott issues and God issues started to drive me equally crazy. Eventually, when Scott and I were together, God would pop into my mind at the most inconvenient times. I would remember that I hadn't picked up my Bible in a week and that my last genuine prayer had been a desperate plea for help with my calculus test. I still had purpose, but it was becoming Scott, and that nagged at me in a way I couldn't quiet.

We dated for almost a year before this really came to a head. I still feel a bit sick inside when I think about our breakup, and I'm sure it's not how either of us had envisioned our exchange of Christmas presents ending. If the look on my face when I opened his present was anything like the look on his when he opened the Bible I'd special-ordered for him, I looked freaked out. He'd gotten me a Russian wedding ring—white, yellow, and rose gold bands interlocked to form a single ring. It was the most beautiful present I've ever received, but I was seventeen! Who buys their girlfriend a wedding ring, even a Russian one, at seventeen? He said the design represented the nature of love. I found out later that it had originally been intended to represent the Trinity, but I can't remember whether I have ever mentioned that particular irony to him. At the time, it mostly just represented scary.

As for the Bible, it only led us back to a discussion we'd had many times before. Scott's parents trudged off to church every week, but neither that nor all their money seemed able to fill the void left after the crib death of his baby sister ten years earlier. The last thing he wanted, he said angrily, was to conform to the formal, lifeless faith of his parents. I said that it didn't have to be that way. But even I could hear that I sounded more forlorn than convincing.

In the end I was the one who said we needed to take a break. Scott was even less of a fan of that plan than of the Bible I'd given him. And all my protestations—that it wasn't him but me, that I felt I cared too much for him, that I had been feeling increasingly lost—came off frustratingly clichéd. His parting words as he dropped me home, delivered in a measured and determined tone, was that we weren't through yet. As I cried myself to sleep that night, I hoped he was right.

After Christmas we settled into an emotionally charged truce that required renegotiating every time we shared the same space. When I entered a room I deliberately didn't look for him until I felt it was clear that he wasn't always the first thing, much less the only thing, on my mind. After about five heartbeats I would allow myself a casual glance. Perhaps he was doing that too, because our eyes usually met at the same moment. Once that happened I could never keep my smile on the neutral side of friendly, and the corners of his eyes would crinkle in warm response.

We weren't together, but we weren't really not together either. We'd casually go out of our way to sit next to each other in class, and

I'd savor and resent the way he could derail my train of thought by simply brushing his arm against mine as he reached for a pen. We still talked, argued, teased. We shared the same study period, lunch table, and friends—who I know watched closely for cracks in the unified front of friendship we presented.

They rarely found any. I don't think they knew either of us well enough to recognize them: my sudden restraint when I caught myself on the verge of forgetting, laughter measured out in smaller doses. The way Scott would look at me sometimes, with his head tilted to one side—as if asking a question without meaning to. Pressed in close behind our easy exchanges I could feel the weight of his expectations and the confusion he'd put on pause. It was a lot heavier than the weight of his ring, threaded onto a chain and lying underneath my shirt, warm against my skin.

When it comes right down to it, this whole mess could be seen as Scott's fault. I would never have gone to Indonesia if I hadn't dated him. I don't like admitting that; after all, it was a missions trip. It would be nice if my main motivation had been sharing the love of Jesus, or at least helping the poor. I'm sure those things were part of it. But any nobility on my part was pretty much buried underneath my need to get away and sort out my head, and hopefully my heart.

When I reached under the bed two months after we broke up, and my hand closed around the slick cover of the rolled-up magazine instead of the missing sock, I didn't acknowledge that what I'd just seized upon was an escape. It was too conveniently prepackaged as service, service sweetened with the promise of adventure. I didn't hesitate.

I spent that evening reading every single blurb and trying to decide where I wanted to go. To Siberia, to teach English to orphans? To Zimbabwe, to help run a sports camp for kids? To Indonesia, to build a church?

While Siberia sounded very appealing, mostly because I had never heard of anyone going there before, in the end I settled on the Indonesia backpack team. I just couldn't get past the image conjured up by *Be part of the first-ever team to Seram. Build a church in a remote village . . . present the gospel using puppets and drama . . . backpack along sandy beaches in Indonesia's famous Spice Islands.*

Sometimes I've wondered whether what happened didn't serve me right. Usually even as I think that, I know it's not true, but knowing this doesn't stop me from wanting to blame Scott for setting it into motion, or Mum and Dad for saying I could go. Even now, though, I find it hard to wish they'd said no. There are so many things I *do* wish had never happened, but I can rarely take my imagined scenarios back beyond the point that means I would never have met the others. I would not trade the nightmares for knowing them.

It wasn't like Mum and Dad agreed immediately, either. They made me work for it. I managed to insert the word *worthwhile* into my introductory spiel four times, but that didn't stop them from grilling me.

I think Mum's first question was whether I'd prayed about it. I told them that of course I had. I didn't know whether they would consider "God, please make them let me go" as prayer, exactly. But as far as I was concerned, it counted.

Divine sanction turned out to be only the first hurdle. Then we went several rounds about team supervision and safety (Dad didn't seem to appreciate my innocent allusions to the comparative risks of living in Nairobi), and even whether I was "jumping into this because of Scott."

In the end I think it was the Kenya card that tipped the scales.

"This is the perfect time," I said during round three. "I've got at least eight months between graduating from high school and starting university in Australia—or here, if that's what I decide. Besides, I've wanted to do a missions trip for *ages*, but something always seems to come up. Like *moving*."

I emphasized that last word, allowing just a hint of blame to creep in. Not enough to get me into trouble, just enough to stir up a tickle of guilt.

Mum and Dad shared a glance. Dad sighed.

"We'll see," he said.

That was the moment I knew that, eventually, they'd say yes.

They were the only ones who said anything resembling yes. My friends said I was crazy and wailed about all the fun I'd miss over the summer. Tanya and Luke moped around the house and said they'd be bored without me. Scott, after he put "three months" and "Indonesia" together, didn't say much at all.

Not about that, anyway. Between exams and the whirlpool of emotion that were the last two months of school, there was plenty to buffer us from having to tackle the topic directly. So we didn't. Even as I was busy buying a backpack, raising support, and packing, I think both of us spent most of the time we were together pretending that I wasn't going.

The day after graduation we met up for one last run as the sun rose. Usually we kept pace evenly and easily, but that morning Scott was on a mission. I gritted my teeth and put all my energy into just keeping up.

"How you doing?" he called back cheerfully, not sounding the least winded.

"Fine." Actually, I thought I was in imminent danger of dying from lack of oxygen.

I managed to make it to the wooden footbridge that would take us over the stream before I had to stop. I rested my hands on my knees, sweat dripping off the end of my ponytail.

He collapsed into the grass, looking satisfied. "That was only three miles!"

"Yeah, in about fifteen minutes!"

When I could breathe again, I sat down beside him underneath the willow tree. The nearby stream whispered, but the soccer field stretched before us green and silent, shrouded by the early morning haze. It was already promising to be a scorcher of a day.

"I brought you a present," I said, pulling a folded prayer card out of my pocket and passing it over. "Sorry it's a bit soggy."

He raised one eyebrow as he looked at my smiling face underneath the heading *Spice Islands Backpack*.

"So," he said, and then paused and tried for a smile. "What are you actually going to do there, apart from helping with the nutmeg harvest?"

"We're not going to be harvesting nutmeg!" I said, although that did sound like fun. I had a brief and beautiful vision of backpacking along a moonlit beach, the hot air heavy with the scent of cloves and cinnamon. "We're building a church for a village."

"Why don't they just build the church themselves?" he asked.

I looked for the sarcasm I expected to be hidden in the words and was surprised not to find any. "Maybe they don't have the money."

"Why don't you get a summer job here, and give them the money?" He sounded infuriatingly logical. "They're probably ten times better at building than you are."

"What?" I was honestly insulted. "I can build."

"You asked me to hang a picture in your room a month ago," he said.

"Maybe I just wanted to watch you use the hammer."

I actually pouted at him; there's no other word for it. Not only had I betrayed my Australian heritage by drawling that line in a southern accent, but I was totally flirting with him.

His lips twitched. Then mine did. Then we were both laughing— out of control, snorting, hysterical, for no good reason, rolling on the ground, laughing. Then I was the only one still laughing, and he was kissing me.

I pulled back, more because I was startled than anything else. He grabbed my arm and brushed his free hand across my neck, scooping up the gold chain with one finger. The ring dangled between us, glinting accusingly.

I looked at it and wilted, suddenly miserable. I don't think that was the expression he was expecting. He pulled me against him in a tight hug, one hand cupping the back of my head, and I didn't resist.

"What?" he asked.

"I'm going away all summer, and it's my fault," I said, wondering with a touch of horror if I was about to cry on him. This wasn't like me at all. I concentrated hard on the trill of a bird in the tree above us, on wondering whether I smelled like a locker room, on anything but how good it felt to have my head resting underneath the curve of his chin.

"Is this really worth it?" he asked. "Is it really worth going to the other side of the world to build a church for people you've never met?"

With my cheek pressed against him I could hear his heart beating. I wanted to say no and clutch him around the waist.

"Yeah," I said softly, hoping I was right. "It is. It's only three months. How hard can it be?"

"Okay," he said slowly and sighed, a small sound of defeat.

I hadn't realized until that moment that he'd actually thought there was a chance I'd change my mind and stay.

"Well, if you can go to Indonesia, I guess I can try and read your Bible this summer."

I grinned against his shirt at the reluctance in his voice and didn't move an inch. I was suddenly and irrationally worried he would take them back if he had any idea how happy those words made me.

"Don't get any ideas, though," he warned.

"Fine."

"I'm still not sure I even believe there *is* a God."

"Fine."

"I'm not just suddenly going to become your brand of Christian just so I'm good enough for you."

My brand? I thought, but could only get out one word.

"Fine."

"Are you crying?"

"No."

"I thought Christians weren't supposed to lie," he said, tracing the curve of my cheek with his thumb and waving the evidence in front of me.

"S'just sweat," I said.

He laughed.

"I'll be here when you get home," he said. "We'll work this out then."

This time I raised my mouth to meet his. For the next five minutes I deliberately forgot to remember that I was supposed to keep him at arm's length.

I guess, when it comes right down to it, the details leading up to why I went to Indonesia in the first place are not the important ones. Scott, Mum, Dad, Tanya, Luke—none of them were there.

It's my story, and Kyle's. And Elissa, Drew, Brendan, and Mark's. And Mani, Tina, Daniel, Mariati, and the others', of course. But they don't come until later. In the beginning there were just six of us—six strangers at boot camp who would become family, bonded with a glue of sweat and tears and blood, bound by fear and need. And by laughter and love too; I don't want to forget that.

Those details, from that first day at boot camp—they're the ones that really matter.

chapter 1 ~

As I opened the car door in the parking lot of boot camp, a sodden cloud of hot sulfur slithered in. The noise followed soon behind it. The parking lot, the wide dirt track that led into the thick squat trees, the clearing I could glimpse in front of the largest tent I'd ever seen—they were all teeming with people. Sweaty, smiling people in khaki pants, T-shirts, and leather boots. Like mine.

"Yuck," said Tanya, wrinkling her nose.

"This area of Florida's mostly swamp," Dad said. "That's the smell."

Somehow, I didn't think that was all she was referring to. I was starting to wonder if this had been a very bad idea. By the time my family had all climbed back into the car after hugs and tears—Mum's—I was almost sure of it. Standing beside my new team leader, surrounded by a thousand strangers, I had never felt more alone.

"Now you're here, we're just waiting for Mark," Gary said, prompting me to pick up my backpack and follow him into the massive tent, silently resenting his cheerfulness.

"Cori, Brendan and Kyle." Gary dispensed with introductions in four whole words as we reached two guys lounging on the floor by a tent pole the size of a sequoia. He moved on to more important matters. "Where are Drew and Elissa?"

"Talking to friends, and bathroom," Kyle answered economically, pointing right, which gave me a clear view of the snake tattoo that wound down the inside of his forearm. It didn't quite fit with the short blond hair and blue eyes, although the dusty bandanna tied around his forehead did give him a certain rakish air.

"Y'all wait here until I get back with Mark." Looking harried, Gary disappeared into the crowd.

Brendan jumped to his feet and held out his hand. I think my mouth actually fell open.

"Six foot five," he preempted with a wry smile, "and pure muscle."

"Half muscle, half Oreo cookies," Kyle corrected, without getting up.

We'd progressed all the way through where we came from—San Diego for Kyle, Colorado for Brendan—and started in on hobbies when a living Barbie doll strolled in and sat down, fanning herself gracefully with a sheet of paper. She was small; her T-shirt was neatly tucked in; her long blonde braid hung straight down her back. She was even sweating elegantly. I felt grubby just looking at her.

"I already know what Elissa's favorite hobby is," Kyle said with a wicked grin. "His name starts with C."

She blushed. "He's more than a hobby, Kyle! Colin's my boy-friend," she said to me, pulling out a picture and passing it over.

"The way you talk about him, I didn't think you had time for any-thing else," Kyle said.

"I do ballet," she said.

That explained the perfect posture.

"What about you?"

"Oh," Kyle said, sighing. "President of the student body, captain of the debate team, captain of the track team . . ."

I thought he was serious until he started to laugh.

"Well, I will be, next year when I'm a senior. What about you, Cori?"

"Underwater basket weaving."

Kyle was the only one who laughed. Elissa just looked politely interested.

"Okay," I capitulated. "Horseback riding."

"Riding!" Brendan said. "We've got horses on our ranch. There's nothing like riding alone at sunset. God's so huge; it's awesome!"

"What's awesome?"

Another girl had arrived in an untidy tangle of arms, legs, and red hair. She crashed down, practically in my lap, and introduced herself as Drew.

"Cool!" she said when she heard my accent. "Another non-American to keep me company. I'm Canadian. Elissa, can I borrow your comb? My hair will not stay put. So, what's awesome?"

"Brendan asked Gary if we could have extra practice on the ob-stacle course every day because we're a backpack team, and Gary said yes. That's what's awesome. We're all real excited," Kyle said casually, looking to the rest of us for support.

Drew, both hands occupied scraping back her hair, looked appalled. "Brendan! Are you *crazy*?"

Elissa stared at the ground, and I stifled a smile. Elissa buckled first.

"Kyle's just teasing, Drew."

Drew went from mad to amused in two seconds. She laughed and threw Elissa's comb at Kyle. It bounced off him and landed in the dirt.

"Oops, sorry," she said as she retrieved it, wiped it off, and handed it back. "Hey, where are the bathrooms?"

Elissa pointed to several port-a-potties near the trees, each one pinpointed by a long line in front of the door.

"Where are the real bathrooms?" Drew asked.

"That's it," Elissa said, not without sympathy.

"Have mercy!" Drew muttered as she got up and left.

"I don't think she has much idea what she's in for," Elissa said thoughtfully.

I did my best to look as though I knew exactly what I was in for.

"She'll be fine," Brendan said. "She seems like a good sport."

Elissa didn't look convinced.

Five hours later I'd stopped wondering whether Drew was going to prove to be a good sport and started wondering whether I was. After Mark had finally arrived, Gary had us on our feet before we'd even finished introductions, although it turned out we had plenty of time for those as we stood in line after line collecting everything from drama costumes, mime makeup, and a portable puppet theatre to canteens and waterproof waist packs.

Mark turned out to be a small, wiry, pugnacious kid from New York. He looked thirteen, although he answered fifteen in response to Kyle's unsubtle query.

"We're going to spend the summer babysitting," I heard Kyle complain to Brendan as we stowed all our new possessions and hurried to line up at the start of the obstacle course.

"See you at the wall!" Gary yelled, as someone entirely too close to my ear blew a very loud whistle.

"Which way? *What* wall?" Drew looked as frazzled as I felt.

"I was on the England team last year," Elissa said, leading the way at a run. "Follow the arrows. Jacob's ladder is the first obstacle."

I'd always wondered what Jacob's ladder looked like. As a kid I'd pictured a wide sweep of steps like the ones leading up to the Sydney Opera House but made out of marble, with angels hovering over them, reverent and silent. According to boot camp, however, Jacob's ladder was a forty-foot-high rope cargo net that we had to climb up and over.

After that disappointment, I shouldn't have been too shattered to learn that Mount Sinai was apparently made out of tires, that the main task of Egyptian slaves had been to transport bricks in a wheelbarrow and build mini-pyramids, and that the Slough of Despond wasn't just a figment of John Bunyan's imagination. It was a large moat blocking our path and filled with muddy water. It was also the last straw for Drew.

"Fun, huh, Drew?" Kyle said, pacing back and forth as Elissa explained that someone would have to jump for the two ropes dangling over the middle of the water.

Drew, sitting in the dirt beside me and struggling to catch her breath, snapped. "This is not fun!" she yelled. "Fun is going shopping. This is torture!" Then she burst into tears.

Silently, I agreed. Where were the sandy beaches? Where was the scent of cinnamon?

Kyle was quick to apologize, and Brendan stuck out a hand to help her up. She batted it away.

"Since you think it's so much fun," she said to Kyle, "you guys can get the ropes."

"No problem," Kyle said, backing up alongside Brendan for a running start. Brendan made it, but Kyle didn't. He snagged his rope just below a large knot, and his hands slipped. He was swinging forward with the force of his jump, and when he went to wrap his legs around the rope he fell. He hit the water with a dull smacking sound and disappeared.

He stood up, looking glazed in chocolate milk, to find all five of his teammates laughing.

"It's slippery," he said defensively, grabbing the end of the rope and swinging it across to us. "You try it."

"Cori, hold it for me," Elissa instructed. "I'll show you how it works best."

She took a run-up, launched herself at the rope, sailed across, and jumped. Brendan caught her on the other side and narrowly saved her from a dunking. Mark wasn't so lucky; he slipped on the bank and ended up wet to the waist, looking decidedly unhappy.

"I hate it here," Drew said.

I nodded slowly, but the expression on my face must have been more transparent than I'd intended, because she looked at me and suddenly, unexpectedly, giggled.

"You can do it," I said. "I'll hold it for you."

She might have made it, except that she forgot to jump off when she reached the other side. Soon she was hanging off the knot above the middle of the pit, barely keeping her feet clear of the water.

"Help! What do I do?" she screeched.

On the other side, Mark was helpless with laughter, and the other three were calling out advice.

"Swing your body to get some momentum," Elissa shouted.

Drew tried, but only succeeded in flopping back and forth, barely even twitching the rope. "I don't want to fall in that disgusting water!"

"It's not that bad," Kyle said. "Just drop off and wade out."

Brendan took a step forward. "I'll come get you."

"Wait," Kyle said reluctantly. "I'm already wet; I'll do it." He waded back into the pit and slogged over to Drew.

"Kyle's right there," I called. "Sit on his shoulders."

"But my boots will go in the water," she said, unwrapping one leg and trying to hook it over Kyle's shoulder.

"Choose." He grunted as he helped her swing the other leg over. "Your boots or you."

I could see what was coming. She was sitting on his shoulders with her arms wrapped around his head, trying to keep both feet out of the water by holding her legs out straight.

"Drew, put your feet down!" I yelled.

Kyle took one step and staggered. She clutched at his head, covering his eyes.

"Drew! Let go!" He swatted at her hands, took one more step, and fell over sideways.

It was like watching a tree fall in slow motion. Drew was screaming as she hit the water. On the other side of the pond, Mark folded gently to the dirt in a heaving, wheezing pile.

Drew only had one word to say when she came up.

Whistle man looked appalled. So did Elissa.

"Young lady," whistle man called, making a notation on his clipboard. "No swearing, please."

"You dropped me!" she accused Kyle, pushing long ropes of hair away from her face.

"I couldn't help it!" he said. "You had your hands over my eyes!"

"I swallowed some of that filthy water," Drew said as Brendan helped her up the bank. "I'll probably get malaria."

"Guys," I called, indicating the ropes, now hanging serenely over the middle of the muddy pit once again.

Kyle started to wade into the water for the third time.

"I'll come and get you," he said, sounding as though he were offering to swim the English Channel on my behalf.

"I can do it by myself," I said.

He retreated, his sudden grin a challenge. "Okay, then, do it."

Suddenly the ropes looked a long way away.

"Cor-i. Cor-i . . ." Brendan started the chant while I backed up.

At least I made it to the rope when I jumped. But it was wet and slick and hard to get a firm grip. Before long I was hanging off a knot in the middle of the slough, up to my knees in water. I could feel it pouring, pleasantly cool, into my boots.

"Want me to rescue you?" Kyle cloaked his taunt in an offer.

"No." It was tempting, but I let go instead, shuddering as the water lapped at my chin and my boots settled into the sticky muck.

"C'mon," Elissa said as I waded out. "We're almost done. Jericho's wall is just around the corner."

"I thought the wall around Jericho fell down," I grumbled as we jogged into a large clearing and I saw the last obstacle, a ten-foot-high wooden wall we were supposed to scale.

Elissa laughed. "Only after days of marching and blowing trumpets. In the meantime, Brendan and Cori, you go over first. Kyle last."

With Kyle boosting from below, and Brendan and me lifting from the elevated platform on the other side, we hauled Drew, Elissa, and Mark up fairly easily. Kyle, however, was another story. Even with a running start, he barely managed to grab one of Brendan's hands. Brendan gave a tug, and I snagged Kyle's other hand. My shoulder felt like it was about to be rudely separated from its socket, and the top of the wall dug painfully into my ribs.

"Cori, no. I'm too heavy," Kyle said.

"Get up here, then."

He planted his feet on the wall, and with Brendan doing most of the work, we managed to heave him to the top. Then we collapsed on the platform, too wasted to think about climbing down the ladder and joining the others. The two guys high-fived each other over the top of my head.

On the ground below us, Gary clicked a stopwatch.

"Thirty-seven minutes and twenty-four seconds," he said. "Not bad for your first try. By the end of boot camp you should knock more than ten minutes off that time."

Drew whimpered. "Can we change clothes now?" she asked.

"Oh, you'll dry out soon enough," Gary said. "We don't hike out to our campsite until after the evening rally. Now, let's hustle. You're late for puppetry class."

I closed my eyes and thought of home. Within two months I would remember how miserable I was on that first day and find it hard to believe I was once soft enough to get teary over an obstacle course.

It was very dark that night on the track out to our campsite. A thick, moist darkness, as if the swamp were breathing around us. It was either raining, or the invisible trees looming above us were crying. Large warm drops hit my shoulders and soaked into my hair. I couldn't see anything beyond the small pale circles cast by our flashlights, but I could hear the others ahead and behind me. Both groups were talking about home.

". . . live with my aunt and uncle," I heard Kyle tell Brendan in front of me. "They're cool. Mostly."

"My folks are the best," Brendan said.

"I'm homesick already," Elissa said quietly. "I miss Colin."

"I miss my bed," Drew said.

Only Mark and I were silent. I was trying to decide whether or not I would eat a live worm if it meant I could go home, when we finally reached our campsite. The small log circle and three tents nestled among the bushes didn't manage to appear cozy, just bedraggled.

"Okay, team. Gather round," Gary said.

His wife, Diane, reached out to take his hand and mine as we made a circle.

As I bowed my head for the prayer, I felt a trickle of cold water creep down my back. Despite Gary's proclamation of collective gratitude, I didn't really feel very thankful for the day. In fact, I was dreading tomorrow.

chapter 2 ~

On day ten of boot camp I woke early, still exhausted but unable to drift off again, already anticipating the shrill whistle I knew would come at five thirty. The birds were offering their first tentative calls, and it was peaceful and cool in the darkness. I started to ease on the same khaki pants and shirt I'd discarded the night before, moving quietly so I wouldn't wake Drew and Elissa. My clothes felt stiff and grainy, but at least they were dry.

I wondered what Scott was doing. Sleeping, probably, like most of the other sane people in this world who hadn't bartered away their entire summer on the strength of a whim. Well, maybe *whim* was a bit strong, but when I compared my "I thought it would be fun" to Kyle's "God told me to come," that's what it felt like.

"God really told you to come on this trip?" I'd asked him, wondering why I sounded so skeptical. If I didn't believe a person could hear from God, what was I doing traipsing off to Indonesia to build a church?

"Yeah," was all he'd said. But his tone implied, *Why, didn't you get the same message?*

Before boot camp I would have said that I was sure that God wanted me to do this. But ten days of blisters, aching muscles, heavy backpacks, no showers, and disgusting food had sent me scrambling hourly to remind myself exactly why. However I looked at it, my decision seemed to have been based on the following syllogism: 1) God wants us to do good things; 2) This is a good thing to do; 3) Therefore, God wants me to do this. If there had been any specific message for me about the trip, I was no longer sure I'd sat still long enough to listen for it.

It seemed I wasn't the only one who had relied on that particularly versatile equation. Drew had collapsed beside me in the drama tent the day before and looked up plaintively.

"I knew this summer would be different, but I didn't know it would be freaky Christian army camp different. I thought it would be . . . I don't know . . . romantic different."

"So that's why you two are really here," Kyle said, laughing. "Romance."

"That's not the only reason." Drew defended us. "We had lots of excellent reasons for coming, right, Cori?"

"Right," I said, trying to remember at least one in case Kyle demanded specifics.

Romance. Lying there in the pre-dawn darkness, I reached up to touch Scott's ring. Getting some space from him wasn't the only reason I was here, though, I reminded myself. I wanted to help people. I wanted adventure. I rolled over and groaned as my aching thigh muscles protested. I just hadn't banked on adventure being quite so much *work*.

It's not like there hadn't been warning signs that it might not be a stroll in the park. In the months after I signed up for the trip, Indonesia was hit with one crisis after another—a drought (which meant bad rice harvests), a huge economic wobble with a 600 percent currency devaluation (whatever that meant), and student protests that culminated in riots in Jakarta that left twelve hundred people dead and the president being forced out of office (which meant, among other things, that I had two very worried parents).

Mark and Drew hadn't even heard about the riots.

"You can't just have a riot if you don't like your president," Drew said when she heard this news on day three.

"What would you do?" I asked.

"Wait until the next election and vote in someone else."

I didn't even try not to laugh.

"He'd been president for thirty years," Brendan said. "And he wasn't elected, either. The election scheduled for next year will be Indonesia's first ever."

"My parents would die if they knew all this!" Drew said.

"I can't believe you didn't know," Kyle said in a tone usually reserved for siblings. "It's because you don't get any decent news up in Canada."

"We do so! I just don't listen to it. Do your parents know, Mark?"

"I don't know," he said, his normally expressive face going suddenly blank. "Maybe."

I didn't miss the glance Kyle and Brendan exchanged, but Drew did.

"Yeah, maybe they shipped you off on purpose," she said.

Mark chewed on his bottom lip and stayed unusually quiet.

"That sounds more like a Canadian family tradition," Kyle teased, diverting her back to herself.

"No," Drew said, a sadness passing over her easy flippancy like a gauze veil. "My parents wouldn't do that."

Mine wouldn't either. Despite the fact that relative stability had returned to Jakarta when the new president took office after several days of riots, I'd had to work hard to convince Mum and Dad to let me stay on the team. Only the facts that Ambon and Seram were five hundred miles from Jakarta and that the embassy reported no trouble in that region had swayed them in my favor.

By a week and a half in, however, I felt I'd learned less about drama, puppets, singing, hiking, teamwork, and the obstacle course than I had about being more cautious in my decision making. If boot camp was what could happen when we got something we asked for, I resolved to be a darn sight more careful about what I prayed for in the future.

My only comfort was that I wasn't the only one struggling, or—if daily bouts of tears were anything to go by—even the one struggling the most. Elissa missed Colin ferociously. He'd started sending her letters before she even left, just so she'd have mail during her first week away. Even after a week of seeing her face light up every time she got a letter, I was still shocked when she confessed that they were unofficially engaged and planned to get married as soon as she turned eighteen.

"Are you *serious*?" Drew had said, sitting up in her sleeping bag in our little tent. "You're only sixteen!"

"Almost seventeen," Elissa said. It was clear she thought eighteen couldn't come quickly enough, and equally clear that Drew thought she was insane. They both turned to me to back them up.

"It's . . . legal. I guess," I said, trying to think.

Drew had not interpreted this as an overwhelming show of sup-port. "You two are boy crazy."

"Us?" Elissa said, incredulous.

It was hard to miss Drew's glances toward Brendan, her total attention when he spoke, the way she maneuvered to sit next to him.

"Yeah," I said, rushing in where Elissa feared to tread. "We're not the ones who came looking for romance this summer."

I'd thought Drew would welcome the opportunity to giggle and debrief.

I was wrong.

"Whatever," she said, prickly. "I don't know what you're talking about."

"Come on." I laughed. "You mean you didn't come here for the guys? Could have fooled me."

These sudden shifts of Drew's felt like summer storms blowing through our tent—intense while they lasted, but usually gone just as fast as they'd arrived.

She wasn't the only one who was intense; Kyle wasn't short on that quality himself. It took us six days to get the real story behind his tattoo out of him. He'd strung us along by concocting all sorts of ridicu-lous scenarios. My personal favorite was the "apprenticed to a snake charmer in India" version of the tale.

Day six's plot involved his running away from home at fourteen, hitching to San Diego with two friends, shoplifting cigarettes, smoking pot, and living on the streets for three weeks before being caught spray-painting a church. He got three months in a juvie halfway house.

Brendan, Drew, and Elissa all laughed on cue when he finished, but I shook my head, suspicious. He looked nervous. Kyle never looked nervous when he was lying.

"That's it, isn't it? You really ran away." This was more story than even I had bargained for.

Mark, who up to this point had been a study in nonchalance, looked deeply impressed.

"What happened next?" Brendan asked, still not sure this was finally the truth.

"The pastor asked the court to assign us to clean it up ourselves. So every Saturday we'd work on that, and every Sunday until we finished we had to go to the morning and evening service, and eat lunch with one of the families in the church. It took us ten weeks."

He looked around, checking that he had our undivided attention as he prepared to deliver the punch line.

"I became a Christian at that church."

"Then did you go home?" Elissa asked, still stunned.

The grin disappeared. "No. The court said I could go live with my aunt and uncle instead. Dad took off eight months ago, and we haven't heard from him since. Mom's probably still as drunk as the last time I saw her."

That was sort of a conversation stopper.

After the high drama of Kyle, Drew's out-of-character reticence, and Elissa's stated intention to become a child bride, Brendan's wholesome stories about growing up on a ranch in Colorado complete with an older sister and a dog named Buster and wearing a suit to church every Sunday seemed straight out of *Little House on the Prairie*. On the topic of home and family, Mark was silent. It was about the only topic he *was* silent on.

In the pre-dawn hush, I reached into my waist pack and pulled out my flashlight and the first letter from Scott. I'd read it so many times in the three days since it had arrived that I practically had it memorized, but there was something about touching the paper and seeing his hand-writing that brought him closer than just thinking of him.

My eyes skipped straight to the first sentence of the second para-graph. *I've done pretty well at getting on with life and only wishing once or twice (an hour) that you were here.*

The ache felt almost physical. I closed my hand over his ring as I heard a sound I was coming to loathe—Gary's whistle.

Four more days, I reminded myself. Four more days, then eight more weeks.

Every one of those remaining four days of boot camp felt like a week on its own, but we survived. We could put on a puppet show, per-form four dramas, sing twenty songs, and recite fifteen Bible verses flawlessly. We could lay concrete, tie steel, and build a brick wall. We could run the obstacle course in twenty-three minutes and forty sec-onds. We could scale tall buildings with a single bound—or something like that anyway.

We had some bad times those last four days.

On day eleven Mark hid Kyle and Brendan's shirts in the bushes, which made us late for the start of the obstacle course, which meant we spent free time that day cleaning thirty portable toilets that had been sitting in the sun for ten days. It was undoubtedly the nastiest experi-ence of my entire life. No one had much to say to Mark that night.

On day twelve we had a huge argument about whether women should be allowed to join the army and fight in combat situations.

"No way," Kyle said.

Not that I wanted to join the army, but I wasn't about to let him get away with that. "Women are just as capable as men," I said.

Surprisingly, it was Elissa who backed me up. "We can do any-thing you can do."

"No, you can't," Kyle said. "Women aren't as strong. And you're more emotional. Just face it; there are some things only men should do. I don't see what the big deal is."

"The big deal is that you're acting like a sexist pig!" I snapped.

"Girls cry all the time too." That was Mark, being spectacularly unfair.

Elissa actually lost her temper. "At least I can go more than one day without getting everyone in trouble!"

"If I had to fight, I think women would be distracting. I'd be more worried about them than about the other guys," Brendan said.

"We don't need to be fussed over just because we're women," Elissa said, flicking her long braid over one shoulder with an angry jerk.

"I think it's sweet," Drew said quietly.

"Well, no one asked you," I said.

"Fine then," she said, glaring at me.

After ten more minutes of this, having to stand next to each other in singing class and practice "Amazing Grace" felt like more of a pun-ishment than a privilege.

On day thirteen Drew ran out of the mini Snickers bars she'd smuggled into boot camp. We huddled in a tight circle, licking the last melted chocolate from the wrappers and keeping a wary lookout for the sudden appearance of Gary or Diane. We weren't interested in cleaning any more toilets.

"Once upon a time . . . ," Mark began, looking sadly at his empty wrapper.

"Once upon a time there was a boy named Jip," I said, looking at Mark's dark, matted curls and the freckles on his dusty face. "Jip was twelve years old and loved chocolate," I added, then paused.

Mark caught on first. "But Jip lived in a land ruled by an evil king named Gary, who hated chocolate," he said.

"Maybe the king wasn't really evil," Brendan said, joining in. "Maybe he was just allergic."

"Well, did he really have to spoil everyone else's fun?" Mark asked. "Besides, he didn't like Jip's pet monkey, Kiki."

From those humble beginnings, the story game was born. None of us had any idea that Jip and Kiki had just become our seventh and eighth teammates, or how far they would travel with us.

Boot camp wasn't *all* bad. But for some reason, even in thinking about all that came later, the good times are not as easy to put into words as the bad ones. Perhaps that's because the good times tended to come in glimpses. Often, right when I felt like I'd been pushed to the edge, there would be a look or a word or a shared laugh that would tilt the scales back the other way.

The commissioning ceremony on the last night was definitely one of the good times. We'd run the obstacle course for the last time that morning, sweated impatiently through our classes, and spent the afternoon packing duffel bags with things like canned food, a portable stove, tent kits, and toilet paper. As I stuffed the first aid kit in and pulled the last strap tight, I finally felt as if we really were going somewhere.

When I walked into the main tent that evening, the usual turbulent roar of two thousand voices all talking at once was muted to a low, rolling hum. Everywhere I looked there were skirts and ties. Faces had been scrubbed and boots shined.

"Everyone looks so different," I said, dropping into a seat next to

Kyle and trying not to stare. The bandanna and his favorite blue shirt
were nowhere to be seen. Between the tattoo and the tie, he looked like
a preppy gang member.

"Clean?" he said, yawning. "I'm beat. Poke me if I fall asleep."

"Like this?" I gave him an elbow.

"No, more like this," he said, returning the gesture with interest.

When the floodlights suddenly went out, it took us all by surprise. Up on stage a fragile, mesmerizing speck of light appeared.

"The light shines in the darkness, and the darkness has not over-
come it."

The bright pinprick moved, and then there were two, four, ten, as
the flame was passed quickly from candle to candle and the light
started to creep through the gathering. I could feel the others close by,
tell who was standing where from the sound of their breathing. The
singing started softly and swelled. Exhaustion, the smell of hot wax,
dancing yellow fragments flickering around us, harmony a thousand
voices strong—it all came together in an intoxicating God-buzz.

That sweet combination of peaceful certainty and confident anticipation lasted exactly twenty-one hours and fourteen minutes, just long
enough to take me from Orlando to 33,000 feet above the Pacific, 1,704
miles from LAX, and heading toward Indonesia.

chapter 3 ~

Peaceful certainty and confident anticipation had long since been replaced by numb exhaustion by the time we finally landed in Ambon. Even the view coming in, craggy green mountains on the right and an azure bay to the left, aroused more terror than excitement.

The small plane bumped and swayed as we circled, left wing hanging low, seemingly headed straight for the side of the mountains—which we could see completely filling the cockpit window through the door the pilot had casually left open. By the time we straightened up at the last minute and touched down gently, I was glad we were staying the night in Ambon with missionary friends of Gary and Diane's and catching a boat out to Seram the next morning. I'd had enough adventure for one long day, and it wasn't over yet.

Outside the door of the plane a different world was waiting.

The air was hot and thick, flavored with car exhaust and warm tar, wet dirt, tobacco, bodies, and spices. There were people everywhere. Short porters in blue uniforms rushed to help us with the bags. Tiny women brushed their mops slowly over the red tiled floor of the small airport. Bearded men in long white tunics and turbans smoked pungent kretek cigarettes and watched us.

Actually, everyone was watching us. Even the Muslim women, many with their heads covered, were openly staring and laughing. More than one person tried to talk to us, stained teeth showcased by friendly grins.

I think the driver of the battered minivan that Gary procured only knew a couple of English phrases, and "slow down" apparently wasn't among them. In the forty minutes it took us to drive around the bay to Ambon City, we came within two inches of vehicles on either side, dodged scores of people talking, smoking, or squatting near mats covered in rice or cloves that had been laid out on the road to dry, and ran a red light at the one traffic signal we encountered.

At every near disaster Drew and Elissa shut their eyes, stopped breathing, and squeezed each other's hands. I think the three guys got as much enjoyment out of watching their reactions as they did seeing how close we could come to actually having an accident.

In the rare moments we weren't collectively mesmerized by an impending traffic disaster, we were flooded with a series of quick images, snapshots of daily life in Ambon. Dirty canals lined with flimsy shacks, mansions surrounded by high walls and iron grille gates that were topped with sharp spikes. Skinny men on bikes. Scrawny chickens scratching in the dirt. Wandering dogs. Clusters of kids in red-and-white school uniforms, laughing. Small somber children slipping between stopped cars at intersections to tap on the windows, begging silently. One little girl had a baby strapped to her front. A small spark of life ignited in her flat gaze when she saw our faces peering down, but we shook our heads and held up empty hands to show that we had no Indonesian money.

I don't think she believed us.

Tim and Alison Stewart's house was down a concrete lane so narrow that two cars couldn't pass each other. The only motorcyclist we met managed to navigate around us without falling into the open sewer on either side.

It was a relief to reach the Stewarts' and find that they had dinner waiting for us. I was almost too tired to be hungry, but the combined lure of chicken curry and the chance to grill our hosts about what we'd be doing over the summer convinced me that bed could wait just a little longer.

Over dinner I was surprised to learn that the Stewarts had been based in Ambon for twelve years—they didn't look old enough for that to be true. They spent most of their time working with the local Christian college and two churches in the area. When Kyle asked why they didn't work in the Muslim areas of Ambon, Tim blinked several times in quick succession, but all he said was that things had been tense in Ambon recently and that it was good we were headed for the island of Seram.

"So we won't be going to Muslim villages either?" Kyle persisted. "Why did we learn all that stuff about Islam then?"

"You'll be talking to Muslims over the summer," Gary said. "We just won't be doing presentations there."

Kyle didn't look convinced. I got the feeling that if this were his show we'd be marching into the Muslim villages wearing big signs that said, *Hi. We've come to convert you all.* For once I was glad Gary was in charge.

"What's the deal with that?" Mark asked.

"Christian evangelism in Muslim areas is technically illegal in Indonesia," Tim said. "You would just alienate everyone in the village and strain already tense relationships with nearby Christian villages and missionaries. Worst-case scenario, your presence, uninvited, could spark a riot."

Tim sure knew how to make a point. Beside me, I saw Alison reach for his knee underneath the table.

"A riot?" Elissa said, hands folded neatly in front of her, nails pressed down hard.

Tim sighed. "Sure, it can be serious. Last month there were a couple of houses burnt down in this area. But it's been simmering along like this for a while now. There's no reason for it to get worse all of a sudden. I'm not trying to scare you. I just want you to know why it's important to respect the local customs."

Alison stood and reached for the bowl of fruit on the counter behind her, neatly changing the subject at the same time. I rested my chin on my hands and drifted, suddenly exhausted. The sun had gone down, but the air being stirred into sluggish motion by the fan was still dense and warm.

No one argued when Diane suggested we head straight to bed after we were done eating. But as I stumbled up the stairs I heard her voice, high and tight, and then the others.

"I don't know if we should have—"

"Seram's quiet. There's never been any significant trouble in Daniel's village."

"Hush. Not yet."

"What is *that*?" Mark asked the next morning, gesturing contemptuously at the oversized canoe moored to the end of the dock. A canvas awning shaded eight wooden benches. On either side, bamboo outriggers stretched out like frail arms. I had a nasty suspicion that "that" was our transport to Seram.

"I've been sailing for years, and that boat is not safe in a storm," Mark said. "It doesn't even have a radio."

His conviction said he had a healthy respect for the ocean. It was nice to see he had a healthy respect for something.

"There's no other way," Gary said. "The big ferry sank two weeks ago, and the new one hasn't arrived yet."

I didn't think that particular line of argument helped Gary's case.

"Sank in a storm?" Mark asked.

"Not storm," said a short, stocky stranger who suddenly appeared in the doorway of the port office, beaming. "Pirate burn. Pirate steal money, then set fire. Close to Ambon. Two die only. But not worry. Pirate gone. Not attack small boat."

Well, that was reassuring.

Tim grinned and clasped the stranger's hand with a warmth that suggested familiarity. "Team, meet Daniel Ayal," he said. "Daniel's the pastor in Batuasa, the village you'll be staying in."

Daniel had an open, gentle face and accented but perfectly understandable English. "It good you are here. Many people excited you are coming. My children also excited," he said, as a young man appeared behind him. Daniel introduced him proudly. "He is my first child, Manuel."

"Mani," Manuel said. He rested the box he was carrying on a wooden pylon. Mani was taller than his dad, about an inch taller than I was; and he had large, gorgeous dark brown eyes that he was using to look us over frankly.

"Want some help?" Brendan offered.

"Thank you," he said, lifting the box again easily and nodding in the direction of the one-room ticket office. "There are more."

He turned and stepped confidently across the wooden plank linking the boat to the dock. It bowed under his weight.

Mark sighed, and I tried to banish a particularly vivid image of the boat splintering apart midtrip and sharks picking us off like so many hors d'oeuvres.

In the end, though, our only problem during the boat ride was sea-sickness—Brendan's, to be precise. He threw up almost as soon as the boat's motor roared to life, and continued to do so at disturbingly regular intervals for the entire trip.

The rest of us spent the time fielding questions from Mani and occasionally getting in a few of our own. When we could get him to talk about himself, he was fun to listen to. Grammatically his English was almost perfect, but his accent emphasized the vowels and softened the harsh consonants, making the words sound somehow round. In bits and pieces we learned that he was a student at the missionary school in Ambon where Tim and Alison taught. Summer holidays had started yesterday.

"What grade are you in?" Mark asked.

"Grade ten next year," Mani said proudly.

"That's like me!" Mark said. "How old are you?"

"Seventeen," Mani said without embarrassment. "We did not come to Seram until I was ten. I was a lot behind."

"You didn't go to school until you were ten? Cool!" Mark said.

"School is very good!" Mani said, puzzled. "You do not like your school?"

"I guess," Mark said, glancing past him out to sea. "I might have to change schools next year."

We all paused respectfully as Brendan rolled over on the floor of the boat and crawled for the railing.

"There's nothing left in your stomach," I said.

"*I* know that. *It* doesn't," he said after he was done retching.

"Poor thing," Drew said, patting his shoulder.

Unfortunately I think he was too miserable to enjoy the sympathy. He was too miserable to enjoy much of anything until we finally reached Seram. The clear topaz of the water as we putted into the tiny wooden dock, moving splashes of color against creamy sand as fish darted away below, the untouched sweep of beach that greeted us—it was all wasted on him. He didn't even look excited at the bevy of motorcycles waiting for us at the end of the dock. Apparently we had one more leg of the journey before we reached Mani's village.

An excited group of kids flocked from the small houses lining the beach as we tied off. They clustered nearby, staring and giggling shyly, hands over their mouths.

"All I want to know is how we're supposed to fit everything on those." Drew was looking at the bikes with the long-suffering air of someone for whom the day could not hold any more surprises.

Mani demonstrated how two people could ride back-to-back on the little wooden platform mounted behind the driver's seat. The extra motorcycles were for our luggage.

"Load them up," Gary said.

"Cool!" Mark said, and set to work willingly for the first time ever.

But loading them up proved easier said than done. Kyle took one look at my efforts to arrange the bags and pushed me firmly out of the way. He then proceeded to give me a lesson on stacking and tying in a very loud voice while he demonstrated his expertise.

The children, who were creeping in closer and closer, seemed to think this was hilarious, even though they probably couldn't understand a word we were saying. "Hello, mister! Hello, missus!" seemed to be the extent of their English vocabulary.

Daniel walked past and grinned at their chatter.

"What are they saying?" I asked.

"Laugh at clothes," he told me. "Think you wear very many clothes when hot, and big shoes. Also think you and Kyle married and you in trouble because not put bags correct."

Kyle seemed to think this was exceedingly funny.

"Tell them we're not married," I said.

"Tell them we *are* married," Kyle said.

He opened his arms for a hug and I ducked under them. The children screeched with glee. Kyle started to chase me around the bike, the shrieks from our little audience spurring him on. I heard kissing noises behind me and ran faster, catching a brief glimpse of our confused driver as I scooted past him for the second time.

Kyle snagged the back of my shirt just as Gary intervened.

"Kyle and Cori," he warned.

Kyle released me, and I stuck my tongue out at him. He winked and blew me a kiss.

Daniel turned to talk to the kids, but a woman in a doorway called out, her voice shrill and commanding, and the children scattered toward the beach, casting glances back.

Daniel looked after them, his sudden sadness obvious.

"What happened?" Kyle asked.

I dug my elbow into his ribs.

"This Muslim village," Daniel said. "I used be Muslim before I be Christian. She not want me to talk to children because I be . . ." He paused, looking for the right word, and Mani moved to fill in the blank.

"Traitor," he said, matter-of-fact.

"Yes." Daniel nodded. He threw it off with a visible effort and ges-tured toward the bikes. "Ready, yes?"

The driver of our bike grinned, exposing what looked like the only two teeth he had left, and showed me how to put my foot on the back wheel and swing myself up. I leaned against Kyle's back and felt him settle against me.

Ahead of us Drew and Mark were laughing and calling out for me to take a photo of them as we putted away along the single dirt road leading out of the village and along the coast.

chapter 4 ~

Dear Scott,

Guess what? I happen to be spending the summer in the very place where agriculture began.

Once upon a time there was a beautiful princess who lived on the island of Seram. She loved a handsome prince who, sadly, did not love her. So she ordered her people to cut her into pieces and bury her. From the places where she was buried, yams, taro, and manioc grew, and people started to cultivate the earth. That's how Seram became the Mother Island of the World.

At least, that's the way Mani tells the story.

Life on the mother island isn't as "garden of Edenish" as you might imagine, at least not in Batuasa, the fishing village where we're staying. Houses are mostly thatched huts made of wood. There are no flushing toilets, we collect drinking water in buckets from a communal tap and filter it, and electricity comes from generators. The concrete schoolhouse also serves as the town meeting hall and, until we finish our project, the church. The three hundred kids here go to school either in the morning or the afternoon—too few teachers, too many kids, so they split the school day in half. Most kids never make it past primary school.

Supermarkets are just one-room stores that stock everything from pens to dried fish to glass bottles full of Coke. Yes, Coke. Every day after we finish working on the church site, we head to the store and buy one each. Well, actually, yesterday Kyle bought three. Gary congratulated us on single-handedly distorting the local Coke economy, but the shopkeeper adores us.

We're camped behind the pastor's house at one end of the village. There's nothing between our tents and the ocean except beach and coconut trees, and behind us, the jungle starts. . . .

I looked up from my letter, searching for the right words to describe the contrast between the sharp fragments of sunlight cartwheeling off the waves and the dusky cathedral hush lingering beneath the tall trees. The first time I ventured alone past the screen of ferns marking the boundary of the jungle's domain, the sudden stillness scared me, and I backed out slowly until I reached the safety of the sun, the sand, and the others' smiles. After the first day the dread had dissipated, but it still never felt quite right to turn my back on those silent trees.

Across the way near Mani's house, Kyle let out a whoop— "Swimming! Finally!"—and I put the letter aside. The sunshine was weighty enough to prickle my sweaty skin and heat my hair. Scott could wait while we enjoyed the beach for the first time since we'd arrived.

Although we technically had some free time every afternoon, so far Mani and Daniel's free-time field trips had included a fishing boat (where we learned we all stunk at casting nets), fruit collecting (where we learned durian tastes almost as bad as it smells), and the village market (where we learned the difference between dried herring and dried tuna, and that Drew would not eat anything with an eye in it no matter how much the rest of us teased). Finally it looked like some plain and simple fun was on the agenda, or perhaps Mani had just given up on making us capable members of society.

The long sweep of beach that fronted the village was my favorite place. During those first days on the island, it became the spot I headed for with my Bible every morning after breakfast, the place I went when I needed five minutes alone. A row of tall coconut trees growing on the fringe of the jungle curved out over the sand like a one-armed embrace, and if you looked back from the beach you could see how the village had settled neatly into the bowl of the valley, as if hundreds of frail toy houses had tumbled down the surrounding hills and come to rest together at the bottom. To the left and the right, the beach and the village ended abruptly in a thick wall of glistening green—the kind of green that makes you think of a wet oil painting.

Down on the beach the boys tore off their shirts and ran straight in, yelling and pushing, sending topaz water sheeting out in white arcs. I dawdled with Drew, savoring the graininess of sand under my bare toes.

"Ready?" she said.

"You're not. Wrong color," I said, pointing to her hair tie.

Drew rolled her eyes as she pulled it loose and dropped it on the towels. "That's just silly. Who really believes that a sea monster will kidnap you if you wear green near the water?"

I half did. At least, I had while Mani was explaining the legend around the fire the night before.

"Come on!" Kyle yelled as Elissa waded in to meet them. Then he gave Brendan a nudge, and the two of them started toward us.

"No!" Drew yelped. "Leave us alone! We're coming in."

I bolted, but I didn't get far before I found myself facedown over Kyle's shoulder.

"You're heavier than you look." He grunted, as he headed for the water.

"You're stronger than you look," I managed. I couldn't get enough breath to struggle, but I could hear Mark laughing and caught a glimpse of Brendan gently herding Drew into deeper water. Somehow I didn't think that was what Kyle had in mind.

He sloshed out knee-deep and tossed me. He really was stronger than he looked. I landed flat on my back, sank, and stayed down, confident that he would come over to check on me. I waited until his shape blocked the sun, then bounced up and deposited a handful of sand down his trunks. But as I turned to flounder away, I landed on something that was bright blue and moved under my foot. I'm ashamed to say I then screamed, jumped onto Kyle, and tried to climb up him.

"A bluebottle!" I shrieked, before it registered that whatever it was, it was about ten times larger than a bluebottle and my foot wasn't hurting.

"Where? Where!" Drew demanded, evidently deciding that I had the right idea and trying to climb onto the nearest person. As this happened to be Mark, all she succeeded in doing was pushing his head underwater.

Elissa floated, feet safely elevated, scanning the sand with a small frown.

"What is a bluebottle?" Kyle asked, obligingly standing still as I reached shoulder height and stopped climbing.

"A stingy jellyfish," I said, already feeling stupid as I slid back down. I couldn't quite get myself to put my feet back on the sand though, so I just hung off his arm trying to look natural.

Mark shook off Drew and came up spluttering.

"You girls are lame!" he said scornfully when he worked out what all the fuss was about, but I noticed he said it while floating.

"It is a starfish," Mani said. He ducked under and scooped one up.

It was bigger than both my hands put together, and its bumpy arms moved in lazy protest at being dislodged. Now that I knew what to look for, I could see dozens of them nestled in the sand, showing up as electric splashes of color.

"You didn't hurt him," Mani said, flipping it over. Underneath, it looked like a lumpy yellow sponge.

"And they can't hurt *you*, silly," Kyle said.

I let go of his arm. "I know!" I said, realizing I sounded like a third grader.

"Are you sure they don't bite?" Drew asked.

"Good *night!*" Kyle exclaimed, grabbing the starfish from Mani and advancing upon Drew.

Total chaos ensued.

It ended with all three girls on the beach by the towels while Kyle, Mani, and Mark mounted starfish offensives on one another. Drew shook herself off like a cat caught in the rain and finally settled down on her stomach next to me.

"Boys!" she said, minus the note of affection that usually accompanied that word.

"Brendan didn't chase us," Elissa pointed out.

Drew's expression softened, and she smiled. I looked over and caught it just before she buried her face in the towel.

"He might have had an ulterior motive in restraint," I said, winking at Elissa over the top of Drew's head. "Like not wanting to blow a week's worth of flirting."

Drew looked up. The smile was definitely gone. "I'm not flirting!" She glared at me.

"I said *he* was flirting," I said, confused as to how I had suddenly landed in such hot water.

"If you want to talk about flirting, let's talk about you and Kyle!"

"What?!" I said. I was so astounded, that was all I got out.

"Guys. Come on," Elissa said. I half expected her next words to be "Play nicely."

"Whatever," Drew said, two bright spots of color burning in her cheeks. She looked away, and her next words were so muffled I almost missed them. "Brendan deserves better."

"That's rubbish!" I said, still mostly focused on the fact that she had put Kyle's and my names in the same sentence as the word *flirting*.

"You have no idea what you're talking about, Cori! The worst thing you've probably done in your life is break curfew by half an hour."

I was insulted. I had done much worse things than that.

"Drew, the past is the past," I said, wondering exactly what was in this past that Drew, for all her open, easy smiles and frequent laughter, was so careful to skirt around. I didn't have to wonder for much longer.

"Easy to say when the past isn't your older sister being hit by a drunk driver walking home from school. Or when you end up in the hospital needing your stomach pumped two years later. Or," she said, crumpling, "sleeping with someone whose name you can't even remember while you were drunk."

I felt Elissa looking at me, waiting for me to say something that would make this right somehow, but I was drawing a blank.

"I didn't know you have a sister."

"I *had* a sister. That's the past now, right?" Two tears left tiny dark starbursts in the sand where they'd landed.

"That's not what I meant. I meant that everyone does things they wish they could change."

"Yeah," Drew said, more sad than angry now. "But some things you can never make right." We all knew she wasn't talking about her sister anymore.

"God can," Elissa said softly.

"But that doesn't change what happened. The past *is* still the past." She got up and started down the beach.

As Elissa and I sat there for a minute, wondering what to say, Brendan left the water and casually sauntered down the beach after her.

Elissa looked worried. "Should we do something?"

I didn't know. "Maybe she'll talk to him."

She sighed and started to get up. "I'll go see if she's okay."

We were interrupted by Kyle, Mani, and Mark as they galloped up and threw themselves down beside us in a shower of cold, salty drops.

"Hey, look." Kyle gestured toward the horizon. "He wraps himself in light as with a garment; he stretches out the heavens like a tent and lays the beams of his upper chamber on their waters."

"What?" I asked. Brendan had just caught up with Drew. I took my eyes off them and focused on Kyle with difficulty.

"Psalm 104," he said. "I was reading it this morning. It's perfect."

I followed his gaze. It was perfect. If it hadn't been for the white streak of distant clouds lying low, I wouldn't have been able to tell where the ocean ended and the sky began. Both glowed.

"We are glad you are here," Mani said. "We have been praying for two years for money and help to build a church. Now Father will not have to preach in the schoolhouse. Many people from around Batuasa will come, and it will be a place of prayer . . ." He stopped and ducked his head, suddenly shy.

I wondered whether I'd ever wanted something that wasn't purely selfish with as much intensity as Mani had just managed to pack into a couple of sentences.

"What are you going to do after you finish high school?" Elissa asked eventually, breaking the silence that had descended upon our little group.

"I would like to go to Bible college," Mani whispered, as if sharing a secret too precious to say out loud. He looked out over the water, unclenched his fist, and let the handful of sand he'd been clutching dribble out.

"My teachers at school know about a Bible college in Bandung. Can you imagine? Three years just to study the Bible and learn about God?" He sounded awed. "But that will take a lot of money, so I will probably come back here and work with Father, fishing. Or maybe I will get a job in Ambon. I would like to come back here, I think."

I looked down and felt small. First Drew, now Mani. My biggest problem was choosing which country to go to university in. And so far I hadn't received any divine answers on that one.

The other three were quiet too.

"Would you like to visit the U.S.?" Kyle asked suddenly.

Mani laughed without scorn, eyes closed, head thrown back, and white teeth flashing against brown skin.

"That would cost more money than a fisherman makes in one year," he pointed out. "More than Bible college."

"Mani!" A little voice piped up from behind me. *"Mama pilang datang langsung!"*

"We should go," Mani translated for us, scooping up his four-year-old sister, Tina, and tickling her until she shrieked with laughter and curled up into a small wriggling ball.

"Here." Mark held out his arms, and Mani passed her across. Tina adored Mark. She wound one hand into his black curls and used the other to poke at his dimple. He growled at her and pretended to bite the persistent finger. She only giggled and snuggled closer.

"There's Drew and Brendan," Elissa said, relieved.

"Well, well, well . . . ," Kyle drawled.

He didn't need to say anything else. They were wandering slowly up the beach, the backs of their hands casually brushing with every second step. Drew looked up at Brendan and nodded, smiling.

I hoped this meant she wasn't mad at me anymore.

That evening brought our first presentation, and what I remember most clearly are the faces of the children as they watched the puppet show. There were easily sixty kids there, sitting in the dust in front of the schoolhouse with the adults standing behind. On the edge of the crowd a scrawny little boy leaned forward on his knees. His black hair was cropped so short that his patchy scalp showed through, and he wore a tiny pair of shorts and a T-shirt so holey it barely hung together. He stared at that simple puppet stage with wonder, too absorbed to laugh, even while the other children buzzed with excitement as the wicked witch was vanquished and happy harmony restored in Puppet Land.

I watched him all through our show. He was equally rapt with our mediocre rendition of "Amazing Grace" in Indonesian, and even hung on every word of Brendan's sermon.

After the performance we retired to the schoolhouse to take off our mime makeup. As I finished scrubbing, I looked up to find Drew watching me.

"Brendan is the best!" she said.

I nodded while I considered and discarded several different responses. Considering where we'd ended up last time, I decided to play it safe and just kept nodding.

She cocked her head to one side and eyed me speculatively.

"You're still mad, aren't you?"

That was too much. I laughed. "I wasn't the one who was mad!"

Drew made a shooing motion. "I wasn't really mad at you. Well, not for long," she amended. "And you were mad, about the Kyle thing."

I stopped laughing and looked around to make sure he wasn't within earshot.

Drew flapped her hands again. "The point is, I love you too much to stay mad with you anyway." She threw her arms around my neck and squeezed.

"I'm capable of loving and being mad at the same time," I choked out.

I don't think she even heard me. Her eyes were sparkling, and her cheeks, under the ghostly patina the white makeup always left on our skin, were flushed.

"I told him about Kelli, and the partying, and the rest of it. Then he said it's the future that really matters." She didn't even pause to check my reaction.

"That's what I told you!"

"Did you?" she said, then shrugged.

"So what's up with you two, then?" I asked, figuring I was on safe ground again.

"I don't know." She beamed. "Come on; we'd better get out there and meet people."

"This conversation is not finished," I promised, following her out into the crowd.

In the middle of the square Mark was pulling long thin balloons out of his pocket, blowing them up, and twisting them into animal shapes. He was surrounded by children clamoring for his creations, and Tina was clinging to his leg and looking proprietary. The little boy I'd been watching was on the edge of the crowd, too small to push his way in.

I wandered over and knelt down. He stuck one finger into his mouth and looked at the ground.

"Hey there, kiddo."

He didn't look up.

"Mark, can you make me a dog?" I asked above the heads of the eager masses.

"Aren't you a bit old?"

"Not for me, dork!"

He flashed a grin as he deftly tied off the end, twisted the blue balloon into the shape of a dog, and handed it over the reaching hands.

"Here." I had to hold it right under the little boy's nose before he focused on it. "This is for you."

He might not have understood what I said, but his smile was sudden and sweet, and when he finally reached for it he clutched the fragile toy to his chest so fiercely I was scared it would burst. As we eyed each other, a pair of bare brown legs appeared behind his small head, and a girl reached down and scooped him up, settling him easily on her hip. She wore a faded dress, and her feet were bare.

"Is this your sister?" I asked him.

The little boy answered with a whole stream of Indonesian, of which I understood not a single word.

Mani, who was standing nearby, stepped in. "This is Leila," he said. "And her son, Budi."

Her son! I'd have guessed she was my age.

Leila smiled shyly at me and said something, using her free hand to gesture to the camera attached to my waist pack.

"She says you are very kind to Budi and wants to know if you will take a picture because she has never had a photograph," Mani translated.

I took out my camera and waved them around so that the setting sun fell directly on their faces, smoothing their skin into a rich chocolate. Leila stared at me solemnly, her weight shifted to one side for balance, a long dark braid falling over her other shoulder. Budi was looking down at the balloon in his arms.

"Now with you," Mani told me, taking the camera and waving me into the picture.

"Smile," I said to Leila, demonstrating. She looked like she wanted to, but she hesitated. Budi had no such inhibitions. He looked up at me and grinned, joy in his eyes, just as Mani pressed the button.

chapter 5 ~

Friday, July 1

D*ear Cori,*

No one's at home today, so I've taken a picnic blanket and a book outside under the big oak tree—where we had the picnic last summer. It's warm and quiet. Too quiet. I wish you were here to make it slightly less peaceful. . . .

Thursday, July 14

Dear Scott,

I just got your first letter here and it made my day! I write to you perched on top of a knee-high plastic barrel with my left foot in a bucket of seawater that Mark just fetched for me. I have blister number five on the exact same spot on my little toe, which has to be close to a world record. At least we're finished working for the day. Now we're just hanging around the kitchen area, getting in Diane's way while she's trying to cook us pizza wraps in the camping oven. Pizza wraps (for the uninitiated) are spam, cheese, and tomato sauce wrapped in pastry. They sound revolting, but they taste okay.

Brendan is wandering around making chicken noises and begging me to cut his hair. I have become the team's official haircutter (due solely to the fact that I volunteered to cut Mark's the other day and told no one that my only prior experience cutting hair was on Tanya's Barbie dolls). Kyle and Drew are trying to get a coconut open with a sharp stone, and Mani is laughing at them.

With the state that our clothes are in, we should be doing laundry, but it's such a perfect evening, I don't think anyone wants to be productive. It's finally cooling down, the sun is setting, and the ocean is all liquid gold. When Gary gets back we might take a dip. We need it. Today was long and hot, and we all smell like . . . like we've been digging in the sun for seven hours. I'm becoming quite the construction worker, though. The first week my hands blistered so badly I had to wrap bandannas around them, but they're toughening up now. I had no idea it would take so long just to dig out the foundations. . . .

Thursday, July 14

Dear Cori,

I haven't received a letter from Indonesia yet, although I practically ambush the postman every day. I know you said that letters could take three weeks to arrive, but it feels like forever since I've heard from you, and it's starting to get boring over here, and I miss you. All right, pity party over, for now. Moving on to more interesting things. . . .

Tuesday, July 27

Dear Scott,

It's right after breakfast and we're supposed to be having God-time, but this morning it's just not happening, so rather than sit here and brood I *thought I'd write a letter. Drew has taken the other option. She's flat on her back in the sand, and from the yawn I just saw, I don't think that it's so she can contemplate the beauty of the sky.*

We're all tired. The whole village seemed unsettled last night. There was a meeting in the schoolhouse that went until all hours, and although we're not camped nearby we could hear shouting and cheering until very late. The mangy stray dogs that hang around were barking and fighting, and the roosters were crowing. All Indonesian roosters seem to be retarded. This morning they started crowing at three o'clock, and they haven't stopped yet. I could cheerfully break every one of their scrawny necks with my bare hands.

There is also a big snake that has taken up residence under the water pump where we fill our buckets, and although Mani says he is harmless, I do not like snakes. I do not like the big spider I saw yesterday, and I do not like digging my own toilet. The novelty has well and truly worn off.

All right . . . sigh . . . unless I want to work myself up into a raging bad mood, I'd better start focusing on some things I do like.

I do like the fact that we are finished digging, and the floor has been poured. We just have to raise the beams that will support the roof, and thatch the roof frame. The church is much bigger than I thought it would be, and it's so exciting to see it take shape. . . .

After the disturbed night, the day didn't get much better. I thought we were done with digging, but I'd forgotten about the posts for the roof frame. So it was back to work with the shovels, carving out foundation holes beside our freshly poured concrete floor.

Not even Budi's visit brightened me up for long. About midmorning I spied him coming in from the beach, hands behind his back and a wide grin on his face. He stopped beside my hole and stood there chanting my name until I paid him some attention.

"Hi Cori. Hi Cori. *Hi Cori!*"

I think it was the only thing he knew how to say in English.

I finally put down my shovel and turned around. We'd tried to discourage him from coming to visit during working hours, but he wouldn't stay away. This time he was soaking wet, his spiky black hair plastered to his head. Even his long eyelashes were beaded with water.

"Look at you," I said. "You're all wet. Your mum's not going to be too happy with that."

He didn't understand a thing I said, but he giggled anyway, and I had to smile. It always surprised me to hear such a deep, rich chortle coming from such a little boy. He brought his hands forward and, chattering incomprehensibly, proudly presented me with a purple starfish.

Mani gave me the short version. "He said he went to find this for you."

Budi had been so disconsolate when his balloon dog finally deflated that I'd dug through my backpack and found the only toy I'd brought. It was a small bear with a bandage over one eye that Luke gave me the night before I left in case I "got lonely." Now Budi carried the bear with him everywhere—and brought me interesting presents at odd moments.

"It's beautiful," I said sincerely, reaching out to take the starfish with only a slight shiver. I was gradually getting used to the creatures, but I still didn't like handling them, no matter how often the guys told me they were harmless.

I looked it over from every angle while its fat arms waved at me.

"What am I going to do with it?" I asked Kyle out of the corner of my mouth.

"I don't know; it's your present," Kyle said, laughing.

"Mani, tell him I want him to put it back in the water, so I can go see it this afternoon when we go swimming," I said.

Budi looked worried as this was relayed.

"He says you won't know which one he is."

"I'll be able to find him, because he's the most beautiful starfish I have ever seen," I improvised wildly.

Budi took it back in his small hands and trotted off happily. We went back to digging.

The morning seemed very long.

"Once there was a boy named Jip," Mark started.

"And he had a monkey named Kiki." Brendan said the predictable second line that had to be uttered before the rest of the story could evolve.

But most of us weren't in the mood to let Jip and Kiki go on yet another adventure to Alaska, sip cocktails in the Caribbean, or learn how to belly dance in Hawaii while we did all the hard work.

"Jip and Kiki were . . . ," Mark prompted.

"Jip and Kiki were digging a never-ending hole on a great big desert island," Drew said sullenly.

That, at least, made me smile.

"And they were digging this hole because . . . ," Mark said, refusing to be sidetracked.

"They needed a new toilet, and the old one was full," Kyle said, already knee-deep in his hole, dusty and sweating.

"Kyle, that's gross," Drew said.

"Full of cocaine," I said. "That's where they stashed all the drugs."

"*They* being the wicked pirates on the island," Elissa said primly. "Because we all know Jip and Kiki are not drug dealers."

"All right," I said. "It was the wicked pirates from the Lightning Gang who hid the drugs in the toilet."

"Yes," Mani said, and we all perked up. Mani didn't often contribute to the story game, but when he did it was always interesting.

"Jip and Kiki were on Laut Seram." He pointed east. "Those islands have many pirates. The pirates stole the spices, like nutmeg and cloves, and also stole many of the people to make them slaves."

"For real?" Mark asked.

"Yes," Mani said. "They were not called the Lightning Gang. That is like in America. I have read about your gangs in America." He tossed up another shovelful of sandy dirt. "I would be afraid of them."

"I guess the gangs back home might be a bit like you guys with the Muslim and Christian villages," Kyle said. "But you get along better than the gangs in the States."

"Sometimes we do not 'get along,'" Mani said, deliberately adopting Kyle's slang. A shadow crossed his face. "Sometimes there are many troubles. But we have the *pela* between the villages. Maybe the gangs should have a pela agreement."

"What's *pela*?" I asked, resting on my shovel and trying to stretch out my back.

"Pela is part of the adat law," Mani said.

We all nodded. We already knew that adat laws were customs and commands that had been passed down from wise ancestors. The week before, Mani had told us a particularly spine-chilling fable about how neglect of an adat law triggered the anger of the ancestral spirits. As punishment, the angry spirits had sent disease and death on the entire village.

I still hadn't figured out whether Mani actually believed these stories or not, but they were pretty spooky when it was late at night and there were just the seven of us huddled around a small fire on the beach. He saved his best stories for when Gary was not around. Gary was all for learning the history and culture of Indonesia, but he wasn't too happy about what he called "that spirit nonsense."

"Pela is the oldest adat law," Mani said solemnly. "It comes from when the people of these islands were mostly headhunting tribes."

"They really used to hunt heads?" Drew asked.

Everyone stopped digging.

"Yes," Mani said. "It used to be that every time there was a wedding there had to be a head taken from an enemy. And also a head was hunted when the important houses in the village were built, to make the spirits happy."

"And you think gangs in LA are scary," Kyle said, almost to himself.

"That's why pela was so good," Mani said. "A Muslim village and a Christian village are pela partners. They exchange a binding oath that they will protect and help one other. Then the important men in the village must drink each other's blood from a special cup after everyone has dipped their weapons in the blood." He patted the machete that hung from a strip of cloth wound around his waist.

"That is the best story yet," Mark said.

Elissa's mouth opened, then shut again, like a goldfish.

"Do you have a pela partner?" Brendan asked.

"Tahima. The Muslim village, five kilometers that way." Mani pointed west. "We have been pela for as long as the oldest village elders can remember." His expressive face suddenly looked sad. "But they say it is different now. Lots of Indonesians from Java have come, and things are different."

I remembered Gary talking about this in boot camp. Over 90 percent of Indonesia's two hundred million people call themselves Muslim, and the Spice Islands are the only area in the country with a significant Christian population (mostly because the Portuguese and Spanish ruling the area during the early years of the spice trade imported Catholicism). Muslims and Christians in the area had co-existed fairly peacefully for centuries, but the increasing numbers of Muslims moving into the region during the last thirty years had begun to disrupt this balance.

"Seram is our home now," Mani continued. "We respect adat. Others do not, and there has been much talk lately." For a minute he looked worried, and then his face cleared. "That's why it was so good of God to send you here to help build a church. He has provided for us, as always. And I got to meet you, like six new brothers and sisters."

He went back to his digging, satisfied.

I wasn't. For some reason, his words left me uneasy.

That night the moon hung low in the sky, painting a luminescent pathway from the horizon to us until the light fractured with the suck and pull of the waves close to shore. The ocean was unusually restless even though the air was still, and the movement of the water was hypnotic. The gathering of each wave sent cold silver racing lightly along the tip of its crest, dancing in the foam, until it was swallowed back into the formless darkness by the rhythmic retreat.

We had our team meeting on the beach. I sat between Brendan and Kyle, enjoying their solid warmth and the cheerful glow of the fire. Drew was snuggled close on the other side of Brendan. Tucked discreetly between their legs, the back of his hand rested lightly against hers, fingers tangling. I hoped Gary couldn't see that from where he was sitting. We'd all heard the "touching people of the opposite sex in public is taboo" lecture at least three times. We were trying, but I'd never realized how often I touched other people, even just friends, until it was forbidden.

"Hey, you two in the boots," Diane said from across the fire, using a team joke and pointing to Kyle and Mark. "I need a letter home from you to send on the boat tomorrow. Okay?"

"Cori will write one for me, won't you, Cori?" Mark smiled angelically.

"Sure," I said. "I'll tell your parents everything you've been up to. And I'll tell them that when I cut your hair I shaved it all off."

"Tell them the mission assignment's been changed, and we're running Bible classes on a cruise ship," Drew said.

"Tell them we switched to a motorbike team." That was Kyle.

"Go ahead," Mark said, with an uncharacteristically bitter note in his voice. "They won't care."

I suddenly realized that Mark hadn't received a single letter since we'd arrived. Come to think of it, he hadn't gotten any at boot camp either.

"A letter. By tomorrow lunch. Written by you," Diane said to Mark as Daniel arrived and settled himself by his wife's side.

Daniel was going to share his story, and while we'd heard bits and pieces from Mani, we were looking forward to hearing the complete version. Two logs in the fire settled lower with a sudden crash, sending a hot shower of sparks up into the night as Daniel began to speak.

"For this, I think best if I talk the Bahasa Indonesian and Mani talk the English. Yes, okay?" In the firelight Daniel's face looked younger than I knew he must be, but his eyes were old.

It was always that way with Daniel. Coming out of our tent once, I'd seen him watching Mani horsing around with Kyle and Mark, and there had been such a yearning in his eyes that I had looked away, not wanting him to know that I had seen through his gentle friendliness to that heaviness, not understanding.

Daniel started to talk, the soft sounds of the words in Indonesian blending together into one soothing stream. Mani translated sentence by sentence.

"I was born in Bandung, on the island of Java," he began formally. "My father owned a store selling wooden furniture. I was the oldest child of six brothers and three sisters. All in my family were Muslim. You know, the word *Muslim* means submission to God. My father was a good Muslim. He taught us to pray, learn the Koran, give alms to the poor, and fast during the month of Ramadan. When I grew older, my father agreed with Mariati's parents that we should marry."

Mariati smiled at that and cuddled Tina closer. Tina's smooth cheek glowed golden in the firelight, her eyes fluttering as she fought to stay awake.

"When Mani was five years old I met a Korean missionary friend. We talked for many months about Muhammad, Jesus, Allah, the Bible, and the Koran. When we were done talking, I became a Christian, along with Mariati," Daniel said simply. "My father was very angry, and my family said that if I would not change my mind, we must go."

Daniel shifted slightly and stared into the fire. Mani translated without hesitation, as if he had heard this many times before.

"My friend organized for me to get a job cleaning the church that many of the Americans went to, and I learned. For four years I studied with them, and then I heard God telling me to come here and make a new home on Seram."

"What about your family?" Brendan asked, voice low.

The night was silent except for the growl of the waves and the crackling of flames. I licked my lips and tasted salt.

Mani started to translate, but Daniel held up his hand and replied in English. "I have never spoke to them for eleven years, except in my heart. To them, we are like dead."

I shivered and felt Kyle touch me lightly on the back, his hand warm.

Daniel started to speak Indonesian again. "For my wife, it was worse. I was not there when she told her family, and her father was very angry, beyond all reason. He beat her and told her to divorce me and marry a Muslim man. She was pregnant with our second child, a son, but he died because of the beating, and she was very sick. For many years we thought we would have no more children, but God has blessed us again with Christina."

I looked at Tina. She was asleep, lips parted slightly and one small hand curled lightly over her mother's. In Mariati's face I couldn't see any hint of the pain that this story represented. She looked peaceful, and when her eyes met Daniel's, the bond between them was almost tangible.

"That's awful," Drew said. She started to say something, hesitated, then said it anyway. "Weren't you angry with God for letting that happen?"

"Angry? No," Daniel said. "I am sad then. Today sometimes I am sad. And for a long time I wonder why. But God show me that I do not need to know why, now. He promise it will all be good."

Even then, before everything else that happened, part of me wanted to dismiss that as simplistic—the words of a man who didn't own a TV, who had never traveled outside Indonesia, who spoke broken English. But I'd seen the look in Daniel's eyes while he was telling the story. I'd seen the way he lived now. How he talked about biblical characters as though they were close friends, and how he prayed all the time —for us, for his family, for the whole village.

It might have been simple, but it rang true.

chapter 6 ~

It was Tuesday night a week later that Diane stopped by our tent to scold Drew and me for staying up too late talking. She seemed perfectly fine then, but the next morning she woke up doubled over, pale and sweating. She could hardly talk. It was obvious that she needed a doctor, and not just one at the small clinic in Hatumentan, twenty kilometers away by motorcycle. Gary had no choice—Diane clearly had to catch that morning's boat to Ambon, and he had to go with her.

The rest of us felt that we did have a choice, though, and we wanted to stay. Even if Diane did have appendicitis and we had to cut the mission short, we could catch the next boat to Ambon in three days, and those three days would be long enough for us to finish the church.

After a brief hesitation Gary agreed, his face drawn and strained as he issued a litany of instructions and stuffed clothes into his backpack at the same time. Daniel's in charge. Help Mariati with the cooking. Here are your passports and money; keep them safe. If I'm not back on Saturday, be on that boat, and Tim or I will meet you at the dock in Ambon. . . . Pray.

Later, after it happened, while we were hiking through the jungle, I sometimes played the what-if game in my head. What if I'd never gone on a missions trip? What if I'd gone to Florida with the church group like Mum wanted me to? What if we'd left with Gary that day? That was always my last what-if; after that, there were no more jumping-off points. Those last three days were a countdown to something far larger than finding out whether we were going to have to head home or stay out the summer. We just didn't know it.

It was weird after they left. We were worried about Diane for one thing, and now that there was every chance we would have to leave on Saturday, thoughts of home popped into my head all the time—running water, flushing toilets, Scott's face when I arrived home four weeks early. But even that wasn't enough to get me really excited. Every time I thought about it, I realized again that leaving meant leaving everyone, not just Mani and his family. Despite the fact that there were odd moments when I would cheerfully have donated one or all of my teammates to any local headhunters still in the area, I wasn't ready to say good-bye.

We spent most of those last three days thatching, but not before we had a fight about it. Kyle and Brendan decided that only the guys should be allowed up on the roof. Brendan was at least reasonable about it and quietly outlined why he thought the three girls should "coordinate the ground operations." Kyle just told us it wasn't safe. Then he lost his temper when I said it was just as unsafe for them. Mark, surprisingly, came to our defense and told them we were old enough to decide for ourselves. I think he was just peeved because the others hadn't consulted him before trying to lay down the law.

In the end I was wishing I'd agreed to coordinate the ground operations after all. Laying prickly bundles of thatch so they fit just right
was not as easy as Mani made it look, and he was kept busy scuttling
back and forth and tidying up after our mistakes. He'd look at our
progress and pause. Sometimes his mouth twitched, but he never said
anything. He just pushed the bundles around, tightened the binding,
slapped the next one down, and nodded.

We finished late on Friday afternoon, climbed down the bamboo
ladders, and stood there looking at it. I guess it really wasn't all that
much to look at—just a concrete floor, wooden walls punctuated by
large open windows, and a thatched roof. But to me it was beautiful,
and I don't think I've ever been as proud as I was at that instant. The
others must have felt the same way, because when Mark threw his bandanna into the air with a yell, we all followed suit.

We had our team meeting in the church that night, to "baptize
it," as Mani put it. The rest of us had looked at one another blankly
when he'd said that we should bless the church, but listening to him
pray . . . it was as if we were not even there. Mani spoke in Indonesian,
but the passionate yearning in his voice was so intense that I felt all the
tiny hairs on my arms go up. Sometimes when he prayed I got that
feeling—a tingling on the back of my neck as if something very power-
ful and slightly unpredictable was hovering just above me. Mani never
prayed casually.

I still didn't know what I was going to say when my turn came
around, and I felt like an idiot. I'd never prayed over a building before.
As I looked around for inspiration, a gentle breeze whispered in warm

through the windows. The darkness was soft and fragrant, and the village was quiet. Everything we'd been hearing about pela, adat, and tension between the villages seemed very far away. In the end I asked that the church would be an instrument of peace.

We sat silently after we were done, listening to the rustle of the palm trees and the constant lisp of moving water. Drew stretched out on the floor and put her head in my lap. I ran my fingers through her hair, and she sighed.

"You pack tomorrow in morning," Daniel said finally. "In case leave on boat in afternoon."

Kyle groaned and rolled over. "But we might not have to leave."

"Maybe. But I think you leave. And I think maybe good," Daniel said, standing up heavily. "I am go now. *Selamat malam.*"

"*Selamat malam,*" we all chorused.

"He wants us to leave?" Mark asked as we watched Daniel's shadow cross to the house and then continue past it, down the road to the village.

Mani stayed quiet, his face turned away from the light of the lantern.

"I think he's just worried," Elissa said.

"Why? The roof's finished. We're not doing anything else hard."

"I don't think it's the building," I said.

"What then?" Mark demanded, looking from me to Brendan and back to me again.

"I don't know." It was hard to put the vague sense of uneasiness into words. I could hear the sound of raised voices again, faint, from the direction of the schoolhouse. It sounded as though the villagers were having another meeting.

"Mani?" Mark said.

Mani stayed silent, all his earlier excitement at blessing the church gone.

"You know what?" Kyle said, in an obvious attempt to change the subject. "The church needs a cross. If we get organized early enough tomorrow, we can go find one."

"There are logs here already," Elissa said.

"But it would be cooler if we found it ourselves," Kyle said.

"I know a good place. About one hour's walk," Mani said. Kyle's idea seemed to have cheered him up a little, but not much.

Drew groaned without opening her eyes. "An hour?"

"If Gary and Diane are back tomorrow, you'll be walking more than that on our first hike this weekend," Kyle said.

There it was again, that big *if*.

Our "good nights" sounded strained, as if we were all listening too hard to hear ourselves say them on what might be our last night in Seram. Mani didn't even say good night. He just turned and trudged off toward the house, alone.

I couldn't get to sleep. Drew was out like a light, and Elissa didn't take much longer, but I couldn't wind down. Finally I got up and slipped out of the tent, holding my breath at how loud the zipper sounded. I didn't need a flashlight—the moon was almost full, spilling light carelessly. I pulled on my boots and headed for the church.

Kyle had beaten me to it. I couldn't see him, but I could hear him. He was speaking quietly but intensely, and I moved toward the sound, concentrating so hard on locating him in the darkness inside that I didn't pay any attention to his words. Suddenly I tripped over something soft, flinging both hands out instinctively and smacking him square in the back of the head right as he said, "Amen."

"Kyle!" I said his name as we tumbled forward, and it probably saved me from being pounded. I won't repeat what he said as we were getting ourselves untangled, but he managed to put words together in ways I'd never thought of doing before.

"What are you *doing?*" he snapped when he figured out who it was.

"What are *you* doing? Who are you talking to?"

"I was praying. I'm never going to get to sleep now. Thanks a lot," he said, still breathing like a winded horse. The hand that was gripping my arm slid down and grasped my fingers. My heart rate, which had started to slow, sped up again.

"Let's go to the beach," I said, ignoring the fact that I knew exactly what Gary would have had to say to that suggestion.

Kyle pulled me to my feet without hesitating.

We walked silently at first, following the strip of pebbly sand away from the village as it narrowed between the ocean and the jungle, watching thousands of ribbons of moonlight skimming across peaceful ripples. Kyle was still holding my hand. I wondered whether I should pull it away, but he didn't seem to think it was a big deal, so I left it where it was.

"Come to Brendan's for the rest of the summer," Kyle said suddenly.

"What?"

We'd just passed one of the village's fishing boats pulled up onto the sand above the high-tide mark. I'd been wondering what my life would have been like if I'd been born here instead of Australia, and what Mani was going to do once we left. Kyle's command came completely out of left field.

"Mark and I are going to Brendan's if we have to leave tomorrow. You should come," Kyle said.

"What are Mark's parents going to say about that?" I asked, seizing the opportunity to fish for some of the missing puzzle pieces of Mark's story. I was fairly sure Kyle had them, and he didn't disappoint.

"They won't care. He says they were so busy fighting when he got on the plane for Florida they almost forgot to say good-bye. They gave him a choice—a missions trip or summer camp. He chose this because Indonesia was further away from home than camp in Colorado." Kyle spoke with grudging respect and a reluctant fondness.

I glanced at him. His hair was frosted silver, his face in shadow. I couldn't see his expression, but I decided to ask anyway.

"Do you miss your parents?"

"My real parents?" He sighed and went silent for a long moment. "Sort of. Sometimes. Maybe it's more the idea of parents I miss than the real thing. They used to fight all the time. When they started up at night I'd climb out the window and go meet the guys in the park down the street. They only caught me twice, and Dad didn't even belt me for it. One night I just didn't go home, you know. But my aunt and uncle are cool. They let me move in with them after everything that happened, and pretty much treat me like their other kids. They're all older, though. Do you miss your parents? And Scott?" There was an edge to that last word.

"I want to share this with him. I want him to meet you guys," I said, reaching up automatically to touch the ring.

"We don't have much in common," Kyle said, dropping my hand. It felt cold without his warmth.

"I think you do. You remind me of him in some ways."

It wasn't that they looked alike. Scott was taller, broader, heavier.

Kyle even moved differently—with a restless grace. One glance at Kyle, and I could tell what he was feeling. With Scott, it was in his voice. That was something they both had—when they were around I automatically tuned in to what they were feeling. I wondered whether it would be confusing if they were both in the same room. The thought was unsettling.

"Sure," Kyle said. "While he was getting his pilot's license I was in juvenile detention. I can see how you could think we're kindred spirits."

"Stop it," I said.

Kyle kicked a fallen coconut and sent it spinning into the dark, dead end of the beach where the jungle kissed the ocean. We'd run out of sand. We turned around and started back.

"I don't think I could anyway," I said, going back to the subject of Brendan's ranch. "My parents are going to want me home before I leave again."

"Have you made your mind up about school yet?" he asked.

I growled at that question, and Kyle laughed.

"Just flip a coin," he said. "Or pick UCLA."

"Another topic," I said, not wanting to tackle the issue of university either and searching for neutral territory. "Ummmm . . . favorite book of the Bible?"

"Revelation," he answered promptly. "It's like the rest of the Bible on acid."

If he'd deliberately tried to shift the mood, he succeeded. My eyes teared up as I tried to laugh quietly. "At some point tomorrow I'm going to ask that again, and I dare you to give the same answer in front of Elissa."

Kyle reached out and took my hand again as we approached the church. He paused at the girls' tent, and I thought he was going to say something, but he just brushed my cheek gently and turned away. His fingers were cool, and I felt suddenly sad.

That Saturday morning was chaotic. We were up with the sun, and it took us until eleven before we were mostly packed and ready to set out on our expedition. I put Brendan in charge of storing all the leftover food in the church while Kyle and I disassembled the camping stove.

"What do I do with these?" Mark held up one of our shovels.

"Leave them with the rest of this stuff," Brendan called.

"I can't find my work gloves," Elissa said.

"And I can't find two of my bras," Drew yelled from our tent.

Mani, working with Brendan to pack the food into boxes, tried to look as if he hadn't understood that sentence, but incomprehension is a hard act to pull off when you already look scandalized.

"They're on our clothesline," Mark said. "You put them there last week when yours was full."

"Is the stove going or staying?" Kyle asked. "Hey. Isn't it malaria medication morning?"

I'd completely forgotten. I looked at Elissa.

"Don't you have it?" she asked.

"I've only got the first aid kit. Diane kept all the prescription stuff."

"Gary must have taken it then."

"It doesn't matter," I said. "We'll take it tomorrow. One day's not going to kill us."

"Can I have some plastic wrap?" Mark asked, far too casually. His left hand, which was holding the handle of his bucket, twitched.

I bent over and took a look at what was inside. "No," I said, gazing at three dead starfish. "You're not taking those."

"Why not? They're dried enough now. It's been ten days."

"They stink," Drew said sternly. "We told you not to take them out of the water."

"But they're my souvenir!"

"Well, you're going to have to find another one," I said. "I've told you before, you can't take them through customs."

"Go and throw them out," Elissa said. Even she sounded annoyed.

Faced with all three of us, Mark trotted meekly off toward the jungle. His coconspirators, Kyle and Brendan, pretended to be very busy with what they were doing.

Daniel let us leave the tents standing and our sleeping bags unrolled when we told him we could get them down and packed in under fifteen minutes. Everything else was nearly sorted. Our little camp, tucked away behind Mani's house, looked bare without full clotheslines and the mini kitchen.

"Come back here by one thirty at most," Daniel said firmly as we got ready to set out.

"Me go!" Tina begged. She and Budi were playing with pebbles.

Budi grinned winningly and held out his stones, inviting me to play.

"You have to stay," Mani told her. "We'll be back soon."

"*Di sini.*" Mariati pressed a woven basket with a broad shoulder strap into Mani's hands and tousled his hair.

"*Terima kasih.* See you soon," he added in English.

I looked back as we walked away and saw Daniel and the two little figures still waving as we disappeared into the trees.

chapter 7 ~

We found the perfect log, and we didn't have to walk an hour to do it either, which was good because it was taking the guys forever to carry it back. It was a bit hard on Brendan, as he was the tallest by at least six inches, and Mani and Mark were a good bit shorter than Kyle.

"I don't know how the Romans' prisoners ever carried their own crosses all by themselves," Kyle panted, using both hands to balance the log on his shoulder.

Brendan grunted.

"This is not even hardwood, not teak," Mani said. "That would be very heavy."

"Correction," Kyle said. "That would be impossible. This is very heavy."

"We would offer to help," Drew said sweetly, "but it's clearly men's work."

"Haven't you heard?" Kyle said. "You've been liberated. You can drink, smoke, vote, and join the army now. Isn't that what you wanted?"

"I couldn't possibly." Drew sounded shocked. "A real lady wouldn't even consider such things."

Mani glanced back at her. It often took him awhile to figure out when we were joking.

"Well . . . ," Kyle said suggestively. Kyle has the ability to take a single word and turn it into a whole sentence.

I rolled my eyes and lifted my camera to take a photo as he grinned at me.

"We're almost home anyway," Mark pointed out.

As he said that, Mani stopped and cocked his head. Mark was right; we were close. But something wasn't right. It took me a couple of seconds to work out that the angry hum I could hear rising and falling through the trees was the sound of voices.

By the time I'd figured it out, the guys had ditched the log and we were all moving, hurrying without knowing why.

In front of me, Drew tripped and went sprawling. Mani, usually the first to help, sidestepped her and raced after Kyle, who was leading the way.

I pulled her to her feet. "Are you all right?" I asked, moving again before I even had an answer.

She nodded, not bothering to brush herself off.

Ahead, at the very edge of the jungle, I saw Mani grab the back of Kyle's shirt with both hands, forcing him to stop, half turning to face the rest of us at the same time. We were almost on them. Drew and I, Brendan, Mark, and Elissa strung out in a line. I think it was Mani's face that frightened me more than anything else. His expression was impassive, but his eyes were frantic.

We all came to a stop. Five small steps from sunlight. Still shielded by the giant ferns and thick brush that choked the very edge of the jungle like a living noose. I could see the back of one of our tents through the green, and the roof of the church to the right.

"Let's go," Kyle said anxiously. "Something's wrong!"

Something sure sounded wrong. We could hear a voice, yelling. Though we couldn't understand what it was saying, the anger came through loud and clear.

"No," Mani said forcefully, still hanging on to Kyle's shirt. He cocked his head and listened, eyes on the rest of us. "Wait here."

"I'm coming with you," Kyle said.

I nodded.

Mani didn't waste time arguing with us. "Stay behind me," he said. Bent almost double, he turned left and wove through the bushes, tracing the edge of the tree line.

I fell in behind Kyle, concentrating on not getting smacked in the face by branches, and almost ran into him when he stopped at the base of a tall palm. The voice was directly to our right, but I couldn't see a thing through the foliage, even though I knew there was only about ten feet of bush between us and open ground.

As the others arrived behind me in a muffled rush, Mani signaled us to stay put, dropped to his knees, and scooted into the leaves.

Kyle followed him without a backwards glance.

Brendan looked at me with a question in his eyes.

I jerked my head toward the noise. There was more than one person yelling now.

"I've got to see what's going on," I whispered. I don't think

Brendan actually heard what I said, but he got my meaning, nodded, and raised his eyebrows in the direction of the other three.

Drew was hugging herself tightly, breathing in shallow gasps. Mark's face was very white against his dark hair. Elissa seemed the calmest.

I caught her eye and pointed toward the base of the trunk. She nodded and grabbed Mark's arm as he took a step toward me.

I dropped to my knees and started to crawl. I felt Brendan follow and prayed that the others would stay put.

We were on Mani and Kyle almost immediately. They were lying flat, side by side, sheltered by broad banana fronds that were hanging low from a stunted trunk. I eased myself down beside Mani, forgetting about spiders and snakes and all the creepy crawlies, and looked out across the grass.

Daniel and Mariati were standing in front of their house, Daniel half a step in front of his wife. Facing them stood a group of men. From where we were lying, I couldn't tell how many, but it was a lot. At first I thought that they were men from our village. Most of them were wearing the usual ragged jean cutoffs and T-shirts. Some were wearing white pants and loose belted tops with white head coverings or strips of cloth tied around their foreheads. All of them had long machetes hanging from the belts around their waists.

One of them, their leader, I guess, was standing between the crowd and Mani's parents, hands waving in the air. It was his voice we'd been hearing. Every time he stopped yelling, the group of men behind him let out a roar of support.

I realized they weren't men from the village at the same instant I heard Mani whisper, "Tahima. They're from Tahima."

Tahima. Batuasa's Muslim pela partner village.

"Allah-u akbar! Allah-u akbar!" the men chanted several times, getting louder with each repetition.

"What's going on?" Kyle murmured on the other side of Mani, his voice so low that I could hardly hear him.

"He says that their Muslim brothers in Ambon sent them news this morning that there is an army of Christ forming to attack Muslim villages," Mani whispered. He paused and listened again, breathing heavily. "He says that the Christians are burning all the mosques. That they are seeking out the houses of Muslims to destroy them, and that many Muslim brothers and sisters have been killed. They are martyrs and are now in paradise."

I saw Daniel trying to speak. His words were drowned out by the crowd.

"Allah-u akbar! Allah-u akbar!" they chanted menacingly.

The back of my neck prickled.

Mani translated without being asked. "God is great; God is great."

The leader started to scream again, his voice shrill, cracking on one word.

Mani's voice was high and tight as he repeated in English. "There's a letter on church stationery that proves that the Christian villages will rise up against the peace-loving Muslim villages. He says that in Mahosi the infidel Christians have burned the house of God and the holy book, the Koran. They have raped and defiled our Muslim sisters. They have dashed our babies against the rocks."

The tirade went on and on, the screaming pounding at me like a fist. Mani's whispered translation washed over me as I stared at the scene in front of us, paralyzed, scrambling to put the pieces together in my mind. It didn't make any sense.

The leader shook his fist in the air, and the crowd raised a new cry in a furious howl.

"Allah-u akbar! Jihad! Jihad!"

In front of the screaming crowd, Mariati reached toward Daniel's arm, and Mani froze, staring at his parents. I had never seen absolute terror on anyone's face before that moment.

"Jihad! Jihad!"

Kyle started to wriggle forward. "We have to do something!" he hissed.

In that instant Mani's eyes cleared and he grabbed Kyle by the shoulder, slamming him down. "No!" he whispered violently. "No! They are calling for a jihad, a holy war. There is nothing you can do!"

"But we could talk to them." Kyle sounded desperate.

"You think your white skin will save you? You will make it worse. If talk can help, Father will know what to say. I promised him I would protect you and Tina. I *promised*." He choked on the force of the words, and Kyle sagged.

"Where is Tina?" Brendan asked, next to me.

I couldn't see her anywhere. Daniel was still standing in front of their house, Mariati right behind him. The church was to his right, between them and the ocean. Even from here I could see Mariati trembling.

"In the house," Mani said hoarsely. "She would be in the house."

The crowd was in front of the house, to our left. From here, we'd be seen as soon as we stepped out of the bushes. I saw the answer the same time Brendan did. He grabbed my arm so hard I almost cried out.

"Back from there, behind the tents. I can use the house as cover and get to the back window," he said.

He was right. If we crawled back around the edge and came out low behind our tents, the house would be between us and them.

Mani had heard the last comment and started to move. "Stay here," he ordered.

"No, wait." Brendan grabbed him. "I'll get her. You stay here." He glanced back toward Drew, Elissa, and Mark. "You need to stay."

I saw the look in Brendan's eyes as they met Mani's, and I wanted to scream at him for thinking what I knew he had left off. You need to stay . . . because if things go bad, if things go bad . . . I couldn't even finish the thought.

"You need to stay," Brendan said again.

"I'll go with you," I said to Brendan.

"No!" they both snapped at the same time.

"Go," Mani said to Brendan, nodding his head. "Go now."

Brendan wriggled backwards and disappeared. Kyle, transfixed by what was unfolding out front, didn't even glance up.

"Allah-u akbar! Allah-u akbar!" The chanting seemed to be getting louder. It made me want to press my hands to my ears and curl up in a ball with my eyes closed.

Some of the men from our village were starting to gather behind the crowd from the other village, but not enough. Many of them were probably out on the fishing boats, or hunting.

"We have to do something!" Kyle said again, his voice shaking.

Neither of us answered him. I looked over at Mani. His eyes were fixed on his parents and his lips were moving, but no sound was coming out. He wasn't talking to us.

About two hundred feet to our right, the ferns parted and Brendan's face peered out.

"What the—?" Kyle looked around wildly, as if he expected Brendan to have suddenly grown a twin brother.

"Tina's in the house," I said over the top of Mani's head.

Kyle looked at the crowd, back at Brendan, and swore. Then he swore again.

We watched as Brendan crawled out, staying low across the thirty feet of open space to end up behind the boys' tent. So far, so good. I held my breath. There was a little voice running through the back of my mind that hadn't stopped since I'd seen the crowd. *God help us. God help us. Don't let them see Brendan. Protect Daniel and Mariati. Stop the yelling. God help us. God help us.*

It must have been only four or five minutes that we'd been watching. It felt like hours.

Brendan paused behind the tent, and I could see him getting ready to make the next dash. It was fifty feet from the tent to the back of the house. I didn't think any of the men could see him from where they were, but I wasn't sure.

Daniel raised his hands and called out strongly, and there was a lull in the chanting. It almost died away, and we could briefly hear his voice over the shouts. We had to prod Mani to get him to translate.

"Father says that no one in this village has harmed any Muslim, that we are also people of the Book, and that we have lived in peace for many years. He begs them not to believe lies told by outsiders."

One of the men near the back of the crowd screamed out again, a shrill shriek that might have sounded ridiculous if it hadn't been threaded with so much hatred.

"He says he knows the reports are true. Father is the liar. He says they must avenge their sisters and the other villages that are destroyed."

Go, I willed Brendan. *Go now, while they are concentrating on this man at the back. Go!*

The man raised his right arm, and the midday sun glinted off the long, curved blade of a machete. There was a pause. It seemed as if everything had fallen silent. I saw the blade, and behind the blade, the rest of the village. The faces of the older men from our village who were coming up the street, their mouths open in shock and anger. The crowd, a mixture of white teeth and eyes, raised fists. But I heard nothing but the sound of my harsh gasping and the frantic pounding of my heart.

Brendan went for it, running, doubled over, straight for the back of the house. I had never seen him move so slowly. Every step seemed to take a minute.

I saw the leader draw his machete and raise it high. Suddenly I could hear again, and the voices of the crowd were raised in one cry.

"*Jihad!*"

Daniel raised his own hand, holding on to Mariati with the other, turning and trying to pull her behind him. The leader whirled. And I saw the direction of that long blade, coming down. And I knew where it was going to fall.

I didn't have to watch. But I couldn't take my eyes off that blade. And when it was raised again it wasn't shiny anymore.

I could hear Mani whimpering. He sounded exactly like one of our puppies in Kenya that the cane rats had gotten hold of one night. The puppy had still been alive the next morning, but it was blind and mauled, crying out helplessly.

Daniel dropped to his knees facing us, his hand still outstretched toward Mariati. Then the leader kicked him hard in the small of the back, and he fell facedown.

There was a great cry from the rest of our villagers, and they surged forward, but they were hopelessly outnumbered.

Mariati stood in front of the open door to her house, but she didn't run. Instead she glanced over her shoulder, then took two quick steps forward, toward them. And then two of them were on her. I can't remember their faces, just the arc of their knives and the way she fell—limp, with one arm flung above her head. And how that didn't stop them from kicking her.

I think I screamed. But it didn't matter. No one could hear us anyway. The crowd had separated into what seemed like a thousand, ten thousand, a hundred thousand screaming men. They were fighting near the church, running back toward the center of the village. I couldn't move. But I couldn't shut my eyes either.

For a little while I forgot the others beside me. I forgot we might be in danger. My mind was completely blank, a black hole of horror that had swallowed every fragment of coherent thought.

Then I saw a young man near the church—he couldn't have been any older than us—light a long strip of cloth hanging out of the top of a Coke bottle and throw it at the building with a wild cry. It broke against the wood with a whoosh. Flames started to climb up the log, and suddenly I could move again, and think.

I realized the thatch roof on Mani's house was on fire too, and felt violently sick. I hadn't been watching for them. I didn't know whether Brendan had gotten Tina out or not. I hadn't seen him running back. I didn't even want to think about the fact that they might be trapped in the house.

"Did Brendan get out?" Kyle asked me urgently.

"I don't know." I shook my head. "I didn't see him. I didn't see!" I was very close to panicking.

"Mani?" Kyle shook him, but he didn't answer.

He was staring at his parents, eyes unfocused.

"Mani," Kyle snapped. "Did Brendan get out?"

"Brendan has Tina behind the tents," Mani said tonelessly.

"Let's go. Right now—we need to move!" Kyle crawled backwards, practically dragging Mani with him. I took one more look. I couldn't believe how quickly the flames were taking hold of the church. They were big logs, and the frame was solid. But a section of the roof nearest the village was already blazing fiercely, a pall of dirty gray smoke climbing into the air. The crowd in front of Mani's house had dispersed and moved back toward the center of the village. I could see men with white headbands running down the main street, machetes in hand, still screaming. As I watched, they caught another villager in the open and struck him. Again and again and again.

In front of her house, Mariati lay still. But just as I was about to turn away, I saw Daniel's arm move slightly.

I rolled backwards through the leaves until I reached the others and sat up fast. "Daniel's alive!" I said to the boys, tripping over my own words in my haste to get them out. "I saw his arm move."

"What's going on?" Mark demanded, his lips trembling.

Drew was sobbing, both hands pressed over her mouth, tears dripping off her fingers.

Mani glanced back through the bushes.

"Wait!" I said. "There's a first aid kit in my pack, if we can get to them."

"You get the kit. We'll get to them," Kyle said, steel in his voice. "Meet you at the back."

"Wait," I said again, willing my heart to stop pounding so I could think clearly.

The shouts were farther from the church now, more toward the other end of the village. I tried not to hear the new sound of the women screaming or think about what it meant.

"Okay, go," I said. "If he can't be moved, come and get me."

Then they were gone, and I was left with the other three. I wondered if I looked as terrified as they did.

"Come on," I said, already moving. I glanced back to see Elissa prod Drew into motion. Then I wasn't thinking about anything but getting to that first aid kit.

Let Daniel live, God—let him live. That was all the little voice was saying now.

I met Brendan in the trees behind the tents. Tina was clinging fiercely to his neck, her eyes wide. I stopped briefly, the other three right behind me.

"Did you see?" I asked him.

"Some of it," he said.

"Get the tents," I ordered them. "Everything in them. All the packs. Food, if you can. Into the trees. Now." My own voice sounded strange, as though it was coming from a long way away.

Tina looked at me and started to cry.

I didn't stop to see if they'd do it. I just sprinted for our tent and dove for my pack. My hands were trembling, and I had trouble undoing the buckle that held the first aid kit in place. Even through the fabric of the tent I could feel the heat from the burning church and hear the dull roar of the flames.

"Come on!" I pulled at it and almost screamed with frustration.

Elissa crawled in beside me just as it came free. "Take everything?" she asked.

I couldn't believe how calm she sounded. "Everything you can get." I grabbed the kit and my towel and backed out fast, running straight into Brendan's legs.

He was staring at the church. It was blazing fiercely. The front section of the church roof nearest the village was just a skeleton now.

As I looked over, it crashed down in a shower of sparks.

"We've got food in there," he said to me.

He was right. We had our team food supplies stored in the back corner of the church where they wouldn't get wet. He was halfway across the open space between the house and the church before I realized what he was planning to do, but then Mani and Kyle came round the corner of the house at a run, and I forgot about the food. They were carrying Daniel between them.

Mani had his shoulders, while Kyle had his arms awkwardly around Daniel's hips. One arm was hanging down, limp. They didn't bring him to the tents, but stopped behind the house, far enough from the flames, and laid him down gently on his side with his head in Mani's lap.

The first thing I noticed was the blood. It was everywhere, all over Kyle's clothes and arms, soaked through the back of Daniel's shirt and already dripping onto the sandy grass near Mani's knees. It was so much darker than I had thought it would be—almost black—until I touched him, and my hands came away red.

There were a couple of big slits down the back of his shirt, and I ripped them further, desperate to get it off and figuring it was easier than trying to get it over his head. The shirt tore easily, the fabric sodden and hot.

Then his shirt, his good blue shirt, the one he usually wore to dress up, was just a rag in my hands, and I could see his back. And the voice in my head, the one that had been asking for a miracle since I saw his arm move, stopped suddenly. And there was only silence in there.

One machete had caught him on the top of his right shoulder, near the neck, and then scored a path across to low on the left side. There was another slash across his shoulders, and more crisscrossed his left arm. I couldn't even see them properly to know how long they were or how deep. His whole back, from neck to waist, was covered in a slick of blood, dirt, and sand.

My hands fumbled with the plastic packet on one of the sterile dressings, too slippery to get a proper hold on it. When I finally got it open, the small square of white seemed pathetically inadequate. I didn't even know where to put it.

I settled on the top of the right shoulder, near the neck, where most of the blood seemed to be coming from. It was soaked through almost immediately. The grass near Mani's knees was much darker now. I put my towel over the dressing and pressed down hard while I tried to figure out what to do next.

"Mariati?" I asked the question in one word, reaching for more dressings.

"Dead," Kyle said beside me, voice flat. Then he doubled over and retched into the grass, crawled away, and retched again.

Daniel's eyes were open and he was whispering to Mani, disjointed fragments in Indonesian. Mani was leaning over him, holding tightly to his left hand, listening. And his eyes were so calm. And I couldn't understand how he could be that calm, because I could feel Daniel dying underneath my hands, and there was nothing I could do to stop it.

Blood was already soaking through my towel and the other dressings. I pressed harder.

Daniel's voice flickered into silence. He just lay there, looking at Mani, his breathing very shallow. And Mani just sat there, looking back. And I couldn't stand the silence, or what it meant.

"Daniel!" I said his name involuntarily. A plea.

His eyes flickered toward me. I don't think he actually saw me, but I know he heard my voice because he said my name, very softly.

"Cori." His chest stopped moving, and then there was another frail gasp.

His eyes moved back toward Mani's face, hovering above him.

"Go with God. He walks with you. *Baku dame jua!*"

He didn't take another breath. I kept waiting for it, pressing down on the towel, but it didn't come.

I don't know how long we stayed there, the three of us. It probably wasn't more than a minute. Mani, cradling his father's head. Me kneeling. And Daniel lying dead between us. But I couldn't let go of that towel.

It was Mani who moved first, placing his father's head on the ground, looking at me. His hand went out to touch my shoulder, but stopped short. I heard Brendan calling my name from far away, but I couldn't answer.

Daniel was so small lying there. So much smaller than I'd ever seen him before. He was wearing shorts. One canvas shoe was missing, but the other one was still on his foot. He'd gotten up that morning and put on his shoes and gone out and not known. For some reason I thought you'd know on the day you died. That you'd look different. Instead of just lying there, wearing the same clothes as always.

Then Brendan's hand was on my shoulder. "Come on," he said from far away. "Come on."

I heard him, but I couldn't move.

Then his arms were around me from behind and he was lifting me up easily, and I was kicking and fighting and he was speaking into my ear. He smelled like smoke.

"I'm sorry. I'm sorry. I'm sorry." It was all I could say.

"There was nothing you could do! Cori, there was nothing you could do."

Brendan said later that he tried to talk to me, but I wouldn't listen. I don't remember. The next thing I knew we were standing in the bushes and he was shaking me, hard, holding both my arms tightly. Hurting me.

"Stop it!" he said. There was a harsh tone in his voice I'd never heard before. "Don't lose it. Do you hear me? Don't you lose it!"

Something snapped back into focus, and I could think again. Sort of.

"I hear you." I had to say it twice before he let go of me.

I looked back toward the church. The tents were gone. Our packs were gone. Even the flames consuming the church seemed lower. Soon the church would be gone too. There would be nothing to show we'd ever been here except a cement floor and three rectangular patches of dead grass. I didn't look at Daniel's body.

"Where are the others?" I asked.

Brendan jerked his thumb away from the ocean, toward the deep jungle. "In there. You all right?" He looked at me intently.

"Yes." I was pretty sure I wasn't, but there didn't seem much point in saying so.

"We've got to get out of here," he said.

"I know."

I could still hear shouting and screaming from the direction of the village, but the noise seemed farther away now. More sporadic.

"Come on." Brendan took my arm, more gently this time, and pushed me ahead of him.

The others weren't far into the trees, but it seemed like a different world. Cool after the heat of the fire and the midday sun. Quiet and shady.

Mark was holding Tina. Her face was snuggled into his neck, and he was patting her and talking softly about going on a camping trip. Elissa and Kyle were trying to bundle up one of the tents. The anchor ropes still had the tent pegs attached. They must have just dragged the whole thing into the trees. Mani was pawing through some of the boxes we'd stored in the church. Drew was sitting still, her legs tucked up and her head buried in her arms.

Elissa looked up and saw us. "Oh, Cori."

That was all she said. But she left the tent, pulled something out of her backpack, and handed it over silently. It was one of her clean shirts.

I looked down. The front of the shirt I was wearing was covered in blood, sticking to me, and my hands and arms were red. For a moment I could feel the hysteria bubbling inside of me, threatening to well up again, but I stomped it down. Hard.

I faced the way we'd come and pulled my shirt off over my head, trying not to let it touch my face. I used the clean backside to wipe at my hands. It didn't help much. I caught myself thinking that Gary and Diane would have a fit if they saw me breaking the rules by changing clothes in front of the guys, and then almost laughed out loud at the absurdity of it.

I pushed away everything I wanted to think about—confusion, terror, and my own wretched helplessness, to think through later. Brendan was right. We had to get out of there. Fast.

Dressed again, I faced the group.

"Here." Brendan shoved my pack into my hands. "Mani's going through the food. We've got to take as much as we can, so just get it in. We'll sort it out later. Load Drew's too."

"What about the other villagers?" I asked. I looked at the first aid kit on my pack. Brendan must have picked it up and strapped it back on.

It was Mani who answered me. "There is nothing you can do," he said flatly. "We must leave."

I felt relieved. Relieved that it looked like the decision had been taken out of my hands. Relieved that I didn't have to go back there. And I hated myself for it.

"But there were children. What about Budi?" I heard myself arguing.

"No!" Mani snapped at me for the first time. "You are my responsibility. Father said. And you are not going back. Here." He pointed to a pile of cans.

I dragged both packs over to him and started shoving cans in the top, packing them down.

Kyle and Elissa finished with the tent, and Kyle strapped it onto the outside of his pack. He still looked sick. Elissa started rolling up the sleeping bags, squaring the edges neatly. It made me want to giggle again. I didn't understand how I could possibly feel like laughing, but I did.

Twelve minutes and we were done. The tents were bundled up, the food packed away, and the sleeping bags strapped on the top of our packs.

"Drew!" I didn't even bother with asking nicely; I just pulled her to her feet. She was still crying. Framed by red, her eyes were very green. She looked right through me.

"We're going. Get your pack on."

"No." She said it dreamily, sagging back toward the ground.

Suddenly I was furious with her. "Drew!" I said again, and slapped her hard.

Her eyes didn't lose their unfocused look, but her hand went to her cheek and she stood up again and let Brendan put the pack straps over her shoulders.

Mani had Mark's pack on. Mark was carrying a day pack on his back and Tina in his arms.

"I'll lead," Mani said quietly.

"Where are we headed?" Brendan asked.

Mani pointed away from the ocean, up to the mountains.

"It's safer," he said, and set out without another word.

We were out of familiar territory quickly and climbing steeply. Mani moved confidently, weaving between the trees, following a path I couldn't see. Soon all I could hear was the sound of my own breathing sawing harshly in my ears and Drew's labored gasps behind me. My face was wet with sweat, dripping off my chin and sliding down my back. When I checked my watch I was shocked to see that we'd only been walking for twenty minutes. It felt like at least an hour.

My leg muscles screamed at me to sit down and rest. Every part of me felt leaden. The pack dragged at my shoulders, tugging me backwards. Soon I couldn't think about anything else but the effort of making the next step. Lifting one leg and putting it down again. Then the other one.

I concentrated on Elissa's back. *If she can do it, you can do it,* I told myself over and over again.

Mani called a break at an hour and twenty minutes, and we collapsed. I couldn't even take the pack off, just leaned against it with my head back.

The only one with any energy left was Tina. She wriggled out of Mark's arms, cast a wary look toward Brendan, and moved over to Mani, touching his shoulder tentatively. He put an arm out, and she snuggled against him.

"Manuel. *Saya betul-betul lapar.*"

He answered her in English. "We will eat soon, okay, Tina?"

"*Ibu di mana?*"

"In English, Tina," he chided her gently, a shadow crossing his face. He paused. "Mama is at home now."

"She come?" Tina continued, tugging gently on his arm.

"No, just us, okay?" Mani's voice was heavy. He closed his eyes.

She left him, wandered back over to Mark, climbed into his lap, and started sucking her thumb.

"Can I dog?" she asked him around her thumb. "Make him dog?" she tried again when he didn't understand.

"Sure, okay." He crawled over to his backpack and pulled an unopened packet of balloons out of a side pocket. "What color?" he asked, showing her.

She thought about it carefully, then pointed to a blue one. "Him."

As Mark blew up the balloon and twisted it into the shape of a dog, I remembered Budi and my throat tightened. My heart rate was slowing, and the full horror of the day was edging its way back into my mind. I was almost glad when Mani got to his feet and heaved Mark's pack up.

No one asked where we were headed or how far we had to go before we stopped. I think we all knew that we had to get as far away as possible before dark. Fortunately, Mani slacked off the pace a bit. The jungle just seemed to get thicker as we climbed. A couple of times we had to stop while Mani and Kyle hacked through undergrowth. Once we had to crawl through a narrow tunnel of leaves. When I reached the other side I didn't think I was going to be able to get up. I stayed balanced on my hands and knees for a while like an oversized turtle, longing to lie down, to rest my cheek on the dirt and go to sleep.

Then I heard Brendan say my name, and I got up and staggered on grimly, hating him. After awhile I stopped thinking and just moved, clambering over the rocks, slipping on the leaves, climbing up. My mind drifted lazily, touching on fragments. The fact that sunlight rarely reached through the canopy to the jungle floor. The way the color of the dirt was so much redder than at home.

One more step, then another.

I thought about a movie I'd seen when I was little. These kids get shrunk by one of their father's crazy machines to about the size of ants. They end up in their own backyard trying to hike home through a for-est of grass stalks that tower above them. That's what it felt like. The trees were so big. Even the ferns were giant, almost as tall as we were.

One more step, then another.

For a while I wondered if we *had* somehow been shrunk. We'd probably been struggling for the last couple of hours to hike across the span of a single footprint. It didn't seem any more bizarre than the rest of the day's happenings.

One more step, then another.

It was Scott's ring that made me think otherwise. I reached up and touched it. It was the same size as always. Warm from my body heat and smooth under my fingers. For some reason I didn't think it would shrink. So I figured I hadn't either.

One more step, then another.

It was almost dark when we reached the stream. I let my pack fall to the ground and went down on my knees, banging my leg painfully against a rock in my haste, water soaking through the knees of my pants.

The water felt icy against my overheated skin, but I plunged both my arms in and scrubbed at them hard. My water bottle had been empty for two hours, and I was very thirsty, but I didn't think I could wait another minute to be clean. Finally, I splashed my face, then cupped the water to my mouth.

When I got up, Drew was still standing beside the stream with her pack on. Just standing, not doing anything. I went over and tugged it off her back for her. She didn't move.

"Are you all right?" I asked, but I didn't have the energy to care when she didn't answer. I just leaned against a tree beside her and watched the others.

Brendan came over and lifted her water bottle. Then he unscrewed it and wrapped her unresisting hands around it. "Drink," he said, kindly but firmly.

She raised it to her mouth.

"Mani says we'll camp here tonight and talk things over tomorrow," he said.

I nodded. I didn't care about tomorrow. All I wanted to do was sleep.

Kyle walked back past me with two tent sacks and snagged my sleeve, pulling me after him.

"Why aren't we camping near the stream?" I asked dully, as I followed.

"Mani says it's not safe to camp near the running water," he answered. "Too much noise."

"Oh." I felt my stomach do a slow, lazy somersault. I hadn't thought about the fact that we might not be safe in the jungle.

"Here." He dumped the tent near the bottom of a huge tree, buttressed with a giant network of spreading roots almost as tall as I was.

There was just enough flat space to pitch two tents in between them.

It was almost completely dark now, and we worked together quickly, spreading the bases, fitting the plastic framework, using rocks to hammer in the tent pegs. When we were finished we walked back to the others silently.

They were by the packs, underneath one of the trees. A small group huddled around a flashlight held low to the ground. I sat down beside Elissa, and she passed over a can and the teaspoon she had been using.

Baked beans.

I looked into the can, and my stomach clenched. I tried to pass it back.

On the other side of her Kyle pushed it back toward me. "You need to eat something," he said.

"I'm not hungry."

"So what. Eat something."

"Don't boss me around," I snapped, pushing the can back into Elissa's hands.

"Well, don't be an idiot then."

"Hey, guys. Don't. Please." Elissa's voice, soft and scared, stopped us.

I reached over, scooped up a spoonful, and put it in my mouth. But I had to turn away and spit it back out before I threw up. Even the smell was making me feel sick.

Kyle didn't say anything.

"Right." Brendan broke the silence when the rest of them had finished scraping out the cans. "We're going to sleep here and figure everything out tomorrow. We'll be all right."

He sounded confident enough, but the words failed to reassure.

It was hard sorting everything out in the dark, whose pack was whose and where all our gear was. In the end we just dragged everything to the tents and left it in a big pile. We pulled the rubber mats free and left the sleeping bags.

We'd pitched the tents facing each other, almost touching. I think everyone wanted to be close that night. If we could all have crammed into one tent, we probably would have.

"You want to switch it around?" Brendan asked me, his bulk more a comforting presence than anything I could actually see.

I almost said yes. I would have felt much safer sleeping by Kyle or Brendan that night, but I shook my head.

"You're right here. We'll be okay."

I felt him touch my shoulder. Then I crawled in beside Drew and zipped the mesh closed after me. I don't even remember lying down. I just fell off the edge of awareness into a black void.

chapter 8 ~

It was just getting light when I woke up the next morning. It was quieter than usual outside the tent. I couldn't hear the ocean. I rolled over and saw Drew lying on her side, looking at me.

"You hit me," she said softly.

At the sound of her voice I remembered where we were, and why. My stomach hurt. My chest hurt. Even breathing against the weight of it hurt.

"I know. I'm sorry."

There didn't seem to be anything else to say.

She nodded carefully.

"Are you okay?" I whispered.

Instead of answering, she asked a question of her own. "They're dead, aren't they?"

I glanced down at my hands. There was either dirt or blood underneath my fingernails. "Yeah. They are."

Drew's face twisted, and tears came to her eyes. She didn't brush them away. "They burned the church?" she asked, as if doubting her own memory.

"Yeah."

There was a heavy silence.

"God," she said to the tent roof. "What happened?"

"I don't know." I was glad she didn't go on to ask the question that had been pounding at me since she first spoke. *What are we going to do now?*

"I'm going to see if the others are up. You coming?"

She shook her head. More tears leaked out, but she didn't seem to notice. She just lay there, staring up.

I crawled out into the pre-dawn gray, careful not to wake Tina or Elissa. It was cold. Thick tendrils of mist curled through the trees and rested gently on the tents, stroking my cheek with a clammy touch. Any other morning it might have looked fanciful. Now it just seemed malignant.

As I went to get to my feet I couldn't bite back a yelp. The muscles in my calves and the fronts of my thighs were ropes of pain. In fact, most of my body hurt in some way. There were new blisters on my feet I hadn't noticed yesterday, and bruises on both arms. I grabbed clean clothes out of my pack and hobbled to the stream.

Kyle, Brendan, and Mani were already there, huddled around a small fire. Its bright orange glow seemed familiar, normal, safe. I hesitated on the edge of the small clearing, not really wanting to face Mani; then I limped over and sat down.

They weren't saying much, just passing a battered tin mug back and forth among the three of them. Someone had cleaned out the baked

bean tins, filled them with water, and rigged up a contraption to sus-
pend them over the fire.

"Here." Kyle passed the cup to me. "We found some coffee in
Drew's pack."

I took a swallow and coughed. It was strong and black, but the
heat was good.

"Are you all right?" Brendan asked.

Despite the fact that I had just asked Drew the same question, I
was sorely tempted to ask him what on earth he meant. Was I all right with
the fact that a whole bunch of strangers had gone berserk yesterday? Or
that we had watched as both of Mani's parents had been killed? Or that we
were in the middle of a creepy jungle half a world away from home? I raised
the palm of my hand to my forehead and tried to grind away the tension.

"I'm okay." I finally managed to do what I'd been dreading and
looked straight at Mani. He was sitting beside me, still, staring into the
fire. I reached over and touched the very edge of his sleeve. The rush of
my own tears was sudden, unexpected, and scalding.

"Oh, Mani. I'm sorry," I managed, before they spilled over. "I'm
so sorry."

We cried separately and silently. Mani's whole body trembled
with the force of it, but he didn't make a sound.

The storm passed as quickly as it had come, and I sat back, curiously empty, gagging on the taste of my tears. Brendan had his arms
around Mani, and Mani leaned into him, still shuddering. Kyle was
standing by a tree at the stream, his back to us. As I watched, he raised
his fist and smashed it hard into the trunk. Then again.

"Kyle!" My abused muscles screamed at me not to move as I
scrambled up. "Don't," I said, my cheek pressed to his back and my
arms wrapped around him.

He could have shaken me off, but he didn't. He just stood there. Rigid.

"Let me see your hand."

"Forget my hand," he said curtly, brushing me off and sitting back down by the fire. "We've got more important things to worry about, like . . . what happened yesterday?"

"Wait awhile," Brendan said quietly, but Mani straightened up, face still wet, but eyes clear.

"I don't know," he said simply.

"What do you mean, you don't know?" Kyle exploded.

He wasn't speaking loudly, but I glanced over my shoulder anyway. The mist, the trees, the wet, dark dirt seemed to swallow noise. Ours, and anyone else's who might be out there.

Brendan saw my movement and shook his head. "We think it's safe. No one followed yesterday."

I nodded, but knew they couldn't be sure.

"They were from Tahima, our pela partner," Mani said quietly. "They'd heard that a Christian army was going to attack the Muslim villages, and that they had already burned a mosque in Mahosi. The letter must have come on the mail boat."

Kyle and Brendan looked as confused as I felt.

"That doesn't make any sense," I said. "A Christian *army*?"

"That's what he said."

"So they just got together and decided to attack you first? Even though you had nothing to do with that? Even after the pela agreement?" Kyle was furious. "What sort of country is this?"

"If a Christian village really did attack Mahosi, if there really is trouble in Ambon . . ." Mani shrugged helplessly. "Trouble can spread very quickly."

"You call that *trouble?*" Kyle asked. "That wasn't *trouble.* That was a massacre."

I stared right through him, not seeing him, seeing yesterday and trying not to.

"I'm sorry," he said after a long pause, his head in his hands. "I just don't get it."

"Why your family?" Brendan asked quietly. "They must have gone right through the village the first time, straight to the church. Why?"

"We came from Java," Mani said, looking deep into the heart of the small fire. "And you know my father was Muslim once. He knew we would be a target for anger if something happened. There has been so much talk lately. That is why he was sending you away today. I mean, yesterday."

"He knew something like this might happen?" Kyle asked. "Why didn't you just leave?"

"He did not know *this,*" Mani choked on that last word, as if the enormity of what it conveyed was too much for him to get out. He blinked twice. "God told him to go to Seram. To our village. There are many in that village who needed him."

"But Mariati, Tina, you?" Brendan questioned. Even he was having a hard time with this concept.

Kyle looked like he was about to blow a gasket.

"Mother agreed with Father."

I poked the fire to cover the silence and tried to tilt the bean can so I could pour some of the boiling water into the mug without touching the hot tin. The others watched me without offering to help.

"Well," I said, giving up and deciding that if no one else was going to ask, I would. "What are we going to do now? If this letter came from Ambon, will there be trouble there too?"

"Maybe," Mani said, sounding exhausted.

"Wait." I remembered something. "When Gary left on Tuesday he said one of the reasons he didn't mind us staying was because he didn't know what was happening in Ambon."

"But we can't get out any other way, can we?" Brendan said, looking to Mani.

"There's no airport on Seram," I said, and Mani nodded. "Gary told us to get on the boat and go to Tim and Alison's."

"Gary!" Kyle said scornfully. "Gary should never have left us here in the first place."

"We don't know the full story," Brendan said.

I stayed quiet. I agreed with Kyle on that one.

"Well, how are we going to get back there?" I asked. "The next boat to Ambon isn't until Tuesday. That's forty-eight hours!"

"If it's still running," Brendan said. "But word has got to get out about what happened yesterday. They'll declare a state of emergency or something. Someone has to be looking for us soon."

I looked around. The mist was starting to slink away, but the trees remained. Huge. Solid. Impenetrable. I could not see the sky through the leafy canopy more than a hundred feet above my head. I had never felt so lost.

"They'll never find us here," I said. "Not even with planes. We have to get to Ambon."

"We can't take that boat. Even if it is running," Mani said softly. "Teharu, where the boat docks, is a Muslim village. Remember?"

I gulped, my shock reflected on Brendan's and Kyle's faces. As far as I knew, that boat was our only lifeline to Ambon.

"But we're Americans," Kyle said, appalled, as if that entitled us to waltz safely into any village we wanted.

Not all of us were Americans, actually, but I didn't bother point-ing that out.

"I don't think that would have stopped them," I said, "if we'd been there when they came . . ."

Mani reached out and traced one brown finger over Brendan's fore-arm. "White," he said, in a tone I couldn't work out. He looked at me and shook his head. "I do not think it would have changed anything."

Except now we'd all be dead, I thought. That, I could picture all too well. Drew running, screaming, Elissa's blonde hair soaked red, Kyle lying sprawled and still . . . I held the back of my hand against the hot metal of the cup long enough to force my mind away from those visions, long enough to really hurt.

"I will go back to the village and check," Mani was saying when I tuned back in, watching as the throbbing white mark on my hand began to glow pink. "But if things are bad, I think we have to go to Halimentan. It is a Christian village. There is a port there."

"But how are we going to get there?" I asked.

"We will walk," Mani said, as if he were proposing a stroll to the nearest ice cream store.

No one said anything for quite awhile.

"How long will it take?" Brendan asked finally.

Mani eyed me dispassionately. "With the girls, and Tina, and packs? Seven or eight days," he estimated. "Maybe more. Many mountains."

Great. Just what we needed. Mountains. Covered by giant gloomy trees. I wanted to go back to our tent and crawl back in beside Drew. Perhaps I could make this a bad dream through sheer force of will.

"Eight days. My parents are going to flip out totally," I said. Thinking about my parents made my throat close up.

"If they even know what's going on," Kyle said.

It seemed incomprehensible to me that anyone could not know what was going on. What had happened yesterday was so huge. So wrong. The whole world should have known what was going on.

"All right," Brendan said, his mind already set on the task at hand. "We need to take stock of what we've got with us."

"I have to go back to the village and see . . . ," Mani said, his voice dribbling away. "I will try and find out some more as well. You get organized. We leave tomorrow."

He stood up.

"I'll come with you," Kyle said.

I got the distinct feeling he didn't want to go anywhere near the village, but he offered anyway. It was the nicest thing he'd said all morning.

"No," Mani said. "I'll go alone. I should be back before dark." He turned away, and a heartbeat later he was gone.

When the others woke up we didn't have as much trouble as I had thought we might. There were no hysterics or tears. Not straightaway anyway. We were all too aware of Tina. We told her that Mani would be back soon, and Mark settled her near the stream with a couple of sheets of paper and a pencil to draw pictures. She seemed perfectly happy with the arrangement.

I found some porridge mix stuffed in the top of my pack, and Elissa took over, putting some in each can, adding milk powder, mixing it carefully with water from the stream and trying to cook it over the fire. It was trickier than boiling water, but we finally had three tins full of the sticky stuff.

It tasted smoky, and I still didn't feel hungry, but I gulped down my share anyway and felt a bit better.

"All right," Mark demanded after he'd finished eating. "I want to know what happened. You guys didn't explain anything yesterday." He looked at us accusingly.

"Yeah. Well, we were a bit busy," Kyle said sarcastically.

"Well, I want to know what's going on."

Mark's voice went up, cracking, and I could hear the fear in it. Suddenly I wasn't annoyed with him anymore. I glanced pointedly at Tina, still absorbed in her drawing.

"She can't understand most of what we say," Mark said. "She's only four, and English is her third language."

"All right." I took a deep breath and sketched out a brief and sanitized version of what Kyle, Mani, and I had seen from the edge of the jungle.

"Well, that was us anyway," Kyle said, looking at Brendan. "What happened with you?"

Brendan glanced at Tina. "I couldn't see anything, but I could hear all the noise. When I got to the back window, she was in the corner and wouldn't come to me. I was hanging through the window begging her, sure someone was going to move around and see me through the door. I could see Mariati's back, but that's all."

"Then Tina came?" Mark asked.

"No. I had to climb in there and get her."

"Did Mariati know you were there?" Elissa asked.

"I think so. Tina started screaming when I grabbed her, and I saw Mariati turn her head; then she disappeared. I'm sure she saw us. Then there was this incredible noise and things started crashing against the house."

"Coke bottles," Kyle said.

The rest of us looked at him as if he'd lost his mind.

"That's what they were throwing. They must have been full of gas or something."

"Anyway, I just about threw Tina out the back window and jumped out after her," Brendan said.

"Mariati stepped away from the door," I said. "Right before they . . . She stepped toward them."

"Poor Mani." Elissa turned toward the trees so Tina couldn't see her cry.

Drew didn't even do that. She just sat there, tears sliding down her face, arms around her knees, rocking slightly. Brendan put his arm around her shoulders and pulled her against him, but she didn't relax.

"Where is Mani?" Mark asked, his voice rough and scratchy.

"He's gone back to the village," Brendan said, and filled them in on the plan we'd started to work out.

"What if he doesn't come back?" Drew said with great effort, then dropped her chin back onto her knees. The next question was muffled. "Do you guys even know where we are?"

I looked at the boys. I didn't have a clue.

"We'd just have to go south, and we'll hit the ocean sooner or later," Brendan said soothingly. "We'll be okay."

I didn't point out that as far as I was aware, no one had a compass, and it was practically impossible to see the sun through the tree canopy.

"This is what we have to do," Brendan said, as the others absorbed the news. "Get everything organized in case we have to hike to Halimentan. But first, I think we should have devotions, like every other morning."

"This is not every other morning," Kyle said, suddenly furious again. His face hadn't lost its hardness. It scared me. He felt very, very far away.

"I know that." Brendan seemed calm, but his gaze was challenging. "The way I figure it, if we've ever needed to pray, now is the time."

"Well, it hasn't done us much good so far, has it?" Kyle asked. "Look at the church. We bless the church, and less than twenty-four hours later it's gone, burned to the ground. Daniel prayed more than anyone else I know, and look where it got him. You can pray if you want, but count me out." He got up and disappeared toward the tents.

Elissa looked scared.

"He'll be fine," I said. "Brendan's right."

I did my best to sound sincere, but I didn't mean it. I hadn't figured out anything that was swirling around in my own head, and I wasn't exactly in the mood to pray either. But I thought the routine act of sitting down with the Bible might provide some normality. And goodness knows we needed some of that.

I finally found my Bible, buried under two tins of ravioli in my pack, and took it back to the stream. Usually I tried to find a spot all alone, but this morning I needed to see the others. I left it closed in my lap for a while and, stretching against the painful pull of tight muscles, shut my eyes and leaned my head against my knees.

All that came to mind were scenes from yesterday. Jerky. Disjointed. They flashed before me in vivid detail. Mariati's two small steps away from the door. The crash of a glass bottle. The glint of sunlight off metal. A shower of sparks, almost pale in the sunshine, as the church roof collapsed in a shower of glowing ash.

Then I opened my eyes and tried hard to focus on something else. I had the feeling that if I let myself think about it too much, I wouldn't be able to move or talk or think. I tried to pray, but I couldn't get past a single cry. "God . . . ?"

It went out into silence.

Finally, in desperation, I opened up my Bible somewhere toward the middle, and my eyes landed on Psalm 55. It was the first couple of lines that caught my attention.

Listen to my prayer, O God. Do not ignore my cry for help! Please listen and answer me, for I am overwhelmed by my troubles. . . .

That's about right, I thought. If You didn't step in and stop what happened yesterday, God, You owe it to me to hear my prayer—if I knew what my prayer was. And I want an answer. I want an answer to the prayer I *should* be praying.

I read on.

My heart pounds in my chest, the terror of death assaults me. Fear and trembling overwhelm me, and I can't stop shaking. Oh, that I had wings like a dove; then I would fly away and rest . . . far from this wild storm of hatred.

I must have read this psalm before, but I knew I'd never read it as I was reading it now, and I didn't want to be reading it as I was reading it now. I didn't want to know what a wild storm of hatred really meant. I wanted to be in my own bed at home, waking up late on a Saturday morning to hear lawn mowers going outside, knowing Mum and Dad were downstairs drinking coffee and cooking Saturday morning pancakes. That was the safest feeling I could think of. I tried to hold on to it, but it proved as ephemeral as the morning fog.

Let death stalk my enemies; let the grave swallow them alive, for evil makes its home within them.

I was completely unprepared for the wave of violent feeling that swept over me when I read that verse. I saw Mariati as she fell, but this time the scene had a different ending. I had the knife, and it was the two men who fell before me. In my imagination I didn't give them any mercy, as they had given her none. I could feel the machete handle in my hand and see the look in their eyes as they went down. And I enjoyed it.

Then it was gone, and I was trembling and sweating. Appalled. I didn't know I was capable of such thoughts. I didn't want to be capable of them. It wasn't a clinical wish for justice. It was a deep longing for violence—to knowingly cause suffering to another person who really deserved it.

I hated myself at that moment.

I didn't read on for a long time. I just sat there, trying to banish that desire I could still feel crouched in the corner of my soul. Wanting a clear head. To think. To plan. But it wouldn't leave. So I went back to the psalm, looking for answers.

Give your burdens to the Lord, and he will take care of you. He will not permit the godly to slip and fall.

That was not an answer I could understand. Kyle's angry words rang in my head, and they rang true. Daniel and Mariati were good people. Mani and Tina were now orphans. Other villagers had died. Children had died. I wanted more of an answer than that. I wanted a reason for what was happening. But the psalm ended with one line . . .

But I am trusting you to save me.

That wasn't a reason.

I shut my Bible with a thump.

The rest of the day passed very slowly. We unpacked everything we'd crammed into our backpacks and spread it out. It made quite a collection. I couldn't believe we'd carried up as much as we had.

"We've got to pack light," Brendan said again, worry creasing his forehead. "We need to carry the food too."

"All right," I heard myself say. I felt numb and heavy, not quite there. "Let's make a list. Starting with the clothes."

"Two pairs of long pants," Kyle suggested.

"Two?" Drew asked without even a flash of her normal spirit.

"You're going to have to carry it," Kyle reminded her.

"Two," Brendan agreed.

I wrote it down. We could haggle over individual items later.

"Two shirts," Kyle continued ruthlessly.

"Three," Elissa suggested.

"Two, and something to sleep in," Kyle countered.

I wrote it down.

We went on like that for ages. Through socks, underwear, jackets, hats, bathing suits, books, playing cards, cooking utensils, shampoo, conditioner . . .

"Water-based products are the heaviest," Brendan said for the third time.

"I cannot go eight days, maybe longer, without washing my hair," Elissa said firmly.

"All right, a compromise," I said. "We'll take one bottle of shampoo and one of conditioner, and share. And one comb."

"I don't want to share a comb with you guys. I'll catch girl cooties," Mark said.

No one laughed.

"What about deodorant?" Kyle asked, holding up his.

"We are not leaving the deodorant behind," Drew said.

"It attracts mosquitoes," I said, remembering something I'd learned during an Outward Bound course in Kenya. Then I shut my mouth with a snap. We were two days overdue for anti-malarial medication.

Elissa looked at me quickly, thoughtfully, and nodded.

"One for the boys, one for the girls," Kyle said.

I made a mental note to make sure all the bug repellent went with us.

"Toothpaste?" Mark asked, waving a tube.

"We're not leaving that," Elissa said desperately.

"We don't need six tubes, though," Brendan said. "We can share again. Three?"

Drew tossed her hair spray onto the leave-behind pile without even looking at it longingly. We were making progress.

"Toilet paper?"

"Three rolls?" Brendan suggested.

"No," I said, remembering that at least some of us had drunk from the stream without filtering the water last night. "A roll each."

I tucked my camera and twelve small film canisters into the side pocket of my pack. Six of those films were already full, and there was no way I was leaving behind our only record of the village. For all I knew, those photos were going to be Mani and Tina's only record too.

Six of the films were still blank. I toyed with the idea of leaving them behind, but in the end I decided we might as well use them, starting now. I pulled my camera out again and took a photo of Elissa and Brendan sorting through our food.

Repacking took us all morning. I had thought I was stripped down to bare essentials when I arrived at boot camp, and I was shocked to see how much stuff we didn't really need.

Tina got sick of drawing and wandered over, wanting to play. We sat her down by the leave-behind pile and let her play to her heart's content. She'd been told so many times not to go into the tents or touch our stuff. Now she combed her hair with a brush, looking at herself in a little mirror, and spent at least half an hour putting on Drew's lipstick.

When we finally finished with the personal stuff, we stowed it away wearily. My pack was about half full now.

"What about dinner?" Kyle said.

We all looked at the pile of food off to the side. It looked big, but I wondered whether it was big enough to stretch over eight days.

"What do we have?" Brendan asked.

"Ritz crackers," Elissa said, rummaging around. "A couple of jars of peanut butter. Rice, canned stuff—beans, ravioli, cheese, spam, tomatoes. Powdered milk, tea bags, coffee, a couple of boxes of pancake mix, jam, Nutella, dried fruit, nuts, M&M's, and some other stuff." She straightened up slowly and carefully, wincing.

"What about wheat crackers and peanut butter?" Mark said.

Elissa shook her head. "They're lighter to carry. Maybe we should eat some of the canned stuff. No chocolate either," she said sternly. "We're saving it for later."

"Two cans of ravioli and one of mixed vegetables," Brendan suggested. "We can mix them together."

Yuck. The thought of that combination was almost more than I could handle.

We were all packed and organised by the time Mani got back. Elissa had even worked out a rough meal plan and organised the food into piles.

"It won't be enough," she said to me as I helped her organize. "Not for three meals a day. Not for eight of us."

"I guess it's not going to kill us to go hungry for a week," I said, immediately regretting my choice of words.

"No," she said quietly. "I guess not."

Mani arrived back so silently that none of us heard him until he dropped the large bundle he was carrying. Tina squealed with delight and ran to him, throwing her arms around his knees and chattering in Indonesian. I only caught the word for mother. He looked too tired even to pick her up; he just laid a hand on the top of her head.

"Come on, little one. Your brother's very tired."

And very sad, I wanted to add. I scooped her up and willed myself not to cry. I didn't know what Mani had come across in the village, but his eyes looked empty and old.

"I'll take her." Mark held out his arms, and I passed her over gratefully.

The rest of us stood, looking at one another, not knowing what to say. It was Elissa who broke the silence.

"Want some tea?" she asked him.

I almost laughed. It seemed so incongruous, but he nodded slowly and sat down by the smoldering fire while Elissa spooned some tea leaves into one of the tins, looking as if she made tea in a baked bean can every day.

I didn't think I was going to be able to hold off asking questions for another minute when Kyle beat me to it.

"What did you find?"

"They're dead," he said expressionlessly.

"How many?" Brendan asked.

"I don't know," Mani said, turning his palms up. "Sixty? Eighty? I don't know."

"What about the rest of the villagers?" Brendan asked.

"I saw some in the forest. Ibu Juati, Peter."

Peter, one of Mani's friends from the village. He would probably have been out fishing when it happened. At least some of them were still alive.

"They stay in the forest," Mani said. "No one is in the village. Peter's mother and little brother were killed."

I found it hard to picture the village silent. Thanks to yesterday, though, it wasn't as hard to picture what eighty bodies might look like scattered through the streets.

A log in the fire crashed down, and a shower of sparks glowed red against the darkness I hadn't noticed approaching. There was a question I wanted very much to ask, but was afraid to. Mani answered it anyway.

"I buried my parents together. Where the tents were, behind the church," he said, then tugged something out of his pocket and handed it to me. It was a little bear with a bandage over one eye. A bandage that was now authentically stained.

"He was still holding it," Mani said.

I handled it gently, as if that could somehow make a difference now. I vaguely heard Drew whimper as she realised what it meant.

"Budi." Mark looked stricken, lowering Tina slowly to the ground where she clung to his leg, scared.

"Peter and I buried him too. And his mother."

I tucked the little bear into my pocket. I needed it out of sight before I completely lost the ability to think. The top of my head felt funny, like it wanted to split apart, bone blooming out like white triangular petals out of place in a red flower. I took a deep breath and held it for as long as I could.

Tina started crying and ran to Mani. He sat down, scooped her into his lap, and lowered his face into the top of her head. Her cries quickly became howls.

"Aku mau mama!"

I want Mama. That much I could understand. I wanted my mama too.

Mani didn't try and explain anything to her just then. He just held her and stroked her back while the rest of us sat with them. Mark, his arms wrapped around his knees and his face hidden, cried with her.

It was completely dark when she finally stopped hiccupping and fell asleep in his arms, her thumb in her mouth.

"Did you eat today?" Elissa asked Mani softly.

When he shook his head, she moved to find something.

"Did they know any more about what happened yesterday?" I asked, trying to take my mind off my own imagination. My voice sounded flat.

"Peter said that the letter also talked about a holy war in Ambon. Some of the men from our village have already gone to attack Tahima," Mani said.

He sounded exhausted. Overwhelmed. As upset by that last fact as all the others we had managed to piece together. There was a glimpse of some fierce emotion on Kyle's face; then it was gone.

Mani shifted Tina so one hand was free and tugged open the bundle he'd carried with him. Something clinked as the wrapping came away.

Four machetes. Three long knives in sheaths.

Machetes. I wondered whether they'd been used yesterday, and what for, and how Mani could handle them so casually—as if their mere presence didn't invite rage and fear to share the circle with us. I don't think I could have touched one, but I wasn't asked to. The machetes were for the guys. It was a knife Mani handed me, and I took that without hesitating and balanced it in my hand. It felt good to have something solid to hang on to.

"No," Elissa said when Mani tried to pass one to her.

"You should take it," Mani said without heat.

"No." She was a little more forceful this time. "I would never use that on someone else."

"Maybe not to use," Mani said. "Just to have. You are a woman. You should have it," he said meaningfully.

"Come on!" Kyle sounded angry again. "Didn't you hear the screaming yesterday? Don't you know what was going on?"

I hadn't remembered until he said that—the sound of the women screaming as we slipped through the trees and away from the village. My fingers closed hard around the handle of the knife.

"I don't want it." Elissa didn't waver.

Mani didn't answer, just handed the knife to Drew instead. Her hands were shaking, and I was glad the knife was sheathed. She didn't look as if she were capable of using it to slice bread at that moment.

"So the plan is to hike to Halimentan, and head for Ambon," Brendan stated more than asked.

Mani nodded.

"But what about what's going on in Ambon?" Mark asked.

"We don't really have a choice," I heard myself say. "Ambon's the only way out and the only place apart from Batuasa where people might come to look for us. And we can't go back there."

chapter 9 ~

Sunday night was supposed to be evening church or movies on TV. It was supposed to be baking cookies or talking to Scott on the phone. It was even supposed to be calculus homework. It was definitely *not* supposed to be hiding in the jungle, sitting in the dirt, eight of us crowded into a hollow formed by buttress roots jutting from a giant tree trunk.

I think we all wanted to leave the fire burning as the gloom gathered under the trees, but no one protested when Mani and Kyle scattered it, carefully smothering all flames. It still didn't make any sense to me. I couldn't work out why anyone would have followed us. But I couldn't make any sense of what had happened in the village either.

I mean, I understood the big picture a bit. Religious tension, pela, foreigners, the government—all the stuff we'd been learning about over the last six weeks. But it didn't make any sense at all close up, when you could smell the blood and hear the glass breaking. It didn't make any sense when it came down to the fact that there were people on the other end of those machetes. People who killed Mani's parents, and Budi, and the other villagers. Other human beings who would have killed us if we had been there. On that level nothing was making any sense, and I knew we couldn't take any chances.

So we sat near the tents, silent. I wondered if the others caught themselves doing what I was doing—straining to sort through the sounds and wondering if there were people out there listening for us. There were a thousand small noises coming from all sides, but I couldn't see a thing. Not even a glimmer of moonlight made it through the canopy.

"What's that?" Mark whispered once, as a stream of scrabbling and chattering swirled above us. I felt, rather than saw, everyone look up into the darkness and hold their breath. None of us had counted on a threat from above.

"Monkeys," Mani said.

After awhile I gave up trying to figure out what each sound was, and whether it was close by. The only thing I could be sure of was the damp warmth of the dirt I was sitting on, and the solid wood behind my back. Focusing on what might be out there made me want to scream. How far would my screams make it, I wondered, before they were hemmed in by the trees? Could they possibly get to the beach? To Ambon? To home? I don't know what time it was when I reached for Kyle's hand beside me. I felt him jump, but then his fingers curled around mine, and it made me feel not quite so much like screaming.

I tried reminding myself of how hard it would be for the men from Tahima to find us by thinking about the fact that Seram was six and a half thousand square miles, almost all rain forest. But that led to thinking about how far from anywhere we really were, how many of those miles we'd have to walk to make it to a port, and what on earth we were going to do from there . . .

I rested my head on my knees and was almost glad for the dark. When the others couldn't see me I didn't have to pretend to be strong.

Finally I couldn't stand the silence anymore. "What are you thinking about?" I whispered to Elissa, beside me.

"Home. Praying. For my family. For Colin. They're going to be so worried," she murmured into my ear, her breath warm on my cheek.

Praying. Good idea. I wished I felt like I could.

I wondered what my parents would think if they could see us huddled in the dirt. Could a satellite possibly pick us out—a small warm cluster parked by a tree? Mum and Dad probably had no idea yet that anything was wrong. How long would it take them to realize we had just vanished into thin air? I didn't want them to worry; I just wanted someone to know what sort of trouble we were in. Just so I felt that we mattered.

"Well, you could pray for us to get out of here and save them some of that worry," I whispered.

"Yeah, that too," came the soft reply. It felt like a rebuke.

"What are you thinking about?" I asked Kyle.

"Praying too," he said shortly.

I felt betrayed. Did everyone have this all figured out except me? Was I the only one sitting here feeling so empty that I didn't think I could pray even if I tried? who didn't even want to try?

"I thought you didn't feel like praying," I said.

"I don't. I'm just letting God know exactly why not."

I slipped my left arm through Elissa's and felt her clutch it hard as she leaned her head against my shoulder. Maybe she wasn't as calm as she sounded, after all.

I don't know what time it was when I finally realized I couldn't sit still for another minute. It felt late.

"I'm going to bed," I whispered into the black hole where everyone's faces were. I might not have been able to see them, but I could hear them. The occasional stifled cough or sniff. The rustling or dull scrapes of someone shifting position. Sometimes the silence had been so heavy I could hear the different rhythms of people's breathing.

"Take Tina for you," Mani said. The strain was really telling on him. I hadn't often heard him make an English mistake like that.

"I won't be able to sleep," Drew said dully.

"You should try." Brendan sounded worried, and I knew what about. Drew had pretty much moved through the day like a sleepwalker.

Mani's voice came low. "I'll keep awake and look."

"Me too," Brendan said.

Kyle said, "We'll take it in turns. One person—one hour. Cori's right. We have to sleep. It's not going to do any good, all of us sitting here all night."

"Me first," Mani said.

"Okay." Brendan passed Mani his watch and showed him how to illuminate it. "It's just after ten now. Wake me at eleven thirty and I'll take over."

I couldn't leave Mani sitting there alone in the dark taking first watch. Not with nothing to think about but watching his parents die and his home burn. I was about to speak up when Mark beat me to it.

"I'm not tired. I'll stay up awhile too."

I lay by Drew in my familiar sleeping bag and stared up into black. Despite what she'd said about not falling asleep, I heard her breathing deepen and even out within minutes of lying down. Elissa's too.

My heart thumped in a steady rhythm. Fast. How could they possibly sleep? I wanted to wake them, but I didn't know what for. Not to talk. Everything else paled into insignificance in the light of what had happened yesterday. But that was the one thing I wasn't ready to discuss.

I flipped from my back to my stomach, feeling the ache in my hips and shoulders, the tight burn of muscles pushed way past what they were used to. The handle of the knife Mani had given me was reassuringly firm under my hand, the sheath cool where it rested against my chin. It smelt like a saddle. I rubbed my thumb over ridged leather, listening for Mani and Mark outside the tent. They were silent.

I wondered if Kyle was lying in the other tent, wide awake. Suddenly all I wanted to do was crawl over there and curl up next to him. I got as far as sitting up and reaching for the tent zipper when I realized that, to do that, I'd have to crawl out there into that living darkness alone. Even though their tent was just a couple of feet away, that was too far. I lay back down again, arguing with myself.

He's ten feet away. Four seconds and you'd be there.

You're safer here. He's probably asleep, anyway.

After everything, you're scared of the dark?

I'm not scared, exactly. Drew and Elissa might wake up and need me.

It's my . . . shirt. And you're not allowed to borrow it. Tanya! I thought I told you . . .

No. Scott.

We've had this conversation before. Why is it so . . . hard?

The ground. There's a stone under the tent. Oh, it's the . . . knife; it's . . . here.

Here on the beach near my grandparents' house. The full moon is high. The sand is cold and white, the scraggly dune grass still. Not a breath of wind. The waves frozen in place, tilted at crazy angles, poised to tumble. A single set of dark footprints track across the beach in front of me. My breath rises in a frosty cloud as I look down. I'm holding someone's hand tightly, my fingers tangled with his. A warm link. Safe. The hand tugs me forward firmly and I step out on numb feet. I feel his smile tingling up through my fingertips, and I'm glad he's there. I look up to see who I'm following . . .

And realize black is fading to gray and I must have slept after all.

I crawled out of the tent wondering how it was possible that my legs felt even sorer than the day before, and almost backed right into Kyle's lap. He gave me a ghost of the smile that two days ago would have been a full-blown teasing grin. I might have felt like I hadn't slept at all, but he *looked* like it.

"Why didn't someone wake me up to take a watch?" I said.

"So much for keeping guard," he said. "I woke up at three thirty, and Mani and Mark were sound asleep."

"Where are they now?"

"Mark's sleeping," Kyle said. "Mani's . . . out there." He threw his arm out in a wide sweep that seemed to indicate that Mani was somewhere between our campsite and Australia.

"Come sit," he commanded, patting the ground beside him.

"What are we going to do?" I asked him quietly, after we'd been sitting shoulder to shoulder for a while watching tree trunks materialize through the morning mist.

His face tightened into a hard mask. "What do you want me to say?"

I looked away and shivered. "How about 'we'll be fine'?"

"That's not answering the question," Kyle said. "Besides, Drew might want that, but you don't."

You're wrong, I wanted to tell him, the shaking growing stronger. That's exactly what I want to hear.

"Cold?" he asked, wrapping an arm around me and pulling me close.

I wasn't, but I nodded, the shivering easing slightly as I rested my head against his shoulder.

"I tell you what we'd do in a perfect world," he continued, his voice low and hot against my hair. "In a perfect world we'd get home. Then we'd come back here with the Marines and blow them away."

"In a perfect world this would never have happened," I said.

His fingers played restlessly with the sleeve of my shirt, pleating and unpleating it.

"What if we'd never gone to get that log?" I said softly. "Or what if we'd taken Budi and Tina with us, or if Daniel and Mariati—"

Kyle cut me off. "What if we'd never come here," he said with real loathing, his arm tightening around me until I let out an involuntary bleat of protest.

"Where's Mani?" Mark asked as he crawled out of the guys' tent. His black curls were tangled and his eyes puffy. There was a long scratch across one cheek.

"Scouting," I said.

"Shouldn't one of us have gone with him? What if they followed us? What if something happens and he needs us?"

Kyle snorted. "Mani needs our help like he needs a five-thousand-pound backpack."

Mark stuck out his lip. "He does so need us. He told me. Besides, Brendan rescued Tina, and you guys helped Daniel."

Kyle flinched. I felt it echo through his whole body.

"Daniel died," I pointed out, more harshly than I'd intended, pulling away from Kyle and sitting up straight.

"What's Mani going to do now? Do you think he's okay?" Mark asked.

Silence again. There had been a lot of silence over the last couple of days. It was like having a conversation in slow motion. Someone would say something, then pause. Five minutes later someone else would answer. Except that, this time, none of us could answer those questions.

"What were you talking about before?" Mark tried again with a different question.

"What we're going to do when we get out of here," Kyle said, the edge back in his voice.

I poked him. I didn't think there was any need to get into specifics again if it still involved blowing people away.

"Do you . . . ?" Mark paused, then started again. "Do you think we *will* get out of here?" He did his best to sound casual, but I heard the quaver on the last word.

"Yes," I said firmly, deciding to offer him the comfort Kyle had denied me. "We're going to get out of here."

"I really want to see my mom and dad." Mark sounded surprised. "Before I would have said that I didn't care if I ever went home again. But now I really want to. I don't even care if they want me there. I just want to go home."

"Yeah, me too," I said.

"At least you two have a home to go to," Kyle said.

"You told us your aunt and uncle love you," Mark said, looking up from the dirt he was stirring aimlessly with a twig. "Stop feeling sorry for yourself."

"You don't think I have a right?" Kyle said, obviously spoiling for a fight.

"We all still have homes to go back to," Mark answered without backing down.

"God could have stopped it," Kyle said, almost to himself.

"God could have let us walk right into the middle of it and get killed," I said absently.

Mark had made me think.

Kyle shook his head and got up, his face grim. "Coffee?" he asked.

Mark and I nodded.

Silently.

The next two days were jumbled. Time seemed to speed up and slow down at odd intervals. Fifteen minutes could be a lifetime of agony. All I could comprehend was the pain of another blister forming on my left heel, the ache of my shoulders as the pack dragged at them, and the burn of the acid in my calves as we climbed. Other times, I'd be jolted by a stumble or a stray branch in the face, and realize I'd just lost hours of my life. Feeling nothing. Thinking nothing. Watching my body walk slowly through a soundless dream. I wondered if I were going crazy.

We walked all day, following Mani, the boys taking it in turns to use their machetes when we came across tangles of vines or thick brush blocking our path. I have no idea how Mani knew where to go. To me, it seemed like we were going in circles. Clambering up, then down. Too much up. But he kept saying we were moving in the right direction. I knew for the rest of my life I would never forget the helplessness of being so dependent on someone else. I had always thought of myself as capable, but I'd never realized how big the difference was between being capable when I could turn on the tap and get water, when I could go to the store and get food, and being capable in the middle of a jungle.

No one spoke much, although Tina still asked about her parents every couple of hours. Those were moments I wished I could miss in that easy automatic fog of numbness. Every time she brought it up, tugging on Mani's pant leg and looking up at him hopefully, he would explain that they had gone to live with Jesus now, in heaven. Then she wanted to know why they would want to go away and live with Jesus without her, and when they would be coming back.

It made Drew cry every time, not that that was surprising. I think she pretty much managed to cry for three straight days, right up until she sat down in the dirt on the afternoon of the second day we'd been walking and wouldn't move.

"I can't."

That was all she said, and she only said it once. Then she was silent.

"You don't have a choice," Kyle said. "It's not like if you sit there long enough they'll come rescue you."

Drew closed her eyes. All of us except Mani tried something—arguing, pleading, commanding, yelling. She didn't even respond to Brendan. I'm not sure she was even hearing us. She seemed to have vanished somewhere deep inside herself, somewhere the rest of us couldn't reach.

As five of us retreated to discuss strategy, Mani walked over and sat down beside her.

"Why?" she asked, five minutes after he'd joined her, and the rest of us hushed.

I didn't know what she was looking for. In my mind there were a lot of "whys" that needed answering, but Mani's response was simple.

"It's what Father and Mother want."

She opened her eyes, and we all held our breath until she finally stood up.

She didn't cry quite as much after that.

I was in that state of pleasant disconnect, my mind trailing lazily behind my body, on the afternoon of the third day of hiking, when Mani stopped suddenly and I walked right into him, knocking him forward two more steps. It's a good thing he had been scanning ahead, and that I'm not heavier, because one more step beyond that and he would have stepped right on it.

I, on the other hand, was not scanning ahead. Not even as far ahead as Mani's back, obviously. Drew evidently wasn't in forward-planning mode either, because I felt her collide with my pack as Mani began to crowd us both backwards down the trail, step by careful step, without saying a word. Despite the fact that my heart rate had suddenly tripled, I had to stifle the inexplicable urge to giggle as I felt the secondary impact of someone running into the back of Drew.

It was amazing the difference four days had made. Before Saturday there would have been good-natured catcalls from the back of the line, and shouted demands to know what the holdup was. Now there was silence. Except for the soft exhalation Drew made as she was squeezed between me and whoever was behind us, the slithery rustle of uncertain footfalls, and birds chattering overhead, there was only a sense of swelling collective tension. I dug my fingernails into slick palms and reminded myself to breathe.

I counted six steps before Mani stopped and sighed, lowering the machete he had been holding two-handed in front of him.

"It is a big one," he said over his shoulder to me.

I looked past him up the trail and couldn't see anything except a tangle of ferns, speckled by sunlight that was falling haphazardly through the unusually patchy canopy layer, and a log across the path.

Kyle appeared at my shoulder and asked the question for me. "What?"

Mani gestured up the path with the point of his machete and answered economically. "Python."

Oh. I looked up the path again and still couldn't see it. I heard Drew whimper behind me.

"Where?" Kyle asked, pivoting with his machete held at the ready, as if he expected to see it coursing down the track toward him like a small train, muscles rippling and mouth open wide.

"There." Brendan pointed forward, awe in his voice. "It's massive. Lying across the path," he added when it was obvious we still weren't following him.

There was another whimper from behind me. Massive was clearly not a word Drew had wanted to hear.

"That?" I asked, pointing to the log, which up until that moment had looked like hundreds of other pieces of wood that we had stepped over. "No way!"

The section blocking the path was about as big as Mani's torso, and both ends were concealed by ground cover. I'd seen a lot of snakes in Kenya, but never one with a girth like that. Goose bumps erupted on the crown of my head and skittered all the way down my body as I realized how close we'd come to stepping on it.

I shuffled farther behind Mani, ostensibly to let Brendan get a better look at it. I'm sure this selfless act was in no way diluted by the fact that it meant if the snake suddenly decided to launch itself in our direction like a giant spear with teeth, there were now three guys between me and it.

"What's he doing on our path?" Kyle asked, sounding violated.

"Maybe it's a she," I said.

They ignored me.

"Sleeping in the sun, or waiting for food." Mani shrugged.

"What are we going to do about it?" Brendan asked. "Scare it off?"

"Yeah," Mani said. "We could kill him maybe. And cook him."

"I am *not* eating a snake," Drew chimed in with her first complete sentence of the day.

"Me either!" Elissa backed her up.

"I'll eat it!" Mark said. But I noticed he was keeping a wary distance behind Brendan.

"We had a friend in Kenya who had a small python," I said. "She went to put a mouse in its cage one day, and it struck her hand instead of the mouse and wouldn't let go, even after she stuck her hand in the freezer. Her husband had to spray it off with a fire extinguisher."

"Is there a point, Cori?" Kyle asked impatiently.

"The point," I spelled out for him, "is that if you Tarzans mess up trying to cut off that snake's head, which you can't even see right now, we have no fire extinguisher. I totally trust Mani to kill the snake if he wants to, but are the rest of you crazy? That thing could probably swallow you whole."

Kyle rolled his eyes. "It could not."

It could easily have degenerated into a third-grade argument. Could not. Could too. Could not. But Mani put his hand up.

"I have heard of two people eaten by pythons on Seram. It would take maybe two days to swallow one person," he said thoughtfully.

I stuck my tongue out at Kyle, and he looked at me as if he was prepared to test out the hypothesis, using me as the mouse.

Mani glanced up at the sky, reading the time, and I looked at my watch. Two forty. Rats. We had at least two more hours of walking to do before we would make camp. Maybe I should have let them kill the snake.

"Just make it leave," Drew begged, and backed up another step.

"Okay." Mani sounded resigned and tucked his machete into the strip of cloth around his waist that served as a makeshift belt.

"Clap," he commanded, demonstrating, "and make heavy steps." He stomped on the ground.

"Are you kidding?" Drew clearly thought she was being taken for a ride.

"The vibrations will probably scare him away," Brendan explained, clapping and stomping with great abandon.

I glanced around, on high alert. The noise we were making was much more frightening than the snake. During the last two days we hadn't heard anything much louder than our own hushed voices. I couldn't see anything out of the ordinary moving in the sea of smothering green that lay behind us.

It was working. We stopped stomping as the snake moved to the right, parting the ferns and slipping into the undergrowth.

Now that it was actually moving, I could see the distinctive tan-and-black pattern overlaying row after row of scales. By the time the thin end of its tail had given a jaunty flick and disappeared, I estimated its length at twenty feet.

Off to the right I heard a shrill cry that was quickly taken up by other monkeys, shrieking and chattering their displeasure. I guessed that meant that one irate snake wasn't circling around to set an ambush for us, but was actually moving away.

"Okay," Mani said, glancing behind us. "Let's go."

We went. I don't know about the others, but I was paying a lot more attention to where I placed my feet. And trying hard not to think about snakes.

It wasn't until I woke up on Thursday that I felt like I could think properly again for the first time since it had all started. Mani was already up and starting a fire. Brendan was using the filter to pump water from the stream we'd found just before nightfall the previous day. The others were still sleeping. Kyle, one arm thrown across his face, twitched restlessly. Drew was curled into Elissa's side, knees to her chest.

"*Selamat pagi,*" Mani greeted me as I pulled a tin of instant coffee out of the top of Kyle's backpack and shook it gently. Already half empty.

"*Selamat pagi,*" I replied automatically, sitting down beside him.

Brendan finished with the pump and joined us, tipping the water he'd filtered into the one saucepan we'd brought with us and standing it on the metal rack we'd improvised.

"What are we going to do if we get to Halimentan and there are no boats, or something's happened there too?" I asked them softly. I'd started thinking ahead last night while I was lying there, listening to the sound of Elissa sleeping. I didn't like where the thoughts took me—too many dead ends fenced in by question marks.

Brendan sidestepped the question with an offer. "May I make you a drink, madam?"

"Coffee. Made from fresh springwater from the mountains of Indonesia."

"You're in luck. That's today's special." Brendan almost managed to smile.

"Good," I said regally. "Then you may draw me a bubble bath and tell my parents I'll be joining them for breakfast."

We'd almost managed to make a joke. But with those last words the thin thread of humor snapped.

I caught my breath. "Mani. I'm sorry," I said. "That was . . ."

"It's okay," he said.

I don't know if he was aware of the tears that stood in his eyes but didn't fall.

He got up slowly and headed for the trees on the other side of the clearing, then paused and looked back. "It is not bad to smile, Cori."

I rested my forehead on my palm as he disappeared and stared at the coffee Brendan had just handed me. A couple of lumps floated on top where the dried milk powder hadn't dissolved. I poked them with a finger that was far from clean.

"I'm an idiot."

"No," Brendan said. "We've been acting like the living dead. We've got a long way to go, and we need each other. We need to start talking more."

He looked around before reaching into his pocket and pulling out a smudged envelope. He tried vainly to smooth out the wrinkles before handing it over.

"Speaking of parents, now's probably a good time to give you this. I found it in my pocket last night. It was on the table in the corner next to Tina, and I grabbed it when I grabbed her. It must have come in the regular delivery that morning, just before it happened."

I stared at the familiar handwriting on the letter I was holding.

Dad's handwriting.

"I didn't think it would be good to wave it around in front of the others," Brendan said quietly.

"Thanks," I said awkwardly, still staring at it, feeling like I'd been punched.

On the back of the envelope Dad had scrawled a short note.

I was thinking about you this morning and finally remembered to post this. I wrote it before you even left for boot camp, but forgot to give it to you before we left. Hope you're well and having fun! Miss you!

I'd tried hard not to spend too much time thinking about the little details of home—like the sound of my dad's voice, or what it would be like to get a hug from Mum or Scott. The big picture of home gave me something to get up for every morning, kept me repeating to myself that we were going to be fine. But the little details hurt too much. They made me want to sit down, curl up into a ball, and stay there until my parents came to find me. And I knew none of us could afford to give in to that.

Just holding the letter made me feel like Dad might be close enough to come walking through the trees. I closed my eyes for a moment, listening for him. I even smelled the letter, trying in vain to catch a trace of home. Nothing but paper. Then I just sat there and looked at it.

Brendan stayed quiet for a commendably long time, then buckled. "Aren't you going to open it?" he asked, gazing at it longingly.

"What if . . . ," I said, then stopped.

I was intensely aware of the swelling early morning chorus that was daily becoming less foreign. The birds. High trills and low, hoarse calls. A harsh screech as a brightly colored parrot preened above us, showing off just for the fun of it. I inhaled that rich loamy smell of damp soil and rotting leaves, looking up. A pair of giant butterflies, the biggest I'd ever seen, skimmed silently between the tree trunks.

Hope on wings, Elissa had called Serum's butterflies the first time we'd seen them. Hope on wings, leading us home.

Home.

"What if this is the last thing I ever get from my parents?" I whispered to Brendan.

He looked around, as if wondering why we were suddenly whispering, then shrugged. "Well, even if it is, not opening it isn't going to change that." Then, "But it won't be," he added hastily.

I almost giggled. Trust Brendan to deflate my melodrama without even meaning to.

There was just a single sheet of paper inside.

Dad to Daughter,

When you were small I would lie very still, half asleep and half awake, watching the black of night turn to the bright of day while you slept peacefully on my chest. Then I would hope that the storms of life that would come your way would be mild, the noonday sun would not be too hot, or the chill of winter night too cold. I would even dream of protecting you from all harm, so your life would be filled with nothing but happiness. But I know that this is impossible.

To even attempt to protect you from all possible pain would be like stopping you from learning to walk just because you will inevitably fall down. I must remind myself that an eagle never soars without leaving the nest. However, I know we don't soar (or walk) alone. The Lord of heaven and earth is with us at all times. He doesn't spare us all difficulties, but He does walk through every situation with us.

God has given us each free will, and it is an unspeakable joy to see you exercise yours to do what you are doing this summer. Experience makes us strong, just as exposure to the elements makes a tree dig deep into the soil and become strong. May God use the experiences ahead to produce a rich and abundant crop of faith, hope, peace, and love in your life.

Love, always.

I hadn't gotten a letter like this, just from Dad, the entire time I'd been away. Sure, he wrote, but it was usually a scribbled note on the bottom of Mum's letter. I should have been overjoyed, but it was too freaky. I wondered whether Dad knew about what had happened yet, about the harm we'd stumbled across. And if this was soaring like an eagle, I was all for finding the nearest nest, crawling into it, and never soaring again.

I pulled the little bear I'd given to Budi out of my pocket and held on to it as I reread the note, then passed it over to Brendan. He devoured it as eagerly as if it had been addressed to him.

"Wow," he said, practically glowing. "This is sort of like a message from God."

"Mmmm," I said. I wasn't ready to think about messages from God yet. I still wasn't sure we were on speaking terms. I poked a stick into the fire, listening to the angry hiss of damp wood resisting flames.

"It's like your own personal psalm," Brendan continued. "Maybe a team psalm."

"But I just don't get it!" I finally said, not wanting to wither his enthusiasm, but unable to contain my frustration any longer. "Dad . . ." I felt my throat close up around the word and coughed before I continued. "Dad wrote that God walks through every situation with us, and we all believe that, right?"

Brendan nodded.

"Then he was walking with Budi, and Daniel, and Mariati. And I just don't get it," I finished lamely.

I didn't say the rest of what was on my mind. If God didn't see fit to save them, who's to say that *we* weren't all going to end up dead in this whole mess? And I hardly saw how that might produce a rich crop of faith, hope, and peace in my life. Unless it was in my heavenly life. Which, as much as I believed in heaven, was hardly a comforting thought.

"Why do you think it happened?" I asked Brendan. I knew he couldn't answer it for me, but I asked him anyway.

"I don't know why."

He paused, and in his eyes I saw some of the same confusion I was feeling. But I also saw peace. With a sudden shock I realized that, on some level, I felt that that peace was a betrayal of Mani's parents, of Budi, of the others who had died.

"I don't know why. But I really think that, in the end, everything will work out okay," he said. There was no doubting his sincerity; he wasn't just trying to make me feel better. That was probably good, because he would have been failing miserably. With every doubt I voiced I was feeling worse.

"Trust?" That one word came out sounding more cynical than I had intended, and with a whole question packed into it. How can I trust when what I see and hear and feel seems like a terrible mistake—the wrong answer to a question that should never have been asked in the first place?

"Yeah," he said quietly. "Maybe you've never really needed to before. I used to wonder how I'd feel if something huge like this happened. It's hard to explain, but I *know* God's still in control. That He's here. That He loves us so much He hurts too."

"I can't get my mind around it," I said honestly. "I just cannot under-stand how God can love us so much and yet not stop something like that. Like the promise in Proverbs 3 that if you trust the Lord with your whole heart, He'll make your path straight. How can that straight path end at the point of a knife, and God just stands by and does nothing?"

"He gave us free will," Brendan said. "People used that free will to make the wrong choice and pick up those knives."

"Aren't you angry?" I asked, almost accusing.

"Yes, I'm angry." His voice rose. "But anger's not going to do us much good at the moment. Anyway—Kyle's angry enough for the both of us."

That was probably true. I glanced back toward the others and almost jumped out of my skin as my eyes met Drew's knees. She'd come up behind me so quietly I hadn't heard a thing. I put a hand to my rac-ing heart as she sat down by the fire and reached toward the warmth.

"Coffee?" Brendan asked, and she nodded.

That was an improvement. The day before she'd been awake two hours before she'd made any sign that she was aware of anyone else's existence. Despite just having woken up, she looked exhausted and pale. There were dark circles under her eyes and dark shadows in them. We'd all been quiet over the last couple of days, but I think she'd been the quietest.

Mani and Brendan were right about one thing, I decided. We needed to start talking more. That, at least, was something I could do.

"Good news," I announced as I passed over a cup. "We don't have to run the obstacle course this morning."

Drew considered that silently for a while. "And I suppose the rest of the good news is that the U.S. Marines are sending a helicopter to pick us up?"

Her voice was scratchy, and I couldn't hear a hint of teasing. But it was a start.

"I don't think the marines have any helicopters. Aren't they water people? Besides, you're a Canadian."

"I don't even know if Canada has marines. I'm not that picky right now."

"Canada has a marine corps, Drew. And the marines do have helicopters, Cori." Kyle's tone was flat as he passed by us. "Too bad there's no way they're using them to come get us."

With that he disappeared into the trees on the other side of the fire. I could have smacked him.

"Can I use your cup?" Elissa asked, as she and Mark sat down by the fire. I nodded, rinsed it out, and filled it with boiling water. Elissa wasn't a fan of coffee, but it was cold enough in the early mornings that even she wanted something hot. She balanced it on her knee with one hand and used the other to pull sticks and leaves out of the braid that hung over her shoulder. One sleeve of her T-shirt was badly ripped. Even she was starting to look frayed around the edges.

"Where're Kyle and Mani?" she asked after looking around carefully.

I jerked my thumb toward the trees.

"What are they doing?"

"I don't know," I said. "Manly things. Secret conferences."

"I don't think that's what Kyle's doing," Mark said, snickering.

I rolled my eyes. I don't know whether it was the shock of what had happened, or the unfiltered water we'd drunk that first night, but most of us had been making regular forays into the trees, and we were going through our toilet paper fast.

"What are we having for breakfast?" Mark asked, looking at Elissa. She had become our unofficial food monitor.

"Not M&M's," she said sharply when she saw what he was holding up. "The same thing we had yesterday, Mark. Porridge."

Mark looked mutinous, but he put the M&M's down, reached for the porridge, and held it out.

I jumped as Elissa reached over and, instead of taking it from him, slapped Mark hard on the side of his neck.

"Ow!" he complained, more hurt than angry at the attack.

"Mosquito," she said, showing him the smear of red on her palm. "You could have just told me, and I would have got it myself."

An hour later the others were back and we were still sitting around, passing my letter back and forth and watching Mark scrape the last of the unappetizing porridge from the saucepan. Elissa read it at least three times, alternatively smiling and crying, but it was Mani who lingered over it the longest. He even translated it into Indonesian for Tina. She sat attentively in Mani's lap, staring up at him, but I think the only thing she really cared about was being close to him, hearing familiar words, low and calm. When Mani eventually handed it back, Kyle got to his feet.

I groaned. I was dreading the thought of having to move, scatter the comforting warmth of the fire, stamp on the sparks, pick up a pack.

"Come on," Kyle said. "You all waiting for a bus or something?"

"There once was a boy called Jip," I said to Kyle as I stretched and tucked the bear into one pocket and Dad's letter carefully into the other one. It felt warm against my leg. "And Jip was waiting for the bus."

"I'm not playing that stupid game," Kyle said. "This is not a time for games."

I gritted my teeth. "This is a time for anything that might help."

"*That* is not going to help," he said, fists clenched.

"Well, neither is that," I said pointedly.

He turned and started downhill.

"Wait," Mani called after him. "Kyle. That way." He pointed up the slope.

Kyle changed direction without slowing down.

"Jip had to take the bus, because otherwise he would have got lost all by himself," Mani continued. His voice was flat, but at least he was making the effort.

Kyle didn't answer or turn around, but I saw Elissa give a small smile.

I resisted the urge to say what would have happened to Jip if he had "got lost all by himself."

"Jip was waiting for the school bus," Mark continued as he pulled Drew's pack up and helped settle it on her shoulders.

I saw her wince, and I knew why. My shoulders were a mass of pain too.

"Jip went to a convent school, and he had big problems with some of the nuns," Brendan said as he tightened his waist strap, leaning forward to take some of the weight off his own shoulders.

Kyle was almost out of sight by this time, still huffing up the hill. We took one more look around our campsite and started to trail after Mani.

"Yeah," I said. "Especially Sister Bertha. She really didn't like his pet monkey, Kiki."

chapter 10 ~

J ip and Kiki didn't go anywhere exotic that day. They caught the bus to school, discovered they'd forgotten their lunch money, ended up eating gross porridge instead of chocolate (that was Mark), and spent the rest of the morning learning their times tables and annoying the nuns. Nice and safe.

Somehow I'd gotten through school without learning my times tables properly. I always started to get confused somewhere around 6 x 8, so I guess I learned something too.

But after we stopped for some wheat crackers and peanut butter around noon, not even Mark had the energy to play anymore. I dropped my pack and sat down next to Brendan, not caring about the dampness seeping through my pants. We couldn't get much dirtier. We hadn't washed properly since Saturday. How bad we were starting to smell wasn't the problem; most of the time I didn't notice that. It was the stickiness that really bothered me. I could hardly remember what it felt like to be clean and dry.

"I'm starving," Mark complained to Brendan in an undertone as he finished his portion in four bites.

My own cracker stuck in my throat, and I washed it down with warm water from my canteen.

"Here." Elissa overheard and tried to pass him half of hers.

"Uh-uh." Brendan put his hand out. Even though he looked tempted to snatch it, his voice was firm. "You eat yours; Mark eats his. And you eat yours," he said, turning to Drew and giving her a nudge.

She jumped, but lifted her hand to her mouth.

I hadn't thought about how hungry the guys must be getting. *I* was hungry. Brendan must have been starving.

"Why can't we just have more?" Mark whined. "There's a whole box left."

"Yeah, and if we eat them all now, we'll be eating nothing but that for the next five days," Elissa retorted, pointing to a fern.

Mani shook himself as if he were shrugging off a daydream and looked at the cracker in his hand. "There will be more to eat tonight," he said in a tone that quelled any argument. He put the rest of the cracker in his mouth and went back to staring into the distance. He looked exhausted.

"Here." Elissa opened our only bag of M&M's and rationed out five pieces each as a peace offering.

I was glad they were in her charge. If they'd been in my pack, the temptation to gobble them all would have been unbearable.

Tina got a kick out of them. I guess she'd never seen M&M's before. She held them in her hands, rolling them around, giggling and chattering to Mani in Indonesian. The only word I caught was *pretty*. Then she went over, crawled into Mark's lap, and showed them to him as if she'd been given the crown jewels.

I was fiddling with a strap on the side of my pack, reluctantly getting ready to move again, when I heard Mark speak.

"I make you him dog," Mark murmured. "You give me the pretties."

I giggled. It felt like the first time I'd laughed in years.

"What?" Kyle hissed at me as if I'd personally insulted him. I motioned him to be quiet.

"You make him five dogs," Tina said firmly.

"I make you one dog. You give me five pretties." Mark was starting to sound desperate.

"Five dogs." She wasn't giving an inch.

"Two dogs," Mark said.

"Ten dogs," Tina said triumphantly, obviously figuring she had him on the ropes. Ten was the biggest number she knew in English.

"Mark, cut it out," Kyle interrupted. "How low can you go, bargaining with a four-year-old for five measly M&M's?"

"I can go very low," Mark said without a hint of shame.

"And an orphan to boot," Kyle said.

There wasn't any need to add that. I shot a glance at Mani, but he was talking to Brendan and didn't hear.

Mark glared at Kyle, but he took one of the M&M's and poked it into the corner of Tina's mouth. She smiled gleefully and poked one right back into his.

"Ten dogs?" she asked hopefully.

"One dog," he said gently, swinging her up onto his shoulders. He looked at Kyle hard. "You back off."

Elissa glanced back and forth among the three of us and sighed. I knew how she felt.

It was a gloomy afternoon. The branches far overhead were choked with flat, shiny leaves as big as dinner plates, greedily jousting for the sunlight I presumed was beating down up there. None of it reached us. It had only been five days since we'd soaked up the sun on the beach, but it seemed like a different lifetime.

The ground we were hiking over was alternately rocky and soggy, often coated with a slick layer of dead leaves. I was getting used to the perpetual twilight, but the trees closing in around me still rankled. No matter which way I looked, all I saw were pale trunks poking up like giant exclamation marks, forcefully punctuating the end of every thought. You are lost! It's just you and the trees! You'll never make it out!

Since these thoughts only led to a combination of panic and hope-lessness, I decided to give up trying to see through the trees, figure out where we were, or catch a glimpse of sky. I focused on the back of who-ever was in front of me, listened for whoever was behind me, and tried not to think past the end of the day.

It seemed especially hot that afternoon, and the air was almost dense enough to eat. I mopped at my forehead with the bandanna that was keeping the hair out of my eyes and shifted my pack straps to the edges of my shoulders in a futile effort to cool down my back, which was also slick with sweat. This stretch was more hilly than mountain-ous, and we were moving uphill at a fairly steady pace instead of stop-ping and starting, scrambling up steep stretches, and having to pay attention to every step. It left my mind entirely too free to wander.

When we'd left Jip and Kiki, they were sacked out on the couch after school watching *The Brady Bunch* and eating potato chips. I checked in with them, and they were still there, munching. They clearly weren't going to be much help. I mentally flicked through the other distraction tactics I'd been accumulating.

I was sick of reciting my times tables. I knew all our memory verses, and when we'd played "let's go to someone's house for dinner" that morning, Drew had livened up enough to describe steaks and ice cream in great detail. We'd all ended up hungry and grumpy.

I raised my hand and touched Scott's ring. The three circles shifted underneath my fingers, sliding smoothly over one another. Warm and solid. It brought him close with a rush. So close I really felt that if I turned my head I would see him pacing behind me, grinning, dimples and all.

A faint breeze brushed past me from behind, carrying a whisper with it.

"Hi." It was so tangible that I didn't turn my head, not wanting to see only trees.

"Hi," I whispered back.

"What?" Elissa said from behind me, confused.

I couldn't help myself. I looked back.

Nothing.

"I was talking to Scott," I said, trying for a laugh. "I'm going mad."

"You're not!" Elissa said seriously. "I talk to Colin all the time."

"Don't you ever wonder whether eighteen is too young to get married?" I asked, seizing upon the distraction from Scott's ghost. I looked back and caught Drew's eye over the top of Elissa's head. She raised her eyebrows. That was a good sign. This might be a topic worth running with.

"Nope," she said. "September 22 next year. That's the first Saturday after my birthday."

"You're crazy," Drew said, walking so closely behind Elissa in an effort to hear us that she was almost treading on her.

"So you don't want to be a bridesmaid?" Elissa said.

"We get to be bridesmaids?" Drew squealed, suddenly more animated than she had been all week.

"Are you guys talking about *weddings*?" Mark asked from behind Drew, incredulous.

We ignored him, but I wondered if the other two felt the same way I did—guilty. Yet we couldn't spend every minute thinking about Daniel and Mariati, or the possibility that there were men out there tracking us. I was worried Drew would shut down again; we all might shut down if we didn't focus, even briefly, on something else.

"What color are the dresses going to be?" Drew asked.

"I was thinking blue," Elissa said. "With pink and white lilies."

Mark made a vomiting noise.

"Dark blue?" I asked, looking down at my khaki pants. There was a rip down one shin, and they were filthy. There were dark brown circles on both knees and, I was sure, on my butt as well. I watched my left foot move forward, a small clump of mud falling from my boot, and felt my toes scrape against the damp graininess of my sock.

"Mark should be the ring bearer," Drew said loudly over Mark's wail of outrage.

"Guys." Brendan dropped back and spoke softly. "Keep it down enough to listen too. Mani says we're in wild boar territory."

He jerked a thumb toward the nearest tree trunk. The pale furrows that had been plowed through the bark and moss neatly underscored the message.

"Mani said they don't usually attack people," he was quick to add. "We just have to be careful not to surprise them."

"Where's Tina?" I asked. Her face, which had been bobbing over Brendan's shoulder since lunch, had disappeared.

Brendan jerked his head back toward his open pack.

I stood on tiptoe and peered inside. She was sitting on the bottom, knees scrunched up to her chin, asleep.

"Lucky girl," I said.

"So," Drew started again, quietly. "What sort of wedding cake are you going to have?"

Despite Elissa's protestations that she wanted a square cake, we decided upon a six-armed starfish and allocated everyone except Elissa and Tina an arm to decorate. Drew finally settled upon a small tent made out of white icing. Mark agonized over whether he could fit both a boot and a toy toilet on his arm. Mani initially wanted a large cross made out of flowers, but changed to a large cross made out of dried fish at Mark's suggestion. Brendan voted for a small campfire with eight tiny figures around it.

Drew banned Kyle from putting a python on his arm.

"You let Mark have a toilet, but I can't have a snake?"

"Yes."

"Fine then," he said. "I want Jip and Kiki."

"You can't have them!" I said. "You don't even like them."

"I do too!"

"I wanted them," I complained, figuring that the machete I had in mind would probably be voted down, and Jip and Kiki would make a good second choice.

"Well, you should have said so sooner," Kyle said, smug.

"You can each have one," Drew said.

"I want Kiki!" I beat Kyle to it. "And a tree."

"Figures!" Kyle said.

"What's that supposed to mean?" I wobbled as I spun around to glare at him, just in time to catch the first real smile I'd seen in days.

"Nothing," he said.

"Great, just great. They're at it again." Drew sounded almost relieved.

We graciously decided to leave the center of the starfish bare so Elissa could put a small bride and groom in the middle. I was trying to figure out how to make a tree out of icing when, looking up, I realized how dark it had suddenly become.

We still couldn't actually see the sky, but the rustling of leaves in a wind that didn't reach to the jungle floor made it easy to guess that a storm was headed our way. Mani slashed at a thick vine and used it to steady himself down the last few steep steps of the ridge we'd been working our way down for the last hour. My legs were shaking and wobbly, my thigh muscles burning. As I let go of the vine behind him, my foot slipped and I overbalanced, throwing my hands out as I crashed down sideways, the weight of my pack pressing me forward.

I lay there for a moment, stunned and taking stock. Then I sat up slowly.

"Cori!" Kyle pushed past Drew and jumped heavily down the slope, slipping and almost knocking me flat again.

"Be careful!" I snapped. All we needed was a broken ankle.

"Are you okay?" Drew threw herself down beside me. I raised my hand, but she shrank back, shocked and shaking. I saw why about the same time I heard the faint patter of drops falling onto the dead leaves between us.

Blood. My blood. Snaking down my arm toward my elbow. Of

course, it wasn't until I saw it that it started to hurt.

"Let me see!" Kyle pawed at me frantically.

"Get off!" I pushed him away and grabbed my wrist with my left hand. My head was spinning. We inspected the damage together. The rocks must have been sharp. It was a clean slice about as long as my little finger along the outside of my arm, just above my wrist. I closed my hand over it firmly again.

"It'll be fine," I said, as the others crowded around. "Drew," I had to repeat. "It'll be fine."

She sniffed and nodded, not looking convinced.

"We need to stop for the night anyway," Kyle said. "It's going to rain, and this area's flat. We can camp here."

The sound of raindrops hitting the leaves above proved him right, but none were making their way down to us . . . yet.

I leant awkwardly against my pack and kept my hands up by propping my elbows on my knees. I knew we weren't making as much progress as Mani had expected, and I didn't want to admit it, but I was beat. My clothes were clinging to me, my legs trembled, and my back ached.

After a few short sentences Kyle's and Mani's voices receded, and I heard Brendan pulling out the ground sheets and the one tent we were still carrying.

Mani had said we'd probably find bamboo lean-tos built by villagers or Alfur tribesmen who wandered the mountains to tend clove and fruit trees. But after Mani's recital of the legends about the Alfur, I was secretly glad we hadn't stumbled across any. I might not be convinced that people could appear and disappear at will, kill their enemies with magic, and fly on sago palm leaves, but I was happy enough not to take any chances.

I rested my head between my elbows and shut my eyes, resisting the temptation to bawl. Despite the pressure on my wrist, I could feel blood still oozing underneath my fingers, just the way it had from Daniel.

No.

I opened my eyes again and looked over at Elissa, sitting beside me.

"You want me to take care of it?" she asked.

I lifted my head with an effort and eased my arms gently out of the pack straps. "I'll do it. Grab the first aid kit from the outside pocket."

It still hadn't stopped bleeding after we washed it off with canteen water and plied it with antiseptic. It was really starting to throb.

"It looks deep," Elissa said. "Maybe you need stitches."

I almost managed to laugh. "Are you volunteering to start a career in surgery?"

She winced. "Maybe Kyle?" She was serious.

"I'll wrap it," I said. "It'll stop eventually."

I hoped I was right.

By the time we'd finished, Brendan had rigged up a giant cubby-house by stretching two groundsheets over the V between a long pair of buttressed roots, and pitching the tent at the edge of the makeshift cave with its entrance facing in. As I dragged my pack over, I felt the first large splash of rain land on my head and heard the sporadic rhythm of drops falling at ground level.

It was surprisingly cozy lying on my back in the tent knowing we didn't have to walk any more that day. Drew crawled in beside me and curled up, her warmth welcome. I don't know how long I zoned out, but I woke again to the sounds of Brendan and Elissa rustling around to the left of the tent.

"What are you doing?"

"We just rigged the other groundsheet for a fire," Brendan answered, appearing in front of the tent. The cubby suddenly seemed a lot smaller.

"Where's Kyle?"

"Just got some wood," Kyle said, crawling in beside Brendan. "How's the arm?"

"Where's Mani?" I answered.

"Hopefully getting dinner."

"What?" Elissa asked from outside the tent, sounding horrified.

"What do you mean, *what?*" Kyle said. "You're not a vegetarian. What's the problem?"

"I don't know," came a small voice. "It just seems weird."

"Well, I'm going to get over the weird factor pretty quickly if it means food," Kyle said, patting his stomach. "I could eat a horse."

"We've got the fire going. Who has the . . . Mani!" Elissa squeaked, interrupting herself. "Take it away!"

"What?" Mani sounded puzzled.

"We are *not* eating a baby monkey!" Elissa said.

"You caught a monkey?" Mark asked, scrambling out to see what was going on, Tina hanging off his shirt.

"Speak for yourself. I'll eat it," Kyle said, following him out.

"No monkey," I heard Tina say with a giggle.

Brendan and I exchanged glances as I tried to figure out if I was hungry enough to eat a monkey. Drew didn't even open her eyes. I figured I had better see it before I decided, so I rolled over and crawled out one-handed.

"It is not a monkey." Mani was dangling the chubby furry body persuasively. "It is a cuscus. Very good to eat."

I shuddered, but reached for my camera. We were going to want a photo of this. The cuscus looked a lot like a koala, but with a flatter face and rounder eyes.

"How did you catch him?" Mark asked.

"Easy," Mani said. "You see them in the tree. You climb up and *bink*." Mani's sound seemed way too gentle to represent the demise of a cuscus, but his gesture left no room for doubt. To make his point he opened his hand and let the limp body fall to the ground with a muffled thump. "Like that," he said. "They move slow."

It didn't look dead. It looked like a teddy bear. Six of us stared at it with varying degrees of horror and fascination. Tina bent over and stroked it.

Elissa put a hand to her mouth. "I can't eat that."

"Mani and I will cook it," Mark said. He seemed entirely too enthralled by the whole hunter-gatherer thing.

"What else did you get?" Kyle asked, checking out the lumpy shapes in Mani's canvas bag.

"Bamboo to cook rice." Mani shook out eight thick cylinders of bamboo, each about a foot long.

"We have a cooking pot," Elissa said.

Mani dismissed the cooking pot with a flick of his hand. "I'll teach you to do it properly," he said. "It's easy."

Easy seemed to be the word of the day, but I figured if he was leading us through the jungle and slaying monkey look-alikes to keep us fed, we could learn to make rice the "easy way."

"How?" I asked.

"It's closed on the ends," Mani said, showing us how each of the cylinders was naturally sealed at either end. He whipped out his machete. Three cuts chipped out a small triangle for the side of the cylinder.

"It's clean inside," he said, sniffing to demonstrate. "You fill it half with rice, the rest with water, put this back on"—he fitted the bamboo triangle back into the slot—"and put it in the fire. Rice cooks in maybe twenty minutes. Easy. Eat rice; throw the bamboo away."

I was impressed. I decided that when we got home I was going to invite Scott for a nice candlelit meal of cuscus and bamboo rice.

"Elissa and I'll do the rice if you take care of the . . . " I pointed to the cuscus, which Tina had by now dragged into her lap and proceeded to pet. I couldn't bear the thought of them skinning it. I hoped they didn't do it in front of her. I also hoped it didn't have fleas.

"How is your arm?" Mani asked, and I held it up to show him. There was red showing through the gauze, but it seemed to have mostly stopped bleeding.

Mani nodded. "That's okay."

It didn't feel very okay, but I guessed I would live.

I would live.

I caught myself wanting my old standards for rationing out self-pity. Failing a math test—that was at least a day's worth of depression. Having to bandage your own bleeding wounds—by old standards I would have deserved a medal, and a week's worth of sympathy.

But I would live.

Dinner was a subdued affair. The bamboo rice, at least, was a definite success. Mani raked the green cylinders out of the fire after the water stopped hissing and steaming around the edges of the triangles.

Then he balanced one end against the ground and used his machete to split each cylinder neatly in half lengthwise, somehow managing not to spill the rice in the process. We spooned stew into the two halves of our long, curved dishes and ate straight out of the makeshift trenchers.

I was quite proud of the stew we improvised out of the cuscus (that looked a lot smaller once Mani had taken off its skin and chopped it up). We boiled it with our last can of tomatoes and the juice of a coconut. Even Elissa ate some in the end, after we told her it tasted like chicken.

You might have thought that finally having a tummy full of hot food would have energized us, but it had exactly the opposite effect. Or maybe it was the weather. It was very dark by the time we'd finished eating, and rain was still falling unevenly through the leaves. Big drops hit the plastic above us with the force of wet pebbles. Occasionally a thin stream of water cascaded down, like a mini waterfall. The jungle was breathing noisily; a wet earthy smell mingled with the smoke.

I leaned back against wet bark, tried to scrunch farther away from the glowing coals of a fire that was fast dying down, and ran a hand over the red head resting against my shoulder.

"I'm cold," Drew said.

"Me too," I said. My legs, closest to the fire, were almost blistering, but the rest of me was feeling the chill.

"You have other clothes in your packs," Kyle pointed out from where he was huddled with Brendan and Mark on the other side of the fire. They didn't fit under the makeshift fire shelter, so they were sandwiched together under another groundsheet that they had used to form an awkward three-man tent.

"Will you get them?" Drew asked in a small voice.

I knew how she felt. The packs were on the other side of the root we were leaning against, somewhere in that wet, noisy darkness under the other groundsheet. The sound of the falling rain was disorienting. I'd gotten used to the regular night noises of the jungle. They provided a steady stream of reassurance that nothing out of the ordinary was approaching. Deprived of that reassurance, the darkness outside the shrinking glow of firelight seemed dangerous.

Kyle sighed and complied. The thin plastic anorak he tossed over to me didn't provide much protection, but it was better than nothing. Drew settled back against my shoulder, her hand tucked into the crook of my left arm. Elissa's warmth was solid against my other side. Brendan placed the last of our wood on the fire, and the flames hissed as they reluctantly took hold of the damp fuel.

"Will you sing?" Mani broke the noisy silence unexpectedly.

"Something in Indonesian?" Brendan asked.

"No. Do you know 'It Is Well with My Soul'? It is one of my favorite hymns in English."

"That's old," I said. "It's my grandmother's favorite hymn."

"Mine too," Brendan said.

"I know it," Elissa said.

"Will you sing it?" Mani asked again, shifting Tina in his lap. She was curled against his chest with her thumb in her mouth.

I really didn't feel like singing, but there was no way I could refuse Mani anything that was within my power. I glanced at the others, and the three of us started on cue, our voices sounding thin.

> *"When peace like a river attendeth my way;*
> *When sorrows like sea billows roll;*
> *Whatever my lot, thou has taught me to say,*
> *It is well, it is well with my soul.*

It is well with my soul.

It is well, it is well with my soul."

Mani joined in on the third line, and when my voice broke at the end, his was steady.

I remembered that the writer of the hymn had penned this just after his four daughters had been confirmed drowned after their ship went down. I breathed deeply against the now-familiar tight ache in my chest and tried to get my mind around such faith in the midst of such agony. The hymn writer, Spafford, and his children. Mani and his parents. Real pain and real peace. It felt like trying to marry two mental magnets; the closer I tried to push them together, the harder they resisted my pressure.

"Where did you learn it?" I asked Mani.

"Mission school. It reminds me of the last thing that Father said to me." His eyes met mine across the fire.

I shook my arm free from Drew's and hugged my knees to my chest.

"You were there," he said to me.

"I know." I quoted the last phrase I had heard Daniel whisper. *"Baku dame jua."*

He blinked, surprised. "You remember."

"I remember," I said, trying very hard not to remember and failing miserably.

Kyle's hand tightened on the edge of the plastic sheet, knuckles shiny, wet and white.

"I don't know what it means, though. I was going to ask you. Someday."

"It means 'walk with peace,'" Mani said, his eyes locked with mine. He looked a lot like his dad.

I remembered the slippery warmth of Daniel's life ebbing beneath my fingertips, and tucked my hands underneath my knees.

"What does that mean?" Kyle asked.

"Father always said the most important thing was to be at peace with yourself and with God. Not to let anything spoil that. So right now I guess it means not to hate." There was a long pause before his voice came again, low. "That is a bit hard, sometimes."

Even by Mani's laconic standards that was an understatement.

Kyle shifted restlessly. "God hates sin, doesn't He?" he said, the angry challenge barely disguised.

"You are not God," Mani said. "And sin is not a person."

Two points to Mani. So why did I still feel like I was on Kyle's side?

"But what is peace, really?"

"No violence?" Elissa said, obviously wondering if it was a trick question.

"Ever? Not even in self-defense?" Kyle asked.

Elissa's eyes flickered toward the machete lying beside Kyle. "Not for me." She said it so softly that I almost missed the hint of uncertainty behind the words.

"I'm not that strong," I said.

"That's not strong," Kyle said. "When peace is impossible, you think it's strong to just let people push you around?"

"Well, peace is never going to be possible if everyone keeps fighting back," Elissa said, looking like she was about to burst into tears. Arguing with anyone always took a lot out of Elissa, but when she really believed in something, she stood firm.

"I think not resisting is harder than fighting back, sometimes. So maybe it is stronger," I said, wondering if I really believed that.

"That's ridiculous," Kyle said, glaring at me.

I glared back, annoyed it was me he seemed angry with. *I* wasn't the pacifist.

"There's got to be more to peace than just not fighting," Brendan said.

"Yeah, like not having to think about things that make my head hurt," Drew grumbled, without shifting from where she was resting against my shoulder.

There was a long, uncomfortable silence. Kyle was the one to break it, finally going to the heart of what we were all thinking about anyway.

"Things between Batuasa and Tahima can't just go back to the way they were, can they?" Kyle appealed to Mani. "You can't just pretend it didn't happen."

Mani nodded his head, his eyes old. "That would not be peace."

"So what do you do about it?" I asked. "How do you get justice?"

"Punishment," Kyle said, his tone as dark as the jungle beyond the fragile circle of light cast by our dying fire.

"But how do you punish and forgive at the same time?" Elissa asked.

"Forget that sort of peace," Kyle said, slowly and deliberately. "Why even bother?"

The last flame subsided reluctantly into the glowing bed of coals, and the darkness drew closer, waiting to take over completely. I snuggled into Drew and shivered.

"We didn't sing the second verse." Mani spoke over the top of Tina's head. "It's my favorite."

I didn't know the second verse.

Mani started softly, and Brendan's deep, rich voice startled me when he joined in. I closed my eyes and just listened.

> *"My sin, O the bliss of this glorious thought;*
> *My sin, not in part, but the whole*
> *Is nailed to the cross*
> *So I bear it no more.*
> *Praise the Lord, praise the Lord, O my soul.*
> *It is well with my soul.*
> *It is well, it is well with my soul."*

I guess that was one way to answer Kyle's last question.

chapter 11 ～

Not even the heavy and irregular rhythm of raindrops falling on plastic kept me awake, although the night was far from restful with most of us crammed into the one tent. Sometime during the darkness a rivulet of cold water found its way into my "bed," and I felt mud soaking into my hair. Kyle murmured when I squirmed sideways, and threw an arm over me before going still again. The contact was warm and comforting, and I pressed closer, not particularly wanting to go back to sleep, feeling the tired ache in my knees and shoulders and the throbbing in my arm.

Every night now was bringing dreams. Sometimes I would see it again exactly as it happened. Sometimes it was my family, or other people I knew, running through the village and calling for help. Sometimes I was leaning over Daniel. My hands were red. Mani was calling desperately for me to do something and, bizarrely, someone was laughing in the background. In that dream I knew it was up to me to do the right thing that would save Daniel's life, and I failed every time.

Kyle twitched in his sleep, and his arm tightened, pulling me closer.

As if I didn't have enough material to fuel the dreams, I had just been awakened from inventing a whole new scene. This time I was standing right there beside Budi, but I wasn't afraid. He was lying in the dirt, wet, as if he'd just been swimming. A man with a machete was standing across him, looking at me. Then he used the knife to spear the bear clutched in Budi's tiny hand, offered it to me, and grinned. I woke to find myself holding the toy.

Despite Kyle's warmth I shuddered as I fingered the bear's fuzzy contours.

God. I felt the word surface involuntarily. It was a plea so fervent that only a few fragmented sentences emerged from the depths.

I'm lost and scared. And in the face of Mani's pain, even that seems so trivial. I need You.

I need You.

It echoed, lingering, and I felt yearning seeping through me, squeezing out my pores, the way I had never felt any need before.

I can't do this alone. Help us.

I don't know how long I lay there in the dark feeling the weight of my need, not even having words to pray when, suddenly, it seemed to lessen slightly and I could breathe more deeply. I don't know whether it was Kyle or not, but as I slid back into sleep I remember feeling a hand smooth my hair.

I didn't dream again that night, and I woke up at a quarter to six feeling slightly more refreshed. Kyle's warmth was gone, and I could hear the intermittent crackle of a nearby fire. As I crawled out from under the plastic shelter I saw that the rain had stopped, even as I felt water soaking through the knees of my pants.

Kyle looked at me critically through misty gray that the dawn light was having a hard time penetrating. "You're filthy."

I put my hand up to my stiff hair and made a face. If it looked anything like Kyle's, it was sticking up at odd angles in artistic mud-sculpted whirls.

"You're pretty grubby yourself. I can hardly even see your tattoo."

"Yeah." He looked down at his arm and grinned suddenly. "Mr. Snake is hibernating. There was a period in my life where I never would have thought I'd say this, but I really need a bath."

We shared a mug of coffee, huddled shoulder to shoulder close to the struggling fire, which was hissing and spitting in the damp.

"So," I said quietly, starting the little routine Mark and I had developed over the last couple of days. "Where are Jip and Kiki going to get to by lunchtime?"

"Quit it. I'm not Drew. I don't need you to baby me."

"What happened to your sense of humor?" I said, stung.

"It's dead. What's happened to yours?" he fired back. "You're trying, but it's not really there. You can fool Mark, but you can't fool me."

For once I managed to resist the urge to snap back at him and just glared. He didn't see me. He was staring through the fire, gazing into the distance. He stayed like that until the harsh screech of a parrot in the trees overhead made us both jump.

"Cori," he said, looking serious, even by the standards of the last week. The rest of what he wanted to say came out in a rush. "I'm sorry for falling apart that day behind the church, with Daniel. I just left you and Mani . . . I couldn't . . ." He stopped, lowered his head, and ground his thumbs into his temples.

"What?" I was shocked. "You were the one who went out the front of the house and brought him back." I could not imagine the strength it must have taken to step out from behind the shelter of the house, within sight of the frenzy in the village.

"It was all the blood," he continued as if he hadn't heard me. He swallowed hard. "Brendan had to drag me across the grass and into the bushes."

"Yeah, me too."

"He said he had to carry you, kicking, and you were saying, 'Let me go, let me go' the whole way."

"I don't remember," I said honestly. "I just remember feeling him die. Just like that. And then I was in the bushes, and I looked back and saw the church burning."

"If I'd held it together, maybe we could have done something." Kyle sounded tortured. "Maybe it would have been different."

"No," I said, suddenly certain. "There was no way. By that time there was nothing we could have done that would have changed it." I caught myself gripping Kyle's arm and made myself let go.

"How do you know?"

"How did you know Mariati was already dead?" I countered.

He twitched. "I just knew. Mani's face. I'll never forget that for as long as I live."

"I'm sorry," I said, leaning against him. Kyle obviously had plenty of material for his own nightmares.

We watched Brendan and Elissa crawl out from underneath the shelter and disappear behind different trees. I tipped some more water into our tin cans and pushed them out over the fire.

"Selamat pagi," Mani said from directly behind me, and I clapped a hand over my mouth to prevent any swear words escaping.

"Sorry." He acknowledged the fright he'd given me with a nod and tossed two furry bodies down beside us. "I found some cuscus," he said casually. To listen to him you would think he'd just been taking a nice stroll in the woods and tripped over the creatures.

"We don't have to eat those for breakfast, do we?" Drew asked, poking a tousled head up over the tree roots.

"No," Elissa said. She wrinkled her nose as she reappeared and headed for the shelter again. "There's still porridge left. I'll get it."

"Mark! Get up!" We heard her command several seconds later in a tone of controlled outrage. "Did I tell you that you could use the porridge box as a pillow? Now it's wet!"

"Leave me alone! I don't *feel* good," Mark whined.

Kyle pursed his lips in a silent whistle. Apparently, even he wouldn't be game to mess with Elissa if she used that tone on him.

"Do you want to eat or not?" Elissa said in a way that made it clear that unless Mark moved instantly it was doubtful he'd ever eat again.

Mark didn't answer, but I heard a groan, and Elissa reappeared holding the porridge. My body betrayed my mind, and my stomach growled.

"I have been thinking . . . ," Mani said gravely, pausing to stir a mug of tea with great concentration.

I tried to figure out exactly what he thought this was accomplishing, since he hadn't put any sugar into it and had already taken out the tea bag.

We sat there, looking at him expectantly. Even Elissa stopped mucking around with the porridge mix. Mani continued to stir his tea with rhythmic precision, staring into his mug. The rest of us looked at one another with raised eyebrows.

"What have you been thinking?" Brendan finally ventured.

We watched as Mani lifted the teaspoon out of the mug and took a careful sip. Only then did he look up and speak, deliberately, in a way that made it clear he had already made up his mind.

"We should not walk to Halimentan. It will take too long. And it is too hard."

I grimaced. With the exception of Brendan and Kyle, none of us were holding up as well as I'd hoped we would be able to. Drew ran out of energy by lunchtime each day. Even Mark was gray with fatigue by the time we stopped every afternoon.

"What other choice do we have?" I asked. "I thought Halimentan was the closest port."

Mani went back to stirring his tea. We watched, hypnotized.

"We can walk down the rivers to the beach, find a boat in a village, and sail to Ambon from the village," he said.

"What are the drawbacks?" Kyle asked.

Mani looked up, confused.

"Disadvantages," Brendan clarified.

"The village boat will not have a motor, just a sail. It will take us about two days to sail that way to Ambon." He met our gaze fully for the first time. "I don't think we can walk over the mountains. The hiking will get harder. Much harder."

I swallowed and glanced at Drew, who had emerged from the shelter just in time to hear Mani's last speech. She looked scared.

"This way," Mani continued, "we hike two days down to the beach, and it takes two days to sail to Ambon."

He stopped there. I hadn't thought too much about what happened after we reached Ambon, but my favorite vision involved the Stewarts welcoming us with open arms, escorting us straight to the airport, and putting us on a plane home. My heart contracted as I looked at Mani. Where was his home going to be now?

"All right," Brendan said slowly. "If you think that's the best thing to do, that's what we'll do."

Mani nodded, looking into his tea again.

He'd almost succeeded in hiding how much of a burden our safety and helplessness was. How he was scared too.

But not quite.

I don't know why it took us longer than usual to get going that morning. We weren't even camped near a stream, so we didn't have to filter any water. Doing the dishes just consisted of wiping at the few utensils with fern leaves, still wet from the rain. It was hard to find a dry place to sit for quiet time, but I finally perched on a rock and leaned back against one side of a broad trunk. After the rain it was almost too hushed, and I was grateful for the small noises the others made as they settled themselves down. Drew was beside me on the rock, and I heard Mark wheezing slightly on the other side of our tree. Two trees away, Kyle hadn't opened his Bible, but at least he was writing in his journal.

I leafed idly through my own Bible, a gift from my parents on my sixteenth birthday. I glanced as usual at the inscription my mother had written in the front.

For Coralie, it said. May these words nourish, guide, and protect your heart, your mind, and your soul. Underneath she had added: Trust in the Lord with all your heart and lean not on your own understanding; in all your ways acknowledge him, and he will make your paths straight. Proverbs 3:5–6

I stared at those words, not finding the energy to pick something else to read. I still couldn't figure out whether trusting God with all your heart meant abandoning understanding entirely. That didn't make any sense to me. We must have minds for a reason. Surely we were expected to use them.

Drew interrupted this familiar swirl of disturbing thoughts by scooting over and nudging me none too gently.

"Ow! That's right where I fell on that rock." I pulled up my shirt to show her the bruise on the top of my hip.

She kissed a finger and touched it lightly. "Kisses heal everything," she said.

"Much better," I replied with a straight face.

"I can't pray," she whispered. "I'm trying, but I just can't concentrate. You know how it says that when we don't know what to pray for, the Holy Spirit intercedes for us with groans that words cannot express? How does that work, exactly?"

"I guess you fill out a prayer request slip, specify the number of groans, and lodge it with the Holy Spirit department," I said.

"Cori, that's dodgy," Drew admonished me, deliberately using one of my favorite words against me. "I don't want to go to Ambon," she whispered. "I just want to sit here until someone rescues us. Isn't that dumb?"

"It's not dumb," I said, realizing I was feeling the same way. Once we'd stopped worrying about being followed, we'd started to feel safe in our little band of eight. Now that it was clear we were heading toward the villages again, even the looming trees were starting to look sheltering instead of menacing.

"We could leave you here with Brendan and Mani," I teased. "Kyle and I will head across to Ambon, commandeer a plane, and come back and pick you up."

"No way!" she said. "You and Kyle would start fighting before you even got halfway. He would storm off, you'd get completely lost and never find the airport, and we'd be stuck here forever."

"Halfway to Ambon is in the middle of the ocean," I pointed out, keeping the joke going so that the word *forever* didn't linger in the quiet. "He's going to have a hard time storming off a boat. Besides, there are worse things than being stuck here. Think of everything you've learned in the last week. You can eat wild rice and cuscus, hunt wild pigs . . . "

"Use leaves for toilet paper," Mark added from the other side of the tree before scooting around and resting his head on my knee. His cheek felt warm against my leg.

"Using leaves is really not that bad," Drew said.

Mark nodded with an evil little grin. "When you pick the right ones," he said knowingly.

Drew and I muffled our giggles, remembering Mark's long spiel the previous afternoon about Kip's adventures with the sharp edges of the sago palm leaves.

Kyle glanced across at us, his expression unreadable.

"I once knew someone who was revolted by even having to use a portable toilet," I reminisced.

"I love port-a-potties," Drew said. "When I grow up I'm going to own two!"

Mark groaned. My stomach turned over lazily and gurgled. I wondered whether all this talk of toilets was activating the foreign bugs to marshal in revolt. We'd had to make seven toilet stops before we even broke for lunch yesterday.

"Besides . . ." Drew thankfully diverted the conversation away from the toilet. "Once you get the plane from Ambon, where are you going to land it?"

"Well, we can't land on the beach. So we'll fly over you trailing a pickup line that you can grab, and then we'll pull you up."

"Ingenious." She commended me.

Mark snorted, reminding me of Scott. I could almost hear the lecture on aerodynamics and the limits of possibility.

"Where would we go then?" Drew asked, snuggling closer.

"Australia, of course," I said. "Although I don't know if they'd let you bunch in. I might have to vouch for you."

"Great," Mark said. "We're stuck then."

I cuffed him gently, and he flinched. "You all right?"

"Headache," he said.

"You want some Tylenol? There's some in the first aid kit."

I felt a headache of my own coming on as I came back to earth to face the reality that we were very far away from Australia. I rummaged through the first aid kit, passed two Tylenol over, and watched Mark dry-swallow them.

"Where's your water?" I said.

"Canteen's empty," he said. "But Mani said we'd find water early today."

Drew passed him hers, and he took a long swallow.

"Ready?" Mani asked, getting to his feet. There were groans all around. Day seven was under way. At least it promised to be mostly downhill.

Just two hours later I had decided again that climbing mountains was easier than hiking down them. My legs were trembling, sweat kept slipping into my eyes when I looked down, and my toes were protesting loudly about being mashed into the front end of my boots.

But I had more to worry about than myself. Mark was walking in front of me, and even from behind I could see that he was struggling. Twice he slipped and fell. The third time I called a rest break.

"I'm fine," Mark said from where he was still sprawled on the ground. He didn't look like he was in any state even to stand up again, much less keep hiking. He rolled over and leaned back against his pack, not even bothering to slide his arms out of the straps.

"Whatever. Open," I said. I pulled the thermometer out of the first aid kit and stuck it in his mouth.

He tried to speak around it.

"Shut up," I said, my bedside manner less than gracious.

I looked across at Elissa and saw my fear mirrored in her eyes. She leaned her pack against her knees and shrugged.

"How far to the stream?" Brendan asked Mani.

"We're close," Mani said, and I thought I saw a hint of the old sparkle in his eyes. "About fifteen minutes. And there is a surprise."

"Can you do fifteen minutes?" Kyle asked Mark.

Mark nodded with his eyes still closed. I saw him shiver.

"101.7," I announced as the little alarm went off. I helped him slip his arms out of his pack straps and stand up. "No worries. You could run a marathon in that condition. Fifteen more minutes will be a piece of cake." I adopted a quavery voice. "When I was a child and I had a fever of 101.7, I still had to walk to school in the snow . . . barefoot."

"Mmmm, snow," Mark managed.

Kyle grabbed Mark's pack and hoisted it onto his shoulders, balancing it sideways on top of the one he was already carrying. He looked like a determined turtle.

"Come on, squirt," Kyle said, nudging Mark forward into line behind Brendan. I dropped back behind Elissa.

"Malaria?" Elissa asked quietly as we started off again.

"I don't know. Maybe." I thought back to when Tanya had caught malaria in Kenya when she was nine. She had almost died. "We don't have any quinine or doxycycline. We've got nothing of any use but Tylenol!" I felt tears of pure frustration in my eyes as I told her what she already knew.

Mani dropped back to join us, piggybacking Tina. "It is malaria, I think," he said, chewing his bottom lip. "Are you taking your medicine?"

"Gary and Diane must have taken it with them," Elissa said.

Mani looked shocked as he did the calculations. "No medicine for seven days?"

"Nine," I said.

"It is malaria," he said more decisively, sounding annoyed. "I thought you were still taking the medicine. If I knew I would have made tea from the papaya tree. It is very good for malaria." He shook his head and sped up again to reclaim his place at the front of the line.

Papaya leaf tea. I felt like screaming. Like stopping right where I was and throwing an almighty temper tantrum. The little Cori in my mind punched the trees. She fell to the dirt and kicked and shrieked. All the little others in my head looked at her like she was crazy. And when she was done she had to get up and keep walking anyway—so I decided it wasn't worth the effort.

"God," I growled under my breath, using a large fern leaf for balance while I stretched my right leg carefully over a sharp rock and down half a foot to the next solid footfall. "I specifically asked You to help us not get sick. You could have at least given us that."

"Are you talking to yourself again?" Elissa asked over her shoulder.

"Sometimes it seems like I might as well be," I said.

"Thank God we have Mani," Elissa said. "Can you imagine trying to do this without him?" She shifted her weight as she prepared to tackle the next stretch of rocks.

The path we were picking through the trees was getting steeper, and the ground glistened with moisture. Even the air seemed wetter.

I felt a sudden overwhelming stab of shame at the difference between our attitudes, and watched as Elissa's braid snagged on a thorny vine and she reached back to flick it free. I heard her words again and banished the voice in my head that scoffed at thanksgiving to the back of my mind.

It growled at me and retreated, sulking.

Thank God we have Mani, I thought, meaning it. *Thank You that Mani was spared. Thank You that we were.*

I saw Kyle reach out and steady Mark, and I was thankful for the fact that there were eight of us. I stumbled and was thankful that we could all still walk. I thought about home and was thankful for parents who were probably frantic with worry and doing everything they could to find out what had happened to us.

All this deliberate thankfulness was calming me down all right, but wearing me out. I suddenly realized just how tired I was and how much I wanted to take a bath, crawl into bed, and stay there for a week.

"Whoooeee!" Brendan's cowboy yell jolted me. It took me an instant to realize he sounded . . . excited.

"Mani—you are the man!" Kyle shouted.

"What?" Drew sounded as bewildered as I felt. She slid sideways down the last muddy slope and disappeared around the immense tree trunk that was blocking my view.

"Have mercy!" I heard her exclaim as I waited impatiently for Elissa to navigate the last section of a track that five previous sets of feet had made more slippery. I couldn't imagine that anything short of a helicopter would be capable of producing quite that much happiness.

Warm, sticky air hit me as I rounded the tree trunk, and I felt a beam of sunlight fall directly on my face for the first time in a week. The others were all standing on large flat rocks beside a murky pond about as big as two backyard swimming pools. It took a couple of seconds to realize what it was—a hot spring!

I had only one question. "Can we swim in it?"

"Yes." Mani smiled proudly at our joy. "It is perfect hotness."

"Temperature," Kyle corrected automatically.

"A bath!" Drew sounded as if no greater gift existed.

"Ummm, guys," Mark said weakly from where he was sitting down. "I don't feel so good."

I turned away from the spring with regret. The bath was going to have to wait.

"You don't look so good either," I told him as I dumped my pack and fished for the thermometer again. "Open."

He didn't argue with me this time.

"We're gonna find a place to make camp," Kyle said. The glance we shared told me he was well aware of what we were probably facing.

"I will go get papaya leaves," Mani said, passing Tina to Elissa.

The thermometer beeped, and I pulled it out. 102.1.

"I have malaria, don't I?" Mark asked, sounding more tired than scared.

"Maybe," I said, trying to sound upbeat. "But Mani's gone to get us all some papaya leaves to make tea with. It's great for helping with malaria, so we're all going to drink some."

"Okay," Mark said, and closed his eyes. He sounded like he had a lot more faith in the restorative properties of papaya leaves than I did.

"I'm freezing," he added, shivering again. "I want a bath."

"All right," I said, stepping over his legs as Elissa sat down next to him. "I'll get the guys."

I had to pause for a moment as I entered the trees again to let my eyes adjust to having less light. Then I set off in the direction that I thought Brendan and Kyle had taken, following the scuff marks in the ground cover and the occasional partial boot print in the mud. We were all getting more confident at navigating; Drew had gone off to get water by herself without even a murmur. It didn't take long before I could just follow the sound of their voices.

"Maybe we should split up," I heard Kyle say. "Two of us could head for Ambon and bring back help."

I stepped into the small clearing behind Brendan, and Kyle acknowledged me with a jerk of his head.

"I don't think it's a good idea to split up," Brendan was saying, worried and clearly working hard to come up with a better plan. "Mani's the only one who really knows where we're going. Mark's the only other person who has any idea about sailing."

"Mark is going to be as sick as a dog in a couple of hours," I said, and saw Brendan jump at the sound of my voice.

"Ahhhh!" he yelped, at a very un-Brendanlike pitch.

I looked around. They had selected a good spot. Flat and almost square, about six paces by seven. Three trees growing close together to the right gave the patch a sheltered feeling, and the ground, although damp, wasn't sticky. They'd laid a groundsheet down between two roots that stretched out from one of the trees like two arms open for a hug. Then they'd draped another over the roots, using a couple of tent pegs to anchor it, creating a makeshift tent that could sleep three people at a squeeze. Our tent was pitched nearby. Three paces away, the other three groundsheets were arranged in a semicircle around what

I assumed was going to be our fireplace. They'd been busy circling it with rocks when I'd arrived. The little clearing looked almost cozy.

"Mark wants a bath. It might be better if we give him a bit of a scrubbing before we put him to bed." I pointed at the two of them. "That would be your job."

"I'm sure Mark wouldn't mind you giving him a bit of a scrubbing." Kyle winked at me.

"Mark's probably too sick to care who's giving him a scrubbing," I said, and then felt bad for jumping on him.

"I'll go." Brendan put down the rock he'd been holding and looked around. "Who has the soap and shampoo?"

"I do," Kyle said, going over and flicking open the side pocket of his pack.

I laughed.

"What?" This time it was his turn to snap at me. "It's not like any of you have used them either!"

"How bad is it going to get?" Brendan paused on his way out of the clearing.

"I don't know," I said, exasperated. Why did everyone always look to me for answers about these things?

"Could he die?" Kyle asked me. It was almost a challenge.

"Yes, Kyle. He could die," I said flatly, suddenly furious with him. He probably knew that already, so why did he have to make me say it out loud?

Brendan just nodded and disappeared. Kyle and I stared at each other across the half-constructed fireplace. He sighed heavily, and my anger disappeared as quickly as it had come.

I took three steps around the rocks and wrapped my arms around his waist, demanding a hug without words. At first I thought he was going to push me away, but then he pulled me close, rested his cheek on the top of my head, and sighed again.

"Hey, guys?" It was the sound of Drew's voice that made us step apart.

"Up here," Kyle called and glanced at me, signaling a truce without words. I wondered if he could read fear in my eyes as easily as I could see it in his.

Drew didn't seem to notice anything amiss. She was red and puffing by the time she'd scrambled up to us, carrying four full canteens looped over her shoulders and trying to balance a saucepan full of water.

"Have mercy!" she gasped, collapsing untidily onto a groundsheet after she'd set the saucepan down. "The water here is definitely heavier than the water at home."

"That's ridiculous," Kyle said.

"*You* didn't just carry it up the hill," Drew said. "I'm speaking from experience. Hey." She changed the subject abruptly, and actually smiled. "There are crayfish in the river. Mani said we could catch them and eat them."

"Not if we have nothing to cook them with," I said, pulling her up despite her protests. "We need firewood."

"Fetch water, fetch wood," she grumbled. "Why do I feel like the world clock's gone backwards several thousand years?"

"Not too green," Kyle called after us bossily.

By the time we'd been back and forth four times with wood, Kyle had a fire going and water boiling. Everyone except Mani had congregated at the campsite. Brendan looked decidedly out of place with his face so clean it was shiny.

"Mark's in the tent," he said, answering my question before I'd asked it.

Mark was huddled inside a sleeping bag when I crawled in. He looked a lot cleaner, but behind his flushed cheeks he was very pale. Even through the sleeping bag I could see him shivering.

"My head hurts," he said, slurring his words.

"I bet it does. Open."

He groaned a little in protest, but opened his mouth for the thermometer.

102.7. I struggled to remember how high Tanya's temperature had gone before the first fever broke. Almost 104, I thought.

"Am I going to die?" he asked softly, not sounding like he cared much one way or the other.

For a moment I wasn't sure I'd heard him right; then I paused another second to make sure I had the right tone of voice.

"No," I said, hoping I was right. "You're going to feel really awful for a while, but you're not going to die."

"Mmm."

I wasn't sure whether he was murmuring in acknowledgment or dissent.

Elissa poked her head in. "Mani's back."

Mani had managed to drag back at least ten shiny green papaya leaves, each as long as he was tall, and was busy slicing them open up the middle of the thick stem on each leaf. Brendan was using his hands to scrape out the white pulp.

"Enough," Mani said after he'd de-pulped three of the leaves and our battered saucepan was half full. He carefully tipped four tin cans of boiling water into the saucepan and set it beside the fire.

"In two minutes it will be ready," he said.

"How's Mark?" Brendan asked.

"His temp's still going up," I said.

Mani nodded. "I have had malaria before. He will be fine, I think. But we can't move for two days maybe. Or three. Or more maybe."

At least two more days. I had known that, but I almost groaned anyway. We were going to have been missing for ten days by the time we got to Ambon. Maybe, I realized with a sudden stab of hope, our parents would even be there when we got there. Maybe they were there now.

"How was the bath?" Drew asked Brendan.

"Amazing," he said with feeling, and then repeated himself. "Amazing."

"Let's go then!" Drew said, turning to Elissa and me and giving the first thumbs-up I'd seen all week.

"Not before we drink the . . . stuff," Elissa said, indicating the brew that Mani was tasting with a teaspoon.

He nodded, dipped out about half a cup, and passed it to Kyle. "Everyone drinks some," he said firmly.

Kyle tasted it and made a face like a gargoyle. Then he held his nose and downed it in three huge gulps.

"Not bad," he gasped, the fact that he was turning slightly green belying his words.

He had lied. When it was my turn, the metallic bitterness made my tongue clench and my jaw muscles ache.

"Gross!" Drew wailed as she tasted her own portion. "Are you sure this isn't poisonous?"

Kyle, who was the only one who'd actually drunk his so far, looked slightly concerned.

"No. It is very good for malaria," Mani said reassuringly. "It has—" He waved his hand, trying to find the right word.

"Quinine," I said. That would explain the bitterness. "It would be better with honey in it," I said, remembering how Mum had crushed up our antimalarial tablets in honey when we were younger.

"We don't have any honey." Drew pointed out the obvious as if she expected me to do something about it.

"We have sugar," Elissa said doubtfully. "But not much." She took another small sip, then another.

"Come on. Don't be such babies," Kyle taunted.

I took a large gulp and gagged. Kyle helpfully pounded me on the back.

Drew didn't rise to the bait, but just sat there, staring mournfully into her cup.

Brendan followed Kyle's example and downed it in one go, but then sat there with his eyes scrunched closed for at least twenty seconds before he sighed deeply and opened them again. Tina seemed to think we were all highly amusing.

I took another swallow and worked hard at not retching. I measured what I had left. One more big swallow would finish it off.

"Just drink it," I told Drew, "and then we can go and have a bath."

At least that thought motivated her to lift the cup to her lips.

Elissa finished hers off with a final sip and passed the cup back to Mani with patent relief. "How much for Mark?" she asked.

Mani measured out almost a full cup. "That first. Another one in three hours. And then another one in three hours again."

"You'll be drinking this every three hours if you get malaria," Kyle said to Drew.

She swallowed. I left her to it and followed Elissa into the tent.

Mark groaned and pushed her hand away as she held the cup to his lips.

"You will drink this, and you need to stay out of your sleeping bag to help keep your fever down," I ordered, hardening my heart and flipping the covers off him.

"I'll get him to drink it," Brendan said, behind us. "You guys head down to the spring."

I backed out of the tent gratefully and handed him the thermometer. "If his temperature goes above 103, start sponging him down with cool water."

I grabbed two towels, my toothbrush, camera, swimsuit, and the other set of clothes out of my pack.

"Who has toothpaste?"

"I do," said Drew, still staring at the remnants of what was in her cup.

"Try not to think about it," Elissa advised sympathetically.

"We're leaving in ten seconds with or without you," I added.

She lifted the mug to her lips, and Tina giggled in anticipation.

"Tina, you want to come for a bath?" Elissa coaxed.

Tina looked confused.

"Swimming?"

"Swimming!" Tina trilled. "Mani come?"

"No, Mani stay here, and we will come back after swimming."

Tina considered that doubtfully for a moment before Mani said something to her in Indonesian, and she took Elissa's hand.

"Done!" Drew slammed her mug down with relief and bounced to her feet. "Let's go!"

"There is going to be a hot spring in heaven," Drew said with assurance, sitting with her legs in the water and both hands busy unbraiding her hair.

I almost slipped climbing onto a large underwater rock and sat down gingerly, letting my legs float out in front of me and trying not to wonder whether there were any Indonesian snakes that lived in hot springs. Mani had been right; the water was perfect, warmer than tepid but not too hot. The stinging of water meeting open blisters started to ease, and I felt myself relax marginally as the heat reached my shoulders. For a long still moment I did nothing but sink into the warmth; then I reached up and took off the baseball cap I'd been wearing for the last two days. My hair felt oily and slick.

Tina squealed in fright when she felt the water and pulled her foot back out again, almost falling over in the process. "Hot!" she said anxiously.

"It's okay." Elissa patted her hands onto the water from where she was sitting on another rock. "Swimming in hot water. It's fun."

Tina looked around expectantly. "Swimming?" she queried. "Mama? Papa?"

Elissa, Drew, and I stopped what we were doing and looked at each other.

"Maybe she thought we were going swimming at the beach," Drew said uncertainly.

"The beach!" Tina crowed.

Her little face fell when we shook our heads, and she stared at us, betrayed.

"Not today," Elissa said, holding out her hand, her voice wobbling.

Tina didn't move. Two large tears gathered in her eyes and rolled down her cheeks. Her mouth shook, and her lower lip stuck out. "The beach," she said hopelessly.

"Oh, honey," Elissa said, tears already slipping down her own cheeks. She climbed out of the water and pulled Tina into her lap. Tina didn't resist. The tears were still coming, but she wasn't making any sound. She cried without energy, limp.

"Want Mama," she said, forlorn. It was more of a statement than a request.

"I know," Elissa said, her own tears dripping onto Tina's dark head. "I want my mama too."

Tina looked up. "Where you mama?" She lifted a hand to touch Elissa's wet cheek.

"I don't know. At home, I think," Elissa said.

"Mani say Mama home in heaven," she said. "The beach," she added as an afterthought, her tears slowing as quickly as they had started.

I wondered what sense a four-year-old could make of the concept of heaven. I saw again Mariati's two small steps away from the door of the house. Trying to protect Tina by walking away from her. I could feel the pressure behind my eyes, but the tears refused to fall. When I swallowed I tasted a bitterness that wasn't only the remnants of papaya leaf tea.

Drew slipped into the water beside me and ducked her head under, coming up with eyes that were almost as red as her hair.

Tina, watching her, scrambled out of Elissa's lap and over to the edge of the water, apparently resigned to the fact that swimming here was as good as it was going to get for now.

"Hot?" she queried Drew.

"Yes." Drew made an effort, but her voice was thick. "Come on in."

Tina looked doubtful but stuck a leg in anyway, then squawked as Drew splashed her.

I grabbed the bottle of shampoo off the rock beside me and lathered a generous amount through my hair. Not even the weight of

Tina's sadness could totally erase the pleasure that brought. When I'd scrubbed my fingertips raw, I piled my hair on top of my head and let it sit for a while.

Across from me Elissa was doing the same. Drew had managed to coax Tina in and was dipping her in and out of the water.

"What are we going to do with her?" Elissa asked, indicating the subject of her question with a flick of her head.

"What?"

"When we get to Ambon," Elissa said. "We can't leave them here. We can't leave her with Mani."

"Do we have a choice?" This was one I hadn't really thought through.

"Mani has no family here now. I don't think he can take care of her by himself. What's going to happen to her?"

"Elissa," I warned her, reading the direction of her thoughts. "We can't take her home. Even if Mani wanted us to."

"Why not?" Elissa said.

"They probably wouldn't even let her into the U.S."

"That's ridiculous," Elissa said with feeling. "She's only four!"

"Besides, who would she go home with?" I knew what the answer was going to be before she said it.

"Me. She can live with my family until Colin and I get married."

"Mani's almost a year older than you," I said.

"So? People all over the world are having babies at sixteen," Elissa argued. "If they can't both come, I want Tina."

I ducked under to rinse my hair off and give me time to think. By the time I came up I knew there was only one answer that made sense.

"They both have to come," I said. "We have to make it work somehow."

Mark's hand felt hot and dry in mine. Every so often it trembled, and his fingers dug into me. Over the last hour the chills had become more sporadic and his grip weaker—but he felt hotter. I shifted in the darkness, trying to ease the cramp in my lower back. My legs were stretched out alongside Mark, and I could just see the tips of my boots in the glow cast by the fire. Huddled around the warmth, the others were speaking softly, the rhythm of their voices as steadying and solid as the tree I was leaning against through the back of the tent. Mark shivered again, and I reached for the thermometer. He didn't even groan, although he did manage to raise a protest when it beeped and I flicked on the flashlight to read it.

103.4.

"Mark, you're going to be fine," I whispered. I couldn't tell whether he heard me or cared.

I had to believe that was true. Despite what I'd said to Kyle earlier, every time I tried to examine the possibility that Mark might die my thoughts would start skipping—like the CD player in a car on a dirt road.

Periodically the darkness, the humidity, and the crushing weight of responsibility dissolved. I would find myself on the couch at home on a Saturday morning huddled under one blanket with Tanya and Luke, watching the Smurfs and eating leftover apple pie we'd smuggled out of the fridge. Or sitting next to Scott with my head on his shoulder, feeling flannel under my cheek and smelling detergent.

"Mom," Mark rasped, yanking me away from visualizing what everyone at home might be doing at that precise moment.

I squeezed his hand and wished with all my might for his mum, for my mum, for anyone's mum. I was sick of being responsible.

"Once upon a time Jip and Kiki were adventuring far from home, in the Australian outback . . . ," I said, deciding no mothers were magically going to appear and that I'd better do the best I could.

Jip was under siege by a whole mob of mad kangaroos, and Kiki was just about to save the day when Brendan stuck his head into the shelter. "Since when do kangaroos wear yellow aprons and ballet slippers?" he asked.

"Have you ever seen kangaroos in the wild?" I asked, knowing I had him there. I pulled up my legs so that he could maneuver. With the three of us it was a tight squeeze.

"I've got some more tea." He reached out in the darkness and guided my hands to the warm mug.

Mark at least understood what that meant, because he let out a mew of protest. I set the mug down carefully in the dirt and flicked on the flashlight again, shielding Mark from the light with my leg. He scrunched his eyes closed anyway. Two patches of red glowed fiercely in his pale cheeks.

"Come on," I said, holding a tablespoon of the milky liquid to his lips. He hardened them obstinately and opened his eyes to glare up at me with as much force as he could muster.

"Mark . . . ," Brendan said sternly.

Just that one word was enough to make him open his mouth, and I dribbled the contents in before he could change his mind.

He gagged. "I hate you," he whispered after he'd swallowed.

"No doubt," I said, tipping in another spoonful with less compunction.

It felt like hours before we emptied that mug, inch by painful inch. Then I sat back, exhausted, waiting for the thermometer to register.

103.6.

"What does that mean?" Brendan asked, sounding uncertain.

"It means we sponge him and pray it goes down," I said, not too sure myself.

Mark had stopped shivering and just lay there on the top of the sleeping bag, radiating heat. Without his shirt on he looked tiny. I could count his ribs. I rolled him onto his side, and he didn't protest when Brendan started wiping him down with a wet towel. I didn't think that was a good sign.

It turned into the longest night I've ever spent. At midnight Elissa replaced Brendan. She was there when Mark's temperature topped 104.

Then Mani. He was there when we realized we couldn't rouse Mark to drink some more tea.

And finally, Kyle. He was there for that hour between five and six in the morning when Mark's breathing was so shallow that twice we thought it had stopped completely. And he was there at 8:04 a.m. when Mark's fever broke and he started sweating.

Kyle cried.

I curled up with my head in his lap, fell asleep, and didn't wake up for nine hours. No nightmares.

chapter 12 ~

It was Wednesday morning. At least that's what my brain was telling me. It didn't feel like it, though. Wednesday morning was getting up early so we could all have breakfast together as a family. Wednesday morning was worrying about the calculus homework I hadn't done.

Wednesday morning was not scrambling downhill following a small animal track that sometimes disappeared completely, leaving us to pick our way through the scrub, weaving around trees, disoriented and trusting Mani completely. Wednesday morning was not having to spend half my energy ignoring the voice in my head that wanted to start most internal conversations with "This time eleven days ago . . ." and the rest with "Ahhhh! A snake!"

I felt cheated.

We'd had a good breakfast, though. Definitely a Wednesday breakfast.

Now that we were getting closer to the villages again we'd decided to have someone keeping watch at all times, and I'd taken the early morning shift. Brendan had shaken me awake apologetically at four. I checked on Mark, who was sleeping soundly, before stumbling out of the shelter into the quiet, chilly darkness and heading straight for the fire.

Brendan must have fed it before waking me, as two larger pieces of wood were just catching alight, small yellow tongues licking at their curves, climbing steadily. I sat down as close to the fire as I dared, my back to the others, my eyes scanning. Above the formless darkness of the bushes nothing but the graceful lines of the tree trunks danced with the shadows. I could hear Brendan's breathing settle into an even rhythm that was almost snoring.

My eyes returned to the fire, too tired to be on high alert. The flames had joined forces, grown in strength, and were busy conquering the last unclaimed twig to which one small leaf was clinging valiantly. It vaporized at the first touch of heat, flakes of ash momentarily suspended, swirling in the light, before scattering.

Something splashed onto my hand, resting on the handle of the knife in my lap, and it took me a moment to realize it was a tear. It was quickly followed by another, and another. I gave in to the luxury of rare solitude and let them slip free, enjoying the warmth on my cheeks, breathing evenly and ignoring the pressure to allow the gentle shower to become a raging storm. The fire slid in and out of focus. One molten yellow ball separated into two and merged again. Then Mani was there, standing across the fire, so suddenly I did not even have time to jump.

I cursed my self-indulgent inattention as he sat down. Some guard

I was! I swiped my left cheek clean on the shoulder of my T-shirt whilst pretending to glance behind me, and the right while smothering a yawn. Mani, digging in the basket he had carried with him, tactfully ignored me.

"Hi," I said, my voice sounding thick.

"*Selamat pagi,*" he replied, looking up. His eyes were so dark in the reflected firelight I could not tell where the pupils began.

"I didn't even know you were gone," I said.

"I could not sleep very much tonight."

He looked so lonely sitting across from me, his shoulders and the corners of his mouth bowed, that I wanted to crawl over there and put my arms around him. But more than the fire separated us. I knew that would only make him uncomfortable.

"Why not?" I asked.

"I was thinking." He sighed and ran a hand through his dark hair, flicking it out of his eyes.

I wondered which particular burden fueled that sigh. His parents? Tina? Us?

I let the silence fall gently, studying the fire again, comforted by his mere presence. The night was fading through gray toward dawn when he spoke again.

"When Father could not sleep, he would get up and go walking on the beach and pray," Mani said. Then, after a long pause, "I miss the beach."

"I know," I said, our eyes meeting briefly. "I'm sorry." I was sorry for so many things, I didn't know which one to pick. "I'm sorry that we're making things so complicated, and that we're such a burden."

"No!" Mani said strongly. "You are a . . . " He paused, searching for a word. ". . . A joy. Just, Father told me to get you home safe."

"We'll be fine," I said with more certainty than I felt.

"Look!" Mani's face brightened as he pulled a package wrapped in fresh green leaves carefully out of the basket. "I was praying this morning, and look what God showed me."

He peeled back the leaves to reveal a dozen small eggs and described, complete with actions, how he'd surprised a foraging jungle chicken and followed it, flapping and startled, back to its nest.

My laughter woke the others.

"Come on! There is no such thing as a jungle chicken. You're pulling our legs," Kyle said after Mani had repeated the whole story.

Mani looked at his hands, which were definitely not attached to anyone's leg. "I am not!"

"He means you're teasing," Elissa translated.

"They're snake eggs, aren't they?" Kyle asked, smirking. I looked at the eggs in a new light.

"Eouwww. Gross!" Drew said.

"Do snakes lay eggs?" Mark asked. He was still pale and listless, but the three days of rest and the many doses of papaya leaf tea the rest of us had forced down his throat seemed to have done the trick. After one last bath in the hot spring, we were leaving the little camp that had become almost homey and hitting the trail again today.

"They *are* chicken eggs! I will show you the jungle chicken nest next time I see one. It is about this tall." Mani jumped to his feet and indicated a height about level with his nose. "Full of sticks and leaves. The chickens live inside."

"No way!" Kyle said. "Chickens can't build a nest five feet high!"

"Indonesian chickens can," Mani said loftily, and sat down again, clearly recognizing that he had the upper hand in this particular argument.

"How are we going to cook them?" Brendan interrupted Kyle and shot for the heart of the matter.

"I would suggest using the fire," I said.

Brendan tickled me from behind and didn't let up until I gave in and gasped for mercy.

"I meant," he said with a great show of patience, "fried, boiled, scrambled, or poached?"

"Or raw," Mark added.

"Dare you," Kyle said to Mark with an evil grin.

Mark narrowed his eyes and raised his chin.

"Scrambled," Elissa said and took authoritative possession of the eggs, thereby relieving Mark of the responsibility of meeting Kyle's challenge.

Too bad. I thought I'd enjoy the spectacle of Mark trying to eat a raw egg.

Now, five hours after breakfast, I was still thinking about how good those eggs had tasted when I tripped over a rock and my thoughts were jerked back to the present. I fell to one knee, staying down for a couple of seconds, hating the weight of the pack that made it so difficult to balance and get up again. I was probably only carrying about twenty pounds, but after three days of sitting around it felt like a hundred.

"Cori?" Behind me, Drew sounded panicked.

"I'm fine." I made it to my feet and wondered how Kyle was managing. In unspoken agreement we'd emptied Mark's backpack and divided the contents among the rest of us. Kyle had taken at least half of the extra weight. His pack was stuffed full and had to be twice as heavy as mine.

"How much longer until we get to the villages?" Drew asked.

"Probably tomorrow," I said. "Depends how much ground we can cover today." I glanced at Mark, walking in front of me. I didn't think we would make it today. Even from behind it was obvious he was struggling, and it wasn't even lunchtime.

We didn't make it to the villages that day, but it wasn't only because of Mark. It was because of Kyle. He should have known better too.

It was an hour after we'd stopped for lunch—the time of day when the air lay thick and hot, close to the ground. The time of day when thinking takes a backseat to willing your legs to keep moving forward.

I was fourth in line with Mani, Kyle, and Mark trudging along in front of me, when it happened. The faint track we'd been following all day took us into a small clearing just like hundreds of others that we had already passed through. We paused for a couple of seconds to let the others catch up. Drew was lagging.

Mani nudged Kyle and pointed across the clearing to an untidy mound of sticks and leaves, almost as tall as I was, nestled in between two tree trunks.

"Jungle chicken nest," he said, turning away to check the others' progress.

"Excellent!" Kyle said. "Eggs for dinner!"

Nine quick steps was all it took for him to cross the clearing and prod at the nest with the tip of his machete.

"Wait!" Mani said sharply, turning back around as Brendan and the girls entered the clearing.

But it was already too late. As Mani spoke there was an upheaval in the nest, and a loud and very angry squeal.

"Pig! Get back!" Mani yelled, struggling to slip his shoulders free of the backpack that held Tina.

Several things happened at once. Kyle's machete blade winked at me as it flew through the air, falling into a bush off to the right. Mani plucked Tina out of the pack and tossed her the short distance into Elissa's arms.

"Hide!"

Kyle took a single step backwards and tripped. As he fell he rolled to the right, onto his side, facing us. He put his hands out to push himself up, struggling against the weight of his pack.

"Move!" I yelled at him, unsnapping the waistband of my own pack and letting it fall from my shoulders.

The boar burst out of the nest like a grunting torpedo and hit Kyle hard. Kyle is not small, but the force of the charge shoveled him along the ground at least a foot toward us. I think it was at this point that I screamed. My knife was out and in my hand, but I didn't have the faintest idea what to do with it.

That boar was the ugliest animal I'd ever seen. Hairy, black, about as tall as my waist, and solid—it looked like an African warthog. Some disconnected corner of my brain took the time to be surprised that it wasn't pink. Its snout was narrow and its head bowed under the burden of two long, stained tusks.

Kyle's face still registered nothing but surprise as the pig worried him from behind. I screamed again and waved my arms as I saw Mani's brown form dance past me, machete balanced in his right hand, and Brendan following.

The boar backed up and glanced at me with small black eyes. I froze. Then he charged again, spearing Kyle's pack with his tusks and tossing his squat head viciously to the left. This time Kyle cried out.

Mani got there first, stepping around Kyle's legs, wielding the machete with two hands in a big overhead arc that caught the boar at the point where its ugly head met muscled shoulders.

It gave a piercing squeal and turned to meet him, mincing lightly on its feet despite the deep wound that I hoped fervently was the source of the drops of blood that had flown through the air in a wide arc as it pulled its tusks free from Kyle and shook its head again.

I saw Brendan's machete come down on it from behind as I reached Kyle, who was half up on his arms, still trying vainly to get to his feet. Over the top of his head I saw a tusk miss his thigh by an inch as the boar wheeled on Brendan. No time. I seized his pack and dragged him backwards over the dirt toward the other side of the clearing, away from the churning and the rotten stink of the pig.

"Are you all right?" I pawed at him frantically, trying to pull the straps off his shoulders, noticing the jagged tears as a toothbrush and a pair of socks slid out of one of the gaping holes in the pack. I didn't want to think about what that force might have done to his back.

Kyle curled his knees under himself and sat up. "I'm fine. I'm fine! Give me your knife!"

Even if I'd wanted to, I couldn't have. I'd dropped it to grab his pack.

I glanced over him to Brendan and Mani. The boar was breathing in big snuffly grunts, its head lowered, and turning in tight defensive circles. Mani's lithe body ducked and weaved around it, feinting and then pulling back. Brendan stood solid, waiting.

God, please!

Elissa's hands appeared beside mine, and between us we eased Kyle's pack backwards off his shoulders.

My legs turned to jelly as I scanned the back of his dirty T-shirt. Wet. But only with sweat. Except for the lower right-hand side.

Blood was dribbling out from under the edge of his shirt, soaking into the waistband of his tan hiking pants. The dark stain was spreading fast. He didn't seem to notice.

I sucked in a lungful of air, my head spinning.

"A knife!" he said, twisting around to glare at us.

I pointed past him to where it lay in the leaves. Elissa just shrugged, open palmed.

"Now!" Brendan yelled to Mani, waving his arms and jumping up and down. Mani took advantage of the distraction and leapt in, striking hard. The boar stumbled and went down on one knee.

"Kyle, you're bleeding," Elissa said, putting a hand on his shoulder in an attempt to keep him from leaping up and rushing into the fray.

"Get the first aid kit," I said to Elissa, and she disappeared into the bushes. I tweaked the side of Kyle's shirt up.

There was a clang, and I saw Brendan's machete meet one of the tusks. All four of the boar's legs had crumpled beneath it, but its head was still tossing.

Kyle batted my hand away.

"Kyle! Get that shirt off. Now!" I said, in a voice I had never heard myself use before.

His gaze flickered to mine momentarily, his eyes wide. He pulled it off and over his head, wincing and catching his breath as he raised his arms.

The tusk had caught him just on the side of his waist, scoring a shallow gash about four inches long from back to front. Rich, dark blood welled up in a steady stream. Higher up on the same side of his back a blue bruise was already forming.

Elissa appeared, fumbling with the first aid kit.

Mani let out a fierce yell as the boar finally toppled over and lay still, panting in shallow, irregular gasps.

I tore open our second-to-last package of thick gauze and pressed it firmly to Kyle's side as Brendan dropped his machete and turned toward us, his eyes frantic.

"Are you okay?"

"Did you get the eggs?" Kyle grinned at him, his voice none too steady.

That was the last straw. I slapped his hand down onto his side over the gauze and stood up. "You absolute bugger! You could have died!" I kicked a stone and sent it spinning into the ferns. Not finding that nearly satisfying enough, I then turned around and kicked a tree. Hard. "And don't you dare take pressure off that!" I turned back around and glared at him.

"It was an accident," Kyle said.

"Some accident. A *stupid* accident! Don't you ever listen? Why are you always the one getting us in trouble?" I yelled, knowing I was being unfair. I stalked over to the pig, which seemed to have expired, and kicked it in the rump, making sure to stay far away from the tusks just in case.

"Like you're perfect!" Kyle shot back at me, his face pale.

"Stinking pigs. Snakes." I kicked the pig again. And again. It was softer than the tree, but not much. "Mosquitoes." There was special venom in that word.

When I turned around again, Drew's and Mark's scared faces were peeping out through the bushes, and Mani was looking at me like I had grown a second head.

"What?" I glared at them and then at Kyle again. "I'd kick you if you weren't bleeding. I'd kick your butt from here to Timbuktu."

"Like you could," Kyle taunted.

It was so tempting to give it a try. I gave the pig an extra-hard kick for good measure before turning around and scooping my knife up from

where I'd dropped it. I saw Kyle flinch as if he weren't entirely sure I
wasn't going to use it on him.

"Cori." Brendan raised his eyebrows and glanced from me to Kyle,
who was still sitting in the dirt.

"What?" I snapped.

"Should we camp here tonight?"

The quiet question grounded me. I sighed. "Yeah. Probably."

"I'm fine!" Kyle interjected.

We both ignored him.

"We'll find a place close by to camp, then. You all right to stay
with Kyle and strap him up?"

"Yeah," I said.

"No," Kyle answered at exactly the same moment.

We stared at each other and spoke in unison again.

"I don't need any help."

"Don't be such a baby."

"Stop it! Both of you," Elissa snapped, her blue eyes flashing.

Chastened, I sat down beside Kyle and lifted his hand away from
his side. The gauze was almost soaked through. I peeked underneath.
The flow had slowed down, but hadn't stopped.

"Half an hour," I estimated.

"We'll be close. I'll be back soon," Brendan said.

Mani nodded. With a backwards glance at the pig, they all disappeared into the bushes.

We sat in silence. I felt my anger drain away as quickly as it had
come and bit my lip hard to keep sudden tears from falling.

Kyle propped his elbows on his knees and rested his head on his
arms. Against the gleaming tan of his arms his back shone white—
except for the angry bruise halfway between his spine and his right side.

I brushed my fingertips over it, and he jumped. "Hurt?" I asked. "No."

Liar. He wasn't even breathing freely. I hoped he hadn't cracked a rib. I looked at his back again, remembering the Technicolor pages of my biology textbook, then glanced over at the curve of the dead boar's tusk.

"You're lucky. That would have gone up into your heart. Or under your spine if it hadn't been for your pack." I saw the gaping holes in his pack and shivered.

Kyle didn't look particularly grateful for that piece of information.

I said what I knew I had to say before it got any harder. "Sorry. I didn't mean it."

"Whatever." He didn't lift his head.

"I was just scared," I tried to explain. I saw the pig hitting him from behind all over again and felt sick.

"Whatever," he said again.

I stopped feeling quite so sorry and had to bite back more cutting words.

Brendan arrived back just as I was finishing strapping Kyle. It was like trying to bandage a mannequin. In the end I just used the elastic bandage, wrapping it all the way around his torso to keep the gauze in place.

He shrugged his shirt on again and scrambled to his feet without taking Brendan's hand. "You want me to take that?" Kyle asked, indicating his torn pack, which Brendan had already shouldered.

Brendan shook his head.

"Which way then?" he asked.

"That way." Brendan pointed over his shoulder.

Kyle disappeared without looking back.

Brendan looked at me, still sitting in the dirt. "You still mad?"

"Sort of."

"You were pretty hard on him, you know."

"I said sorry," I grumbled.

Brendan laughed.

"What?"

"You look like you've just sucked on a lemon."

I borrowed a phrase from Kyle as I took Brendan's hand and let him pull me to my feet. "Whatever."

Barring any further accidents, it was going to be our last night in the jungle. I looked at each face in the firelight. Mark was hypnotized by the flames. Kyle wouldn't meet my gaze. Drew looked especially exhausted. Brendan had said that she cried the entire time it took them to find a campsite and set up. The smothering clutch of green pressed in closer than usual around us. I hoped bush pigs weren't attracted to firelight.

Mani was gazing at the fire too, the slump in his shoulder betraying his fatigue. His arms curled protectively around Tina, who was asleep in his lap.

Elissa stirred the makeshift kettle, a tin can with the string of a single tea bag protruding.

"Are you sure you're all right?" Drew asked Kyle for the second time in the last hour.

"Drew, I'm fine," he said, more patiently than he would have answered me. If he'd answered me at all.

We'd exacted revenge on the pig by eating him for dinner. After the boys dragged him back through the trees, they made me take a photo while they all posed with one foot propped on the carcass. Drew told them they were the most pathetic-looking hunters she'd ever seen.

As I watched Mani butcher the pig while we rigged up a makeshift barbecue, I toyed with the idea of embracing vegetarianism, but changed my mind during the eternity it took to cook the meat over the flames. It ended up burnt on the outside. By that time it was too dark to see whether it was raw in the middle or not, and I wasn't taking any chances. I toasted my portion bite by bite. Tough and gamey. It wasn't worth the effort.

Elissa said it reminded her of *Lord of the Flies*, only we were much nicer. I hoped so. I remembered Piggy's sad end and Jack's crazed flight through the forest onto the beach.

School. It seemed like a movie plot, not reality. Gleaming hallways smelling of bleach, gym clothes, and books. Lovingly prepared lunches in brown paper bags. The overwhelming stress of the impossible French assignment due the next day. Reading *Lord of the Flies*, safely snuggled into a bed with clean sheets.

Reality wasn't school anymore. In just two weeks it had shrunk to these seven other people sitting around the fire with me. Reality was looking at Kyle, Brendan smiling with his eyes without moving his lips, Drew's whisper in my ear, Elissa speaking volumes with a single glance, Mark tickling Tina, Mani's quiet strength. Reality was smelling of sweat and campfire smoke, sore muscles, chapped lips, dirty clothes, and Kyle's blood still underneath my fingernails. It had nothing to do with school. That could have been a different lifetime. A different me.

Jack was met on the beach, I remembered. Saved. By faceless adults. I wondered whether there would be any adults to meet us on the beach tomorrow. Somehow I didn't think so. Sometime during the last twelve days I had stopped believing that adults could bail us out of this.

"Tomorrow we get to the village," Mani said.

"What then?" Elissa asked.

"I will go and see whether it is Christian or Muslim village. And get a boat."

"What sort of boat?" Mark asked, snapping out of his trance. "Like the one we came over on?"

"Smaller probably," Mani said. "Maybe a fishing boat."

Across from me, Brendan's mouth tightened, carving grim lines down toward his chin.

"How are you going to get a boat?" Elissa asked.

Mani shrugged. It was one of the few times I'd seen uncertainty in his face.

"We have money," Elissa said. "It's not right to steal someone's boat."

"American money. I think it is safer to borrow the boat," Mani said diplomatically. "I will come back and pay for it later."

Elissa and I looked at each other. He wouldn't be coming back if we had anything to do with it.

"How much sailing have you done around here?" Mark asked, suddenly looking older than his fifteen years.

"This side of the island?" Mani looked down and said the last word quietly. "None."

"Have you ever sailed to Ambon by yourself?"

"No. Just fishing at home."

"How far from here to Ambon?" Mark asked, returning his gaze to the fire.

Mani shrugged. "Maybe a hundred kilometers. It depends if we land on north shore and hike over the mountain or sail around into Ambon Bay."

"The airport's on the bay, isn't it?" Kyle said, still shirtless. His short blond hair was sticking straight up, his blue eyes narrowed in thought.

"Yes."

"Why wouldn't we just sail around to the bay then?" Brendan asked, his mouth twisting on the word *sail*, probably remembering how he'd spent the prior voyage hanging out the back of the boat.

"Coral reefs."

"Reefs."

Mark and Mani answered at the same time.

"Pirates too," Mani added. "There are more near the entrance to the bay where the big ships come in."

Drew clutched Brendan's hand. "That's not funny, Mani!" she said, blinking back more tears.

Brendan jumped in before Mani could say anything. "It's just a joke, Drew."

Mani stayed quiet. From the sideways glance Kyle shot me before he remembered he wasn't speaking to me, even nonverbally, I knew he realized Mani hadn't been joking.

Great. Sounded like sharks were the least of our worries. We were about to steal a boat that would then be piloted across a hundred kilometers of open sea by a seventeen-year-old fisherman and a fifteen-year-old who hadn't managed to make it through a single day of boot camp without getting into trouble.

Mani has already saved your life more than once in the last two weeks, I reminded myself. Stop borrowing trouble. What was that Bible verse? Don't worry about tomorrow, because today has enough trouble of its own? Or don't waste time worrying today, because tomorrow will bring enough trouble of *its* own? Neither version was particularly comforting, but both made sense. I yawned hugely, deciding the best way to leave behind the trouble of today and hasten the trouble of tomorrow was to sleep.

"Come on." I climbed up and pulled Elissa after me. "Who's taking first watch?"

"I will," Kyle said, studiously not looking at me. "I'm not tired yet."

"Wait," Mani said, fishing out the familiar white pulp we'd scraped out and sealed in one of our few Ziploc plastic bags. "Papaya leaf tea."

"Yuck!" Drew wailed, burying her face in Brendan's shoulder.

"Love the papaya leaf tea," Mark warned her with feeling. "It is your friend."

"I'll sit up on watch with you," I said to Kyle, reaching out instinctively to put a hand on his arm. It was the barest flicker of movement that warned me that it would not be welcome contact. I dropped my hand.

"No," he said. "You need your sleep too."

The others were all very quiet. I felt like I'd been slapped.

I lay awake for a long time that night, watching the rise and fall of Kyle's back as he sat silently by the fire. Home had never felt farther away.

I could smell it before I could see through the trees into open space. Salt water. And suddenly I was scared again. Pigs or no pigs, I wasn't sure I wanted to leave the jungle.

In front of me, Mani stopped and lowered the pack he was carrying. "The village is close," he said quietly, pointing off to the right.

We clustered around him, suddenly hesitant.

"What do you think we should do?" Brendan whispered.

I swallowed hard and noticed Kyle rolling his shoulders carefully, wincing.

"Kyle and me will go see it," Mani decided. "The rest of you stay."

"I don't want to split up," Drew whispered.

Mani shook his head. "It's more safe this way." He glanced at Kyle and nodded. "Ready?"

Kyle looked as surprised as I felt at how quickly everything suddenly seemed to be moving. "Yeah," he said. "I guess."

Wait! I wanted to say. I balled my hand into a fist to keep from reaching out and clutching. *Look back*, I willed him, as they turned to leave. *Don't walk away from me still angry.*

Kyle didn't look back. Just brushed through ferns that slid softly back into place behind him. All I'd gotten was a light touch on my arm as he slipped past, so light it could have been accidental.

Drew's hand on my arm snapped me out of my trance as I stared after them.

"He's pretty mad, huh?"

"Yeah. When he does something, he does it well."

"Well, you did call him stupid."

"I've done that before," I said.

"But this is the first time he thinks it's true," Elissa said.

I had a lot of time to think about it that afternoon. It didn't take very long to eat our last portions of cold rice, and then we just sat. It felt hotter than usual, and my feet were sticky and uncomfortable, trapped in my boots.

Mark leaned back against his pack and fell asleep, his legs twitching. Tina sat beside him, playing quietly with the last balloon, which

Mark had twisted into the shape of a giraffe. Elissa pulled out her diary and started writing.

Drew crawled over to me and laid her head on my shoulder, grabbing my hand. Hers was cold. "Jip's scared," she whispered.

I considered that for a while. I didn't have to ask why. "One boat ride," I said, "and he'll be safe."

"Do you think anyone will be there to meet us in Ambon?" she asked.

"Maybe. It won't matter if they're not. We're just going to head for the airport and get on a plane anyway." I hoped that was true. "How's Kiki doing?" I asked. "Does he want to stay in the jungle with the other monkeys?"

"No way! He wants to go home with Jip and hang out with his friends there and eat shop bananas."

"That's a bit tame, isn't it?"

"He's not a wild monkey." Drew defended him. "He's never known anything else."

"What's the first thing Jip's going to do when he gets home?" I asked.

"Make an appointment with my therapist."

In my mind I saw a big leather couch in a quiet office. Instead of Jip, I was lying on the couch. I was dressed in muddy boots and dirty clothes, sweating all over that expensive leather and staring at the dark wooden walls.

"And how did you feel then?" came a bored voice from the tall chair at the head of the couch. "How did you feel waiting for Mani and Kyle? Wondering if they'd come back . . . or just disappear?"

"No," I said out loud.

The couch vanished, leaving me in the dirt again. Familiar territory.

"Jip's not going to a therapist," I whispered into Drew's hair. "He's going to throw a big party to celebrate being home, eat a ton of ice cream, and have a bubble bath." And then, I continued mentally, he's going to curl up under his bed and stay there for at least three days.

"I love my psychologist," Drew said. "Although she did encourage me to come on this trip. We're definitely having words about that."

"When did you start seeing a psychologist?"

"After I ended up in hospital that time. Mom and Dad were desperate, I think." She sighed.

"Did it help?"

"Totally. I still see her sometimes."

"What did you talk about?"

"How Kelli getting hit by that car wasn't my fault. How I was hurting myself in different ways. We did this collage with pictures and stories about her life."

Drew's grip on my hand tightened. I rested my cheek on the top of her head and wondered whether Tanya would do that for me if—

"I still miss her, you know. I sometimes wonder whether she can see me from heaven. You're lucky you're so strong."

Strong. The only thing that felt strong about me right now was the grip on my throat that tightened every time I thought about Kyle and Mani. I didn't know what to say. So I just squeezed her hand, closed my eyes, and tried to be blank.

The next thing I knew it was dark, and I was flailing against a touch on my shoulder. It took me a couple of seconds to realize it was dark because my eyes were closed. And that the touch on my shoulder had been Brendan.

"Ow!" he said, half seriously. "That's some right hook you have."

"Sorry," I said, confused.

"The others are back." He rubbed his chest again.

I let out the breath I felt like I'd been holding since they disappeared, and sat up.

It was starting to get darker, although the heat hadn't lifted yet. I felt slow, stupid, and very thirsty.

Elissa looked around as we assembled ourselves in a rough circle. I knew how she felt. It was strange to have one of these conferences without a fire burning and a cup of tea brewing. But Mani had said we were too close to the villages now to take the risk.

"So?" I said, as they sat down.

Mani sighed deeply and took a long drink out of the canteen Brendan passed him.

"It's a Muslim village," Kyle said.

Drew bit her lip.

"But there are boats," Mani added quickly.

"What else?" Brendan asked.

Mani and Kyle looked at each other. This time Kyle deferred, and after a long pause Mani spoke.

"There is trouble in Ambon."

chapter 13 ~

I lay flat on my stomach, peering out at the village from underneath a bush. Well, actually, all I could see was the backside of some small cement houses in the distance, and a long stretch of beach. The fishing boats were coming back—an untidy migration. It didn't look like anyone had caught more than he could carry. In the near darkness the men were indistinct as they leaped around the boats and out onto the buttery sand, but their voices carried in the wind. I heard a burst of laughter.

A Muslim village. They hardly looked like a bunch that would take machetes to us without a second's hesitation. Even after what we'd seen at Mani's village I was having a hard time understanding that someone might hurt me deliberately. But Mani said we had to stay hidden until after dark. Everyone would know we were Christians because we were white, and he wasn't taking any chances.

Now that was irony—Jesus' skin color would have been a lot closer to Mani's than mine, yet everyone here would assume I was Christian because I was white. I rested my forehead in the dirt and shut my eyes. They were aching from the effort of trying to peer through the dusk. In the dark world bound by the sound of my breathing, the pounding of my heart, and the moist, dusty smell of the soil, I felt a hand on the back of my neck, kneading gently.

Kyle.

He'd come back from that foray with Mani . . . settled somehow. Different. Without saying a word he'd made it clear that things were okay between us again.

I reached up and brushed his wrist with my fingertips in acknowledgment. He gave my neck a final squeeze, and the hand disappeared, but I felt a bit better. I also made a mental promise to Jip that as soon as we got home we were going to a masseuse.

It was almost completely dark when I opened my eyes. Drew, Elissa, and Mark were getting better at fading into the jungle. I couldn't hear a sound from where I knew they were waiting by a tree ten feet behind us. With Mani's permission I'd crushed up one of the pain tablets that had codeine in it from the first aid kit and given it to Tina. When I broke my wrist in Kenya codeine had always put me to sleep, and I hoped it would do the same for her. She was usually good at being quiet, but none of us wanted to take that extra risk of loud tears when we were in the middle of stealing some poor fisherman's boat.

I could hear Kyle and Brendan breathing on either side of me. Mani was invisible on the other side of Brendan. They had tried to get me to stay back with the others, but I just couldn't. I know they thought I was being unnecessarily brave, but it wasn't courage. The opposite. I couldn't stand sitting back there, not being able to see what was going on, feeling completely helpless and sick to my stomach with the tension.

I took a deep breath and tried to relax. My stomach had felt like a ball of tightly knotted yarn ever since I'd heard those words.

Trouble in Ambon.

There had been silence for a long ten seconds. Drew put a hand to her eyes. Elissa bit her lip and looked at the ground. I stared at Kyle. He stared back and nodded. Maybe we were all hoping that if we didn't actually ask for more details they wouldn't exist. Ambon was supposed to be safe.

"Define trouble," I finally heard myself say, my voice distant against the thrumming of my heart.

"Riots. Churches burnt. Mosques burnt. The city under curfew."

Kyle stopped there, but I knew what went with that. People killed. He opened his mouth, closed it, then opened it again.

"The airport might be closed," he said.

"No!" Elissa said softly. "But . . . " She paused and took a deep breath. She was shaking. "No."

Brendan shook his head, tearing his gaze away from the trees over Mark's head, and reached out for her hand.

I didn't even know where to start asking questions. Who did they find this out from? Should we still go to Ambon? Should we stay here for a while instead?

"I talked with a man from the village while Kyle hid," Mani said. "He thought I was Muslim. He said there has not been trouble here, but he has heard that there is trouble in Ambon and in other villages. *Demonstrasis*," he said, using the Indonesian word for riots.

"Why?" I asked.

"He was not sure. But he thinks it started in Ambon about two weeks ago."

Two weeks ago. Around the same time we'd fled the village. Days after Gary and Diane had arrived in Ambon.

"There was an argument on a bus," Mani said. "And then the Muslims went into a Christian area and burnt a church. Then the Christians went into a Muslim area and burnt a mosque . . ." He spread his hands, palms up, in that universal gesture of helplessness.

"Well, if it started two weeks ago, maybe it's stopped now," Elissa said, her voice small.

She did have a point. There had to be only so many churches and mosques on the island. Perhaps they'd burnt them all, and no one had been hurt, and then they'd all gone home peacefully to discuss the spectacle. Yeah. Sure.

"The Indonesian army might be there too," Kyle continued, grim.

Drew took her hands away from her face and stopped rocking back and forth. I was surprised to see that her eyes were dry. "That's good, right? They'll tell everyone to stop. They're all breaking the law, right?"

Kyle and Mani looked at each other.

"Maybe," Kyle said.

I raised my eyebrows at Kyle in a look that told him I knew he was dodging. He stared back, impassive. I wondered what Mani had told him.

"You know the situation better than anyone else," Brendan said to Mani. "What do you think we should do?"

"We've got three options," Kyle said. "We can all go to Ambon and try to find the Stewarts' house. We can stay here, hike back into the jungle, and camp out another week. Another two weeks. See if things change. Or we can split up. Two or three of us can head to Ambon and get help. The rest stay here."

Great. So we could all steal a boat and sail into the darkness, heading for chaos. Or we could hike into the forest and hang out with the pigs and the mosquitoes while our parents continued to wonder whether we were dead or alive. Or we could split up and have the best of both worlds.

I resisted the urge to stand up and say very loudly just what I thought of those three options.

"It's a Choose Your Own Adventure mission trip," Mark said, his eyes still closed.

No one smiled.

"I used to cheat on Choose Your Own Adventures," I told him. I didn't say that eight times out of ten the hapless adventurer ended up being devoured by rabid squirrels or something equally horrific.

There was a long silence.

"I don't think we should split up," Drew finally said. "It might be the most sensible thing to do, but I just don't want to."

"I agree," Brendan said.

"I don't want to stay here either," Elissa said. "I want to go home."

I wondered whether she would have been as quick to say that if she'd watched the crowd at Mani's village. I wanted to go home too, but maybe it was best to take our chances with the pigs and mosquitoes.

Brendan and Kyle hesitated with me.

"What do you think?" I asked Mani.

"I don't know," he paused, his lips pressed tightly together. "I have been asking God. I think perhaps we should go. Mark may get sick again from the malaria."

Mark groaned in acknowledgement. I had the feeling if he had

had any extra energy he would have queried the "again" part of that statement.

"This is something we all have to decide," Brendan said, looking around. "We have to agree."

"I agree," Drew said.

"Me too," Elissa said.

"Yeah," Mark said.

"Can we get more information first?" I asked, stalling.

"That is dangerous," Mani said. "The man I spoke to was outside the village hunting. I told him I was from Java and traveling to visit friends. He said to be careful. Everyone is afraid of strangers."

I looked at Mark, thought about my parents, and nodded.

"Okay."

Kyle and Brendan nodded too.

So here we were. I couldn't see the beach or the boats anymore, just fragments of light from the village. Suddenly I wondered whether the villagers would have set a guard over the boats.

Mani's whispered "no" didn't do much to set my mind at ease. He didn't sound too sure.

I rested my cheek on my forearms. The thought of being out in that salty moving darkness by ourselves on a rickety wooden boat was paralyzing me. Prayer came a bit easier this time. Not even the hypocrisy of only praying when I was flat-out scared bothered me.

It seemed like hours later when Mani and Brendan began to stir. Mani slipped back for the others while we stood at the very edge of the jungle, rocking backwards and forwards to restore some circulation, jerking on already-tight pack straps. There was plenty of blood being pumped out of my heart, but none of it seemed to be reaching my toes or fingers.

As the others moved to lift their packs, I heard the sharp *clink* of two metal buckles meeting, the keening slide of polyester over polyester, the crunch of a heavy weight landing on a fallen palm frond. How could they not hear us in the village? On Ambon? I grabbed Kyle's hand, and his fingers closed tightly around mine.

We hesitated for a long time at the edge of the trees.

Mani moved first, and Kyle and I followed him together.

Stepping out from behind that tree, moving through the ferns out onto the open sand, was one of the hardest things I have ever done. Even with only half a moon I felt like we were center stage, awash with silvery light, with a breathless audience waiting to be entertained.

· And now for our latest trick, ladies and gentleman—the Christian mission team will steal a boat from an impoverished fisherman. Thank you, thank you very much. No applause, please.

I concentrated on the back of Kyle's white shirt, only now thinking that he should have been wearing a darker color. The village, off to the right about a hundred meters, was mostly dark, quiet shapes. My ears felt like they were growing by the second. Soon, I was sure, I would have twin satellite dishes attached to my head.

I pictured the seven of us in a little line, struggling through the unfamiliar soft sand that was dragging at every step, waiting for the shout of alarm, of anger.

None had come by the time we reached the line of boats that were tugged up onto the sand past the tide line. I rested my hand on the damp hull of the first boat in line, the farthest one from the village. The wood was cool and solid beneath my fingers.

Mark and Brendan slipped forward in response to Mani's signal, and they moved away up the line of boats, stopping to examine each one until their shadowy figures became indistinct blurs.

"I'll be right back." Kyle's warm whisper startled me.

"Where are you going?"

"Nature calls."

"Now?"

"Now." Incredibly, there was a hint of laughter in his voice.

I went back to staring after the others, willing them to hurry.

"Cori?" This time it was Elissa's voice, hesitant.

"Yeah." I didn't look around.

"Ummm—" The tone had me turning my head before she'd even finished. "Someone's here."

The man was standing about ten feet away, back along the beach, staring. Possibly he was wondering why there were three white girls, loaded with packs like giant sea turtles, standing near his village. Just a guess.

We'd been staring the wrong direction! I'd been so worried about people coming from the village. Where had he come from?

The four of us stared at one another for long, frozen seconds. He was wearing pants and a ragged shirt. About my height, but a fair bit skinnier. A machete hung from his waist, but he made no move to reach for it.

Behind him I saw a white blur move. Kyle.

I tried to speak. Swallowed and tried again.

"*Selamat malam.*" Good evening. Dipping my head in the manner of a respectful greeting. As I raised my eyes again I saw the white blur behind him, closer, pause.

The man took a step backwards and asked a question in Indonesian. Rapid, incomprehensible, too loud.

I racked my brains for any Indonesian phrase that might help buy us some time.

"*Apakah anda berbahasa Inggeris?*" Do you speak English?

I could see the blur moving faster now. Almost here.

The man was stepping backwards again when Kyle tackled him from behind, clapping a hand over his mouth and spilling them both onto the sand, pinning him with his weight.

"Elissa—go get the others," I said, going down on my knees beside them. Muffled squeaks were emanating from underneath Kyle, the man's legs thumping helplessly.

"Shhh. We're not going to hurt you," I hissed uselessly.

"Get his machete," Kyle grunted, directing some phrases in Indonesian to the struggling figure underneath him. "*Kami kawanmu; bukan mush. Kamu tidak akan disakiti.*"

I think he said we were friends. That might have been a bit of a stretch, but the legs stopped kicking quite so hard as I slipped his machete free of its leather loop and handed it back to Drew, wilting in relief as I heard the others arrive in a rush.

Mani dove down beside me.

"Tell him we're not going to hurt him," I said, but he was already speaking. The kicking stopped, and Mani motioned Kyle to let him up.

Kyle rolled him over awkwardly and sat up, one arm wrapped firmly around the man's torso, the other over his mouth. The moonlight glinted off the white of his eyes as they darted between us.

Mani started speaking again in a low voice. Hands moving. I glanced around, wondering whether he had been alone, and noticed Brendan doing the same. Nothing but empty beach.

The nod of the man's head against Kyle's restraining hand, and then a shake, drew my attention back to Mani.

"I've told him who you are. That you were staying at my village when it was attacked and that we have been walking for two weeks and we have to go to Ambon. I told him we will not hurt him. He said he will not scream if we let him go."

I glanced around at the others. It seemed like a big risk, but what other choice did we have?

"Is he a fisherman?" Brendan asked suddenly.

Mani put the question to our captive.

He nodded.

"Can we buy his boat?" he asked.

"Wait," Kyle said. "Can we pay him to take us to Ambon?"

I nodded. That way we wouldn't be leaving him behind to raise the alarm.

Mani started talking again while I reached beneath my T-shirt and rummaged in the flat pouch that was belted against my skin. My fingers slipped over the warm plastic of our precious passports and closed on cash.

"One hundred American dollars," I said, knowing that was probably more money than he made in a year.

I hadn't thought the man's eyes could widen any farther. I was wrong.

He nodded, and Mani motioned Kyle to release him.

Kyle slowly loosened his grip. Apart from raising a hand to rub at his mouth, the man didn't make any effort to move. He looked straight at Mani and asked him a question in a low voice.

Mani looked down for a long moment, then began to speak in short sentences, his voice flat.

The man shook his head, lifted his hand, and rested it gently for a second on Mani's shoulder. Then he spoke again.

Mani nodded and turned to us. "He wanted to know why we were hiking through the jungle, what happened. I told him. He will go and tell his wife where he is going. He promises, by Allah, to return and help us."

The darkness made it hard to tell what the others were thinking.

"I don't know," Brendan said.

"He said she will be very worried if he does not come home for four days. She is pregnant," Mani said.

Still we hesitated.

"Alone," Kyle said. "He returns alone."

The man nodded and spoke again as Mani translated.

"By the name of Allah. He will help us," Mani said.

Mani nodded, and the man scrambled to his feet and took off for the village at a trot.

Brendan sighed and clapped Kyle on the shoulder. He groaned.

"What?" Brendan asked.

"Jolted my side when we fell. Do you think he's really going to help us?" Kyle asked, moving to what was on all our minds.

"Yes," Mani said. "He promised."

I hoped he was right. There was nothing to stop him charging back up the beach with all the rest of the men in the village and taking our money, or us, by force.

I remembered that brief touch on Mani's shoulder and felt slightly reassured. Slightly.

"Let's just go back," Drew whispered. "Hike to the next village. Please."

Even in the darkness I could see her trembling. Brendan put an arm around her and pulled her close. She buried her face in his chest.

"No," Elissa said. "We have to get home." There was just as much urgency in her voice.

From my knees I looked longingly toward the solid black safety of the tree line. Listened for the muffled thump of feet running on sand. For raised voices. There was nothing but the gentle splash of baby waves reaching up toward us.

We probably should have retreated to those trees. Waited to see what would happen and who would come back. Been ready to flee again. Back up the mountains.

But we didn't. We stayed there, all of us, waiting exactly where the man had left us on the beach. Drew crying silently into Brendan's shoulder. Mark leaning listlessly against the boat. Tina, curled up inside a pack like a hibernating baby squirrel.

Sitting on my knees, my legs folded underneath me, I ran the cool, damp sand through my fingers. As I stirred it with my hands I thought about making sand castles at my grandparents' house in Australia.

I saw Luke and Tanya playing together on the beach one bright summer's day. That was the day I deliberately stepped on a sand castle that Luke had spent ten whole minutes perfecting, a lifetime for a three-year-old. He had looked at me, sitting bowed beside his ruined castle, shocked and betrayed. Tears had filled his big blue eyes.

I had laughed at the time, but now I wished desperately that I could tell him how sorry I was for doing that. That I would help him make a hundred sand castles if it would make him smile.

Kyle put his hand over mine, and I let the fistful of sand I'd been clutching dribble out, grasping him with grainy fingers.

I slid my other hand under the edge of his shirt, checking the dressing on his side. He sucked his breath in when I touched it, but I couldn't feel any fresh warmth. It was still dry.

"You okay?"

"My shoulder hurts," he admitted.

I felt my way up his back, feeling the extra heat radiating from the bruise over his ribs, the slight swelling under smooth skin. His shoulder moved restlessly under my touch as I laid my hand over it, absorbing some of the heat. I leaned forward just a fraction and rested my forehead against his shoulder.

He bent to whisper something in my ear; I turned my face at the same time, and my lips met his cheek in a brief kiss. He dipped his head forward, brushing his cheek gently against mine. It was rough. He hadn't shaved since the hot spring. I felt his other hand reaching underneath my braid to rest on the back of my neck.

"Kisses heal," I whispered, borrowing Drew's theory.

"Hmmm." He considered that for a while, then breathed into my ear. "It *really* hurts. I think it's going to take more than one."

I felt, more than heard, a bubble of laughter vibrate through him. Then the laughter was gone, and it was tension rippling through his body, muscles tightening up underneath my touch.

I raised my head and let go of his hand. A dark shape was loping over the sand at a steady pace. It was the man, and he was alone.

It all happened very fast after that. There was a brief exchange between Mani and the stranger; then we were moving down the beach. Lifting packs over the side of the boat, trying not to let them thump on the bottom. Being boosted awkwardly over the edge, pulling Elissa and Mark after me. Crawling on the wooden planks, banging my forehead against a low, flat platform covering half the boat. A swaying jolt as Brendan, Mani, and the stranger shoved the boat free of the beach. The sucking sound as the clinging sand released the hull. The sharp smell of the salt water slapping the wood. The world tilting underneath my knees, righting itself, then tilting again. Holding Drew in my arms. Elissa's hand linked through the curve of my elbow. Splashes as Mani and the stranger gave one final push, knee-high in water, and swung themselves on board.

And we were adrift in a dark, moving world.

Leaving Seram.

chapter 14 ~

I opened my eyes just at dawn. My hip was sore from being pressed against the wood all night. I was cold, and my mouth tasted like hyena droppings, but I felt better. Lighter.

I pulled my arm free from Drew and crawled out from under the flat roof that I remembered running into the night before. The boat was bigger than most of the fishing boats we'd seen on the beach, about twenty-five feet long and six feet wide. The back half was open, but the front was shaded by the wooden platform.

Drew, Elissa, Tina, and Mani were still asleep on the floor of the boat; the others were on the roof. Mark's head was propped awkwardly on one of the packs, which was pressed up against a thin wooden railing six inches high—all that was preventing it from sliding off and into the ocean. Kyle and Brendan were both flat on their backs, Kyle with one hand thrown above his head.

I reached for my camera and wished I could take a scratch-and-sniff photo. The strong smell of fish really added something to a scene that was already surreal.

Mani was lying at my feet, sprawled between me and our guide—who was perched at the back of the boat beside a small motor, which wasn't on, his hand on a wooden rudder. Mani's eyes popped open as I sat down beside him. My head just cleared the side of the boat. Behind me I heard the gentle smack of water against planks.

"Go back to sleep," I whispered.

He shook his head and sat up, rubbing bleary eyes. "I slept a lot," he said, leaning against the opposite side of the boat, our knees almost touching.

"Yeah, right." In between waking up every time one of us rolled over.

I nodded at the man we'd tackled last night. He nodded back shyly, dropping his eyes. He was scrawny, his tunic-style shirt cinched in with a colorful woven belt.

I looked up.

The sky.

It was huge, stretching in one unbroken arc from behind my head to a lumpy, cloud-shrouded horizon over Mani's shoulder. Above us it was deep royal blue. I could just make out the last remaining stars, the brightest ones. To my right the horizon was catching fire, orange tracing the low unbroken line where the water met the air. Pink battling blue. Darkness was slowly giving ground.

I gulped at the salty air and just looked. The gray, mist-shrouded mass behind us was Seram. Looking at it, I couldn't believe we'd survived two weeks in that foreboding cloud. I couldn't see Ambon.

Mani, reading my mind, jerked his thumb toward the front of the boat, where the view was obscured by the roof frame. "That way," he whispered.

"How long?"

He glanced at the fisherman and asked him something in Indonesian. Bony shoulders shrugged.

"Depends on the current," Mani said. "We will not use the motor until we get closer to Ambon, to save petrol. Maybe twenty hours. Maybe more."

Australia must lie directly behind me then. About a thousand kilometers. I looked over my shoulder again, but nothing marred the straight harmony of the horizon.

The bottom of the boat quivered as Kyle swung himself down off the roof and landed lightly on one foot.

"Brendan's awake," he said as he slid down beside me, his leg touching mine. "But he says he's going to puke if he moves. So he's lying up there staring at the sky."

"I didn't realize how much I missed it, the space. We could just stay on the boat and sail to Australia," I said, wishing that were an option.

"You've gotta know how bad it could be in Ambon," Kyle said without preamble.

I stared out over Mani's head, ignoring him. The last star in the blue tapestry winked and disappeared. The clouds hanging low over Seram were picking up the color of the sunrise, scalloped edges glowing a dull, angry red.

"Cori," Kyle said, insistent.

"Can't we just watch the sunrise?" I muttered, knowing it was already ruined.

"Do you want to talk about this with Drew and Elissa then?" he asked.

I sighed, not taking my eyes off those ominous, hypnotic clouds. I pulled my legs up against my chest and wrapped my arms around my knees. "No."

Kyle put an arm around me and pulled me against his shoulder. I heard what he was saying with one ear and felt the warm vibrations with the other.

"Tell me, then," I said.

It was like uncorking a bottle of warm Coke.

"He said it started almost three weeks ago over an argument between a taxi driver and a passenger."

I glanced at Mani. He looked grim.

"It spread. Muslims came into the Christian quarters and burnt a church. Christians did the same to mosques. Houses, shops, cars, all burnt. The market area's trashed."

Mani nodded. Kyle was obviously summarizing what they'd talked about last night.

"Supharti also says Ambon is very bad," Mani said, gesturing toward our fisherman guide, who broke in with some rapid Indonesian. "He says Ambon is not safe."

"Well, Seram isn't safe either, is it?" I pointed out.

The fisherman shook his head slowly, pointing forward toward Ambon and back to Seram.

"No," Mani said. "He says that he would not hurt us, but that lots of people are acting crazy. Even in his village, in his home, it is not safe for us."

"Tell him we are sorry about last night," I told Mani. "We didn't know he wouldn't hurt us."

Mani did, and Supharti smiled shyly and ducked his head again.

"Back to Ambon," Kyle said. "The airport might be closed."

I didn't want to think about that just yet. "So the trouble in Ambon started before what happened in our village," I said, still trying to work out the timeline in my head.

"Yeah. So if Diane had appendicitis, she might have been flown to Darwin, right?" Kyle looked at me.

I nodded. Darwin would be the nearest big city where good medical treatment was available. "Gary might have gone with her, and then couldn't come back the next day," I guessed.

"Good timing."

"Not for us." I swallowed hard. Not for Daniel. Not for Mariati. Not for Budi.

"But what about the Stewarts?" Kyle said. "This is what's bugging me. If they left without even trying to come and get us, it must be bad."

"Maybe they thought we were safer on Seram."

We fell silent.

"The riots on Ambon," I said softly. "Are they *just* burning things?"

This time it was Mani who answered. "No."

"What about pela?" I asked. "How can this happen?"

Mani shrugged again and smoothed his hand over his forehead. It didn't erase the lines of tension. "Pela is for Moluccan Christians and Muslims. Since 1950 lots of Javanese Muslims have moved here. The village heads don't have as much authority as before."

"What about the army?" I asked. I was with Drew on that one. I didn't see how the presence of the army could possibly be a bad thing if Ambon was such a mess.

The fisherman, who'd been following our three-way dialogue through Mani, broke in, shaking his head. The only word I caught was *hati hati* —be careful.

"The army is doing bad things, especially in the Christian areas," Mani translated for us. "We should go to the Ambonese police. They are mostly Christians and will help us."

"But the army has to help us," Kyle argued. "That's their job."

"Maybe they will help you because you are white. But Supharti says Tina and me . . . we do not matter so much," Mani translated without emotion.

Kyle's arm tightened around my shoulder.

"Why are you helping us?" he challenged Supharti directly.

The answer, when it came back through Mani, was gentle.

"We are all people of the Book—Christians and Muslims, children of one God. Allah would want me to help you. What has happened to you . . . " Supharti glanced at Mani, sitting alone across from us. "It is not right."

It was a long day. After two weeks of filtered light, the sun was harsh, pouring straight down in hot waves, bouncing a thousand arrows of light off the gentle swells of water. My eyes ached.

Mark and Brendan lay side by side underneath the wooden platform. Brendan was right. He'd thrown up as soon as he moved, but he had no choice. It wasn't long after dawn that we realized he would fry like a piece of bacon if he stayed up on the roof. The rest of us sat alongside them, cramped, or at their feet in the remaining slice of shade. I'd thought it would be cooler being out on the water, but the breeze was fitful and the swell flat and glassy as we rocked gently along.

We spent the morning just sitting and sweating. I'd woken up tingling with impatience, ready now to conquer Ambon and get home. That had mostly evaporated during the first hot hours of daylight, sitting on the wood with my boots and socks off, watching my pale squished toes wiggling like so many unearthed slugs. Now I just felt tired, and angry that we had more to deal with in Ambon.

None of the others asked directly about the plan. Not verbally anyway. Elissa looked long and hard at me over the prone bodies in the middle of the boat. I nodded. She nodded back. And I felt like a hypocrite for pretending that everything was going to be fine when I really had no idea.

It was Mark who saved our sanity that morning. Lying flat with his eyes closed, he suddenly spoke into the heavy silence. "Once upon a time there was a boy named Jip."

Drew opened her eyes and raised her head. She lifted her braid and fanned the back of her neck. "And Jip had a best friend. A monkey named Kiki."

"Jip and Kiki had been hiking for two weeks in the wild woods of Neverland," Mark said, plagiarizing shamelessly.

"And now they were ready to go home," Elissa said.

"But first," Kyle said, "they had to cross an ocean."

"Luckily," I said, "they met up with Tinker Bell in Neverland, and she decided to hang out with them for a while and help out."

Tinker Bell's fairy dust is going to come in handy if the airport really is closed, I thought, anticipating the plotline. They'll be able to fly from Ambon to Australia. Probably not all the way to America. The magic powder can't possibly be that strong.

"Um." Mani raised a diffident hand, two familiar creases between his eyes indicating that we had suddenly lost him.

Jip and Kiki were temporarily abandoned to their own devices while we filled Mani and Tina in on the essential background to *Peter Pan.*

"Oh," Mani said, grasping the possibilities. "This fairy, can she turn back time then?"

"No." Brendan spoke without moving his head or opening his eyes. "Not even in Neverland."

"Okay," Mani nodded, patting Tina's shoulder. She sat in his lap, sucking her thumb, staring at us with wide dark eyes.

"Anyway," Mark said, bored by the scientific laws of relativity in fantasyland. "There they were, on the beach, staring out to sea."

"How are they going to get off Neverland?" Drew asked, the hint of laughter in her voice reflecting relief that at least we were safe on this side of that adventure.

It took us most of the morning to get Jip and Kiki off the island. They tried paddling off using banana fronds as canoes and hollowed-out coconut shells as paddles. But they didn't get twenty meters from shore before Kyle (who had ridiculed the banana leaf idea from the beginning) sank them, and they had to swim back. They hardly made it ashore before Drew and Mark retaliated with an attack by a whole herd of wild pigs. Jip barely escaped with his life and was saved only thanks to the heroic interventions of Kiki and Tinker Bell. About noon I left them in the throes of fashioning jet skis from forest material and clambered up on the roof to peer toward Ambon.

We didn't seem to be moving. Beneath the boat the water stretched straight down below us, deep and unfathomably blue. I pressed my fingertips against the scorching planks. They were all that stood between us and those silent depths.

"Wait."

I heard Mani's voice below me.

"A jet ski is like a small, fast boat, but only for one person?"

"Or two," Elissa said. "Like a motorcycle, but on water."

There was a pause, then Mani's voice again, puzzled. "But what do you *use* them for?"

"Nothing, really," Mark said. "You just ride on them really fast. It's awesome fun."

"Huh. Well, how do you make them out of wood then?" Mani asked.

"Excellent question. And what are you going to use for fuel?" Kyle asked. Always the realist.

"Coconut milk," Drew said defiantly. "It would work, wouldn't it, Cori?"

"Sure. It's high in natural fruit sugars. Fructose," I called down, struggling to remember the correct term from my nutrition classes in Kenya. I knew that it would come in handy someday. "We could burn it for energy like ethanol."

That last bit was a whole load of what my dad would have called codswallop. But why stick with realism all the time? It's so boring.

"You can't burn coconut milk for fuel!" Kyle sounded outraged.

"Cori said you can," Mark said, as if that sealed the argument.

Kyle swung himself up on the roof to continue the discussion with the original authority. "You're being ridiculous," he said, but the statement had lost its energy. He was staring at the same thing I'd been looking at for the past couple of minutes.

Ambon was still a distant mass rising from the water, its edges blurred and indistinct. But even through the haze that hung over the island it looked like there were three separate smudged pillars of . . . smoke.

"So?" Drew said.

"Fine," Kyle said, distracted.

From underneath us there was laughter and the smack of two wet hands meeting in a high five.

The even roll of the boat checked briefly as Mani joined us on the roof. None of us said anything. I strained my eyes, turning my head one way, then the other. It didn't make any difference. Even if it was smoke, there was no way to know what it meant.

"What are you doing up there?" Elissa called.

"Sunbathing," I answered.

"You're going to burn," she warned.

She was right. I scooted backwards and swung down carefully, balancing with one foot on the side of the boat. Despite the sunshine it had seemed cooler up on top.

"See anything?" she asked.

"Ambon. It's a long way away yet. I wouldn't go up there. Your skin's a lot fairer than mine."

She sighed, brushing sticky tendrils of blonde hair back off her neck.

Mani vaulted off the roof with careless grace and started talking to Supharti, who was still perched on the back of the boat.

"Do you think the airport will really be closed?" Elissa asked quietly, underneath the three-way discussion that was still going on about jet skis.

"I don't know. But there have to be other ways to get out," I said. "If the army is there, they'll be on the lookout for us. Our parents must have contacted the government."

"I'm hungry," Kyle said, appearing suddenly.

Elissa grimaced. "We're sort of low on food."

"What do we have? We won't need it after today."

Now that was a strange thought.

"Two tins of beans, half a jar of peanut butter, some dried fruit, some cooked rice, a bunch of squished bananas from that tree last night, and some pancake mix—which isn't going to help us here."

"Rice, beans, and peanut butter. Banana for desert. Yummy, yummy," Kyle said, actually sounding like he meant it.

Brendan groaned.

After everyone except Brendan ate something, Drew, Mark, Brendan, and Tina fell asleep. Kyle was up on the roof again. Elissa sat against the wall writing in her journal. I opened mine, but then got stuck. I'd hardly written anything during the last two weeks. Every time I started, I just ended up scribbling down questions or doodling.

My mind danced from topic to topic like a water bug skating over a pond.

Ambon. Burning.

The airport.

Mani. Tina. How could we leave them?

My parents. Where were they? They must be so worried.

My pen moved of its own volition over the top of the blank page.

Dear Mum, Dad, Tanya, Luke . . .

We're on a boat somewhere between Seram and Ambon. I just realized I don't even know the name of the ocean. How ignorant is that? But I thought you might like to know we are off Seram.

I stopped. Every which way I turned mentally, I ran into something I wasn't sure I wanted to write about. I felt like a fifth grader at camp, writing my first letter home. Actually that fit too. I could just write . . .

Dear Mum and Dad,

My friends are nice, but I hate it here. Please come and get me and take me home.

Love,

Cori

P.S. Bring chocolate.

I sighed and drew a flower. Across the other side of the boat, Elissa didn't seem to be having any trouble.

"What are you writing about?" I whispered.

"Letter to Colin."

Okay. I chewed on the end of my pen. It tasted salty. I could do this. I put the pen to paper and started moving it, not letting myself think about what came out.

This has been the longest two weeks of my life. Deep down, where the others can't see, I've wondered every day whether we would disappear into that jungle forever, like a pebble tossed into a deep pond, with no one but God to watch it sink.

I stopped again, frustrated. I wasn't saying what I wanted to say. I didn't know *what* I wanted to say. I folded the piece of paper and stuck it beside Dad's letter. Maybe I should write to Scott. But this time I only got as far as his name on top of the sheet before I got stuck.

I threw the paper down and bounced the pen off the floor of the boat for good measure. Elissa glanced over and raised an eyebrow, but didn't say anything. "I'm going up to see Kyle and Mani."

I didn't wait for her nod, but planted a foot on the edge of the boat and scrambled up, widening the tear in the knee of my khakis and collecting a splinter in the process.

Ahead of us the sun was setting. To our left, Saparua Island was close. Uncomfortably close. To our right, the shores of Seram pressed in.

"So we're in Seram Strait now?" I asked.

"Yes," Mani said. "We will pass Saparua, then Haruku Island, then Ambon."

I couldn't actually see Ambon anymore over the bulk of Haruku Island.

I hadn't realized it was so late in the afternoon. The sun was sinking fast, touching the haze over the land ahead of us with red, unrolling a narrow, bright carpet of light that stretched across the water to our boat. I didn't want the sun to go down. The thought of being all alone on this small boat out in the middle of the ocean for another long, dark night was suddenly very scary.

"Supharti thinks it is maybe better for us to sail into the bay, near the airport." Mani's voice was uncertain. "But he has only done that one time before now."

"So the plan is to float through the strait tonight. Then early tomorrow we cut left and sail into the bay." Kyle sounded reassuringly certain.

"So we might be at the airport by noon tomorrow?" This seemed to be the one part of the plan I was having trouble grasping.

"Yes," Mani said, his expression blank.

"You've got to come with us," I said to him suddenly. "Even if you decide to come back later. Just come for a while."

Kyle put his hand over mine, curling my fingers into his.

"I will go with Tina to the mission school," Mani said, not meeting my eyes. "We will be all right."

I felt an actual physical pain in my stomach. "But you can come live with any of us. Please come with us. Please." I stopped, choking.

"This is my home," Mani said. "Father would have wanted me to stay."

Not anymore, I wanted to scream at him. It's lost that claim. This place is not fit to be anybody's home. Not yours. Not Tina's.

"Daniel wanted you both to be safe. To walk with peace, remember? How are you going to do that here? Now?"

Kyle's fingers tightened over mine, and I stopped. The wood creaked beneath me as Elissa climbed up and slid forward to lie flat beside me. The four of us, pressed shoulder to shoulder, stretched right across the width of the boat.

"Mani's not coming out with us when we get to the airport," I said, ruthlessly dragging Elissa into this, knowing she was an ally.

"Why not?" Elissa sounded calm, but I felt the tension in the arm that was pressed against mine. "What about Tina?"

"Tina should stay with me." Mani sounded less certain on this point.

I knew what Elissa was thinking—Tina could have a better life with one of us. Grow up in a family. Far away from her culture, her brother. How do you weigh what's best for someone like that? How do you ask a friend who has just lost both his parents to give up his sister as well?

"No," Elissa said, her face tight and pale. She started to speak, bit her lip, started again.

"You have to come with us. You have to." That was all she got out before the tears started to pour down her face, and she buried her head in her arms, her whole body shaking, repeating a single word over and over again.

"No."

Kyle and Mani both looked at me. I think they were expecting me to do something about the situation, say something to make her feel better. Their faces were blurry. I thought it was just the dusk until Kyle reached up and touched my wet cheek.

I shook my head. I couldn't speak.

"Hey." Kyle scrambled over me to reach Elissa and pulled her awkwardly into his arms. "It's all right."

"It's not all right," she said as she sobbed. "We can't leave them here."

"Mani." I scooted over closer to him and gulped back more of my own tears, searching for something that might help him change his mind. "You could finish school first; then you could come back. You'd be like part of our families."

"I have family here too," Mani said, glancing back at Seram, his face set. "Peter has no mother anymore either. I do not know what happened to a lot of the people in the village. I have to go back."

Ahead of us the sun kissed the horizon and started to sink beneath it. The boat tracked steadily forward, sliding along the liquid golden path. I realized again that I would probably never grasp everything Mani had done for us.

"Mani, you're only seventeen. Do you really think that your parents would have wanted you to go back by yourself? With Tina?" I hated myself for hurting him more, but I loved them too much not to try.

"I don't know." His voice, usually so low and even, cracked. "I'm tired," he whispered, almost to himself.

"What about Tina? What's best for her? Any one of us would take her back with us and give her a home," I said. I nodded to Elissa, who was still curled up in Kyle's lap, weeping in ragged gulps.

"I wish I could ask them," Mani admitted, not a trace of self-pity in his tone.

"Pray about it, all right?" I said. Personally I hadn't received any divine revelations lately, but Mani seemed to be a bit more in touch, and I couldn't conceive that God wouldn't be on our side on this issue. "Can we just see when we get to the airport?"

"Okay," he said.

We lay there silently for a while, listening to Elissa's sobs gradually grow further apart.

"I would miss you all," Mani whispered to me. "You are my brothers and sisters now."

We watched the last of the sun sink below the narrow slice of horizon bracketed by the two islands ahead. With it went the last glimmers of the lighted pathway. As darkness closed in more rapidly than I had thought possible, the water in front of us just looked cold and black again.

chapter 15 ～

No one slept well that night except maybe Supharti, who curled himself up into a ball on a corner of the roof and didn't stir for hours. Mani took his place at the tiller, while Kyle and I filled the others in on the plan. It was very dark inside the makeshift cabin. All I could see were the two neat strips highlighted by the bars of moonlight falling through the open windows. One bar of white light fell across Drew's knee and the fingers of her left hand, entwined with Brendan's. The other rested gently on Tina's face. She was snuggled under the crook of Elissa's arm, staring out the window up at the moon.

"So Mani thinks it's the best thing to take the chance of sailing into the bay?"

"Yeah," Kyle said.

"Can you see Ambon?" Brendan asked, probing. He knew we weren't saying everything.

"We did earlier," I said.

"What did you see?"

There was silence, and then Kyle and I spoke at the same time. "Smoke."

My hand reached out for Kyle's and found it.

"So if we sail around into Ambon Bay, we'll be close to the airport?" Drew asked.

"Mani said we can get within a short walk to it," Kyle said.

"And we'll get in about dawn?"

"Fewer people around."

"I think we should do it, then," Elissa said.

There didn't seem to be much to talk about after we'd all agreed. Thinking forward meant thinking of safety and home. That felt just out of reach, something that could be pushed beyond our grasp by careless words.

Home was something I desperately wanted, yet didn't want. It meant being surrounded by family, yet not having the others within arm's reach. And they were the ones who made me open my eyes in the morning now.

Thinking backwards was hard work. The world was divided into before it happened and afterwards. Even before it happened every action, every interaction, since we'd started this trip seemed somehow touched by the death of that hot Saturday in Mani's village. Even our laughter. And there had been a lot of that. How could we not have known, not have understood what might happen?

So we were stuck in the now. The now was the warmth of Kyle's fingers wrapped around my hand, the feel of his arm resting solid against mine, the dull throbbing in my wrist where the cut was slowly healing. The now was rough wood against the back of my head, water lapping against the other side of thin planks that were all that was keeping me from a deep, wet darkness. The now was the dense familiar smell of salt water and the taste of peanut butter, all we'd had for dinner.

I reached up and touched Scott's ring. The smooth circles were warm beneath my fingertips. But they were not the now anymore. They had lost the ability to anchor me. I let them slip away and rested my head against the shoulder I knew was there beside me in the dark. Kyle shifted slightly as he lifted his other arm to reach over and stroke my hair, running gentle fingers down my cheek.

"Go to sleep," he whispered.

"I can't." I wanted to cry again. "Tell me a story."

He paused. Then the shoulder under my cheek shifted as he leaned away from me. I heard him undo a pack buckle and pull something out.

"Check this out," he said softly, wiggling back over and pressing something into my hands.

I could tell straightaway it was a book, probably a Bible, from the feel of the pliable leather cover. But there was something very odd about it. I leaned forward and held it out in front of me, into the white river of moonlight pouring in through the window.

It *was* a Bible, small but thick, bound with worn black leather. The front cover was intact, but the back . . . the back was neatly punctured, the leather pushed in. My fingers sank deep into the cone-shaped hole, feeling the torn edges of fragile pages.

"What happened to it?" I asked.

"I found it the day before yesterday, while I was waiting for Mani near that village. It must have been on the back edge of my pack," Kyle whispered.

"What?"

"When the pig . . . ," he said.

I remembered that charge. How the tusks had disappeared into the pack. How Kyle's legs had flopped as he was shoveled along the ground. And the blue bruise over his ribs.

"This was almost your heart," I said, pulling it out of the light and handing it back to him. I didn't want to touch it anymore. It made me feel sick.

"I know." He sounded awed. I could hear him flipping through the pages. "He got all the way to Numbers."

"Figures," I said, still not wanting to think about what it meant. "I always get stuck in Numbers too."

Kyle snorted.

"It's awesome," he said. "I mean . . . it's just awesome!" For once he was stuck for words, but there was no misreading his tone. I couldn't hear a trace of the anger that had been simmering for the past two weeks. It was just . . . gone. Kyle sighed. It was a peaceful sound.

That should have made me happy.

Instead it made me feel lonely.

"Go to sleep," he said softly. I could hear him still playing with the ragged edges of the paper. He shifted, and one arm reached back around me. "We're going to be fine."

I closed my eyes against the dark, concentrated on nothing but the feel of his fingers in my hair, and drifted.

I don't know whether it was the throb of the engine turning over, catching, then failing, or the sound of Mark's voice, high pitched and scared, that jerked me awake.

"Try again," Mark urged.

Same result. A whine, the promising slide toward a deeper, steadier mechanical hum, then nothing.

I sat up. The moon hung low in the sky, bathing the back of the boat in light. Supharti was crouched over the engine tinkering with something, swaying as the boat shifted and rolled. The swell had risen while I'd been asleep. I felt abandoned as Kyle crawled over me and out of the cabin without a word.

"What?" I heard Brendan ask.

"Engine," Mark answered as everyone else began to stir. "We need the power to get around into the bay."

"Supharti says no problem," Mani said.

"What time is it?"

There was a green fluorescent flash as Kyle lit up his watch dial.

"Four thirty."

Supharti waved the others back and yanked on the cord. This time there was nothing. Not even a whine. He nodded and went back to tinkering. I could hear the clink of metal on metal and started to sweat.

"You have to be joking!" Drew said.

"Supharti says no problem," Mani repeated, sounding a little less calm.

I crawled out of the cabin and stood up, bracing myself against the swell. Ambon was there to our left, a dark, solid mass rising from the water. Straight ahead of us there was only black space.

"So where are we going?" I asked Mark.

"Around that, hopefully," he said, pointing to the tip of Ambon. "Not unless we've got power, though."

"Otherwise what?" Drew asked, coming to stand beside me, holding on to the edge of the roof.

"I don't know," Mark snapped, turning back to Supharti. "We'll probably end up in Africa."

"No, we won't," I said, tucking my free arm through hers as I heard her groan. "Indonesia's made up of fourteen thousand islands, remember? At least some of them have to be between here and Africa."

"So we kidnapped a fisherman, stole a boat with a broken engine, and are going to end up shipwrecked on an island somewhere," Drew said, sounding completely resigned.

I felt cold spray hit the back of my legs as a particularly large wave slapped the right side of the boat.

"No," I said, trying to stifle a hysterical giggle. "Stick to the facts. We hired a fisherman, and his boat, which is only having temporary difficulties. And there will be no shipwrecking."

"All right." Drew took a deep breath. "If that's Jip's official version."

Supharti yanked on the cord again, so hard I was afraid he was going to break it.

It caught, almost died, then settled into a low sputtering growl. I started breathing again. The nose of the boat swung right, into the swells.

"Are you sure the bay's there?" I asked Mark.

"Up around the headland," Mark said. "But it's low tide, so it could be rough going in."

The noise of the motor was shockingly loud. I wondered whether there were villages we couldn't see on the beaches we were fast approaching, people out there listening.

"You're shaking," Drew said, surprised.

I let go of her arm. "I always do when I'm having lots of fun," I said.

"Fun?"

"A moonlight cruise in tropical seas. You're not having fun?"

It worked. She laughed.

I shivered, goose bumps rippling up my arms and down my back.

We were so close now I could see the sharp edges of rock meeting water, the dark, impenetrable tangle of trees hugging the coast. The nose of the boat edged right, cruising parallel to land.

"The entrance of the bay is just around this cliff," Mani said, pointing straight ahead.

Then suddenly we were there, swinging left again, nosing past the spit of land jutting firmly out of the water. Only I couldn't see the bay or land beyond, just scattered fragments of white, undulating gracefully in midair at eye level. Under the putter of the engine I heard a deep pounding *boom*.

Beside me, Mark used language I'd only heard from Kyle before.

I was struggling to make sense of the shifting shapes. Then I lurched as the boat tipped forward sharply, and I understood.

I dropped to my knees, clutching Drew as the first wave hit the boat head-on and sluiced up over the bow. The force of it was broken by the shelter of the cabin, but enough water washed onto the deck to leave our legs soaked.

Brendan yelped, then coughed.

"Hey!" Elissa called from the cabin as I stared into the next wall of water that was about to hit us.

Drew screamed as it slammed into us side-on, washing straight over the right side of the boat, soaking us to the neck. I couldn't make a sound. My only conscious thought was that I couldn't let go of Drew's arm, wet but solid in my grasp.

Then the planks tilted underneath us and we were sliding back-wards, awash in water.

"Out! Get out! We're getting swamped," Mark yelled, sliding forward into the cabin and tugging on someone's leg.

Another wave hit us from behind, rolling us forward. The engine whined shrilly as the back of the boat came out of the water.

"Left! Left! Turn left!" Kyle yelled from the roof.

I looked over my shoulder. The next wave towered as tall as the cabin. We didn't even have a hope of turning to meet it head-on. It broke onto us, knocking us flat.

My shoulder and then my cheek smashing onto the deck. Red stars exploding against the inside of my eyelids. Drew's arm still there. Water drowning my hair, closing over my head. Choking on coppery salt, warm in my mouth.

As the boat dropped I felt the crunch shudder through my whole body, echoing in my skull, and thought for a moment that I was hear-ing the sound of my own bones breaking. It wasn't until I remembered how to move, lifted my head, and gulped air that I realized that the pain wasn't going to come. It wasn't mine.

"Left!" Kyle was still yelling.

I don't know how Supharti was doing it, but we were turning left into the empty blackness of the bay. The next wave curled over the back of the boat, water closing over us again. Drew and I were still flat on the deck. Elissa and Brendan huddled just ahead of us, clinging to the side of the boat. I don't know where I found the thought space to wonder whether Brendan still felt sick or whether it had been scared out of him.

Another wet push from behind. Drew and I slid forward, coming up hard against the wall and reaching up to grab it.

"Clear ahead," Mark yelled. "Go! Go!"

I didn't understand how we were still afloat, much less moving forward.

"Stay down," Kyle yelled. He didn't have to tell us twice.

Up. Down. The crash of invisible waves against the rocks. The steady vibration of the motor. Long strands of hair washing forward, then back.

One minute. Ten. It was hard to tell.

Then we weren't getting so wet. Within a few waves we had stopped being swamped, and I suddenly stopped believing we were all going to drown. Until I stopped believing it, I didn't realize how certain I had been.

I unwelded my fingers from Drew's arm and pulled myself up against the side of the boat. My hand slipped on the wet wood and my arm plunged over the edge, splashing into water. The side of the boat was clearing the water by about four inches.

"We're sinking," Mark said, appearing between me and Mani. "We came in too close to the reef! We're lucky we didn't get tossed against the cliffs."

"I know," I heard my voice say, remembering the crunch, watching myself in surprise as my legs moved obediently to stand up and I reached up toward the roof.

"Kyle," I demanded.

He gave me a pull up.

"There's a beach up there." He pointed, and I saw the sheen of moonlight on pale sand.

It was hard to tell how far it was in the dark. Maybe two hundred meters. Maybe more.

The motor coughed, bubbled, and went silent as the intake sank below the water. We were left with only the pounding menace of the waves on the reef behind us. I felt the boat begin to sag to the left.

"There's a beach to the left, ahead of us," Kyle called down. "We're going to have to swim."

"Leave your boots off. Stick together," I said into the silence, talking to help myself avoid thinking about having to jump alone into that wet darkness.

"Supharti can't swim," Mani said.

Life jackets? No.

"But he's a fisherman!" Kyle said.

"He can't swim. Most Indonesian fisherman can't swim." Mani sounded too calm.

"Kyle and I will tow him," I said. "Tell him to float on his back. Not to try and hold on to us. We'll hold on to him."

Between the two of us we should be all right, I thought. We were both strong swimmers. We had raced at the village almost every day. He always won.

"I'll help you with Tina," Brendan said to Mani.

"My diary!" Elissa wailed. I heard her scrabbling in her pack. Good idea.

I dropped back over the edge of the roof and reached for mine, scooping out the small notebook, all the film and my camera, and stuffing them into the waterproof pouch around my waist. Everything else had to stay. I felt a small stab of satisfaction at the imminent fate of my hated boots.

Water started to pour over the left side of the boat, and we listed farther.

"Go," Kyle said, landing heavily beside me.

"I can't." Drew gasped.

There was a splash as Brendan dropped into the water, followed by Mani and then Elissa.

"Go! Or we'll lose each other," Kyle ordered, helping her forcefully over the side. Her yelp was cut off as the water closed over her head before she reappeared, bobbing behind the others.

"C'mon." I grabbed one of Supharti's arms as Kyle grabbed the other, and we jumped.

It was warm. A black bath.

"Hey!" I yelled, treading water, wet salt slopping into my mouth, Supharti's arm weighing me down. I kicked away from the boat. Supharti started to twist in my grasp, his hand scrabbling, pulling at me.

"Here." Brendan's voice drifted back from somewhere in front of us. To the right maybe.

"Kyle!" I gasped, just before my head went under.

Kicking against soaking clothes, my world shrank to the three of us thrashing in the water. I lost my grip on his arm, and Supharti's hand closed on my shoulder, pushing down. I kicked hard, connected, and felt the grip loosen. In that instant I didn't care that he couldn't swim. I just wanted air.

My head broke the surface again, and the blurry moon swayed in front of me.

There was a dull smacking sound, another one, and then Kyle's voice, rough. "Turn him over."

Supharti was limp as we rolled him onto his back.

I trod water, panting, a hand under his head.

"He was going to drown us," Kyle said.

"I know."

"You okay?"

"Yeah." I coughed against the salt.

"Is he breathing?" Kyle asked.

I tried to find a pulse in his neck, but I couldn't tell.

"Hey," I yelled. "Brendan! Mani!"

Nothing. They couldn't be that far away yet.

"Which way?" I asked, not recognizing the shrill voice that I knew must be mine. I couldn't see anything from water level except more water, and my legs were already getting tired, my chest tightening up. I tried to take a slow, deep breath and had to spit out more water.

"Face the moon, to the left," I heard Kyle say.

I slipped my right arm through Supharti's, near his shoulder, and started to kick, trying not to think about what would happen if Kyle was wrong.

Keeping Supharti's face above water was harder than I had anticipated.

Breathe. Kick with both legs. Stroke with my left arm. Breathe. Eyes stinging. Face burning. Trying to see. Nothing but the moon. Hating the weight between us. Kick with both legs. Breathe.

I don't know how long it was before we paused.

"Brendan!?" Kyle bellowed. "Drew? Mani?"

I didn't think I was ever going to be able to get enough oxygen again.

"Here . . . " The word drifted back. "Over here . . . "

Kyle grunted.

"Let's go." He kicked forward again.

I can't, I wanted to say. But I felt my legs moving even before my mouth had a chance to form the words. Against the darkness I saw our backyard in Kenya. Our pool. Tanya, Luke, and I used to challenge one another to see who could swim the most lengths underwater with a single breath. I did four and a half once. Luke had done five just after me, and I'd never been able to break that record, although I'd spent hours trying.

Hours. We swam for hours. Surely I'd broken the record by now.

I felt Supharti's arm twitch, his head turned, an eye half open. We paused again. My lungs clawed at my chest.

"Don't move," Kyle commanded in a terrible voice.

At least the tone translated. He didn't move. But he held his own head up.

"Kyle? Cori?" Brendan's voice sounded closer. He yelled something else. All I caught were the words "straight" and "beach."

"Here!" I tried to call out, but my voice was faint and scratchy. The red stars were back, circling lazily around the moon. Graceful somersaults. Like the ones I could only do in water. Endless somersaults in the pool under the hot sun. Ten in a row, and we'd come up dizzy and laughing. Deliciously sick. The grass a green carpet around us. Barnabas leaping around crazily, barking, trying to catch the sparkling drops we splashed his way.

"Cori?" Kyle's voice sounded a long way away.

I'm fine, I told him.

"Cori! Answer me!"

I did, I wanted to protest. What's wrong with you? It wasn't worth the energy, though. We could argue about it later.

"Brendan!" he screamed.

Just swim, I said. I'm sure I said it. It's okay. Just one more length. We'll break the record.

I put my face down and kicked. Opened my eyes. Black. Silent. I wondered how deep it was. It wasn't scary anymore. There was nothing to be afraid of. The stars below me winked gently. Yellow and red now. Multiplying. Swirling peacefully. The sky. The water. It didn't matter. Same thing. Friendly stars.

Hard fingers in my hair. Wrenched my head up. Flipped me onto my back. The pain forced me to breathe.

"Float," Kyle said.

I wanted to tell him about the stars.

"We're almost there," he said.

Shut up. He was chasing them away. The pain was spreading. My face throbbed. My chest was full of knives. I'd swallowed stars. They were angry.

"A hundred feet maybe," I heard Brendan say beside me.

"Take him." Kyle gasped.

Water touched my face again. I coughed, starry fragments gouging my lungs. My knees coming to my chest. Twisting against the grip in my hair. Eyes underwater. The stars were there, mocking. Reaching out. Dragging me down.

Purple, the color of panic.

Cold fireworks.

Nothing.

The moon was calling my name. Which way? I kicked out lazily toward the light, following the silver path. Beyond the moonlight the darkness was soft and silent. I couldn't hear anything, not even the sound of my own strokes through the water. Nothing but my name, echoing gently, tugging me forward.

Then I reached up and touched the moon and it dissolved around me, flooding me in light. And feeling came back.

Choking. Hot water gushing out of my mouth and nose. One

breath. Then cough. One more breath. Someone's hand was warm on my back. Another hand on my head. The rest of me was freezing. Kyle calling my name from a long way away. I rested my forehead on the sand. The shifting graininess was firm and reassuring.

"Just breathe. You're okay," Brendan was saying.

My eyes were burning, and getting them open was hard work. I rolled over and tried to sit up. Brendan helped me.

It was just on dawn. Pink fingers were reaching up into the blue. The pale light sent pain stabbing through my head, but we were all there, even Supharti. Soaking wet and shivering. No shoes. Hair draggling over pale faces. Wide eyes standing out white.

"Where's your shirt?" I asked Kyle. It was the first thought that popped into my head. I heard my words slurring and had to try twice to make them come out right.

"Supharti's stronger than he looks." Kyle tried to smile.

The left side of my face hurt. I put my hand up.

"Don't." Kyle pushed it down again.

"Did you do that?" I asked Kyle, confused.

He looked horrified. "No!"

"Oh, yeah," I said at the same time, articulating carefully. "I hit the deck. Do I have a black eye?"

"You will. A beautiful one," Kyle promised.

I took another breath. A bit deeper this time. I hurt all over. Someone had scoured my sinuses with steel wool, and my stomach ached.

"What happened?" I asked.

"We were almost to the beach. Why didn't you tell me you were in trouble?" Kyle demanded.

I shrugged. "I didn't know." It sounded ridiculous even to me. "Did I pass out?"

"I couldn't even tell if you were still breathing." He was furious.

"Did you try mouth-to-mouth?" I asked.

"Cori!"

I was shocked to see tears in his eyes.

"It's not funny." He jerked his hand back and turned away.

"I'm sorry," I said to his back. He didn't answer. Brendan squeezed my shoulder.

My head was pounding. I thought about the remaining painkillers in the first aid kit. They were probably on the bottom of the ocean by now. I wanted to curl up and go to sleep.

"So what do we do?" Elissa asked.

If I never heard that question again, I didn't think I'd miss it. I never wanted to have to make another decision about *doing* something again. Should we head for the bushes behind us or walk along the beach? Or sit there until something just happened? That thought was too tempting, and I stood up, dragging heavily on Brendan's shoulder and willing my legs to stop shaking. My mental commands were about as effective at controlling my legs as they had recently proven in controlling my emotions. I hoped the others would think it was the early morning chill that was making me shake.

As opposed to the fact that I had just very nearly drowned.

That thought made me sit down again, hard.

"You okay?" Elissa asked.

"You scared the holy Moses out of us," Drew said, tears welling up.

"Did you see a light?" Mark asked.

"No. Just stars."

"That is really cheesy," he said.

"Big ones. Red and yellow. They were dancing. Besides, who are you to make fun of my near-death experience?"

"Sorry." He looked stricken.

I had intended to make a joke. Was nothing I said coming out right?

"Come here." I reached up and squeezed his hand. It was shaking about as much as mine.

Apart from our little band, the beach was deserted. I wondered how long it would stay that way. To the east the sky was brightening.

"How far from the airport are we?" Brendan asked Mani.

"The airport is over there." Mani pointed across the bay. "We'll have to walk around."

We sat in silence. No one asked how long that would take.

"What about Supharti?" Elissa finally said.

"He says he will walk back over the mountains and catch a boat from the other side back to Seram," Mani said.

I fumbled in my waist pack and pulled out all the cash I was carrying. Three hundred dollars. Enough to get him a new boat.

"Here." I shoved it at Mani. "Tell him thank you, and we're sorry about his boat."

Supharti smiled and ducked his head. I could see he was going to have quite a shiner too. I remembered the panic of his hands pushing on my shoulders and shuddered again.

"He says to tell you thank you for saving his life."

"I didn't." I nodded toward Kyle.

"Tell him to learn how to swim," Kyle said without turning around.

Drew laughed. It had a hysterical edge.

"We lost you right at the boat," I said. "It took us awhile to sort out how we were going to tow Supharti."

"What happened?" Drew asked.

"Kyle hit him," I said.

"No, I meant with you."

"I don't know. I was just following the moon." I couldn't tell them when I'd stopped following the real moon and started following the one in my head.

"Kyle had to drag you up the beach," Drew said.

"He dragged me?" I was having a hard time concentrating on anything but the trivial.

"He was beat," Elissa said. "He couldn't even say anything except your name."

"I thought that was the moon," I said. "Weird."

Drew dropped down beside me and wrapped her arms around my shoulders. The extra warmth felt wonderful.

I dug my toes into the cool sand and looked back out over the water. To the right I could see the water roiling around the cliffs, smacking against the rocks. There was no sign of our boat. To the left the coast continued. Sand gave ground to rock again about half a mile down the beach. If those rocky cliffs hadn't been broken by the cove, there's no way we would all have made it to safety.

Across from us the other peninsula was visible. I knew that meant Ambon City itself was several miles to the left. I couldn't see the city. Just a green haze. Indistinct. But the dark oily smudges against the horizon in that direction, like sooty thumbprints against the clarity of the morning sky, could only be smoke.

On the bright side, I guessed that meant we wouldn't get lost finding the city if we needed to.

I wondered suddenly about the Israelites and all those years of God's miraculous provision in the desert—leading them by night with a pillar of fire and by day with a cloud of smoke. Did they sometimes worry that those signs that served as their guides would also serve as markers to draw their enemies to them?

Back then, I thought, God was a bit more generous with His miracles. Manna, the Red Sea. They may have been a bit more trusting with regard to their personal safety.

Maybe not. I guess they did end up worshiping a golden calf.

A little bit of water out of a nearby rock wouldn't go astray right now, God, I thought, staring at a large pebble near my foot.

Nothing.

"C'mon." Kyle's hand blocked my view of the pebble as he reached down to help me up. "Let's move."

chapter 16 ～

I walked behind Mark on a narrow track that was covered by a layer of fine sandy dust. I couldn't remember when I'd hurt more. My face throbbed and I could hardly see out of my left eye. Breathing just felt wrong, and my damp and sandy clothes chafed. My mouth was gummy and salty, and I was very thirsty. Even my feet, which had initially celebrated the rebellious liberation from my boots, were ruing their loss. My watch told me we'd only been walking for forty minutes.

If Mark can do it, I repeated to myself, *you can do it.*

I glared at his back, willing him to put his hand to his head, stumble, and call for a break.

It took me awhile to work out why I was so jumpy. The track cut a close green tunnel through thick brush, but the deepening blue of the sky was visible above us, and glimpses of the sea occasionally peeked through the leaves to our right. It left me feeling claustrophobic and too exposed at the same time. The noises were different too. Gone was the sucking squish of a single footfall into damp ground cover, the soft rasp made by brushing a shoulder past a tall fern leaf. I couldn't even hear many familiar birdcalls. Instead, the constantly changing lisp of water meeting rocks, meeting sand, tracked us. It masked other sounds I had grown used to hearing and filled in all the cracks in the dawn silence.

We hadn't seen another person yet, although I knew we must be coming upon the first of the villages soon. Supharti's warning rang in my head. *Hati hati.* Be careful.

I wished fruitlessly for Jip, Kiki, and Tinker Bell to sweep us up and fly us away.

What happened instead was that Mani held up his hand and we all froze, well trained by now.

"I think this is Christian village," Mani whispered, tired eyes sunk back into his face. "You wait. I will go." He turned and loped off without waiting for a reply.

I figured I couldn't get much dirtier and joined Mark and Brendan on the ground, lifting an exploratory hand to my face. The left side felt huge and alien.

"Cori." Kyle's tone was sharp. "Poking at it is not going to help."

I glared at him. If he had almost drowned that morning, I was sure I would have treated him much more gently. He wouldn't even meet my eyes, and I was seized by a new fear.

"Drew." I yanked on her arm until she leant down and I could whisper in her ear. "Am I really ugly?"

She looked at me like she was wondering if I had knocked a few more screws loose than anybody had realized. "You're fine. It's just starting to turn blue from here to here." She ran cool fingers lightly in an arc from above my eyebrow down to my cheekbone.

"In that case," I said, relieved, "I think we should take a photo."

"You saved the camera?" Mark asked, perking up slightly.

"Yeah, and the film."

That coaxed a small smile out of Mark and Brendan.

"What's the occasion?" Drew asked.

"Surviving a shipwreck."

"Yeah—some of us almost didn't," Kyle muttered.

"Shut up," I said. "It wasn't like I did it on purpose."

"You could have asked for help."

"I didn't think I needed it."

"You never think you need it."

"Guys, just stop it." Drew sounded resigned.

"Fine," I said, as if I didn't care. "Write down the caption then. Film 10, photo 7." I handed Kyle the small notebook.

"Fine," he said, in a way that told me this particular discussion wasn't finished yet.

"Why is this dry?" he asked suddenly, curiosity temporarily overcoming annoyance.

"Waterproof, remember?" I patted the small waist pack where I'd stashed the film and camera beside our passports.

"Good thing you didn't drown," Mark said. "I need my passport."

"Brendan has yours," I said dryly. "But I gave away all of your money and mine to Supharti to buy a new boat."

"What am I going to tell my parents?" Mark said. "They told me not to spend it all at once." The little imp grinned at me before closing his eyes again. He must have been feeling a bit better.

I was reaching up to hand the camera to Drew when Mani appeared, and I froze.

There was another man with him. An old man who was hobbling along at a remarkable pace using a rough cane. A stranger. A stranger who was wearing the traditional round cap of the devout Muslim. Had Mani gone mad?

We must have made an interesting still-life tableau as they drew closer. Barefoot and ragged. Kyle shirtless, with his tattoos showing dark against white skin, notebook in hand. Mark with his chin propped on his knees. Tina clinging like a small brown limpet to Brendan's back. Me with my swollen face, holding up a camera.

The man's gaze skimmed over us and landed upon the camera. His face lit up and he started talking, nodding emphatically.

I looked sideways at the others without moving my head, only to find them doing the same thing.

Mani nodded and kept walking toward us. It was the look on his face that frightened me more than anything else. Until that moment I hadn't fully realized how I relied upon Mani to know what was going on, to know what to do. One glance now, and I knew he hadn't planned this. His eyes were wide, his hand gestures jerky.

"This is Haji Kembang," Mani said hesitantly. "He is one of the village elders of Tuleha. The village elders wish us to go into the village. I didn't tell them much—that I was your guide and that we had been on Seram for two weeks. Now he thinks you are journalists, and he invites you to come and hear what has happened so that you can tell others what is happening here, and the fighting will stop."

Drew's voice was quiet as she pointed out the obvious. "We're not actually journalists."

"We are now," Kyle said. "It's doesn't look like we have much choice."

"If we do agree to go into the village, how will they guarantee our safety?" Brendan asked. "Won't they think we're Christians because we're white?"

The old man looked almost affronted as Mani translated, and answered without hesitation.

"We will be honored guests," Mani told us.

"Can't we just go around it?" Elissa asked, chewing on her lower lip.

"I don't think so," Mani said, glancing at Tina. "I think we should go. I don't think they'll hurt us."

That did it for me. We'd followed Mani this far and, as I saw it, he probably had more to lose than we did by going in there. I stood up, holding the camera casually and doing my best to look like your everyday barefoot and bedraggled journalist.

"Hey." I poked Kyle in the back as we followed Mani and the spry village elder back along the track. "This is your chance to evangelize in the Muslim villages. Isn't that what you wanted?"

He ignored me.

"Can you not say *evangelize* in quite such a loud voice, please," Elissa whispered, agonized.

"Have you figured out which news service you work for yet?" Kyle asked her. "I'm with the Associated Press. Mark is my assistant."

"I wanted to work for CNN," Mark said.

"There's no way," Kyle told him.

"Assistant!" he complained.

"Yeah, the worst one I ever had. You're fired as soon as we finish this assignment."

Mark faced forward again and huffed.

That drew a small nervous giggle from Drew. "I always knew you had more talent for acting than you displayed in drama class, Kyle," she said.

chapter 16

"Who do you work for?" he asked.

"I dunno. I'm a model?" she offered, her voice tight and high.

"Sure. Dare you to tell *that* to the village elders."

"I think you would make a good model," Brendan whispered.

Drew actually blushed.

"I'm a freelance photographer," I said.

"This is all lying," Elissa said.

"It might not be," I said. "If we get out of here people might publish these photos. Then I would be."

Besides, I thought, it's just a baby lie, and one that might save my life. I have no problem with that. Would God? The way I saw it, being needlessly stupid was probably also a sin. Therefore, being scrupulously honest when a small lie wasn't hurting anybody else and the truth might cost you your life could be considered needless stupidity, and might actually count as a bigger sin than lying.

I knew my dad would say that any justification that complicated should make you examine your motivation.

I didn't need to examine very hard. I was just plain scared.

I could hear from the quick gasps behind me that Elissa was too.

As the village appeared ahead of us, I heard the crash of glass and the whoosh of flames in my head again, and that fear grew. I reached forward and hooked two fingers through the belt loop on Kyle's pants, needing to be close. He reached back and squeezed my wrist gently.

Tuleha looked a lot like Mani's village, only bigger. As the elder led us down the wide dirt road and into the village, bodies and heads started appearing from windows and doors. Men stared, smoking and squatting, leaning against walls in the shade. Quick glances showed

272

some curious gazes, some hostile. For an early morning it seemed unusually quiet. Even the children weren't out playing. The younger ones clung to their mothers' long skirts in doorways. A group of boys about ten years old huddled near the open window of a small general store and stared at us sullenly. The pungent smell of dried fish drifted out as we passed, and my stomach growled.

Haji Kembang led us past the store and into an open area that was ringed by houses built out of large cinder blocks that looked like they had once been white. The village square, I guessed. In the middle of this square stood a large tree beside a well. He motioned excitedly for us to sit, and disappeared toward the largest of the houses at a hobbling trot.

Mani passed Tina to Elissa and unobtrusively motioned Drew, Elissa, and me to move behind the guys. We sat cross-legged in two neat rows. Mani squatted easily in a way none of the rest of us had managed to fully master. More and more faces were appearing at the edge of the square. I looked at Mani and hoped fervently that he knew what he was doing.

I was expecting Haji Kembang to reappear with the other village elders. I was expecting the crowds that were gathering to suddenly surge forward and attack us. What I wasn't expecting was for two young women to appear from the big house. As they reached us, the first knelt gracefully to offer us water in chipped, grimy glasses. Brendan glanced sideways at Mani; then, obeying his almost imperceptible nod, reached out, picked up a glass, and drained its contents in four gulps.

Please don't let this make us sick, I thought, as I received my share after all the guys had drunk. I was so thirsty that my hands were shaking. It tasted like the purest filtered water.

"*Terima kasih.*" I thanked her in Indonesian and placed the glass back on the tray.

The young woman, who didn't look much older than me, clucked softly as she took in my eye. Her gaze was gentle, and I smiled tentatively at her. Her eyes answered me, but her lips didn't move.

It was only once I had drunk that I could spare any attention for the second, younger woman. She was carrying a bundle of rubber flip-flops, new ones, and a shirt for Kyle. She glanced doubtfully at Brendan's feet, looking embarrassed.

"They are a gift from the village elders. They are sorry to hear that we have lost our possessions," Mani told us.

Brendan hesitated, then with a resigned shrug selected the biggest pair and tried them on. They were too small by several sizes, and I heard several titters from the onlookers.

Brendan ignored them and thanked the woman gravely.

The pair I was given fit perfectly, and the sudden urge to weep took me as much by surprise as the gift of cheap shoes from the villagers.

The girl before me ducked her head, then rose gracefully and walked back across the square, disappearing back into the dim interior of the biggest house.

"Who were they?" I whispered to Mani.

"The village elder's youngest wives, I think," he answered without turning around. "It is a respectful welcome."

He fell silent as Haji Kembang and three older men approached. The four boys stood up, and Mani motioned the rest of us to stay seated. After shaking hands slowly and deliberately, the men all settled down.

Maybe Haji Kembang was half blind as well as lame, but I was convinced that the other village elders were going to know straight off that we weren't journalists. They didn't turn a hair, though. If they doubted our story, it didn't show. Polite greetings were hardly over before Haji

Kembang was talking again, the others nodding and adding comments, Kyle solemnly taking notes.

As the halting conversation progressed through Mani, I slowly forgot about how scared I was. I forgot I was not supposed to make eye contact with the men. There was a deep weariness as the elders talked about what had happened in their village, the weight of it dragging at their words. As they finished their narrative they named the men, women, and children who had been killed and injured during the last two weeks.

Usman, he was six. Son of Wakano. Killed the night the mosque was burnt down.

I thought of Budi and bit my lip.

Yusuf, father of Ani, who is four and Hamid, who is two. Husband of Prima. Killed returning to the village the day after the troubles started.

In the surrounding crowd, heads nodded as different names were mentioned. Kyle carefully wrote down each one in the notebook, checking the spelling with Mani.

By the time they had recited the tenth name I wanted to put my hands over my ears, but they kept going until Kyle had made thirteen neat notations. Thirteen lives gone. Thirteen families shattered in this village of maybe four hundred people. Everyone here would have known someone who had been killed.

Haji Kembang's voice jerked me away from my thoughts. Compared to the funereal solemnity with which the other elders had spoken, he was animated and passionate. He jerked his thumb emphatically, pointing Indonesian style. Pointing at me. Some of the other elders looked doubtful. One shook his head, but Haji Kembang seemed determined.

I looked at Mani.

Mani looked uncertain again, but leant over to speak to me in a low voice. "He wants you to go and take photographs of the mosque and the graveyard, and"—he swallowed hard—"and what happened last night."

What happened last night? I wanted to ask, but Mani's attention was elsewhere again, back on the elders, one of whom was still shaking his head. Now Haji Kembang switched tack and gestured toward Kyle.

"He says that you work for Kyle, and that you will take the pictures and Kyle will write the story."

"What? Kyle might work for me!" I whispered.

Mani's look told me that now was not the right time to argue for the equality of women in the workplace. "Will you go?" he asked.

"Do we have a choice?" Kyle said.

Mani shrugged; then his face tightened and he turned away, listening, before turning back. "The others wanted to know where the rest of our cameras and equipment are. Haji Kembang told them that we lost everything else when the boat sank last night."

I watched Haji Kembang, fascinated. He was obviously describing our shipwreck. Sculpting waves with his hands, bringing the boat crashing down onto the rocks. He could have been there.

"He says that if we tell the story to the rest of the world, then the fighting will stop. He says Australia will come and help."

Big call. For one, I was amazed that a Muslim would *want* Australia to come and help. For another, we weren't journalists. But maybe he was right. If we got out of here we could tell people what had happened. Maybe they would do something. For the first time since this had started, I thought that maybe we had a responsibility beyond ourselves.

"We'll go," I said to Mani.

Kyle nodded.

"We will all go," Mani said, making a quick decision. "Then we will keep going. I have told them that I am guiding you to the airport."

As Mani relayed our assent, Haji Kembang smiled a wide gummy smile that revealed the only three teeth he had left. He nodded firmly, then shook his head and pointed to the sky before holding up four fingers.

Mani frowned, but all he told us was, "Haji Kembang will take us himself."

It soon became apparent that he meant to take us right now. He rose from the little three-legged wooden stool he had been sitting on and motioned impatiently toward the east.

Mani thanked the rest of the elders in Indonesian, and I dipped my head respectfully before turning to follow Haji Kembang.

"He said there have been no planes flying over for four days now," Mani said. "Not even army planes."

I glanced behind me. They'd all heard. No one said anything.

I turned back around and followed Mani and Kyle up the road toward the mosque, the rest of the crew trailing behind.

Someone had sure done a number on that mosque. It would easily have been the largest building in the village, and highlighted against the night sky, the bonfire must have been quite something. I remembered the pale ferocity of the flames reaching up toward the thatch on our church roof. Five weeks' worth of work—gone in minutes. Lives worth a lot more than that—gone in less.

This mosque hadn't been thatched, and the minaret hadn't burned but had come crashing down onto the floor of the worship house and shattered. White ceramic fragments mixed with the dark piles of ash.

Two back walls were still standing, leaning precariously inward, but not much else was. I stopped in what had been the entrance and raised the camera, trying to find the best angle to record the devastation. Then, stepping carefully over the debris, Kyle and I circled around the outside of what was left of the building. I lined up a shot that framed the very top of the minaret, still pointing up toward the sky from the floor, with the two remaining walls on one side and a view of the village on the other. I was getting the hang of this photojournalism thing.

"What happened?" I asked.

"About twenty men came to the village late at night. It was burning before anyone really knew what was happening," Mani translated.

"Who were they?"

"He didn't know them. Christians, though."

"How does he know they were Christians?" Kyle asked, defensive.

"They were wearing red bandannas and yelling about how Muslim infidels had burnt down their church," Mani said.

I nodded and, stepping over broken glass, moved to the rear of the mosque and stopped.

The graveyard was full of freshly spaded earth and thirteen neat, new graves. I felt Kyle's hand on the small of my back and leaned into the comfort of his touch. I thought about how Mani had buried his parents and Budi near the church. Was there a similar-looking graveyard there?

Moving around the graves, I raised the camera, waved Kyle out of the shot, and took a picture across the cemetery with the mosque in the background.

Suppressing a shiver, I crossed to Kyle and walked back out into the sunlight from behind those two walls. Mani was with Haji Kembang in the doorway of the ruined mosque, both staring quietly into the ashy silence inside. On impulse I raised the camera and took a photo of the two of them standing side by side. The old Muslim man, cap askew, leaning heavily on his wooden cane. The young Christian, balancing his baby sister on his hip, her face buried in his neck.

The expression on each of their faces was the same. Incomprehension, fatigue, and grief so deep that it went far beyond words.

We were still at the mosque when we heard shouting from the outskirts of the village. Then the wailing started. One woman's voice climbed easily over the angry shouts of the men. It was a primal scream of anguish that came without reservation.

The back of my neck prickled, and the hair on my forearms stood straight up. Within seconds we'd subtly readjusted our little band and clustered together. There wasn't a single person who wasn't touching someone else. I was jammed between Kyle and Brendan. Drew, Elissa, and Mark were so close behind us I could feel Drew's breath tickling my ear. Mani held Tina, who had one arm wound around his neck and was firmly clutching Elissa's blonde braid with the small brown fingers of her other hand.

I glanced around, wondering whether we could melt away, slip backwards between the couple of little houses that were all that stood between us and the edge of the village, and just fade into the bush. Into the silent green solitude. Away from that screaming.

But the voices were already coming closer, and Haji Kembang, already bowed, stooped a little lower.

"They have found Daoud," Mani reported to us in a low whisper. Who was Daoud?

As they appeared, I raised the camera and took a picture. I wasn't playacting anymore. Somehow when I viewed the scene through the camera lens, neatly bounded by the square edges of the viewfinder, it didn't seem quite so immediate. I could control the placement of the two angry faces leading the little group. They were evenly spaced on either side of the long heavy bundle they carried between them. And behind that bundle I saw a woman's tearstained face framed by the dark head scarf she was wearing. Behind her, like a little green crown, the top of a palm tree. It was the tree I concentrated on as I pressed the button.

As I lowered the camera, the men laid Daoud before Haji Kembang. The woman pushed her way forward and fell to her knees, the action pinning her long dress tightly over her rounding stomach. She must have been at least six months pregnant. She reached out as if to draw back the plastic covering his face, then hesitated, hands hovering, searching for somewhere to rest. Eventually her fingertips settled gently on the shrouded shape, and she closed her eyes, mouth open, wailing.

Feeling like a voyeur, but not knowing what else to do, I took another photo. I don't know whether anyone actually heard the click of the camera amidst all the yelling and crying, or whether it was my movement, but it was at that instant that they noticed us for the first time. All except the woman. She wasn't noticing anything at that stage.

They stopped talking, literally froze midgesture. Then there was nothing but the raw pain of the woman's grief and a sickly sweet smell that seemed to coat the back of my throat with foul grease.

It was Haji Kembang who stepped into that silence. He spoke for what seemed like ages, although it couldn't have been longer than a minute.

The black anger on the faces of the men didn't abate, only now it was turned toward us. One of the men who had been carrying Daoud rested his hand on the handle of his machete. He was the one who finally interrupted Haji Kembang by spitting loudly on the ground and gesturing contemptuously in our direction.

"He says the best way to get the attention of the West is to kill the Western journalists, and they might pay some attention," Mani translated out of habit in a barely audible voice.

There wasn't a sound from any one of the six of us. Not even a whimper.

Mani's voice, however quiet, drew the attention of the crowd, and the man motioned him to come closer. He took a step forward, and Tina, in his arms, tugged hard on the braid she was still clutching. Elissa gasped and her hands shook as she worked loose Tina's grasp.

Mani's voice was steady as he moved to stand beside Haji Kembang and answered the man's questions. I couldn't understand a lot of what they were saying, but I knew enough isolated words to know when they asked him if he was a Christian. And I knew the word for yes.

I stopped breathing. There was total silence. Even the kneeling woman had stopped keening.

Mani spoke again. I only understood the words for *parents* and *Seram*.

Still no one spoke. I couldn't tear my gaze away from that one man. His eyes were glittering with a combination of pain and rage, his chest heaving and hands shaking with it.

Then several things happened at once.

Brendan stepped forward to stand beside Mani, towering over him by a full foot. The man reached for his machete and started to pull it out. The other men moved closer, some reaching for their own knives. Haji Kembang put up his hand and moved with speed I would not have thought possible to stand between us and them. And the widow of

Daoud opened her eyes and put her hand on her swelling stomach. She looked at Tina, who was half-strangling Mani, and said, *"Tidak."*

That "no" carried all the force of the rage and pain evident on her young face, swollen with crying. And it stopped them in their tracks.

Then she really let them have it. She screamed at them from her knees with utter conviction, a vein throbbing in her temple. The force of her tirade pinned every one of us in place as she pointed to Mani, to us, and down to Daoud. She glared at the ringleader, eyes blazing, until he let go of the handle of his machete; then she flicked her wrist at us with authority.

"Ayo pigi!" she said to Mani. Leave.

There were a few horrible seconds when I wondered whether my legs were going to obey my brain's command to move. Then I was backing away, eyes pinned to the tableau before us until the two remaining walls of the mosque blocked them from view, and I was free to turn and follow Mani between the houses and into the bushes.

Mani led us straight inland, barely pausing as Kyle lifted Tina from his arms and swung her round to piggyback her. We crashed through the thick brush for what seemed like hours. Thorny vines snagged my clothes and dragged at my legs. Thin trails of blood mixed with the dust and ran down my bare ankles, staining the cheap rubber flip-flops, but I couldn't feel a thing except the heat. Cut off from any ocean breeze, the thick humid air was stifling, the sunlight baking us slowly.

No one spoke.

I wondered if the others were doing what I was doing—replaying it again and again in my head. Wondering whether Haji Kembang and the young woman's words had been enough to stop them from following us. I felt my heart throb in my chest and opened and closed my fists to check that my hands still worked. This body didn't seem to belong to me.

Ahead of me, Brendan put his hand to his head and stumbled. If it had been Mark I would have been worried then. But not Brendan. He had always seemed invincible.

So I was mostly amazed when he swayed again, then collapsed to his knees and fell forward without further warning.

Get up! I willed him as I pushed forward, listening with one ear for sounds of pursuit. Drew and Mani had already rolled him over by the time I got there.

"Brendan!" Drew hissed desperately, patting his cheek.

He was breathing evenly, but the color had faded out of his face, neatly highlighting dark blue circles under his closed eyes.

"He hasn't eaten anything for more than two days," Elissa said.

Behind us I heard snatches of raised voices. My heart felt like it had suddenly ballooned to twice its normal size, and with one giant thump it pumped out a huge rush of blood. I choked on my own fear, cold metallic trickles of it sliding down my throat.

Drew heard it too. She steeled herself and slapped his face.

His eyes fluttered open.

"You have to get up," she said.

He looked at her blankly and closed his eyes again. Drew went back to pleading. Mark sat down beside her, silent, and rested a hand on Brendan's other arm.

I strained to hear past everyone's ragged breathing, listening for more voices. I couldn't hear anything, not even birds. The wet heat seemed to have smothered every living thing.

"What was she saying?" Kyle asked Mani in a low voice.

Mani shook his head, his normal vivacity dulled, his hands hanging limp.

"She said that it was enough. That we had not killed Daoud. And did they want to be responsible for the child"—he nodded toward Tina—"growing up with no one, the way their baby would now grow up without a father?"

"So who did kill him?" I asked.

"They said he was stopped near one of the villages near Ambon City by a group of men and killed. And burned," he added as an afterthought.

So that had been the smell.

Brendan's eyes opened again.

"Where are we going?" he asked.

"The airport. Ambon. Remember?" I said, looking behind us again.

"I know," he said, frustrated. "I mean, why aren't we following the coast?" He sat up slowly, some of the color back in his cheeks. Trust Brendan to wake up out of a dead faint and ask sensible questions.

"They said that this track goes to one of the Christian villages, and then back down to the coast near the airport," Mani said.

"Come on then." He scrambled to his feet as the sound of more voices reached us.

He didn't have to tell us twice.

chapter 17 ～

By the time Mani finally led us off the narrow dirt path and stopped beneath a tall palm I was long past the point where I could spare energy for worrying about phantom voices behind us.

We collapsed.

Brendan closed his eyes and fell asleep. At least that's what it looked like. It may have been a coma instead. Mark took one look at him and followed his example.

I wanted to think about what we should do next, but I was too thirsty. My mouth was sticky, and my tongue felt like a dead furry thing. I thought that once I acknowledged how thirsty I was I would be able to ignore it and think clearly, but it wasn't working. Instead my thoughts were limping around in circles.

I wonder where the village . . . Man, I'm really thirsty. Is anyone following . . . Really, *really*, thirsty. Is Mark . . . Would chewing on leaves help?

Mani stood, swaying slightly. Maybe he thought if he sat down he'd never get up again. "I will go and see the village," he said.

There was silence, and then Kyle spoke slowly from where he was leaning against the tree. "I'll come."

"No." There was no particular force behind Mani's refusal. It was just a tired statement. "It will be easier by myself."

No one even nodded. We all just stared at him until he disappeared. I summoned up the last of my energy from somewhere, crawled across to Kyle, and put my head on his leg. The last thing I felt was his hand coming to rest on my shoulder. I wanted to tell him to take it off because it was too hot.

But I fell asleep.

Waking up was a long struggle toward the light with only one thought in my mind. Water.

All the other thoughts that would normally have registered as a matter of course—that I was stiff, that my watch told me I'd slept almost two hours, and that Mani, who had just arrived back with a canvas bag slung over his shoulder, looked shattered in a way I hadn't seen since those first hours after the death of his parents—they all had to wait. I grabbed the plastic half-liter bottle Mani threw across and gulped, my hands shaking, spilling some of the precious water down my chin and my shirt in my greed.

I finished the bottle before I lowered it and looked at Mani properly. His gaze was unfocused. He tried to look at me, tried to talk. Nothing came out but a low whispered stream of Indonesian. His voice cracking, he fell silent, shook his head, and started to cry. As a steady stream of tears welled up and slipped down his cheeks, he didn't wipe them away. His dark expressive eyes were blank pools of misery.

I woke Kyle, Elissa, and Tina up, crawling over their legs to get to him. Mani didn't lean into my touch. He didn't even seem to notice I was there. He just kept rocking back and forth.

With my free hand I fished two more bottles of water out of the bag and threw them across to the others. Tina stood beside me for a minute, looking at Mani with a grave face, before tugging on my sleeve.

I let go of Mani to open a new bottle and feed her some water.

"Cori, Mani sad?" she asked me seriously after she'd drunk half the bottle.

"Yes," I told her honestly. "Mani's sad."

She pushed past me decisively and climbed into his lap, looking up into his face. Reaching up with little hands she wiped his cheeks, trying to brush away the tears.

"It will be okay," she told him carefully, using the phrase every one of us must have used on her at some time or another during the previous three weeks.

The tears didn't stop, but his eyes focused on her upturned face, and he smoothed the dark tangled hair out of her eyes.

"Terima kasih," he said, adding something else in Indonesian that I didn't understand. Leaning forward, he kissed her gently on the forehead.

She nodded and climbed off his lap, crawling into mine instead.

With a single nod at the rest of us, Mani lay down, rolled over, and fell asleep.

Kyle, Elissa, and I looked at one another wide-eyed. No one asked the question they knew the others couldn't answer, but I knew they were also wondering.

What could have made Mani so upset after everything we'd already been through?

Drew moaned in her sleep and rolled over, snuggling closer to Brendan's back. Mark didn't stir.

Tina, cuddled in my lap, seemed the most unconcerned of any of us. She looped her free arm up around my neck and took her thumb out of her mouth only long enough to issue an order. "Jip and Kiki!"

Tina loved it when we talked about Jip and Kiki. I don't know why. She couldn't have understood most of what we were saying, but she'd sit there, looking back and forth between us as we spoke, nodding when we nodded. Sometimes when the debate got particularly heated she would intervene. The first time she'd acted as judge, Drew and Mark had been arguing about whether Kiki could communicate with snakes.

"No!" Mark said firmly. "Everyone knows that monkeys can't speak snake language."

"Kiki's not just any monkey," Drew had yelled from across the campsite. "She can talk to Jip. How do you explain that? Plus she *has* to talk to the snake to convince it to let go of Jip."

"Being able to talk to Jip is because of the gift of tongues. And you only get one tongue, so she's going to have to find another way," Mark shot back.

"That's just stupid," Drew shouted, losing her temper and stamping her foot. "Why should you get to make a rule? It's *my* section of the story. And if you're going to get all legalistic, why would a monkey get the gift of tongues in the first place?"

Sitting by the fire, the rest of us had just watched. I was hoping that Mark would keep needling and needling until Drew really snapped. On the rare occasions that happened, her face would turn scarlet and you could practically see sparks come out of her ears. It was always very entertaining.

We were all surprised when Tina stood up in the middle of the show and held up her hand. "No," she said in a small, clear voice.

Drew and Mark both stopped yelling and looked at her.

She looked between them, and then nodded regally at Mark. "Mark," was all she said.

Mark threw his hands in the air in a big **V** for victory. "I win!"

Drew had spent the following half an hour trying to reason with Tina, who refused to be corrupted into changing her vote. When Tina wanted something, she knew her mind. And right now, she wanted a Jip and Kiki story.

Elissa pleated the end of her braid nervously, picking leaves out of the tangled hair. "Hmm, Jip and Kiki were . . . "

I didn't blame her. I was having a hard time thinking of a suitable story line too. Jip and Kiki were stuck. Between sinking boats, villages, and closed airports, I didn't see much hope for them.

"Once upon a time," Kyle said, "Jip and Kiki were minding their own business when Jip's dad asked him to take a message to his group of brothers, who were out on a long fishing trip to another island."

Kyle looked at me meaningfully, but for once I didn't have the foggiest idea what he was talking about.

"Um, so they got in a boat and went to deliver this message?" I offered.

"Right!" Kyle continued. "And Jip was the second youngest son and his dad's favorite, so his dad gave him this awesome fisherman's hat striped all different colors."

Elissa and I got it at the same time. Tina giggled as Kyle described the hat in great detail and topped it with a balloon dog riding proudly on the brim. I don't know whether she understood him or was just laughing at how ridiculous he looked acting it out.

"But," Elissa interjected in a somber tone, "Jip's brothers were jealous of his beautiful hat and of how much their dad loved him. So when he arrived with the message, they sank his little boat and sold him as a slave to a passing ship headed for Jakarta."

"Jip was very sad," I said. "When he got to Jakarta, he and Kiki had to work in a factory making cigarettes for two whole years. He missed his dad and the village. He worried that he was going to spend the rest of his life just making cigarettes. He wondered if God had forgotten him and Kiki."

During the next twenty minutes Jip became foreman, then owner of the factory. As soon as he was owner he closed it down, freed all the indentured servants, and dynamited it as a protest against smoking. Soon he was the country's leading antismoking crusader and shortly afterwards, the Indonesian minister of health.

"When his brothers came to see him because a strange disease was making everyone sick on their island, they didn't even recognize him," Kyle said, gazing at Tina.

I felt her grip on my arm ease. She was falling asleep.

"He could have taken revenge," I said. "Made them pay for sending him away from home as a slave and telling his dad he was dead."

"But he didn't do it," Kyle said.

"He forgave them," Elissa said.

With a little help from his mentor, Joseph, Jip came off more nobly in this particular story than was usually the case.

We fell silent. My legs and stomach were sweating where Tina's body was pressed against me, but I didn't want to put her down. It was two o'clock, and the sun was still strong. The palm we were sitting under didn't provide much protection.

"Do you reckon you could?" I asked them.

"Nope," Kyle said.

"I can't imagine my brothers and sister selling me into slavery," Elissa said, wrinkling her forehead.

"I can," I said. "I'm sure there have been times when mine would have given me away for free. But that's not the point. How do you forgive something like that and still hold on to love?"

"Those people in the village were really angry," Elissa said, her voice shaking, taking us directly to the one topic we were all thinking about anyway.

"Of course they were angry," Kyle said, grim. "Wouldn't you be if it had been one of us?"

"But . . . they were going to . . . to . . . us." She paused. "We didn't kill him. I don't understand."

I raised my eyes to meet Kyle's blue gaze. I thought I understood a little. But how does it ever stop, then?

"That woman, Daoud's wife, probably saved our lives," Elissa continued.

I think Elissa was amazed that she'd needed to.

I was just amazed that she had. If I had been her, I'm not sure I would have been in the mood to save anyone's life.

"It doesn't make any sense," Elissa said.

I tried not to roll my eyes. Almost three weeks after what had happened in Mani's village, and she was only now coming to that conclusion?

"Bet it didn't make any sense to Joseph either," Kyle said.

"And Joseph didn't have Jip and Kiki," I said, trying to cheer her up. She was sounding really rattled for the first time.

"Joseph never made it home," she pointed out in a quiet voice, arms folded.

"We'll make it home," Kyle said.

"You can't know that." Elissa flared at him, tears springing to her eyes. Then, "Sorry," she apologized immediately, clearly feeling even worse now. "It's just that you guys always seem to know what to do, and I've been trying and trying, and I just don't think I can anymore. I just want it to be over."

I was stunned. "What are you talking about? You're always the one who stays calm, no matter what's going on."

"That's not calm." She sniffed. "That's just being too scared to do anything."

"Elissa, everyone's scared." I eyed Kyle, daring him to disagree with me. He didn't even look tempted. "I'd take calm-scared over out-of-my-mind-crazy-stupid scared any day."

"She should know," Kyle said. "I think you should listen to her."

At least that brought the shadow of a watery smile to her face.

My stomach growled loudly, and I wished Mani had brought food with him. He was still fast asleep. What had he seen? All the possible answers to that just made me feel . . . more scared.

Mani was back when he woke up two hours later. He was a little like a slow-motion version of himself. He gestured as if lifting his arms was an effort. He even blinked slowly. But he was back, and he had a lot to tell us.

There hadn't been any welcoming party or spry village elders to meet him in Hanima. The village was almost deserted, the doors to some of the small houses hanging half open, the few panes of real glass in the windows of the small general store smashed. He couldn't figure out why it was so quiet, but he thought he'd grab some food and water and hightail it back to us. The store was a mess, cans knocked off their shelves, bundles of dried fish pulled down off the rafters and scattered.

My stomach growled again at this stage of the story. Even dried fish was sounding like a tasty banquet.

He was chucking bottles of water into the bag when he found the store owner huddled in a corner behind the large bin that held sago flour. It had taken half an hour of sitting on the floor beside him before he had managed to talk the old man out of his hiding place.

Soldiers, the elderly shop owner told him, trembling. Soldiers came late the night before and ordered everyone out of their homes. He'd been awake and visiting the toilet when the truck roared along the dirt road and into the small village. He'd seen them pull up right in front of the door to his house before he'd slipped in the back door of the store and hidden behind the bin.

After that he hadn't seen much, Mani said, but crouched in the dark by himself he'd heard the thumps of the soldiers on the doors, loud laughing, and the orders for everyone to assemble in the church. Then screams, running feet, shots, more screams, drunken laughter. It went on for a long time, he said. The old man was convinced that the soldiers hadn't left and were waiting for him to come out.

"So what happened after that?" Brendan asked, when Mani paused and seemed to lose his train of thought.

"We went to the church," he said slowly. "And they were dead."

We sat still until Mani roused himself and continued.

"The old man said that a lot must have escaped in the dark. They must have tried to set fire to the church afterwards, but it didn't burn too well. Tin roof."

"How many?" Kyle asked in a low voice.

"Maybe thirty." Mani's voice cracked. "The shopkeeper's wife was there." He dropped his head into his hands and stared at the dirt.

"Soldiers?" Drew spoke for the first time since that morning. "Army soldiers?"

Mani nodded without looking up. "Probably. Or maybe members of a Muslim group like the Lasker Jihad, in army uniforms."

"But I thought that the army was supposed to be stopping the fighting. Isn't that what martial law is all about?" Drew sounded totally bewildered, and I didn't blame her.

From what we'd managed to piece together, it had all started over a simple argument. Now the Muslim gangs were killing the Christians. The Christian gangs were killing the Muslims. The army was killing the Christians. The militant Muslim forces were killing the Christians. It was getting very hard to keep track, but one thing was sure: The Christians seemed to be on the losing end of this equation a lot.

"Well, what are we going to do?" Brendan asked, sounding like he was talking mostly to himself.

"I don't know," Mani answered, not even looking at him. "I don't know." His voice was hollow, and he sounded completely hopeless.

Drew and Elissa looked at me, wide-eyed. We'd never seen him like that, not even in the first hours after leaving his village.

"I guess we head for the airport," Brendan said.

"The army is at the airport," Mani reminded him.

"The army can't all be bad," Drew said.

"No," Mani said flatly.

"You want to take that risk?" Kyle asked her.

I didn't know what to think anymore. Surely our parents had been pestering the Indonesian government to find out where we were. We had our passports. And when it came right down to it, we had our white skin, which would probably still count for something, even though it shouldn't. But Mani and Tina didn't have any of that. No passports. No identity documents. No white skin. No foreign family. What would the soldiers do with them?

"No," I said. "There has to be another way."

"What? Swim?" Elissa sounded like she was trying hard not to panic.

"Maybe Tinker Bell's going to save us?" Drew wasn't even trying not to panic.

Brendan put a hand on her arm. but she shook him off.

"What?" she asked him, her hands balled into fists. "Maybe Jip and Kiki can make water skis out of coconut leaves, and we can all ski out of here behind their jet skis."

"What about a boat?" Mark suggested suddenly.

"Yeah, sure. Good one. And I guess you're going to sail us single-handedly to Darwin in a dinghy?" I snapped.

He answered me more patiently than I deserved. "No. A proper ship. Won't there be other people wanting to get out? With the airport closed, how else are they going to do it?"

I felt like an idiot. We'd completely overlooked the obvious. I guess we'd just been so focused on the airport this whole time we hadn't thought of the fact that Ambon was a sizeable port. There were bound to be boats bigger than fishing dinghies.

"A refugee ship," Kyle said, eyes gleaming.

Brendan groaned.

Mani looked up, some signs of life flickering in his brown eyes for the first time that afternoon. "There are docks near the airport. You could get on one of those boats. We will go around the village and go there."

I hadn't realized how angry I was until I started to speak. "We can't just go around the village!"

They all stopped and stared at me.

I held up the camera, which was looped around my wrist. "The *army* did that. No army should ever be allowed to do that. We're going to get out of here. People are going to pay attention. We need proof."

"Are you insane?" Drew asked. "The whole world is going crazy, and you want to go and take photos of more dead people in a church?"

"Maybe Haji Kembang was right," I said. "Maybe something we say can convince people to come in here and help."

"Help like the army is supposed to be helping?" That was Kyle being cynical.

"I'm not going anywhere near that village," Drew said wildly.

Elissa nodded.

I didn't even know why I was arguing for this. I didn't want to go into the village either. Just the thought made my stomach turn over and fresh sweat bead my forehead. I could almost hear the angry voices that the old shopkeeper must have heard, huddled in the dark, afraid for his life. But I felt surer about this than I had of anything since this whole turned-upside-down mess had started.

I could tell by the look on Brendan's face he was on Drew and Elissa's side, so I preempted him. "And we need food."

"We don't need food that badly," Drew said.

"Brendan does. He hasn't eaten anything in two days, and the rest of us do too. It could take us days to get to the port."

It was an unlikely dual-purpose mission. Go see a massacre in a

church and pick up some dinner while we were at it. I wasn't even hungry anymore, but it was a good enough argument to make Brendan nod
his head reluctantly.

"No!" Drew wailed.

"You don't have to come," I said. "I'll just go with Mani."

"And me," Kyle said.

"And me," Mark parroted.

Hmmm. We'd have to see about that one.

"It's not that." Drew started to cry. "What if something happens
to you?"

"We'll be fine," I said. "Mani said the village was practically
deserted."

"Come on then," Kyle said, standing up. "In and out in an hour.
Then we head for the docks."

The sun was setting as we reached Hanima. We'd parked the others ten minutes back down the track, and I'd unwound Drew's arms
from around my neck and left her practically hysterical with Brendan.

Now that the sudden surge of anger that had fueled this whole
plan had cooled, I had to admit that it seemed a lot more stupid. And
thoughtless. I hadn't even asked Mani whether he'd be willing to take
us back into the village. At the front of our small group he was moving
like a sleepwalker. I'm not sure he would have noticed if he'd led us
right into an army patrol.

Kyle would have noticed, though. He was wound up, crackling
with energy.

"So we get in there. Take photos. Grab food and head out, right?"
he kept repeating under his breath. Then came the litany of questions

I couldn't answer and didn't have the energy to think about. "How will we find a refugee ship? Will they take us on board? Where will the ships be heading? How can we get word home?"

I let them wash over me. He was talking more to himself than me anyway, thinking three steps ahead and turning the details over in his mind.

I was having trouble thinking one step ahead, much less three. My imagination kept taking me into the small store, like the one in Mani's village, and plonking me down right beside that shopkeeper in the pungent darkness. I could practically smell the dried fish. My stomach rumbled again, loudly. I was appalled at myself. Violent death and food didn't go together in any world I knew. Then again, the world I knew had changed a lot in the previous three weeks.

"Can you keep it down up there?" Mark hissed from behind me.

I ignored him. I hadn't wanted Mark to come. Telling him that in a reasonable voice should have been enough, but it wasn't. He'd simply replied that I wasn't his mother. In response to that, I'd thanked my lucky stars. Things had gone downhill from there.

"Why do you always have to be so bossy? And who appointed you queen of decision making anyway?"

I almost sank to his level and told him Jip had. But then I decided to be mature and call him a little brat instead. That eloquent comeback was spoiled a bit by my turning around to storm off, only to walk straight into the trunk of the tree behind me. Thankfully Mark had the sense not to laugh, or I would have belted him.

"Fine," I said, nursing my abused nose. "Come then. But don't expect us to hold your hand."

"Oh, Cori," Elissa said.

She didn't have to say any more than that. I knew what she meant.

We needed one another more than ever. But I was just so tired. And worried. This was my idea, and if something went wrong because I'd made us go back into the village, it was going to be my responsibility—whether I'd wanted him to come or not.

Mani raised his hand, and we paused, listening. It was quiet except for the harsh sound of our panting. Way quieter than a village should have been.

"You sure you want to do this?" he asked us.

I nodded, my mouth suddenly too dry to talk. I wanted to scream no, run back down the track, and tell Drew she'd been right. Leave this place and forget about soldiers and guns and churches.

"Okay then." Mani seemed to reach down deep inside himself. "We'll go straight through the village to the church first, get food on the way out."

Then he was moving, stepping out from the screen of the palms into the bright light of the setting sun before I was ready for him to go, and I gasped, wondering whether I was going to be able to get my legs to move.

Kyle heard me and turned his head sharply. "You okay?"

I nodded.

"Hey." He curled a hand around the back of my neck and squeezed. "I think you're right."

It was those four words that got me moving. That, and the fact that I couldn't bear to let Mark see me freeze now, after the way I'd acted.

Stepping silently, we followed Mani between two small shacks and found ourselves on the wider central road. Just wide enough for a small truck. I looked down the road, and there they were, about twenty feet away—the clear marks of heavier tires in the dust. Mani had been right. Windows were broken, bottles had been smashed against the walls of houses, and glass glittered in the street. Some of the doors had holes through them, low, as if they'd been kicked hard.

I fumbled with the camera.

Click.

"Wait," Kyle said, as Mani was about to walk on. "If we're trying to make a record of this, shouldn't we take a picture of those?" He indicated the almost perfectly preserved tire tracks.

The truck had obviously driven in, stopped, and then backed out again at a slightly different angle. There was no space to turn around.

"Who else but the army would drive a big truck in here?"

Click.

It didn't take us long to find the church.

There were people there. I was stunned. It was so quiet I'd thought that they must all be in hiding. Or dead. But there were eleven villagers in the square in front of the church. An older woman sat with two small children by the pump. Three teenage girls and two boys stood across from the church entrance, their arms linked. Two men and a woman stood in the doorway of the church. The woman sagged into the embrace of one of the men, not even lifting her head as we arrived. An old man with impossibly white hair and an equally white goatee sat on the ground with his back leaning against the church wall. The old shopkeeper, I guessed.

The woman may not have noticed our arrival, but the others sure did. The teenagers circled closer and backed away. The woman by the pump lumbered to her feet, children grasping at her skirt. The men in the doorway whirled, their hands going to their waists. I don't know what they might have done if Mani hadn't greeted the shopkeeper in a low voice. It seemed to take an eternity for the old man's gaze to focus on him, and his nod of recognition was slow in coming.

Mani crossed over to the men in the doorway, and I let my breath out.

"For a second there I thought we were toast in a Christian village," Kyle said.

I tried to imagine a distraught Drew trying to explain that one to my parents. Somehow I didn't think they would have appreciated the irony.

"Okay," Mani reported back. "They say we can take photographs and look. They don't know much more. Just that it was army soldiers. They escaped and hid until just now."

"Here." I shoved the small notebook into Kyle's hands. "Ask questions."

"What can you ask people who've just found out half their village has been killed?" Kyle asked me. "How do you feel?"

He had a point.

"Go." Mani gave me a gentle nudge. "I have told them that you are taking photos and will tell their story to try and get justice for them."

I counted my steps as I approached the door of the church.

Ten.

It was symbolic.

I grew up ten years as I stepped through that doorway. Or maybe a hundred years. Or a thousand.

The smell wasn't strong, but it still made me gag and breathe through my mouth. Just the faint scent of something rotten, but slightly sweet. I guessed the sunlight, falling in long gentle bars through the empty windows that fronted the building, had done that.

There was a small girl, maybe seven years old, sitting just inside the door beside the body of a woman. She had the woman's hand in her lap and was stroking it slowly, over and over again. She looked up at me as I entered, but I don't think she saw me. She looked right through me. She wasn't crying. Maybe it would have seemed less terrible if she had been. The silent weight of the shock and grief I saw in her face pulled me to the edge of the abyss I was suddenly terrified was there. Inside me.

For a second I swayed there. Then I raised the camera and took her photo.

Later that would turn out to be the only photo inside the church that I actually remember taking. The girl's small face is looking up at the camera, holding her mother's hand, which was miraculously free of the blood and gore that seemed to have bloomed from the woman's chest and touched everything else inside that building.

I can still look at that photo and bring that little girl back. The way her dress had been neatly patched, perhaps by the very hand she now held. How a long lock of black shiny hair fell forward across her face, half covering one of her eyes. The way her small lips parted, as if she wanted to speak, and then closed again.

I can see her mother too. See what she looked like sprawled awkwardly on her back in a parody of sleep, her expression blank, as if mildly surprised at the damage the bullets had done to her chest. But I still can't see the twenty-one others who were in the church that night. I know they were there. I photographed them all. But the pictures could have been taken by somebody else.

Later, all I would remember were the abstract shapes made by the jumble of limbs lit orange by the last of the setting sun, the feel of the blood still sticky against my feet as I walked among the dead, and the silent presence of the young girl keeping me, and her mother, company.

chapter 18 ~

I don't remember much about the rest of that night. Kyle told me later that when I didn't come out of the church, he came in to fetch me. Apparently I was just standing there, the film all used up. I do remember the warmth of his hand and turning to follow his voice. I tripped on a woman's arm, and I felt so bad about that, even though logically I knew she was dead. I have a distinct memory of apologizing, but Kyle says I didn't say anything.

In fact, I didn't speak for hours. Everything got jumbled. I saw or heard something, like Mark holding my hand and rubbing it, his lips moving but no sound coming out. Then the kaleidoscope twisted half an inch; all the tiny crystals that made up my world reassembled themselves silently and smoothly, and next thing I knew the scene had changed and Drew's arms were around my neck. She was crying. Again.

Fragments of conversation came out of the darkness.

"It was soldiers. They're sure it was the army."

"Yeah, she did. A whole roll. Thirty-six photos."

"Three days to get to the port."

"We'll have to move at night."

"We'll rest a couple of hours, then move out. There probably won't be any patrols out by then," Brendan said.

No one pointed out that there had been patrols out late last night.

Last night. I could not believe that it had only been twelve hours since we washed ashore.

"Open," Kyle said to me.

I felt something pressed against my lips and opened. Tasteless. But I swallowed anyway.

"Come on, Cori. Focus!" That was Kyle again, and he sounded angry.

I wondered vaguely whether I was supposed to care.

Then we were walking through the darkness, my fingers grasping the back of Kyle's shirt, my mind drifting. As if I were looking backwards through a long dark tunnel, I saw the thin thread of decisions that had led me from there to here. I could even hear ice rattling against my bedroom window, the way it had the night I'd first found the brochure. I knew I'd been torn up about Scott, but I couldn't really remember what that felt like. It didn't seem to matter anymore.

Say no, I willed Mum and Dad as I saw us discussing it over the kitchen table and chocolate cake. But they had nodded.

Pick a different team, I told myself. But I had sealed the envelope and dropped it into the mailbox.

I tasted my tears from that first night at boot camp. Quit, I thought. Quit now. Tell them you made a mistake and that you want out. But I had gritted my teeth.

I could hardly remember what had been so tough about boot camp. It hadn't even included any near-drowning experiences or animal attacks. When we got back, we would have to help them redesign the obstacle course. There should be a bush-pig barricade on the track between Mount Sinai and the last wall. That place was perfect for surprise attacks.

What else? The obstacle course referees should have the power to point to any team member at any time and cry "Malaria meltdown!" Then the other team members would have to carry them the rest of the way.

I giggled out loud at the thought of the five of us trying to get Brendan over the wall.

"Enjoying yourself?" Kyle whispered as if from a long way away. I felt him duck and followed automatically.

One thing we did do enough of at boot camp, though—memorizing Bible verses. I remembered the first one on the list.

Be strong and of a good courage; be not afraid, neither be thou dismayed: for the Lord thy God is with thee whithersoever thou goest. Joshua 1:9

Whithersoever. That had to be the coolest word in the English language. Score one for the King James translation.

"Be not afraid," I repeated, surprised to discover that I wasn't afraid for the first time in ages. With the click of the camera when I took that little girl's picture, I had simply ceased to be afraid. My thoughts shied away from the church, and the kaleidoscope spun again.

It was like my own private slide show. Stumbling along behind Kyle, my legs moving automatically, I saw the others as I'd gotten to know them during the last two months.

Brendan at boot camp, perched on a log and grinning up at Drew and Kyle. We had just been assigned to dig a ditch as punishment for something one of the other teams had done. The rest of us had been hopping mad, even Elissa, but Brendan just grinned and shrugged philosophically.

"What's the big deal?" he'd asked. "We just have to do it and get it over with."

"But it's not *fair*," I said.

"No," he agreed. "But stewing about it for the whole hour isn't going to make it any better."

Mani, biting his lip as he looked at some of our handiwork on the church roof or watched us try to work the fishing nets. Poor Mani—he always seemed to get stuck wondering how to tell us we'd done a rotten job without hurting our feelings.

Elissa, sitting cross-legged, giving Drew and me "the look" the time we said that Jip felt called to write a new book for the Old Testament called Hezekiah.

"What will be in this book?" Elissa asked, suspicious.

"The usual Old Testament stuff," Drew said, winking. "Violence and sex."

"And Kiki worship," I added while Elissa was still in the silent stages of being appalled.

Mark, the morning he whacked me on the head with his Bible, exhorting me to "feel the love of Jesus." Vehement protestations that he was worshiping hadn't saved him from, yet again, getting in trouble with Gary.

Kyle . . . Kyle could make me madder than almost anyone else in the world. But it was Kyle I wanted to tell first when I found the turtle tracks down on the beach, Kyle I wanted to be near when I felt overwhelmed,

Kyle whose hugs made everything feel a bit better no matter how bad the situation really was. Kyle whose passion for knowing God better had inspired me so much at the start of this trip. Kyle I loved.

I don't know whether it was the shock of thinking that last word, or the sudden pain of a palm frond sliding past Kyle's shoulder and smacking into my face, but as reflex tears filled my eyes, the kaleidoscope settled firmly into place and images stopped dancing past me.

Feeling like I had some sort of control over my thoughts again was nice. Feeling scared again was not so nice. Because the instant I started caring again, the fear was back—coiling low in my stomach like a heavy weight, the weight of knowing that all the questions nagging at me had to be answered, and that there was no one around to do that but us.

We were walking single file down a narrow path. It was very dark, and the bush was quiet around us. Very quiet. I could hear Mark breathing behind me in quick shallow gasps, but I couldn't hear the sound of water, so we weren't back near the coast yet. I couldn't see my watch, but the moon wasn't overhead anymore, so it must have been sometime after midnight. My legs were burning, and my feet hurt.

The second I thought about my feet, they became all I could think about—how nice it would be to sit down, dangle them in cool running water, massage scented moisturizing cream into the bruises.

I tried to recapture that easy state where my mind drifted free while my body did all the work, but it was no use. My mind was firmly anchored back in my body and bent on paying attention to every ache and pain. And there were a lot of those.

Kyle stumbled in front of me and cursed. "Watch that root," he hissed.

Kyle. With one hand still twisted into the back of his shirt, I reached up with the other and fingered the ring, wondering what Scott was doing at that moment, whether he was thinking of me. The links slipped through my fingers, oily and smooth, and touching them brought him a little closer. His crooked smile appeared as if through a pane of thick glass. I tried to reach out for him, to pull the image closer, scanning for that familiar tug on my heart that was always part of thinking about him.

It didn't come.

I wondered when the wall had gone up. When had I stopped conjuring up his face to help me through the rough spots, and reached out for Kyle instead?

It was still dark when Mani stopped, made us backtrack several meters, and then let us sit down. We all collapsed onto the track. Actually, I don't know if you could call it a track anymore. Somewhere along the way we'd stumbled onto a dirt road big enough for a small car.

Ahead of me I could hear Drew panting in little hiccups, and Mark's breathing had become steadily more ragged. I didn't have much energy to spare for worrying about them, though; I was beat. I sat cross-legged, trying to stretch out my thigh muscles as I leaned forward to rest my forehead on Kyle's back.

We were about thirty feet from the main road that curved around this side of the bay, and about two miles from the airport, Mani said. Halfway between here and the airport we should find a smaller road that branched off up into the hills, and then wound down again to the main port area. That was where we were headed.

"Unless we've changed our minds and want to take the chance and go to the airport," Brendan said.

I touched the camera I'd fastened securely to one of the belt loops on my pants, and Kyle, Mark, and I spoke in unison.

"No!"

"But I'm sure they wouldn't hurt *us*," Elissa said. "We're all exhausted. What if Mark gets sick again?"

"I don't care," Mark said. "You can go if you want. I'm not going near the army."

"That's not what I meant," Elissa said. "I would never go without you guys."

"Well, we're not going," I said flatly. So much for consensus decision making and listening to everyone's opinion, but on this issue I just couldn't bend. The thought of facing soldiers armed with the type of weapons that had been used in that church made the drawstring around my throat pull tight.

"Fine," Elissa said, sounding defeated.

"How about we pray?" Brendan said.

"Yeah," Drew said.

"Fine, I will," Brendan said, after a silence that no one else volunteered to fill.

"We walk one more hour, maybe two," Mani said after Brendan was done. "Then rest. If we stop now we will not be able to cross the big road during the day. It will be busy."

There was silence. One more hour! I didn't think I could get up, much less walk one more hour. In that dark void before dawn, surprisingly, it was Mark who took the lead. I don't know where he found the energy, but it was truly heroic.

"Come on, you bunch of . . . what did you call us the other day, Cori? Kangaroos?"

"Jackaroos," I muttered, thinking of Dad. That's what he always called us. Man, I wanted my dad.

"Let's make like jackaroos and hop on out of here."

"Mark, that was really bad," Drew said, sounding like she was on the verge of tears again.

But it got us moving.

We'd thought carefully through all the options, we'd made a decision, we'd prayed, and we were thinking only of getting through another torturous hour so we could collapse and sleep. That's why it was such a shock when we were caught.

The big road Mani led us out onto was paved. It wound along the ocean, but it wasn't exactly hugged by a gentle sandy beach that stretched down to the water. The right side of the road dropped off sharply in a jumble of rocks and shale. At the bottom, about seven feet down, hungry little waves surged against the rocks. The noise they made drowned out all the other familiar sounds of night.

On the other side of the road, thick bushes choked every available inch of space between the palm trees. Together they formed a textured black wall.

The road, curiously flat beneath feet that hadn't touched tarmac for almost two months, was the only way forward. And we took it. Trudging wearily, heads down, not noticing the wild lonely beauty that surrounded us. Not even noticing the low rumble of an engine until it was too late.

We had about five seconds between when the truck first appeared around the sharp bend only a hundred feet down the road and when those impossibly bright headlights swung around to focus straight down the stretch onto us.

We all froze except for Kyle.

"Run!" he screamed, tearing his hand out of my grasp and leaping forward.

I just stared down the road, stupefied by the sight of those twin beacons turning inexorably toward us. Now I understand what happens to rabbits and kangaroos caught unawares.

"Go. Go!" Kyle's voice reached me again from out of the haze, and this time it shocked me into action.

We might have all made it into the bushes without being seen in those few seconds we had left if it hadn't been for me.

I ran the wrong way.

And Mark and Elissa followed me.

Kyle had been holding my right hand, and now I turned toward where he'd been and ran. I was so charged up I would probably have run right off the road and ended up on the rocks below if someone hadn't grabbed my shirt from behind and yanked me back, steering us toward the other side of the road just as the headlights settled on us. That was a weightless white blow that blinded me completely.

I put my head down and bolted, but we were only halfway across the lonely stretch of open tarmac when I heard startled shouts from the truck, much closer now, and the squeal of brakes.

I had the sense to put my arms up as I crashed into the bushes, finding time to be thankful I hadn't run full tilt into a tree.

But that thought, along with most others, was wiped from my mind by the unmistakable sound of gunfire, unbelievably loud. Two shots.

Behind me, Elissa started screaming and didn't stop.

I would like to say that I went back immediately, but I actually took three more steps forward, still blinded, fighting the creepers that were clutching me in the dark, wanting nothing more than to get farther into the bush and hide until it was all over.

"Stop! Don't shoot!" Mark called out desperately.

Whoever had the gun obviously didn't take much notice of him, because I heard a third shot. Finally I stopped, turned around, and went back just as fast. I didn't know what I was going to do when I got there, but I did know that if I didn't get there before I let myself think about it I would freeze, safe in the darkness, but safe by myself.

I burst back out onto the road into the light.

Mark and Elissa were facing me, lit up brilliantly. Both of them had their hands up. Elissa's arms were moving so much with the force of her screaming she looked like she was waving.

Another shot went off and Elissa stopped screaming, just like that. The sudden silence was almost scarier. She was still standing, though, so she hadn't been shot. Since I hadn't felt a bullet hit me in the back, I figured I hadn't been either. That realization didn't make me feel much better.

I put my hands up slowly and turned around, squinting. I couldn't see anything and my ears were ringing, but I could still hear enough to know that there were men yelling at us from that truck, and they didn't sound happy.

I backed up slowly so I was standing beside the others as shadowy figures carrying big guns started to appear around the edges of the light. Their guns were pointed at us.

I glanced toward the bushes lining the side of the road and then forced myself to look away. Where were the others? I didn't have the nobility to be thankful that they'd gotten away; I just wanted them close by.

The voices were getting more strident; the men were motioning with the rifles. I was having a hard time looking anywhere but at all those gun barrels waving around.

"I think they want us to kneel down," Mark muttered.

Bits of tarmac poked hard into my knees as I knelt. God, I don't want to be shot! I knew exactly what that would look like. And we must have made such perfect targets.

I opened my mouth and tried to speak. It was so dry I had to lick my lips and try again.

"*Kami tidak bisa berbicara Bahasa Indonesia.*" We don't speak Indonesian.

There was a low buzz; then one of the men stepped forward. I couldn't see him very well; his back was to the light. But he was dressed in an army uniform, and his tone was commanding. "Where other people?"

I didn't know how to answer that question, so I decided not to. "Are you going to shoot us?" I asked, trying to sound casual and failing miserably.

Head Honcho threw back his head and laughed, repeating something in Indonesian to the men behind him. They all started to chuckle.

"No," he said, when he'd laughed enough.

"Then why were you shooting at us?" I yelled, losing my temper. For a moment I had been sure we were going to die, and the laughter just undid me completely.

"I heard it," Elissa whispered, through white lips. "That first shot. I heard it go right past my head. I heard it."

Head Honcho waved his hand, nonchalant.

"Oh, accident. You should not run away, you see. We think you naughty people. You break curfew. What you do here?" He looked completely mystified—and why not, when three white faces suddenly appeared on the road in front of him in the middle of the night.

We looked at one another. Since they said they weren't going to shoot us, I guessed we may as well tell the truth. I didn't think these guys were going to believe we were journalists.

"We were camping on Seram," I said finally.

"What for, camping?" he asked.

I sighed.

"Building a church on a mission trip," Mark said.

Great. Now the cat was really out of the bag. I hoped they meant it when they said they weren't going to shoot us.

Comprehension dawned, and he turned back to the men behind him and spoke rapidly. When he faced us again he was flushed and excited.

"How many you are?" He held up six fingers. "This many? From the United States?"

I nodded slowly.

An excited clatter of voices broke out behind him, and I saw at least three gun barrels go down.

"Where other people?" he asked again.

"Here," Kyle's voice answered from the right. "Don't shoot. We're coming out."

"No shoot!" the man promised, doing a little jig.

Kyle's head poked from between two leaves, and then the rest of his body materialized into the light, just like the Cheshire cat. The others followed him, Drew, Brendan, and Mani, carrying Tina.

The soldiers were very excited. There was lots of chatter that I didn't understand, and big grins all around.

The eight of us huddled in a little group, still lit up by the head-lights, shivering with shock and cold as the sweat started to dry. The sky to the east was starting to lighten, and a cool breeze was coming in off the water. We were all talking at the same time.

"I was yelling *run* and you all just stood there!"

"I thought you were right behind me, but when the shooting started I looked back and there was no one!"

"I couldn't see anything!"

"Me either."

Of all of us, Elissa was the most upset. "I heard it," she kept repeating, touching her left ear. "That bullet. It went right past my head. Right here."

"I'm sorry," I said miserably.

"Yeah, that was really dumb," Kyle said. "What did you think you were proving?"

"I got confused."

"You got confused, and so you just happened to run back out onto the road right in front of people with guns?"

"What?" Brendan asked.

"You ran right past me, back out onto the road. I thought they were going to shoot you," Kyle said to me.

"So did I," I said, then realized that made no sense at all. "I had to," I tried to explain my apology again. "It was my fault we went the wrong way."

"Yeah. Thanks a lot! And then you—" Mark said, glancing at Elissa. "She just stopped. I ran right into her back. Then it was too late."

Elissa grabbed my hand. "I was glad to see you."

"Next time, don't yell at the men with guns," Mark advised.

Kyle groaned again. "You guys wouldn't last a day living on the streets."

"Hey," Drew said, holding up her hand and looking confused.

We all paused.

"It's okay. I think we're safe."

Wow. I'd been so busy worrying about the fact we'd been caught I hadn't realized what that meant. Between one breath and the next, as I eyed the brightening strip that heralded the rising sun, the pressure dissolved. I wouldn't have been surprised to look down and find my feet hovering gently above the tarmac. I could feel every part of my body, even the brush of my eyelashes against my cheek as I blinked. Nothing hurt.

The next breath of that cool salty air was an act of worship.

Of course, it was Kyle and his overactive imagination who wrecked it. I think he'd watched too many war movies.

"Or we're prisoners of war," he said.

My feet hit the tarmac again with a painful thump. The left side of my face throbbed. My arms stung where I'd just picked up a new collection of scratches.

"No." Mani, who'd been keeping half an ear out for what the soldiers were saying, shook his head.

Head Honcho left the rest of the men and sauntered over, relaxed now, rifle down. We eyed him warily.

"You been missing long time," he told us, as if we didn't know. "Your family very worried. Army tell us to see for you."

I think we all let out the breath we'd been holding. So it was true. Drew's eyes gleamed. Brendan proved that his arms were long enough to hug Drew and Tina at the same time. Standing a little apart from the rest of us, Mani wilted, like a potted plant that's gone too long without water. Elissa sat down hard, as if her legs had been knocked out from underneath her. Kyle let out a whoop and high-fived Mark, then grabbed me and danced me around in a clumsy circle.

I cried.

I cried harder than I ever remember crying before in my life. The kind of out-of-control crying that grabs you by the throat and leaves you choking and gasping for air.

When I was fourteen we spent Christmas in Australia. At the beach early Christmas morning I stripped down to my swimming cozzie and ran headlong into the ocean. But a storm the night before had undercut the coastline I thought I knew well, and I was quickly in over my head, caught halfway between the solid sand and the relative safety of the open water out past the breakers. Panicking, and forgetting to dive down to the bottom and hold on to the sand to avoid the force of the waves, I got absolutely pounded. Bouncing off the sand and tumbling in the backwash, arms and legs whirling, not knowing which way was up and which down, ears and lungs creaking under the strain, seeing nothing but a cloud of white water, and feeling the bubbles fizz past my face.

That's how it was that morning as the first rays of the sun peeped over the horizon. Caught in the grip of some violent feeling I couldn't even identify, I was helpless to stem the storm of tears.

Then it just stopped.

And I haven't cried since.

chapter 19 ~

I have to say they treated us well. Very professionally. To fit us in the back of the truck three of the soldiers had to walk, and they stood there smiling as we climbed aboard and waved us off like long-lost friends.

We were quiet during the truck ride. I was pressed so close between Drew and Kyle that I couldn't tell where their body heat ended and mine began. That was the only familiar thing I had to hold on to. Everything else—the cool hard touch of metal against the back of my legs, the surge of power beneath us as the truck accelerated, the cloying stink of diesel fuel, the excited curiosity of strangers—it wasn't just the language they were speaking that was foreign.

I hadn't yet started to think about home. It was still too far away, and the thought of its clean serenity felt just as foreign. Almost against my will I did start to think about my parents, though. Maybe, just maybe, they were close by.

It didn't take long for us to get to the airport. After that, things seemed to happen very fast.

The large hall that Head Honcho ushered us into was empty except for a long line of soldiers who swung toward us as we entered, handling their rifles far too casually. I couldn't help but wonder whether any of them had been in that church—whether one of the clean-shaven, youthful, neatly uniformed soldiers had looked into the face of that young girl's mother and pulled the trigger.

The church.

I felt for the camera.

It was still there, dangling from my belt loop.

I unhooked it and tucked it into my pocket.

The man hurrying across the room toward us was older than most of the soldiers standing around taking in the show. His uniform was spotless, buttons polished, and crisp hat perched jauntily on his head.

Everyone except Kyle was doing what I was doing, nervously smoothing down T-shirts and hair. I wished I could do something to hide the big rip over my left knee. It was only then that I noticed how grimy my fingernails were. Black half-moons accused me. I folded them into my palms.

"*Selamat datang*, welcome," the suave soldier said, waving his hand expansively. He spoke much better English than Head Honcho. "You must be tired, yes? Can we get you some tea?"

Drew's sudden snort sounded very loud.

"Yes, please," Brendan answered, sounding very grown-up.

"And we would like to phone our families as soon as possible.

Please," I added. The instant we stepped into the hall it had suddenly seemed unbearable to go one more minute without hearing their voices.

"Oh!" Elissa gasped, grabbing my arm.

Mr. Suave ignored me and directed his comments toward Brendan, who towered over him by at least six inches.

"Yes. Yes. Tea first. Then we will talk."

"But we have to call our families now. They must be wondering whether we're even alive," Drew said.

Mr. Suave's smile didn't falter, but tiny creases at the corners of his eyes deepened. "We have already passed the news of your rescue on to Jakarta," he said dismissively, eyes still upon Brendan.

Rescue! I seethed.

"While they were busy 'rescuing' us, your soldiers shot at us. We could have been killed," I said loudly.

That got his attention. The flat gaze he turned upon me was not exactly unfriendly, just hard.

I squirmed.

"That would have been unfortunate. However, they did not know who you were, and you were breaking curfew and running away," he said. "They were forced to fire friendly warning shots over your heads."

I glanced at Elissa. Her face was white, her lips pressed together. She shook her head.

Kyle pinched me hard, and I shut up.

So we drank the tea in big tin mugs that Head Honcho personally carried over to us on a tray. He beamed at us proudly as we sipped the sweet brew. I was actually sad when he disappeared back out the door we had come in.

We sat at a rickety table in the middle of that cavernous room and listened as the major interrogated Brendan about everything that had happened to us since we had fled into the jungle on that hot bloody Saturday afternoon, three weeks and a lifetime ago.

Mani offered to translate, but Mr. Suave paid no more attention to him than he had to us girls. He seemed eager to show off his English, and I had to admit it was excellent. Almost as good as Mani's.

The bit about Kyle and the bush pig excited the first show of genuine curiosity from him. He made Kyle pull up his shirt and examined the bruises on his back. The one over his ribs was as big as my fist, livid and purple. The soldiers lining the walls murmured.

"You are very lucky boy," he announced.

"God may have had something to do with it," Kyle said.

I almost fell off my chair. If you ask me, that statement was almost a bigger miracle than the tusk hitting the Bible.

Mr. Suave raised one eyebrow and went back to taking careful notes. When Brendan talked about the boat sinking, he snapped his fingers and issued a crisp order. A map arrived and was unfurled with great ceremony.

"Where?" he demanded.

We all stared at it blankly. Those clean black lines on fresh white paper didn't seem to have anything to do with the terror of waves that had pounced upon us from out of nowhere, with that warm dark swim against fear and exhaustion.

"About there," Kyle estimated.

Mani nodded.

Something changed. It wasn't obvious, but Mr. Suave's shoulders tightened. His lids dropped lower, hooding his eyes.

"Where did you go then?"

I could tell from Kyle's quick glance that he noticed it too.

Brendan named the Muslim village and described what we'd seen.

"What next?"

Don't tell him, I willed Brendan, staring at the tabletop and not trusting myself to look at him. It was a cheap, white plastic veneer. One corner was chipped off, exposing a dark pulpy underside. I was no longer scared for our lives, but if it *had* been soldiers in Hanima, I couldn't imagine the army would be too pleased with the knowledge that we had been there.

I needn't have worried. Brendan skipped smoothly over our detour and went straight to our encounter on the road. I looked up.

Mr. Suave didn't let it go.

"You didn't see Tehani village?" he asked casually.

"No," Brendan answered calmly.

"What about Hanima?"

At that name my heart migrated upward and settled, fluttering, somewhere near my voice box.

Brendan didn't waver for an instant. "I did not see any other villages at all," he answered truthfully.

Kyle, Mark, and I didn't make a peep.

"Why did you run away from the soldiers?" Mr. Suave demanded.

"We didn't know who you were," Brendan said. "And we didn't know who we could trust."

Mr. Suave relaxed and leaned back in his chair. "Well," he said, his smile back in place. "It is lucky we found you, yes? We have been watching for you for two weeks, but it has been hard with everything going on, you see?"

We didn't see, not really. It wasn't until later that we would realize the lethal extent of the man-made chaos that had engulfed Ambon and spread to Seram and surrounding islands.

"What will happen now?" Brendan asked.

"There is a military plane leaving this morning, soon. It has been waiting for you. You will go on that to Jakarta. We have contacted your embassy. They are very happy to hear of your safety."

There was a collective gasp from the six of us.

"Just like that?" Kyle asked.

Mr. Suave looked puzzled. "Did you think we would make you swim?" He laughed heartily at his own joke, slapping the table. "No, I think you have done very well. Enough swimming. I also am very happy that you are safe."

And I think he actually meant it.

Quick on the heels of the best news we'd gotten in three weeks came the worst. That probably sounds callous in light of everything we'd seen and heard about, but I'll stand by it. To us, at that time, it was the worst.

This was not an abstract, formless, incomprehensible anguish— grief for those I had not known, shocked confusion at what people were capable of, guilty fear that under the right circumstances, or the wrong ones, I could do something similar. That was already a horrendously potent combination. But this hit us personally, when we were at our weakest, just when we'd let our guards down. It shattered the exhaustion, the dizzy relief that was starting to take hold, and burnt like acid.

Mani and Tina had to stay behind.

I'd been so occupied by unfolding events that I hadn't thought about it since that night on the fishing boat—what our safety meant for them. I've never felt so selfish in my entire life.

It was Elissa who asked the question. She'd been silent all morning, but now she spoke up, her voice shaking.

"We're all going to Jakarta, right?"

Startled in the act of pushing back from the table, Mr. Suave looked at her.

"Of course," he said, eyes taking in the six of us and skimming right over Mani. It was that casual skip of his glance that was our first warning.

Elissa gathered the last threads of her courage and pushed the point. "All eight of us, right?"

"What? No, six."

There was one second of silence, and then all six of us howled. For once we were completely unified.

"Absolutely no way!"

"But Mani and Tina have to come!"

"We're not going anywhere then." That was Kyle, halfway out of his chair.

"Please. Please!"

Tina, who was in Elissa's lap, added to the din with a loud squawk of protest at being clutched too hard. Mani just ducked his head, folding silently into himself.

Mr. Suave took half a step backwards, perhaps wondering whether we were about to jump over the table and attack him. The soldiers lining the walls shifted uncomfortably. He held up his hand.

"They are Indonesian citizens, and Ambonese. They live here. We cannot send them to Jakarta on a military plane."

The brief window of silence we'd given him to speak disappeared again.

"Why not—I thought you got to give all the orders around here?"

"That's rubbish!"

"No way!"

"Guys, wait," Brendan interrupted. Obviously striving for some semblance of calm, he turned to face the major. "He saved our lives. Don't you understand we wouldn't be here without him? We can't leave them behind. They don't have anyone else."

"It is good that he saved your lives," the major said, implacable. "But he cannot go with you. Wait!" he said with authority, staving off another outcry. "It is not just Indonesian government policy—it is yours too. He cannot go with you to the United States."

"What about as a refugee?" I asked desperately.

The major gave a short, humorless bark of laughter. "There are thousands of people trying to get out of here. Should we fly them all to Jakarta? We cannot. What will they do? Sit there in a refugee camp for three years until the papers are all done? Enough—the plane is waiting. Anyway, it is safe for them here, now that the army is in control."

That last statement was so patently untrue that it stunned us all temporarily into immobility.

"It's okay," Mani said quietly, repeating that familiar stabilizing phrase.

Only, not for the first time, it was clearly *not* okay.

Now we were fighting on two fronts, and we were down to three strong. Drew, Elissa, and Mark were already crying too hard to talk. Tina, overwhelmed, screwed up her face and joined them.

Despite the major's growing impatience, it was Mani himself who finally put an end to the pleading and arguing.

"It is the right thing."

I thought he was dead wrong. How could he know enough to make that call? He didn't know anything about life outside of Indonesia. I guess I had always thought that if we got out of this mess, it would be our turn to save him.

Brendan, after a long look, finally backed him up. "It's your deci-sion," he said slowly.

It shouldn't be, I wanted to scream. Not when you're so obviously making the wrong one!

After ten minutes of this Mr. Suave was getting seriously agitated. He clearly hadn't counted upon any resistance to his grand "rescue" plan.

"It is time to go now," he said sternly. "The plane must leave."

"We need some time to say good-bye," Brendan said, dignified.

I don't know how he did it. I wanted to grab the major by his starched collar and shake him until his teeth rattled. I wanted to smash that jaunty cap down over his eyes, leave him writhing on the tiles, and smuggle Mani and Tina aboard—while the other ten soldiers just stood calmly by and watched, I guess.

Instead I just ground my teeth and hated him.

"Two minutes," he said. Then he turned smartly on his heel and stalked off.

Two minutes. Later I was to wish we'd defied the major and taken ten minutes, twenty, an hour, to tell Mani everything that was on our hearts. But the fight had gone out of us. It wouldn't have been enough time anyway, and we would never have found the right words.

How do you express such a mixture of grief, fear, and thankful-ness? As usual with me, it was to be the grief and fear I thought of first—grief that we were leaving them with no home to go back to, fear that we were leaving them in the backwash of all the violence that we'd seen. It was monstrously unfair that right when we were starting to grasp the fact that we could finally relax, we were leaving him to fend for the two of them by himself.

The thankfulness came late, when it was my turn to grab his hands and bumble my way through a good-bye.

It was a horrible scene. Maybe, in the end, it wasn't all bad that we only had a couple of minutes. Everyone was crying, except me. My tears had all been wasted on the tarmac. They were long gone, little piles of useless salt.

"Where will you go?"

"The mission school. Maybe there are some people left there." He shrugged, uncertain again.

My heart clenched.

"Maybe back to the village."

I fumbled for my little notebook, ripping out the front couple of pages where Dad had carefully written down our home phone number, address, my grandparents' address in Australia, all the embassy contact details—everything was there except my favorite color, and I'm sure he would have written that down if he'd thought of it.

"Here." I handed them over. "Write. Please."

He nodded, wordless.

"Wait." I reached up, unhooked the clasp around my neck, slid the ring off, and dropped the gold chain neatly into his hand.

"Cori, no."

"Mani! Sell it," I said in my *don't be ridiculous* tone, and he tucked it into his pocket.

There was a pause.

"Thank you, for everything," I said, hoping he could glimpse even a fraction of what was in my heart. Thank you for your strength, your patience, your faith, your unflagging efforts to get us safely home.

Then Mani, who'd given so much already, gave me one last present. *"Baku dame jua,"* he whispered, giving me a wobbly smile through the tears.

I did something I'd never done before. I leaned forward and kissed him on the cheek.

Then I turned away.

Tina was bawling and being blubbered over by Drew. Her small face was covered with tears and snot. I don't know whether she really understood what she was crying about, or whether she was just joining in on the general mood.

Either way, when I held my arms out she came to me willingly enough, her sobs slowing. I sat her bottom on the edge of the table and used the hem of my T-shirt to scrub at her face.

"Where you go?" she asked me, hiccupping, eyes screwed up with worry, one hand clutching my sleeve. "Heaven?"

I knew what heaven meant to her. It meant people went away and never came back.

"No," I said matter-of-factly, pulling a chair over so that we were eye level. At least, I hoped not yet. "America."

"Me come?" she demanded.

"I will come back and visit. I promise," I told her, not knowing whether it was a promise I could keep. Knowing it was not one I wanted to keep. Apart from her and Mani, there was nothing here I felt like I would ever want to come back to. Ever.

"I have a present for you," I said, eager to distract both of us.

Present was one word she'd learnt from Mark. Her eyes lit up hopefully. "Dog?"

"No." I pulled out the ring.

She smiled, long black lashes spiky with tears. She had often pulled out the ring and played with it when she sat in my lap. It was probably even as good a present as a dog.

I slid it over her middle finger and curled her fist over it.

"Look," she commanded someone behind me, holding it up.

I felt Kyle's hand pass over my hair before he swept her up in the air. "That's beautiful," he said gravely.

I leant my head on the empty edge of the table, closed my eyes, and wanted to feel . . . nothing.

chapter 20 ～

It all happened too fast. Within six hours of being spotted on the road we were landing five hundred miles away in Jakarta.

As the tires touched down with a screech and a bump, I felt a sudden surge of hope mixed with fear. Would I ever feel just one emotion again? I was desperate to see my parents, but I was already scared of what that meant—going home—alone.

Occasionally when we were hiking on Seram I would let myself picture this moment. In all the TV footage I'd seen of returning soldiers or hostages, they'd walked down the plane stairs and stepped onto the tarmac to see their loving family bolting across that black expanse to meet them, faces radiant with joy and excitement. Pulling my boot free from a particularly sticky patch of mud, surrounded by trees and the chattering of monkeys, I'd play that movie in my mind.

The reality was nothing like the movie. For one, we didn't walk down stairs; we walked off a ramp and out the back of a giant cargo plane. For another, no one rushed lovingly across the tarmac to greet us. Instead we were met by yet another taciturn soldier who ushered us into the airport building and through two doors.

There, fifteen feet away behind a flimsy wooden barricade, were some familiar faces, but not the ones we most wanted to see. I hardly noticed the flashbulbs going off. Later, at home, Mum showed me some of the news footage of us coming through that door. Tanya told me afterwards that Mum had been walking around in a daze ever since they'd gotten the call from the embassy hours earlier telling them we were all safe, and that she started crying the minute she saw us appear through that door on the TV and didn't stop for an hour.

"Did you cry?" I asked, trying to picture them in those hours after they'd gotten the news.

"Maybe," she said, gazing off into the distance. Then she shook her head and returned to form. "But I was mostly crying over all your clothes and the CDs I knew wouldn't be mine anymore."

She couldn't fool me. In that second I'd seen a glimpse of how much she really cared, and just how scared she had been. I tackled her to the floor and tickled her until she was screaming and purple. It was one of my happiest moments in those first weeks home.

The news footage showed Brendan barefoot and limping badly. Drew was hanging on to one of his arms, and on the other side of him Mark was holding the edge of his shirt. Kyle and I were holding hands, and Elissa had an arm hooked through mine. Our faces were grubby, our hair tangled, and our arms covered in scratches and bruises. I had, as Kyle had promised, a doozy of a black eye. Kyle's relatively clean T-shirt stood in stark contrast to the rest of our clothes, which were filthy and torn. We looked exhausted, thin, and dazed. Not one of us focused on the cameras; our eyes scanned the rest of the crowd nervously.

Afterwards I think Mum was sorry she'd shown me. I ranted and raved for half an hour. It was the newscasters who set me off. First they stated that we'd been found wandering through the bushes near the airport and had been rescued by the Indonesian army. Mr. Suave would have been pretty happy with that.

"Wandering!" I yelled, incensed.

Wandering? How did they think we got from Batuasa to Ambon —we just "wandered" hundreds of miles? They made us sound like idiots.

Then they said we were too traumatized to answer questions. That wasn't fair. I don't know about the others, but I didn't even *hear* the questions. I had more important things on my mind, like looking for my family.

They weren't there.

I think we all came to that realization at the same time, just before the Stewarts and Gary ducked under the wooden barrier and reached us. The Stewarts were an oasis of calm, but Gary was a mess. He hugged each of us over and over again, sobbing.

I wanted to find some words to reassure him that we really were fine, but all of a sudden I found I didn't even have the energy to raise my arms and hug him back.

After the stranger who had been waiting with Gary and the Stewarts ushered us through the crowds and into a minivan, there was a brief, awkward silence. Gary had stopped sobbing, but he still looked tortured. I think he'd lost more weight during the previous three weeks than we had.

"Where are our families?" Brendan asked for all of us.

"At home," Tim said. He looked back at us from the front passenger seat as the driver piloted the van through the traffic. The close press of cars, buses, and motorcycles, most of whose drivers appeared bent on either suicide or homicide, was unnerving. "Your father was here, Cori, the first ten days after we realized you were missing. Yours too, Mark, and your mom, Brendan."

I caught my breath. My dad! Suddenly there were so many questions that needed answering.

"My dad was here?" Mark sounded amazed.

"We did everything we could think of," Tim said. "We talked to the embassies, the army, the government, local mission staff in Ambon. No one had the faintest idea where you were or what had happened to you."

"When you didn't come on the boat that Saturday afternoon as you were supposed to, we were frantic," Alison said. "We were holding off on being evacuated until you arrived. We were at the docks, with police protection and everything, and then you weren't on the boat."

She and Tim shared a glance.

"Then you know what happened at Mani's village?" Brendan asked.

Another glance.

"Bits and pieces. We had some radio contact with one of our bases on Seram after that."

They paused. It was obviously our turn to speak. I didn't even know where to start.

Kyle summarized. "We hiked with Mani and Tina from Batuasa to Rikit and took a fishing boat from there to Ambon. We were going to try and get on a ship."

The Stewarts, Gary, and the silent stranger all gaped at us.

"You hiked all the way to Rikit?" Tim said, apparently not believing what he'd heard. "That's mountain territory."

"We know," Kyle told him dryly.

I felt the first warm stirrings of pride. Maybe we hadn't done so badly after all.

Each group was so eager to get information from the other that the conversation became a verbal tug-of-war.

"Is Diane all right?" Elissa asked.

"She's fine, but she did have appendicitis," Gary said. "We were airlifted here, and she had surgery. We never even made it to Darwin. It was only two days! Then I couldn't get back into Ambon. Where are Mani and Tina?"

"Those army creeps in Ambon wouldn't let them come with us," Kyle spat out. "Why couldn't you get back in?"

"It was crazy in Ambon," Tim said. "It went from nothing to crazy so fast. We stayed another four days hoping you'd turn up. We sent people over to Seram looking for you. Nothing. After that we had to leave. Your parents were already in Jakarta when we got here."

"Why didn't mine come?" Elissa asked in a small voice.

"And mine?" Drew asked, sounding much more peeved.

"Oh, honey," Alison said, reaching back to pat Elissa's leg. "They all wanted to, but they talked to Gary and decided that it was really only necessary that two or three of them come out."

"How were they?" I asked, hungry for any tidbit from home.

"Worried," Gary said in a strained voice, and I had a sudden glimpse into how awful these last weeks must have been for him in particular. I wouldn't have wanted to face my parents, having made the decision to leave us on Seram.

"Mark, your father threatened to sue me for everything I had."

Mark looked positively delighted at this further evidence of parental affection.

"Why *did* you leave us behind?" Kyle asked. I knew this was something that had been bugging him from the beginning.

Gary put his hands to his forehead. "It was the wrong decision," he said. "But everything happened so fast, and I knew things were heating up in Ambon. I just thought you'd be safer on Seram with Daniel until we could figure out what was going on."

"Safer?" The anger came from Drew. Gary was just the most convenient scapegoat. "We hike miles. We have to eat those . . . those monkey things . . ."

"Cuscus," Brendan said, a stickler for details.

She ignored him and kept going. "Daniel and Mariati are *dead*. Mark gets malaria. We get attacked by bush pigs. The boat sinks, we almost drown, soldiers shoot at us, and then Mani can't even come with us. You're darn right it was wrong." She sat back and folded her arms, staring out the window.

There was silence; then the stranger spoke for the first time as the van slowed before the high metal gates of the U.S. embassy. "There's clearly a lot we haven't heard. The other embassy officials will be most interested to hear it too. Then you can rest. You're safe now."

It was that promise of rest that got me through the following hours.

The embassy let us call our families as soon as we arrived. It was almost 2 a.m. at home. It was fantastic to hear their voices, but it turned out to be a bit of a weird conversation. So many times I had ached for them to know what was happening, and now that I had the chance to tell them, just like in the van, I didn't know where to start. I ended up not saying very much.

Mum cried most of the time she was on the phone. "How are you?" was pretty much all she got out.

I cast around for the right word. *Dirty* was the one I finally settled on.

Dad swung into organizing mode. "I'll be there by late tomorrow night. Is there anything from here you want me to bring?"

"I dunno," I said dully.

"Me! Take me!" I heard Tanya yelling in the background. "Cori!" she suddenly squealed in my ear, obviously having wrenched the second phone away from Mum. "You're famous. You guys are on CNN! We're going to have a huge party when you get home, and what happened to your eye?"

"I banged it while the boat was sinking," I said.

There was an awed silence. "Wow. Wait—Luke—let go!"

I heard a scuffle, and then Luke was on the line.

"All the hamsters are still alive, and I prayed for you every night," Luke announced proudly. "And Tanya's been wearing all your—"

He didn't get to finish the sentence. There was a thump, and then Tanya was back.

"Don't listen to him," she said. "You know what he's like."

Yeah, I did. Earnest and pretty much incapable of deceit. But they'd done the impossible and made me smile.

"Hey, I have to talk to Dad for a minute."

"Tanya, hang up the phone," Dad commanded.

There was a sigh and a click.

I touched the camera in my pocket. "It's safe to talk to the embassy, right?"

"Yes."

"About anything? Even the army?"

"About anything."

After a pause, which I didn't fill, his worried voice reached me. "I'll see you tomorrow night. We love you."

The rest of us were already eating by the time that Brendan and Elissa finished on the phone and joined us. We couldn't wait. The minute I'd hung up and walked back into the meeting room, my stomach sat up and begged.

Chips, sandwiches, pasta, chocolate bars, fruit. Oh, and olives. Random. I grabbed a plate and plopped down beside Mark, who from the looks of things had a significant head start on me. The American who'd met us at the gate and two other embassy officials were in the other corner of the room talking in low voices.

"Did you talk to your parents?" I asked Mark, after I'd consumed a sandwich, a bowl of pasta, and a Mars bar in the space of five minutes.

He nodded, stuffing the last of his pasta in his mouth and reaching for more chocolate.

"My dad's coming. They sounded *really* upset," he said complacently, licking the bottom of his plate of pasta salad, and then lowering the bowl slowly, one hand going to his stomach.

"What about your aunt and uncle?" I asked Kyle.

"I'm going home with Brendan, and they'll drop me off in LA on their way," he mumbled with his mouth full, annoyed. "I told them I could catch a plane by myself. Honestly, after everything that's happened, you'd think they'd trust me to get on a plane."

"Guys," Mark interrupted, looking green. "I don't feel so good."

I looked around desperately.

"The trash can!" Kyle commanded, pointing across the room.

Mark just made it there, then vomited noisily.

I was too tired to go over and play nurse. Besides, I didn't feel too hot myself. I took another sip of Coke and decided I'd better drink it slowly.

The embassy people in the corner looked worried. "Is he okay?" they asked.

"He's fine," Kyle said, disgusted. "He just ate too fast."

What little savages we must look like, I realized. I hadn't even taken the time to wash my hands.

"Maybe it's the malaria," Mark argued.

"Yeah, the malaria plus two sandwiches, one plate of noodles, and two cans of Coke," Kyle said. "I counted."

I gaped at him.

"What a waste of good food," Mark said mournfully.

The adults shared shocked glances and went back to whispering.

They might have been expecting that after letting us call home and feeding us, we'd be all energized to give them a blow-by-blow account. It didn't quite work that way.

Instead, our brains pretty much shut down.

After eating two more sandwiches, a bit more slowly this time, Mark put his head on the table and went to sleep. Drew only picked at her food, wondered aloud whether Mani and Tina had anything to eat, then started to cry. Elissa was all keyed up because she'd spoken to Colin, but even she wilted within half an hour.

We should have put our foot down and demanded to be taken to the Stewarts' new place so we could sleep, but I think we were all so stupefied by the speed with which things had happened, and relieved to be in the presence of adults and have the responsibility of decision making suddenly lifted, that it just didn't occur to us.

So we sat there yawning, trying to answer questions, while some doctor they'd called in dragged us off to the next room one by one to check us out.

Tim looked more and more impressed, and Gary looked increasingly horrified, as the story unfolded in bits and pieces. We managed not to argue about details too much. Kyle did initially make it sound like the bush pig had burst out of the jungle chicken nest and attacked us for no reason at all, until I pointed out that being stabbed by the tip of his machete was probably a pretty valid reason for it to get all worked up.

By the time we got to landing on Ambon we were stumbling over our sentences, slurring our words, and getting confused.

Kyle and I paused when we got to the bit about Hanima. I raised my eyebrows. He shrugged his shoulders. The whole reason we'd gone in there was so that we could let people know what really happened, and I guessed we might as well start. Of course, we hadn't banked on Mani and Tina being stuck in Ambon when we were thinking about ratting out the army. I said their names in my mind, a silent prayer; then I opened my mouth.

"There were twenty-two people there. They were all dead. Shot. By the army."

The embassy staff all froze, even the one taking notes.

Then the guy who'd been asking most of the questions cleared his throat. "The TNI?" he asked. "The Indonesian army?"

We nodded.

"That's a very serious accusation," he said. "How do you know?"

Something about his tone set me off. You could tell he thought we were making it up, that we were a bunch of hysterical teenagers who'd gotten a bit confused after all they'd been through. So when I yanked the camera out of my pocket and slapped it down on the table, I guess I spoke a bit more forcefully than I had intended.

"Because we went in there and took photographs."

Gary twitched as if he'd been poked by a branding iron.

"What?"

"How did you know it was the army?"

"Did you see anyone in there?"

The embassy people were falling all over themselves.

I left it to Kyle to answer their questions while I reached into the waist pack that had come so far and brought out the other eleven rolls of film, lining them neatly up on the table in front of me.

"We have other photos too," I said, suddenly spent.

The oldest man, the one who'd identified himself as the ambassador, reached across for the film and placed his hand on the camera. I didn't let it go.

"You'll take care of it," I said. It was more an order than a question. "We promised them."

"I promise," he said, looking me straight in the eyes, all skepticism gone.

I let go, feeling bereft, and rested my forehead on the table. I'd just relinquished the only thing of value we still owned.

They wanted to keep us there, but Alison was fantastic. She suddenly decided that enough was enough. The doctor backed her up.

There was some talk about putting Mark in hospital for observation, but he didn't want that and neither did we. In the end we all swallowed antimalarial tablets and went home with the Stewarts.

"Papaya palm sap." The doctor kept shaking her head and repeating herself. "I'll be. You're one very lucky young man."

I scored a couple of painkillers for my eye, which actually didn't hurt too much, and Kyle got dosed for his ribs, which I think were still hurting a lot more than he let on.

She also clucked over my wrist. "It should have been stitched, but it's a bit late now. You'll have a scar there."

It was a very quiet ride to the Stewarts' house. Gary didn't say a word. I didn't really care. That might have been because I was so beat that I could hardly keep my eyes open. The traffic, noise, exhaust fumes —everything swirling past was making me carsick. But I also didn't for one second think we had done anything wrong. He hadn't been there, and he had no right to judge. Just three weeks earlier I would have quailed at the thought of Gary being angry with me. Now it didn't seem to matter.

"I'm sorry," Alison fussed after we arrived. "I don't have anything but mattresses and sheets. We're still setting up here after the evacuation."

I just collapsed onto one of the mattresses and closed my eyes.

"Can I have a shower?" I heard Elissa ask.

I wanted one too. The thought of hot water and soap was almost enough to get my eyes open again.

But not quite.

chapter 21 ~

I slept for seventeen hours without stirring. In the end Drew and Elissa woke me. I think they were worried I'd fallen into a coma.

I was my usual charming morning self. "Go away," I mumbled, hugging the pillow to my face.

A pillow. Wow. I cracked one eye open so I could look at it. Elissa was perched cross-legged on the bed, and Drew was sitting beside me.

"It's ten in the morning. You've been asleep for ages," Drew said. "There's some counselor coming to see us soon."

"That's a good reason to stay asleep," I said.

"Anyway, you stink."

No wonder. We had sweated a lot since our dip in the ocean. The combined lure of a drink, some food, and a shower made me sit up.

Elissa disappeared into the bathroom across the hallway and came back with a glass of water.

"So what else is happening?" I asked, after I finished it.

"Alison's on the phone organizing tickets for us to fly home. Gary and Tim went out. Your dad gets here at seven tonight. My mom's coming in about eight thirty, Brendan's mom and Mark's dad get here about nine, and Drew's mom arrives tomorrow morning sometime," Elissa summarized for me.

"Canadian flight schedules," Drew said glumly.

"Where are the boys?"

"Downstairs," Drew said. "Probably still eating. Piggies."

She was obviously in a funk with all of us.

"Where'd you get the clothes?" They were both so clean they glowed.

"Alison," Elissa said, lifting a small pile beside her and handing them to me. "Go have a shower."

I could write pages and pages about that shower. The smell of the soap. The way the hot water ran smooth off my skin, stinging a thousand small scratches, and pooled brown against the ceramic floor. My hair, slick with conditioner, slithering through my fingers. I leaned my forehead against the tiled wall and stayed there, letting an army of drops beat down onto my shoulders, until the water faded through warm to cold.

I was ready to go back to bed after that, and I stood there for a full minute before I found the energy to get dressed. It was weird putting on someone else's clothes, a long light skirt and a white shirt. At least the underwear looked new. The bra didn't exactly fit right, but it was all a darn sight better than the stinking heap of clothes I'd dropped on the bathroom floor as I stepped into the shower. I didn't even want to touch them.

I brushed my hair back with both hands, left it dripping down my back, swiped the steam mist from the glass, and looked in the mirror for the first time in weeks.

My face didn't seem to belong to me.

It wasn't just the eye. That was a beauty. The swelling had gone down enough so that the eye was almost fully open, but it was Technicolor. A blue-and-purple circle tracing the line of my eyebrow all the way down through my cheekbone.

Actually, I guess it was the eye. Both eyes really, but not the surrounding bruises. It was what was in them as they stared back out of the mirror.

Or what wasn't in them.

They were empty.

The day dragged.

It shouldn't have; there was plenty happening. But although it was all focused on us, it mostly seemed to swirl around us.

I was surprised to learn that there was yet another type of tired. On Seram we'd had physical tired. The type of tired when a thousand muscles are screaming at you to quit walking, sweat's running off you, and only the energy you manage to generate from gritting your teeth helps you take the next step.

That type of tired can keep the emotional tired safely at bay—the tired when sadness is a physical weight, a thick smothering, aching thing. That was the dangerous type of tired we couldn't afford on Seram. That's the type of tired that makes you want to sit still and listen to despair.

But it was this type of tired that was the most overpowering.

When the danger was gone, and I didn't feel responsible for helping make the thousand and one decisions that could mean the difference between life and death, the fatigue was total.

I couldn't seem to break through it.

I watched myself going through all the motions.

Eating. With proper utensils. At a table.

Sitting with the others listening to Patrick, the counselor. Nodding in all the right places.

With Kyle and the embassy staff, answering more questions. Speaking clearly into a tape recorder. My voice flat. The most horrific details of what we'd seen falling from my lips with no inflection.

Some small corner of my brain was quite impressed with how well I was coping, especially compared to Drew. She could barely get out two full sentences without dissolving into tears. Brendan faltered at times, dropping into long pauses for no apparent reason. Even Kyle went pale talking about the church, his lips twitching, searching for words.

There was only one thing that came close to reaching me during those first hours. As they were finally leaving about five in the afternoon, one of the ladies from the embassy touched me lightly on the shoulder.

"I am so glad you're safe," she said, looking me straight in the eyes. "I just want you to know that my kids and I have been praying for you guys every night since the news came through that you were missing."

It almost broke through.

But not quite.

I was too tired. Too tired to even say thank you.

I just nodded.

I hope she understood.

It lifted a little as the time for Dad to arrive drew closer. At least I was feeling something. It wasn't exactly the overwhelming joy I'd been expecting. More like anxiety. But it was something.

"Sit down. You're making me dizzy," Drew said, looking up from the Scrabble board where she was playing with Brendan, Mark, and Kyle. Elissa was curled up next to them on the couch, writing. We'd been so edgy during dinner I think Tim and Alison were glad to leave us to our own devices in the living room. We'd wanted to go to the airport to meet our parents, but that had been vetoed. So Gary was picking them up, and they were coming to us.

"Mark," Kyle said. "What is a *blund*?"

"A small blunder," Mark said defiantly, aware he was on thin etymological ice.

"That's not a word," Brendan told him gently.

"It could be." He stuck out his lip, suddenly looking his age.

"It could be," Kyle said, with exaggerated patience. "But it's not. So change it."

"What about dun or bun?" I said.

"Don't help him," Drew howled. "He's already beating me."

I froze and forgot all about Drew's Scrabble woes as headlights flashed across the window and paused in front of the imposing metal gate that seemed to be part and parcel of houses in Jakarta.

The four on the floor looked at me, wide-eyed; then there was a mad scramble to the window beside the front door. Drew, Elissa, and Mark peered around the edges of the curtain. Kyle pulled the door open and stepped out onto the wide veranda.

I was stuck by the Scrabble board with Brendan.

"What's wrong?" he asked me.

It seemed too complicated to explain. I felt shy. The prospect of seeing Dad made me realize how much I'd changed over the last couple of months, how complicated everything now was. I was scared too, I think, that with Dad's arrival I would lose the last thing I was holding out for and collapse completely.

I didn't work that out right then; it came later. But in that moment I think Brendan understood me better than I understood myself.

"Go on." He stood and gave me a little push. "We're here."

They were too. They didn't come rushing down to the driveway with me, but I could feel the weight of five sets of eyes as I walked down the three shallow steps that led up to the house.

The car came to a gentle stop and then —Suddenly. There he was. With a hug that smelled like peppermint and Old Spice.

It was that smell that made it real for me.

I raised my arms and hugged him back, resting my cheek against his shoulder. We stayed like that for quite awhile, not saying anything. I felt him shaking and realized, shocked, that he was crying. I couldn't remember ever seeing Dad cry before.

"We were so worried," he said, holding me away from him and scanning my face.

He looked the same. Tired, but the same.

I grabbed his hand and tugged him toward the steps. We'd done everything together for the last two months. I didn't see why reunions should be any different.

I think Dad was a bit startled to step into the living room, lighted bright against the warm darkness outside, and find himself attacked. Drew flung her arms around his neck. Brendan grabbed his free left hand and pumped it enthusiastically. Elissa was giving little hops of excitement. Only Mark and Kyle were more restrained.

He knew who was who already; I hadn't banked on that.

"Tea?" Alison asked as she and Tim came rushing in to add to the tumult.

"That'd be great," Dad said.

Since when did Dad start drinking tea?

"How's everyone?" I asked, the minute there was a pause.

"We'll catch up later," Tim said, handing over the tea Alison had passed to him.

Dad looked at it blankly.

"We'll be in the kitchen," Tim said.

"Come on." Kyle dragged the Scrabble board across to the other side of the room and shooed the others away. They resumed play, but I could tell most of their attention was on us.

Dad sat down and started to pull stuff out of the duffel bag he was carrying. "Your mother sent you a book to read on the plane."

Anne of Green Gables, one of my childhood favorites.

"Tanya sent clothes and makeup and nail polish." Dad's tone was dry.

I recognized the clothes. Cream jeans, a black scooped-neck shirt, and black summer sandals. She'd included a gold bracelet that I didn't recognize, and the nail polish was bright red. That was a color I used to like putting on my toes.

I set it aside.

"Luke wanted to send you Humpty and Dumpty."

I smiled at the thought of Dad putting our hamsters through the airport x-ray machine.

"But he agreed to send Ezekiel instead."

Wow. Luke pretended he was too old for teddy bears, but Ezekiel was special. I couldn't remember Luke ever sleeping without Ezekiel nearby. I held the ragged teddy gently.

"Scott sent you a letter." Dad's eyes twinkled. "I think you'll be very happy."

I reached out and took the envelope, holding it awkwardly.

I didn't miss the way all of the others glanced surreptitiously at Kyle.

No one missed the way that he got up and left the room.

Dad looked confused at the sudden silence.

"More tea, Dad?" I asked.

Friends of Tim and Alison were hosting our parents for the night. I think Dad had expected me to stay with him, but there was no way I was leaving the others on our last night together. Elissa was tempted to go with her mum, but after a long look at the rest of us she decided to stay too.

I think Dad was a bit hurt, but he hugged me without protest when Alison gently shooed them out the door shortly after midnight. We were all glassy-eyed and overwhelmed by then, like little kids on Christmas Day coming down off a sugar high.

I plopped in the wicker chair in the upstairs sitting area outside the bedrooms while I waited for my turn in the bathroom. The house was finally quiet. Undoctored by an air conditioner, the air in the alcove where I sat hung heavy and humid, warm against my bare arms. I curled my legs up, despite the protest of tight muscles, and tucked my bare feet under the long cotton skirt.

I stared at the envelope in my lap. Heavy cream paper. Sealed and unaddressed. Thick.

I didn't even need to see his handwriting for memories to come sneaking back.

Scott laughing with his head thrown back and his eyes closed, one dimple winking.

Me reaching up to kiss that dimple.

Figures. When I had stopped looking for it, when I had stopped wanting it, there it was again—that familiar tug on my heart. Faint, but definitely there.

I reached up and touched my neck before remembering that the ring wasn't there anymore.

I shook my head, slid my finger underneath the flap, and pulled it open, ripping the envelope raggedly.

It was a long letter, and I was surprised by its intensity. This was something I'd noticed on the phone home too. It's not like I wasn't relieved to be out of there—I was. But that's exactly what it was, a relief, a letting go of the fear. Missing was the wild joy, the ecstatic buzz that I'd expected. It was everyone else who seemed to have that.

Dad, everyone at home, Scott . . . they had that. It came through loud and strong in Scott's letter, four pages of it, describing what the last three weeks had been like, outlining plans for when I got home. More than anything else up to that point, it gave me some insight into the limbo of helpless waiting everyone we loved had been plunged into.

But that wasn't what had me still sitting on the couch ten minutes later when Kyle came out of the guys' room, glass in hand, moving confidently in his bare feet, and wearing only a pair of shorts. His blue eyes stood out against the sunburn we'd all picked up during the last couple of days.

He paused when he saw the pages scattered in my lap.

"Scott's become a Christian," I said, hearing myself speak as if I were a long way away.

Kyle looked at me, expressionless, for several long seconds before dropping his gaze and nodding once, very slowly.

"That's great," he said.

Then he turned and went back inside the room, closing the door gently.

I felt very alone.

Drew and Elissa were both asleep by the time I entered our bedroom. Drew, flat on her back, breathing noisily. Elissa, curled on her side, silent. I considered waking them up, then realized that I didn't know what I'd say.

Something along the lines of . . . I know we've all been through hell during the last couple of weeks, we don't know where Mani and Tina are, and people may be dying in Ambon as we speak, but what I'd really like to talk about right now is my love life.

Actually, they'd probably love it.

I'd just feel ridiculous.

Clutching Ezekiel to my chest, I stared up into the darkness.

Scott. Kyle.

Kyle. Scott.

Surely it was a moot point anyway. I was going home the next morning. Kyle would not be there tomorrow. Or the day after that.

I forced myself to repeat that several times. The repetition didn't make it less painful.

I rolled over and stared at the crack of light sneaking under the heavy wooden door and thought about all the talking I'd have to do when I got home to try and make them understand what had happened, and the things I'd leave out.

I remembered Kyle's voice in the water, his hand on my shoulder in the church. I wished the guys were closer. I wasn't used to not being able to hear them nearby and know whether they were asleep or awake, peaceful or dreaming.

I thought about what the counselor had said that morning. Normal reactions to an abnormal situation—that was his pet phrase. He also said that we'd face a lot of people at home who loved us and hadn't been able to do anything to help us while we were missing, but wished they could. Once we got home they wouldn't mean to take over and try and run our lives, but they might anyway. Our job wasn't going to be making everyone feel happy, but concentrating on doing what was best for us and getting on with life.

Mark had grinned at that one. I could just picture him telling his parents that the counselor had said it wasn't his job to make them feel happy and that they shouldn't be running his life.

Actually, maybe not. He had been pretty rapt when his dad had arrived, and you could tell his dad was moved, even though he didn't say much.

Somewhere in the middle of thinking about Mark and his parents, I must have drifted off. It was still dark when I woke again, thirsty, with the friendly butterflies I'd gotten to know well frolicking in my stomach. In the distance I could hear faintly the Muslim call to prayer. My eyes felt gritty when I blinked, but I wasn't tired. There was no way I was getting back to sleep anytime soon, so I got up to get a drink.

Apparently Kyle couldn't sleep either. He was sitting on the couch in the dark, staring at the small blank television screen across the room as if it were on.

I padded across and curled up next to him, resting my head on his shoulder. I felt him stiffen briefly, as if he were going to pull away; then his hand dropped over mine and squeezed.

"What time is it?" I whispered.

"About five."

We'd gotten used to talking like this, close in the dark. Not looking at each other, just our voices, soft, the warm linking of our hands, and an unspoken permission to say anything.

"What are you thinking about?" I said.

There was a long pause before he answered.

"Mani. You guys. Home."

"Are you okay your aunt or uncle aren't coming over?" I asked.

"They can't afford it." He paused, shifting restlessly. "It's not like I want to stay here. But I'm not ready to go back either. It's stupid."

"I thought I was the only one," I said. "Elissa's not thinking of anything else. Though I guess she's got Colin to go back to."

"What about Scott?" Kyle asked, so low I hardly heard him, even against the silence.

I sighed. "I just don't feel the same way. Everything's changed. Things are never going to go back to the way they were. I almost wish that it wasn't that way, but it is."

There was a charged silence. I wondered if Kyle knew how tightly he was gripping my hand.

"So you're not going to get back together with him?"

"I don't know," I said, trying to be totally honest, but knowing it was the wrong choice of words the minute I said it. What I meant was, maybe—in six months, a year, maybe there would be a chance. Who knew how things would change, how Scott would change, how I would change?

I don't think Kyle heard it that way. He let go of my hand.

"What do you mean, you don't know? You're just going to get home and wait and see if he can talk you into it?"

"No!" I lifted my head off his shoulder. In the reflected light spilling from the bathroom, I could see him clearly. He looked about as mad as I felt.

"What I meant was not anytime soon. How could I when it's *you* I'm always thinking about, and *you* I want to talk to all the time? You're the one I feel really understands me. It's driving me crazy!"

It was so typical that we were finally having this conversation, and we'd already managed to turn it into a fight. It wasn't destined to be a long fight, though. He cocked his head to one side and studied me carefully.

"That could be a problem," he said finally.

I punched him in the shoulder. Hard. "Kyle! It's not funny. I'm confused."

He reached for my hand again, and I batted him away.

"All the time doesn't sound very confused. And you definitely said *all* the time."

"You should be a lawyer," I said.

"If it helps any," he said, "I'm not confused. I haven't been from the very first day at boot camp."

"It doesn't help," I said, starting to smile in spite of myself.

"Come on." His tone was suddenly coaxing. "Let's not fight. Not now. Let's kiss and make up."

I was going to tell him I wasn't ready to make up, but I got distracted. He kissed me.

I once licked a battery after Tanya dared me. I'll never forget the way that spark raced through my tongue, making my jaw ache instantly and my eyes squint up against the energy. I could feel the tingle for an hour afterwards.

Kissing Kyle was like that, in a good way, of course.

I could have pushed him away. Maybe I should have, but I didn't want to. It was so nice to feel something alive and warm and good. To feel my heart beat fast, and not because I was scared. To feel his lips gentle against my swollen cheekbone and know he remembered the terror of that night too. In that moment I felt alive, and that in the end it would somehow be okay. For once, my emotions were speaking without my brain getting in the way, and they were saying good things.

Later, in the days to come, I could sometimes rekindle that feeling of hope by remembering that dark, warm moment on the couch. It helped.

I don't know how long we would have sat there, or what we would have said afterwards. It's not like the kiss resolved anything. Kyle was headed back to LA, and who knew where I was going to end up next year, not to mention Scott.

But we didn't get the chance to talk about any of that. Some small sound made me open my eyes. There was Mark, standing in the doorway to the guys' room and grinning like a Halloween pumpkin.

"Kyle and Cori, sitting in a tree . . . ," he chanted softly when he saw us looking at him.

That was as far as he got, because Kyle left the couch in one bound and shot toward the door.

Mark squeaked, pivoted a hundred and eighty degrees, and bolted back into the bedroom.

The light from the bathroom fell directly across the hall and into the room, so I could see what was going on by the time I reached the doorway.

Mark had obviously taken a flying leap onto Brendan's bed and was now occupied with squirming down behind him, underneath the sheet, as fast as he could wiggle, cackling.

"Shut up," I begged in agony. "You'll wake up Tim and Alison."

"What . . . ?" Brendan started, confused and still half asleep.

"Help! Save me!" Mark yelped.

But it was too late. Kyle had a firm grasp on Mark's legs and dragged him, flopping, onto the next mattress. He pinned his arms and leaned in close. I couldn't hear what he was saying, but I could imagine Mark was being threatened with bodily harm if he told the others.

"What is going on?" Brendan asked me, rubbing his eyes and managing to string a full sentence together for the first time.

I shrugged.

"Okay! All right!" Mark said. "Get off me."

Kyle let him up.

"What did you do?" Brendan asked Mark, interested.

Mark looked outraged. "What did *I* do? Nothing! Jeepers creepers!" He stomped off toward the bathroom.

"Seriously, what'd he do?" Brendan asked us.

"He woke up," Kyle said.

Brendan looked very confused.

Behind me, the door to the girls' room cracked open, and Elissa slipped through.

"What's going on?" she asked, obviously wondering why we were all wide awake and having a yarn at five thirty in the morning.

"Don't ask me," Brendan said. "I was sound asleep until Mark jumped on me." Brendan sounded a lot less cranky than I would have been if I'd been yanked abruptly out of a peaceful repose.

"We're calling a team meeting," I improvised. Somehow I didn't think Kyle and I were going to get the chance to end up back on the couch for a private little chat. Maybe that was a good thing.

"Now?" Elissa asked, yawning. "You wake up Drew then. I'm not doing it."

"If we're having a team meeting, I have an announcement," Mark called out from behind the closed bathroom door.

Kyle tried the door. It was locked.

"Mark . . ." Kyle growled through the keyhole, packing a heavy dose of threat and promise into that one word.

"Or I could just make it now," Mark said, clearly figuring that he held the upper hand as long as there was a locked door between them.

Kyle glanced back and forth between me and the door. I couldn't help it; I started to giggle. Elissa looked at us both as if she was wondering whether we'd lost the plot overnight.

I turned and fled.

After I finally managed to get Drew moving, we padded silently down the tiled steps, through the living room, and out the back door into the small grassy courtyard. Mark trailed the group by several feet, keeping a wary eye on Kyle.

The air was almost cool as we stepped outside, but instead of the wet dirt smell of the jungle, the faintest scent of rotting garbage and car exhaust underlay the perfume from the flowers growing in carefully tended beds along the wall. The moon had already gone down, but the pale cement walls that divided this house from its closely packed neighbors were reflecting light from somewhere, pooling it in the garden.

"What are we doing out here when there are perfectly comfortable beds upstairs?" Drew asked.

"I can't sleep in a bed anymore," Kyle said, throwing himself onto his stomach and propping his head up with one arm.

"It's almost time to get up anyway," Elissa said. "It's getting light."

That was a bit of a stretch, but I appreciated her support.

"So, who called a team meeting?" Brendan asked.

Kyle looked at me.

"Jip did," I said.

"Oh. Of course. Why?" Brendan said.

"Well, Patrick said yesterday we should talk about happy memories. Jip thinks that would be a good thing to do." I held my breath.

I wasn't sure whether the others would go along with the idea. At least I could count on Kyle to back me up this time. Of all of us, he would have been the most likely to dismiss this as psychobabble.

I gave them a minute. I'd needed some time to work backwards through all the awful memories before I found some good ones myself.

Drew spoke first. "I have one. Remember when we did the cancan to 'Amazing Grace' with coconut shells? Remember the spider?"

I did remember. When he noticed the spider on his arm, Brendan had screamed and leapt around in a radical departure from his usual calm. Even after Kyle flicked it off it took him ten minutes to calm down. The rest of us had ended up rolling on the ground, hysterical.

"That," Brendan said, "is not one of my good memories. That was the biggest spider I've ever seen. As big as the coconut."

Drew laughed, honestly laughed, something I hadn't heard her do for ages.

"Fine then," Brendan said. "I have one. Swimming in the afternoons."

That was one of my favorites too. Rushing down the beach, relishing the feel of warm sand on bare sweaty toes, that first cool shock, the sting of salt on the scrapes we'd picked up during the day's work.

"I have one," Kyle said.

"I bet I know what yours is." Mark smirked.

Since I was the one sitting beside him, I poked him. He stuck his tongue out.

"Building the church," Kyle said. "I know it got burnt. But building it, watching something we were making ourselves grow. And that moment when we finished . . ."

One day, I thought, before remembering we were supposed to focus on the happy memories and trying to push the sudden bitterness aside. One day was all it had stood for.

"I got one," Mark said, suddenly serious, "but I don't know if it counts."

I was going to make a snide comment but, thankfully, I bit my tongue.

"It was when I was so sick," he said.

I wondered exactly how you manage to make a happy memory out of having malaria while lost in a jungle.

"I felt like . . . well, I felt *really bad*, but I remember waking up the next morning. You were there." He nodded to me. "And Kyle. And I could hear Brendan talking. And I knew that as long as you all were there, I was going to be okay."

I felt a sudden wave of affection. Maybe all his brattiness was just attention seeking. Maybe he was just a lonely kid, starved for love. I suddenly had a hard time remembering why he could drive me crazy.

Then it all came rushing back.

"I have another one," Mark said quickly, as if eager to atone for his sudden vulnerability. "When I came out of the bedroom this morning and saw Kyle and Cori kissing."

There was a moment of startled silence.

"Really!?" Drew threw her arms around me.

"So that's what was really going on this morning!" Brendan said, punching Kyle in the shoulder.

Elissa cast me a worried glance and didn't say anything.

My face must have looked like a plum. Kyle met my gaze and shrugged helplessly, but there was definitely a twinkle in his eyes.

"My turn," I said, hoping to distract everyone's attention from any budding romance. I don't think it worked, but they played along and quieted down.

"Once upon a time there was a prince named Jip who traveled with a monkey named Kiki and eight knights of his court. First, there was Brendan the . . ." I paused and looked around, waiting for them to catch on.

"Strong," Drew suggested at the same time that Elissa said, "Trustworthy."

"Then there was Elissa the . . ."

"Loving," Kyle said.

If it hadn't been for the smile he sent my way, a smile that warmed me right down to my toes, I might have got a bit jealous over that one.

"Pacifist?" Brendan said.

"A pacifist knight?" Kyle said.

"Affirmative action," I ruled. "Elissa the loving pacifist. Mark the . . . court jester."

"Mark the rat fink," Kyle said.

"You guys!" Elissa said. "Mark the unsinkable."

We settled on unsinkable jester for Mark, droll and sensitive for Drew, passionate and brave for Kyle, and candid and courageous for me. I suggested confused would be more apt, but I was overruled. Tina became the royal mascot, and after Mani was simply dubbed heroic, there was silence. I knew the others were also wondering where Mani and Tina were, whether they were okay.

"Jip, Kiki, the eight knights, and their trusty steeds had many adventures and faced many dangers together," Kyle said.

"Until the day came when they had to return to their own lands."

"Then," Drew said just as things were getting too depressing, "they were called upon to face their most dangerous trial alone . . . airline food."

We howled.

It was so ridiculous, but it was either laugh or cry. We were still frantic and heartsick over Mani and Tina. All the bad stuff was still there, hovering, a heavy, dark presence. But I'm glad that in that moment we drew enough strength from one another to choose laughter, or let laughter choose us. Because that's how I like to remember us saying good-bye. Not the strained scene hours later with tearful hugs, promises to talk soon, and the awful suffocating pain of letting go of Kyle's hand for the last time.

But in the garden, laughing, as the sun came up.

chapter 22 ~

It's taken me six weeks to write this. I'm not dreaming every night now. But even on nights free from nightmares, I still don't sleep very well. Usually about four thirty I'll be dragged awake. Sometimes abruptly—from dreams so vivid I wake expecting to hear the birds and feel cold ground against my cheek. Sometimes slowly—from a foggy darkness so heavy that I panic, struggling against a lethargy so complete I get scared that I'm paralyzed. Or that I'm only dreaming that I'm waking up, and that I'm actually dead, and that being dead is this slow struggle from blackness to light that goes on and on forever. And you never quite reach your goal.

I don't actually believe that about being dead. Or I hope I don't. Sometimes I'm not sure what I believe anymore.

I guess you could say I fell into a bit of a hole after getting home.

It wasn't a slow, steady slide either. I was fine on the flight. The airline had heard about us from someone, Alison probably, and upgraded us to first class, which was awesome. I drank so many cold soft drinks I got hiccups that wouldn't go away for an hour. They even served us ice cream sundaes.

I was fine arriving home. Scott wasn't there. Dad said he was away with his family when they got the news and wouldn't make it back until later that day. But Mum, Tanya, Luke, and people from our church—people I didn't even recognize—turned out to meet us at the airport. Tanya ducked under the security railing and sprinted up to meet me, Mum and Luke only two steps behind her. For at least a second or two I think I felt pure joy.

I was fine the rest of that day, and the next. I prowled around my bedroom, waiting for it to feel familiar again. I noticed things I'd never appreciated before—the beautiful music of a toilet flushing, how amaz-ing clothes smell when they come out of the dryer, how much food we could store in one fridge. I missed the others with every breath. I *ached* to share being home with them, but I can say that it was a good day.

The second night back the dreams started again, and I woke up alone, feeling I would never be happy again.

Mani and Tina were still in Ambon, and I was here. People were dying over there, and I was here. I turned it over and over in my mind. Surely there was something we could have done differently. Should have done differently.

The cloud didn't lift. Mum took Tanya and me to the mall for some of what Tanya called retail therapy.

I just couldn't connect.

"What about this?" Tanya kept asking, holding up one top after another.

I wasn't interested in any of them.

She finally headed for the changing rooms with an armful of clothes for herself. I wandered, ending up in front of rack upon rack of fake jewelry—gaudy, horrible, shiny gold earrings. Suddenly I felt angry and sick at the same time. How could we spend money and time making and buying such trash when there were people who didn't have enough to eat?

That anger didn't go away.

Tanya, Luke, and I were playing Monopoly the next day when I noticed that Tanya had underpaid the bank by a hundred dollars. That was it; I started screaming about cheating. I'm pretty sure she had been cheating, but she yelled right back that it was a mistake. Then (I'm embarrassed to write this down) I flipped the board, threw a handful of little green houses at the wall, and kicked the couch. It wasn't until I saw how scared Luke was that I managed to stop. I pushed past Mum, who'd come to see what all the fuss was about, slammed the door to my room, and spent the rest of the day finishing *Anne of Green Gables*.

Not even Scott was spared. He came by again the day after that, and I dragged myself downstairs to the kitchen.

". . . just not herself."

I caught the tail end of what Mum was saying as I entered and glared at her.

"Scott's here to take you out for a milk shake," she said brightly, in the tone of voice you might use for a kindergartner. I half expected her to add, "Isn't that nice?"

She didn't, but I rolled my eyes anyway.

We were quiet as we walked out to the Jeep. It was the first time I'd left the house without a family member since my return.

"How has today been?" he asked as I buckled my seat belt.

"Weird. Okay." There was a long pause. "So tell me more about what happened while I was gone."

So Scott did the hard work. He chatted about school stuff while we drove to the same restaurant that had been the scene of our big breakup. I thought about it briefly as we entered and was mildly surprised to feel . . . nothing. It could have happened to someone else.

Scott's classes started the next day at Georgetown. He'd decided to take philosophy instead of German.

"Didn't your dad flip out?" I asked.

"He wasn't very happy," he admitted. "But it's what I want. I was so mad at you for going away this summer, but it really made me think about making my own decisions and not letting other people make them for me."

"Take German then," I said. "Look what happens when you make your own decisions."

He leaned across the table and took my hand. It lay limp in his, a cold dead thing. "I really want to understand."

So I tried. I talked about the village, the church, Daniel, Mariati, Mani, Tina, the others. But I ran into trouble when I got to that Saturday. I slipped a hand into my pocket and fingered Budi's bear, which I carried with me everywhere. It didn't help me find a way to explain what it was like to be so completely alone after that, alone with seven other people who were all that stood between you and insanity. I fell silent in the middle of talking about that first dark night under the trees.

The story line was there, but the emotion had gone out of it. It, too, could have happened to someone else.

"Just take me home, please," I said.

He did, promising to return the next day.

I went upstairs and lay on my bed for the rest of the afternoon, too tired to read. Too tired even to call Kyle.

That was when Mum started ringing psychologists.

And Amy told me to write it all down.

And I started to feel something again. Since then I have often wondered whether numb is better.

Early in the mornings when the house is still and the silence dense, I have a lot of time to think. I usually think about what I'm going to write that day, retrace every step of those particular events in my head. Sometimes when it's especially hard, like the days I wrote about Hanima, I leave the house, needing to be outside. I slip out of the front door while everyone else is still sleeping and follow the track Scott and I used to run. It loops through the neighborhood, across the soccer field, and down to the little wooden bridge over the stream.

There, in that quiet darkness before dawn, I stand on the bridge and stare down into running water. I listen for the first sounds of the birds waking up, and let the peace that surrounds me battle with the images in my head.

On those days when I can't find the words to pray, and don't even know whether I want to, God sometimes finds me there on the bridge. Afterwards, on a good day, I return to the house able to make eye contact, talk in some sort of normal way, sometimes smile, sometimes even mean it. That's my miracle for that day.

Today I lingered too long, and the sun was already up when I let myself back into the house. So was Dad. He was sitting at the kitchen table with his Bible open in front of him. Deep creases of worry between his eyes relaxed fractionally when I walked in.

He got up and reached for another cup from the cupboard. "Coffee?" he asked.

I nodded, standing awkwardly in the doorway.

"Sit," he said.

I sat. Stared at the clay fruit bowl I helped Mum make when I was eleven. I remembered how proud I'd been when she let me glaze it. I could still pick out the irregularities in the glaze that I'd dripped down the left side. Dark shiny splotches of blue. It would have been a far more perfect bowl without my help.

"I was worried," Dad said, pouring boiling water into my mug.

"I was just down at the creek."

"Don't you think that might be a bit dangerous by yourself?"

"Dad . . ." I actually laughed.

He let it go, distracted by something else.

"This came yesterday from the American embassy." He tapped a small box lying on the table, and my stomach tightened. The photographs. Finally. The embassy staff had been fobbing us off for weeks.

"Did you look at them?"

"Yes. And I read the interview transcripts," he said slowly, sliding the box over to me.

I stared at him blankly, letting the box sit on the table at a safe distance.

"The interviews you did in Jakarta at the embassy," he said.

I don't know what I expected after that, but it wasn't what he said next.

"I'm very proud of you. We're both very proud."

"You're not mad that we went into that village?" I asked, surprised.

"No." I think there were tears in his eyes, but they didn't fall. "I'm just sad that it happened at all. That you had to see it. They're investigating because of those photos and the notes Kyle took. Apparently they caused quite a stir with some human rights organizations."

"Yeah?" I perked up at that, eager to focus on anything that would help me to avoid thinking about the stack of faces in that box. All the smiling ones. All the dead ones.

"Yeah. They're putting pressure on the Indonesian government to identify the soldiers responsible and try them."

"It *was* soldiers then," I said.

"Well, the government said it *might* have been rogue elements of the army. The army says it was militia using hijacked army equipment, nothing to do with them. But the international human rights organizations think it was TNI soldiers."

"Are they going to get them?" I asked.

"I don't know," Dad said. "The only time any Indonesian soldiers have ever been tried for human rights abuses was after East Timor. And most of them got off."

"They deserve—" I stopped. There was no way to express what I thought they deserved without sounding like a bloodthirsty little fiend, and I didn't want Dad to add *homicidal* to all the other adjectives they'd had reason to apply since I got home.

Dad nodded. "You probably aren't going to be all that welcome in Indonesia anytime soon."

"They'd actually stop us from coming into the country?" I asked, hurt.

"That's a problem?" Dad looked confused.

"No. I guess not," I said, wondering why I cared. I thought I never wanted to go back.

"So do you want to look at them now?" Dad asked gently.

I stared at the box and shook my head.

Not yet.

I went to see my psychologist again today. I've been going twice a week. Usually we just talk about what I've written since my last visit. How I felt then, how I feel writing about it now, and how things are going at home. I was expecting more of the same today, but no such luck.

Amy sighed deeply, kicked her shoes off, and switched on her kettle. "Tea?"

"Tea would be good," I replied, staring at the new print she'd hung since my last visit. "What kind of flowers are they?"

"Daffodils." She smiled. "Adds some color to the place, doesn't it?"

Not that the place needed more color. The walls were a light purple. There were framed pictures of flowers everywhere, a large blue beanbag, and a bright red two-foot-high exercise ball in the corner. On my third visit I'd told her that she should be able to pick the mood of her clients by where they sat. The other armchair was the safe, middle-of-the-road choice. Balanced on the exercise ball meant a hyped session. On the floor in the beanbag was probably a bad sign. She had laughed and said she'd keep that in mind.

Today I really, *really* wanted to choose the beanbag. So I had to sit in the armchair instead.

"Did you finish it?" Amy asked, bringing over my tea and curling up in the armchair opposite mine.

"No." I stared at the floor. "I can't. It's not finished."

"Where did you get up to?" she asked, flicking through the sheaf of pages I knew she'd read later.

"Yesterday."

"How has it been, writing about the days since you got home?"

"Harder. It just gets harder and harder." I didn't tell her that yesterday I'd sat in front of the computer for an hour before I typed a single word.

I stared balefully at the beanbag.

"I know you're hurting," Amy said with an unusually firm edge to her voice.

I raised an eyebrow, but she didn't tell me she knew how I felt.

"You have every right to. But you also have a responsibility to start picking yourself up out of this emotional heap you've fallen into since you've gotten home."

I thought about arguing with her, but it was too much effort.

"Look, it's natural," she said. "You felt a lot of responsibility in Indonesia for the others. You had to make a lot of quick decisions. Taking a month off as a break from that is fine, but you can't check out on the rest of your life."

"I'm not checking out," I said, stung.

"You're sliding toward depression," she said bluntly.

"Can I help that?" I shot back, knowing I sounded surly.

"Yes," she said. "To a certain extent you can."

That was the last straw.

"This is pathetic," I raged, wanting to throw something. "Who knows where Mani and Tina are or what they're coping with while I'm sitting here talking about how bad I *feel*. And how I should be working to get back to normal—whatever that is."

"Do you feel that you're betraying them by starting to move forward, even in a small way?"

"Stop psychoanalyzing me," I snapped.

"You're not, you know—betraying them. Just sitting around

feeling sorry for them isn't helping them or you."

"And I suppose now you're going to ask me whether you think that's what Mani would want."

"Is it?"

"I thought this was what counseling was all about. I get to sit and talk about how much I'm *hurting*, and how much life *stinks*, as much as I want. It took you long enough to get me to do that in the first place," I said, remembering the first day I'd really broken down.

That was the day I'd told her about thatching the roof of the church, the day Budi gave me the starfish. She'd sat with me for forty minutes, listening to me babble about the starfish and how I wished I'd taken a break from work to pay more attention to him, and how all the work on the church was wasted anyway. I'd definitely been in the beanbag that day.

"The pain is always going to be there in some form," Amy said. "You are *always* going to carry this with you. Talking about it is good, but it's never going to make it go away completely. I want you to think about whether it's time to make room for something else besides the pain, something more constructive. I'm not saying you have to make big changes right away, but next time I want to talk about what form that might take. And"—she tapped the bundle of pages—"how you are going to finish this."

There's no way of predicting what it will be that gets to me at odd moments. Once it was seeing Mum dish up rice for dinner. The other day I saw a durian in the imports section of the grocery store. On Sunday at church it was "Amazing Grace."

I squeezed past Scott and out the door, hoping everyone would just think I was headed for the bathroom.

It was peaceful outside. The empty cement steps heated by the sun. The silence, a balm.

"Hey," Scott said, sitting down beside me five minutes later. "You okay?"

"Yeah," I said slowly, surprised to realize that it was truer than it would have been a week ago.

He sat beside me quietly.

"Did I ever tell you what happened to the ring?" I asked, the thought sparked by the warm gold of the early fall leaves. They were just starting to change color with the bite of impending fall.

"No," he said. "I thought it must have been lost with everything else when the boat sank."

I shook my head. "I was wearing it on a chain around my neck, right up until the end. I gave the chain to Mani and the ring to Tina. She loved it. I couldn't walk away without giving her something."

Mani and Tina, I thought. It was a three-word prayer. The fact that we'd had to walk away at all was still bitterly raw. We hadn't heard a word in the six weeks we'd been home. They had just vanished. All our inquiries had led absolutely nowhere.

"I'm glad," Scott said after awhile.

"It helped, you know," I said, wanting him to know how important it had been. So, stumbling a little, I talked about that first crazed flight into the trees. How I'd reached for the ring. How it had anchored me. "I talked to you too," I said.

"You missed me." There was relief in his voice.

"Of course I did. Right up until that day, I wanted you there. I wanted to show you . . ." I paused, trying to find the words to convey how violently everything had shifted. "Then everything changed. And it became . . . harder to think about what wasn't right in front of me."

"You miss them?" he asked, after another long moment of sunny silence.

"Part of me is still missing," I said. "It's weird not having them around."

Scott took a deep breath. "Especially Kyle." he said. It wasn't really a question.

I nodded slowly.

"You together?" he asked evenly. He always had been good at that, staying calm when he was tense.

"No," I said.

It was the truth. Kyle tried to bring up that kiss shortly after we got home, and I shut him down. A couple of days later he circled back around. I shut him down again. It was becoming our own little long-distance ritual every couple of days. I still wasn't ready to think about it.

But I knew that Scott would understand that behind that one little *no* was a whole story that wasn't finished yet. I hadn't shut him out of the stories in my life during the last two years. It couldn't have been a fun feeling.

"I'm sorry," I said, reaching for that familiar hand. He took it.

"For what?" he asked.

"Everything's changed," I said.

"Some good," he said, looking up at the wispy clouds. "Some not so good, maybe. But there's time. You're coming to Georgetown in January, right? You're not going back to Australia, not now?"

I shook my head. "I don't know. I still haven't decided."

We heard the final hymn finish inside and stood up.

"I missed you so much," he said, looking at me as the doors above us burst open and people began to spill down the steps, parting around us. "I still miss you."

I hugged him fiercely. Losing my balance as we were jostled by the tide. Letting go quickly to avoid falling.

"I missed you too," I said.

But by then there were other people between us, and I'm not sure whether he heard me over the crowd.

The next day I heard the mail drop through the slot in our door and onto the mat. No one else was home, and I almost left it there. But I was thirsty anyway, so I put the book down and got up.

I knew it was from him the minute I saw it. The envelope was cheap and grimy. The stamp, Indonesian.

I sat down hard, back against the front door, and ripped it open with shaking hands.

Dear Cori,

This will be fast. There is someone leaving soon who says he will carry mail for me. There is no other way from here.

We are in Manado, North Sulawesi. The camp is called Kibang. I used the gold to allow us on a refugee ship from Ambon. I did not go back home. After you left I went to Ambon City. The mission school was empty except for the old workers. When they heard about what we saw they said to take Tina and go far away until peace returns. I cannot write much, but I know you will understand when I write I hope you showed them out there, and told what happened. I have heard since that it happened the way we thought. Maybe that will help.

I missed you all, but I am thankful you were gone then. Ambon City was fearful. But we seem to be safe here, and there is enough rice. I do not know where we will go next. School is supposed to start soon, but everyone is saying that there will be no school this year. Perhaps not for many years. Someone gave me a math book and an old book in English, so I am studying by myself sometimes, and I teach Tina. Maybe I can get a Bible soon.

I do not know what to do right now, but I am waiting for God the Father to show me. Sometimes the waiting is hard. I think about all of you, and Tina always asks where you are. I pray this reaches you. Would you write to us? I long to know that you are all safe too. Please pass this news to the others.

Baku dame jua.

Mani

I didn't really believe it until I heard myself tell Kyle.

"They're safe. They caught a refugee ship, and they're in a camp in Sulawesi."

There was silence on the other end of the line, then a sound that could have been a sob, or a cough.

"Read it," he said.

"Thank God," I heard after I finished. "Thank God!" he said again, louder, followed by a whoop.

"We have to get them out of there," I said, sitting at the kitchen table and staring out into the sunny green peace of our backyard. A couple of leaves drifted past the window. The empty house creaked.

"We will," Kyle said strongly. "I know . . . !"

"Tim and Alison," we both said at the same time, knowing they'd do it. They had to. I wondered why we hadn't thought of it before.

Kyle carried it one step further. "We need to do those interviews. They'll need the money."

I hesitated. We'd been deluged with offers for interviews since we got back. It was so bad for a while that I'd learned to let someone else answer the phone. But the six of us had been talking, and there were a couple we were considering. We hadn't been able to decide whether we'd be helping Mani or putting him in more danger by talking to journalists.

"He said it," Kyle said. "Mani said tell the story. And we have the photos now."

"Have you looked at them?" I asked. I knew the other five had received identical boxes.

"Yeah. Haven't you? They came three days ago."

"No," I said.

"They're not all sad, you know, and some of them are really good. I know we were just pretending, but you would make a good photojournalist."

"I'll think about the interviews," I said. "We need to tell the others first."

"Okay," said Kyle, signing off casually the way we'd grown accustomed to doing. "Love you."

I sat at my desk that night, the door closed, and turned on the computer. The day deserved to be written about. I'd conference-called Drew and Elissa, and we'd talked for almost two hours, buzzing with ideas for how to get Mani and Tina safely to Tim and Alison's in Jakarta. Or here, if he'd come.

We were still talking when Mum and Tanya arrived home. I think they were slightly confused to walk in and see me smiling and giggling. I saw Mum look surreptitiously around the kitchen, checking for evidence that I'd gotten into the liquor, or worse.

When they heard the news they celebrated with me. Pulling the ice cream out of the freezer, we sat around the table with three spoons, eating out of the carton.

"Well, now you know where Mani is, you can talk about it, right?" Tanya said with her mouth full, chocolate sauce dripping down her chin. "You're famous. It's sickening. The principal asked me today whether you'd give a speech on speech night."

"About what?" I said, struggling to keep up.

"What do you think?" She shot me a disgusted look. "What you ate for breakfast yesterday, probably."

"What did you tell him?" I asked, still too happy about the letter to be annoyed with her.

"That if you wouldn't, I would." She tossed her head. "I could give a speech on what it was like to put up with Mum and Dad while you were missing. And what it's like to live with you now you're home and walking around like the living—"

"Enough," I said, swatting her as I saw a shadow cross Mum's face. "If anyone's giving speeches, it won't be you."

"Why not?" She sulked. "I'd probably do it better than you anyway."

Not for the first time I wished Mark lived closer, so I could introduce him to Tanya and watch the two of them learn to get along.

I sat in front of the empty screen that night, not finding the right words. We were finally at a point where we could *do* something again, and I wanted to do something *now*.

I got up from the computer and wandered over to the window. It was dark; the street was empty. I pushed up the window and let the night air in, welcoming the chill. It smelled of damp leaves and . . . smoke.

Someone nearby must have built a fire.

I looked at the box. Sitting under the lamp, Budi's bear perched on top of it.

"Okay," I said to no one in particular as I picked it up.

I spread the photos out on the floor of my room. At first I was methodical, laying them out quickly in neat rows. But it wasn't long before I was captured by a moment.

Drew was laughing. In a rare show of masculine solidarity, Brendan and Kyle were holding her firmly in place while Mark drenched her with a bucket of water. Behind them, Mani was leaning on his shovel, looking puzzled. Elissa stood beside him, pointing.

Drew had stacked the guys' toilet paper rolls on an ants' nest, I remembered, and hidden ours.

I smiled. Kyle had been right. They weren't all sad.

But too many of them were.

By the time I finished it was after midnight. The rest of the family was sleeping. And I was tired of crying.

I looked at the photo of Budi in the arms of his mother, clutching his balloon dog, smiling up at me.

Suddenly, I knew what I was going to do about it.

My computer beeped at me, and I uncurled myself from the floor, stiff.

It was Mark, at home in New York and on the instant messenger.

YOU THERE? KYLE AND I ARE CHATTING, the screen said.

MARK, WHAT ARE YOU DOING AWAKE THIS LATE? I typed.

He ignored the question. Instead what came back was . . .

ONCE UPON A TIME THERE WAS A BOY NAMED JIP.

Kyle followed quickly with, JIP'S BEST FRIEND WAS A MONKEY NAMED KIKI.

BUT JIP WAS LONELY, Mark typed. HE WAS USED TO HAVING MORE

THAN JUST ONE FRIEND WHEN HE WORKED IN THE CIRCUS.

We were a circus now?

HE USED TO HAVE MANY ADVENTURES WITH THE LION TAMER, Kyle typed.

YEAH, HE REALLY LIKED THE LION TAMER, Mark typed. IT'S TOO BAD THAT DURING AN ESPECIALLY DANGEROUS STUNT THE LION TAMER GOT HIS ??? BITTEN OFF.

I could just imagine Mark's grin as he keyed those question marks in.

HIS BUTTONS, Kyle typed back. THE BRAVE LION TAMER SCOFFED AT DANGER. OCCASIONALLY HE'D GET SO CLOSE THEY'D BITE HIS BUTTONS OFF. BUT HE WAS A PROFESSIONAL. THE SHOW WENT ON.

SO THERE WAS JIP, KIKI, THE LION TAMER, AND . . . , Mark typed.

A HIGH-WIRE ACROBAT IN A LEOTARD, Kyle typed.

Ha! He wished.

I picked Budi's bear up and perched him above the computer, so that he could look down and watch me.

CORI? Mark finally prompted me.

JOURNALIST, I typed.

WHAT??? Kyle flashed back. IT'S A CIRCUS. WHAT DO WE NEED A JOURNALIST FOR?

PERHAPS TO PUBLICIZE THE DARING ANTICS OF THE LION TAMER. P.S. THIS IS AN AUSTRALIAN CIRCUS, I typed back, feeling something click into place inside of me.

They might not like it.

But we are just going to have to work it into the story.

Because that is my decision.

epilogue ∼ ⌣

It's been almost four months now since we got home, and I keep coming back to the computer every couple of days, waiting for this to be finished. But I'm starting to realize that what I said to Amy that time was truer than I knew. It's not finished. It might never be finished in the way I've been wanting. There's not going to be a neat point when I can type the last word, hit *save*, and proclaim, "It's complete." That's probably a dangerous phrase anyway. I mean, look what God still had ahead of Him when He finished creating the world. His troubles were just beginning.

When I first started writing, I used it to hold on to everything that happened during the long, crazy summer, to make it real, even to myself. It allowed me to go back there every day. The village, Seram, Ambon.

That had become more real to me than life here, and I didn't know how to let go.

But as I got further into the story, to all the awful bits, I ended up wanting to shut the lid on what had happened and just let life get back to normal. I wanted to be able to go to the grocery store without comparing it to the village markets. I wanted to be able to chat to Scott and my other friends about everyday stuff, to concentrate on what they were saying and be interested in their lives. I didn't want to be so serious all the time. Tanya was right; I was no fun. And it was exhausting.

I can't really have either extreme, though. I have to find a way to live without the others nearby all the time. And I have to do it without blocking it all out. I'm working on finding a new normal.

Of course, I still have bad days. Days when I wake up and life seems hopelessly grim and I don't want to get out of bed. Times when my smile is just a mask pasted to my face. Some weeks it seems I have more bad days than good. But lots of things are helping. I'm slowly amassing a store of "good things" to think about that can shift the darkness. Sometimes.

Knowing Mani and Tina are safe, or as safe as anyone can really get in this crazy world, has helped me more than anything else. Things happened fast after we got Mani's letter. Tim flew to Sulawesi and went to the camp. The three of them left the next day. Mani and Tina are now living with Tim and Alison in Jakarta and are both back in school. Mark's dad has insisted on paying for everything, so the rest of us have put some of the money we've been earning from interviews into a Bible college fund for Mani.

I know it's not what Mani wanted, but I'm so glad they're with Tim and Alison, where Tina can have some sort of a mum, and where Mani won't have to carry the whole load by himself.

Ambon is still a mess. It's hard to get news, but the last reports filed suggest that hundreds, probably thousands, of people have been killed in the last couple of months. It's even harder to get news about Seram, although in his last letter Mani wrote that he thought there hadn't been any more violence in his village since we left.

Yes, that's one thing I can say with certainty. I am happy they're in Jakarta. Mani's too young to cope with all that alone.

The others all seem to be doing okay. I saw everyone two weeks ago when 60 *Minutes* did a section on the turmoil in Indonesia and "our rescue," and flew everyone to New York for the interview.

Mark was the last one to arrive at the hotel, and when he did we all pounced on him at the same time. He hugged us back fiercely, and I'm sure I saw tears in his eyes even though he denied it vehemently.

Mark's dad stood back, watching quietly. I knew Mark's parents had separated, but he was living with his dad and seemed much happier with how things were going at home. I'm sure the look I saw on his dad's face had something to do with that. I think before Indonesia, Mark wasn't sure whether his parents cared if he was alive or dead. He knows the answer now.

They'd booked us all separate hotel rooms, but Drew, Elissa, and I all stayed in one room, too excited to sleep alone. We admired Elissa's engagement ring, but told her we still thought she was crazy to get married at eighteen. She stuck her nose in the air and told us we were just jealous. Drew and I laughed at her.

It was good to hear Drew laugh. I got the impression she hadn't done much of that lately. She had thought about deferring university, but her psychologist recommended she start on time. I asked what her fellow freshmen thought about her summer.

"I dunno. I don't talk about it much. They wouldn't understand, you know?" she said, looking up at the ceiling.

"I know," I said.

"You dating anyone?" Elissa asked.

Drew blushed. "No. But . . ." She stopped there, and we had to tickle it out of her. "Okay, Brendan and I are writing, but nothing's going on. We're just friends."

"Same here," I said when it was my turn. "Just friends."

"Sure," Drew said with a smirk. "How often do you and Kyle talk on the phone?"

"Every couple of days," I said, defensive. "Besides, I leave for Australia in two months."

"Oh, yeah." Both their faces fell, and they looked at me, glum.

"Why?" Elissa asked.

"It's a home I've never known. If I don't go now I probably never will. There's a great journalism program in Sydney, and I can take some human rights courses too. I just feel like it's the right choice," I finished lamely.

From the looks on their faces I could tell they weren't convinced.

"What did Kyle say?" Drew asked.

"You mean after he stopped yelling?"

They both giggled.

"Yeah, he wasn't too happy."

That was the understatement of the year. My stomach hurts every time I think about being that far away from him, but I really think it's the right choice. I can always come back after a year if I hate it.

"Scott?" Elissa asked.

"Him either," I said. "But it's not their life."

"That's so neat about Scott becoming a Christian," Elissa said.

"Yeah." I sighed, thinking back to Scott talking about the moment when my parents had rung his house with those two words . . . *They're missing.*

"I was already halfway there," Scott had said, still not managing to smile about it. "But that was it. That drove me to God. There was nowhere else to go."

I still cringe every time I think about it, because I feel like such a fraud. How did he come out of those three weeks closer to God, while I came out feeling further away?

"You're so brave." Drew flopped on her back, long red hair spread out over the white bedspread like a fan. "I wouldn't want to go halfway round the world by myself."

"Can we talk about something else?" I begged. It might be the right decision, but that doesn't mean I'm not nervous.

"I think you'll make a great journalist. You've been doing all that writing. You always sound like you know what you're talking about in interviews." Elissa wrinkled her nose. "I hate them."

"When are we going to get to read it anyway?" Drew asked.

"Not yet," I said.

Maybe never, I added to myself. Kyle is the only person besides Amy I've let read any of this so far. And even he hasn't seen all of it.

The two of us spent that afternoon sitting by the pool.

"It's good," he had said thoughtfully, tapping the pages. "But it's heavy."

I listened to the happy screams of kids splashing nearby.

"Yeah," I agreed, wishing for a moment that I hadn't let him see it —which is a bit silly since he knew most of it anyway.

I know he thinks it's simple. Well . . . simpler than I make it. He says you just have to make a choice based on what you know about

God. And relax and trust for the rest of what you don't know.

At this point in the conversation I usually remind him about the time he almost put his fist through a tree and talked about blowing people up. And that he had been really Angry with a capital *A* until a pig put a tusk through his Bible.

"Yeah," he says, as if I'm thick. "That's why I understand. And why you should listen to me."

I might miss him, but he can still make me mad.

I didn't expect what he said next.

"Our prayers were answered, you know," he said.

"What?"

"The church. I think it's touched more people by being burned than it would have if it was still standing."

"I asked that the church would be an instrument of peace," I said, remembering that warm night, the hiss of the kerosene lamp, everyone's face glowing in its light.

"Maybe it has been," Kyle said. "Think about the letters we've gotten from people who've heard about it."

"Maybe," I said, reluctantly. It's still not the sort of instrument I would choose.

"You know, life's a journey," Kyle said. "Some questions get answered later. You can't stop traveling just because that's not now."

I raised my eyebrows at him.

"Where'd you get that?"

He grinned at me, undaunted. "I read it somewhere, can't remember where, but that bit on the end is mine. I've been waiting for the right time to use it."

I kicked him halfheartedly. "I haven't stopped traveling," I said.

"That's good," he said, the glint in his eyes forewarning me. "I think you should travel somewhere right now."

"But I don't have my swimsuit on," I said, knowing exactly what he had in mind.

"Poor planning on your part," he said, reaching for my arms and dragging me toward the pool.

As I hit the water I felt the tickle of round bubbles of laughter fizzing past my face.

Rising.

About the violence
in Ambon ～

The characters in this story are fictitious, but violence in the Maluku Islands of Indonesia has, unfortunately, been a reality for much of the past decade. The fighting that broke out between Christians and Muslims in Ambon, the capital of Indonesia's Maluku province, in 1999 triggered a virtual civil war that soon spread to other parts of the province. Since then, at least 5,000 people (perhaps as many as 10,000) have been killed and at least 500,000 (about a quarter of the population in the area) displaced from their homes.

There have been recent positive signs of recovery. In May 2007 the Jakarta Post reported that several *latupatis*, local traditional chiefs, established a council to assist in the reconciliation of local Muslim and

Christian communities. It is expected that peace in the Maluku Islands will gradually return. However it is still too early to generate any definitive predictions that this fragile peace will hold. Although relative calm seems to have been restored and people are beginning to return, sporadic outbreaks of violence still occur.

Acknowledgments ～

Thank you . . .

My parents, for always loving each other and "us kids." For daring to take us to live in challenging places. Also for not freaking out when I rang you up after finishing six years of university and said I didn't feel like getting a job as a psychologist in Australia and was going to come and live with you in Manila for six months, volunteer for a nonprofit, and work on this novel. Dad, special thanks for letting me use a letter you once sent to me in this story. I could not have conjured up better words for Cori's own father.

Since then, this story has evolved across four continents. Along the way I have been blessed by the encouragement of many wonderful people.

Thank you to . . .

Michelle and Matt. For being home to me, no matter where we are in the world.

My teammates on the 1994 Teen Missions International backpack team to the Philippines, especially Jon, Steve, Steven, Fiona, Maryann, and David. For sharing boot camp, hiking, laughter, stories of coconut fairies, and displaying more good grace than I often managed. "Special blessing" to you all. Paul and Beth—thanks for being brave and crazy enough to spend two months on Camotes Island with thirty-two teenagers.

Tash, Ani, Paul, and Emma. For being there in Thailand in 2001 when Jip and Kiki were born. Special thanks for Tash for reading all the various drafts and talking about these characters as if they were real people.

My fellow Peace Studies classmates at Notre Dame. For pens, chocolates, shoulder massages, sangria, tango lessons, advice about dinghies, and many late night discussions that were sometimes far from peaceful. You expanded my world.

Robert and Ruthann Johannsen. For enabling me to spend some of my time at Notre Dame writing this story, and for using some of your time to encourage me.

Brock and Bodie Thoene. For encouraging words at the right time.

Friends from North America—Jenn, Dayla, Araba, Sharla, Joe, Charisse, Brad, Ed, Grace, Carol, Nick, Erica, Robert, Steve, Tiffany, and Robin. For reading drafts and saying you liked it (or at least not saying that you didn't like it). Ryan, special thanks for your honest, constructive, feedback. Apologies in advance to those I am quite sure I have forgotten to name.

Stan Jantz and Bruce Bickel. For being mentors when I needed it, and for your vision and ongoing encouragement and enthusiasm.

Missionaries and humanitarian workers who have spent years in Ambon, and who asked not to be named. For sharing your stories.

Finally, the team from Moody . . .

Andy McGuire. You once laughingly told me you'd rather be mean than wrong. In my experience you've never been one of those, and only rarely the other. Thank you for picking this story up and going to bat for it, for making me edit it ruthlessly, and for being a cheerful, insightful, and unstinting voice of support. You have been a blessing. LB Norton. Thank you for helping me push through with the last round of editing, and for your instincts, your questions, your meticulous attention to detail (and for telling me you loved the story) —and for taking time to help me understand more clearly why I shouldn't write sentences like this one. Randall Payleitner, Lori Wenzinger, Pam Pugh, and the rest of the team. You're all awesome—that's all there is to it.

Discussion Questions ~

Background Note: While the characters in this story are fictional, they experienced a real-world conflict. Events very similar to those depicted in this story have occurred in the Maluku Islands of Indonesia within the last decade.

1. To what extent do the characters of this book remind you of yourself or someone you know?
2. What scene(s) did you find had the most emotional impact? Why?
3. Did any part of the story make you uncomfortable or angry? If so, why?
4. What themes and/or questions stood out to you as you read this book? How did different characters in the story interact with these themes?

5. How do the various characters react to the massacre in Mani's village and the events that followed? Did you learn anything about the experience of trauma through their stories? Which character did you identify with most?

6. Marooned in the jungle, what was Cori thinking and feeling as she read Psalm 55 (pages 117–119)? Have you experienced events in your life that could have prompted similar questions and feelings? How did you react in those times? How do you address such questions in your own life, now?

7. How did Cori repond to returning home? Why might she have reacted the way(s) she did? Were you surprised by any of her reactions? How were they similar or different to experiences you or others you know have had after returning from spending time overseas?

8. How have the various characters changed by the end of the novel? What changes were "positive/negative"? Why?

9. Has reading this book prompted you to reconsider some of your views or investigate further some of the issues raised (e.g. faith-based or sectarian conflicts, post-traumatic stress)?

10. The title of this novel was taken from a line on page 95. Do you think "my hands came away red" is a good title for the book? Why or why not? What are some of the images and meanings the title evokes?

11. Where did you see laughter, joy, and hope in this story? Where did the characters find them? When things seem darkest in your own life, where do you tend to find those things?

12. Throughout the novel, the characters frequently make up their own stories about a boy named Jip and his pet monkey, Kiki. What did Jip and Kiki come to mean to the characters in the story? What role(s) did they play as a literary device?

13. What can you do to better understand people who have a different faith or worldview?

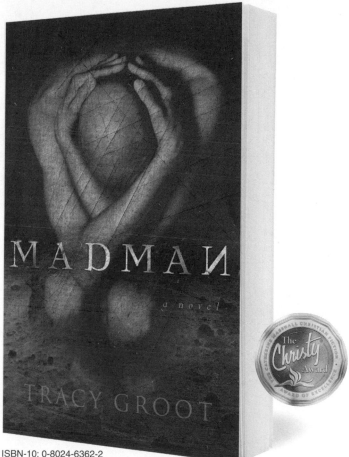

ISBN-10: 0-8024-6362-2
ISBN-13: 978-0-8024-6362-3

A close encounter.

If there is a way into madness, logic says there is a way out. Right? There is only
one scholar left who knows what happened to their prestigious Greek Academy
and the rest of his colleagues. But he is the one who needs the most help . . .
a madman.

by Tracy Groot
Find it now at your favorite local or online bookstore.

www.MoodyPublishers.com

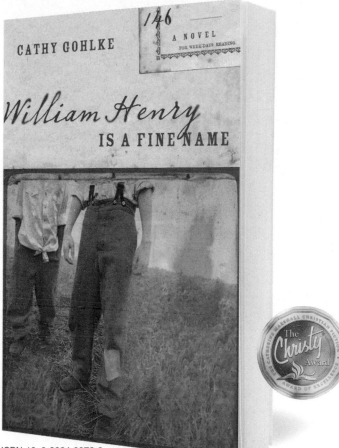

ISBN-10: 0-8024-9973-2
ISBN-13: 978-0-8024-9973-8

Colorblind.

They told him his best friend wasn't human. And the one thing he couldn't do was nothing at all. In the Pre-Civil War South, 13-year-old Robert's feelings of justice and loyalty have forced him to try and make sense of the surrounding chaos.

by Cathy Gohlke

Find it now at your favorite local or online bookstore.

www.MoodyPublishers.com